Messenger's Mischief

Blessings!
♡ Julia

Wells Fargo West Series

"There was one very powerful business rule. It was concentrated in the word courtesy."

-Henry Wells, 1864

Escape to an Era Where True Love Prevails

Other Books by Julia David

Wells Fargo West
The Messenger's Mischief
The Station Keepers Surrender
Coming soon!
The Passenger's Promise
Coming soon!

Love's Pure Gold Series
Truitt's Truth.

Morgan's Medicine.

Ian's Empire

Leaving Lennhurst Asylum Series
Available on Amazon and Kindle Ebook
Love Covers *Book 1 Elias*
Love Flies *Book 2 Patience*
Love Protects *Book 3 Anna*

Other Historical Romance Books by Julia David
Mighty One Series
Available on Amazon and Kindle Ebook
Burgundy Gloves
Broken Chain
Black Coat

Come visit: https://www.juliadwrites.com for behind the scenes, photos, videos, newsletters, release dates and fun giveaways.

The MESSENGER'S MISCHIEF

Julia David

Field Runner Press

"My body faints for You in a land that is dry, desolate, and without water."

Psalm 63:1 NLV

Chapter 1

Miss Elaine Balderhoff's heart pounded straight down to her deerskin moccasins. Chewing on her bottom lip, she stared at the strange pallet she'd been left to stand on and tapped her toe ten times. The wagon master called it the "stage platform." The small square of wood lacked a bench and looked like the rest of the town—lonely, desolate, and run down.

Taking a deep breath to settle her nerves, she recited her favorite Psalm in her head. *The Lord is my Shepherd. I shall not want.* Except she was in complete want—want to find an outhouse, want to believe if she found one, she would not miss the next stagecoach to Virginia City.

"*Meow.*"

Laney turned to see her cat, Moses, sitting in his box on top of her wide trunk.

"I know Mo, but the man said the next coach would be along in an hour. It's a Wells Fargo coach, and he said they are never late." She slid her fingers through the slats on the wooden cat box and tried to scratch under Moses's chin. "But, I have to find the outhouse." Pulling her fingers out, she scanned the area. Two other travelers had been picked up by a hay wagon and already rolled away. *Little hospitality did they offer.*

She quirked a frown at Moses. "The mercantile seems like the safest bet."

Stepping off the platform, Laney looked long over the hot desert of dirt and sagebrush. At least she could see the entire flat landscape from left to right. Not a swirl of dust to be seen. "Keep a watch out for the stagecoach, Mo. I'll be right back."

A few minutes after the store owner pointed out the outhouse behind his store, Laney re-entered the back door and thanked him for the help.

"Just you traveling, Miss?" His plump cheeks rose with a smile.

"And my cat." She answered. Pulling out a dime from her pocket, Laney purchased some jerky and a jar of milk. "My aunt made the trip to Cherry Creek with me, but her varicose veins were hurting immensely. She got a hotel bed and will head back to Nebraska as soon as she is better."

"And you?" He nodded at her. "What brings you this far from home?"

"I am the new schoolmarm for Virginia City."

"No." He stopped dusting, and his jowls lowered. "Are you sure about that?"

"I am." Laney straightened. "I even have the school board's agreement in my trunk."

The storekeeper waited while scrutinizing her. "You seem a bit young. Have you ever been to Virginia City?"

"No, sir. But I have read about the town, the mining, and the sudden growth due to the Comstock Bonanza. I understand a Mr. Feldon was the previous teacher, but I suppose he could make more money mining. I shouldn't speak so freely." Laney looked around the empty store. "But I suppose it is unusual to hire a woman. With all the men leaving to mine, they likely had no other options."

"So you *are* a teacher, then?" His voice held little confidence.

"Yes, sir. My second position." Just as the sentence flew from her confident mouth, Laney felt her entire body tense. Why did she just let that slip out? Before he could ask why she wasn't still at the first position, Laney took her items on the counter and quickly told him her cat awaited her return.

Keep everything in order, and God will keep you. The words weren't scripture but often helped to quell her nerves. The afternoon sun hit her face as she walked back to the platform. She'd let her employment history slip to a stranger—so what? She would never see him again. Pulling her shoulders higher, Laney found her trunk and the boxed cat just as she'd left them.

A scripture came to mind as she pulled off some bits of jerky and fed them to Moses. *"For, therefore, we both labor and suffer reproach because we trust in the living God, who is the Savior of all men."* She sat on her trunk next to her cat box. "I've suffered enough reproach," she said to Moses. "You will be the only one who will know my past." She popped some jerky in her mouth and chewed. "And you are my most trusted friend, never tattling the things I've told you or correcting me for talking while I chewed." Laney took a sip of milk and recounted her decision.

Living with her mother's constant scowl, strict manners, and with her Aunt Lula's incessant sour opinions had left her desperate for a change. Surely God was prompting her to go and possess her own land or at least her own opinion. Even in this strange day, sitting with the unknown, she would take the arid wind across her face over the confines of their small, suffocating house in Nebraska.

"I do love them," Laney told Moses. "You know, I do. It was just time to leave the nest. Leave the gossips and naysayers." Laney stood and moved Moses's box to the wooden platform. "Let me find your bowl and my parasol." She flipped the heavy latches. "We shouldn't have to wait too much longer."

An hour later, Laney rapidly tapped her fingers over her parasol handle and looked over her thick skirt layers. Two men rode by on horseback, and both gave her a long stare. She knew her moccasins were unorthodox for a young woman, but certainly her hem easily covered them. They were the last gift her father had bought her before he passed away. Knowing this trip was rough on the body and feet, she'd chosen to be comfortable. "Wearing Indian objects" was on the list her last position sited for termination, among other things. *Forgive ye others as Christ has forgiven you*, caused her chin to raise higher. God has given me a new assignment, a new town, new children to educate, and the benevolence of my great God.

A distant pounding caused her shoulders to straighten. It had to be the Wells Fargo and Company Express. She was surprised others had not joined her on the simple platform, for everyone across the states knew the sturdy coaches brought mail and newspapers from far and wide.

"The stage is on time, and everything is in order," she huffed to Moses. "Nothing to fear. God is on our side. He is the stronghold of my life, of whom shall I be afraid?" She rolled her lips and chewed on her bottom lip as the team of black and brown horses slowed to a pace that made the dirt billow around the imposing gold and red stagecoach. Two rugged men sat high atop the bench. One held the reins and pulled them backward. The other held a gun atop his thigh.

The clamor of hooves quieted as the large coach rolled behind her. It was certainly a powerful sight to behold, but strangely it stopped nowhere near the platform she'd waited on. Turning around, she watched as four men came from the livery and brought buckets of grain and water for the horses. The two Wells Fargo men stood on the stage roof and untied boxes and barrels. The storekeeper she met earlier pulled his own boxes out of the store for loading, she presumed. The men from the livery reached up as the two stage men dropped boxes and satchels into their hands. The loading and unloading was a great synchronized event until the storekeeper stacked the last box. Pointing across the broad road of dirt, he signaled the men standing on the stage roof to her location. In unison, they turned to see her, and she sucked in a small gasp.

Like a skittish lizard on a rock, Laney forced herself steady. *Should I walk to them?* Or would they turn the entire stagecoach to pick her up? Before she could decide, the man that held the gun earlier frowned and shook his head while staring at her. Laney opened her mouth to explain—Aunt Lula's veins are very menacing, and otherwise she wouldn't be traveling alone. Of course, she knew it wasn't proper. Both men atop the stage swung legs down, hitting footholds before they landed on solid ground.

"Oh, Holy Moses," she murmured, thinking they were coming her way. But all the men seemed to finish their tasks and disappear inside the livery door. "Why am I breathing so hard?" A weak snicker escaped. "Even though I have to ride through the darkest valley, I will fear no evil, for thou art with me. And it's not even dark, Mo. I'm sure we will make it to Virginia City before dark. Really now, we'll be fine. We've come this far. No need to worry."

Laney brushed a strand of brown hair from where it poked her in the eye. She shoved her hand inside her skirt pocket, finding her hankie. Pinching it ten times, she finally brought it out to dab the perspiration from her temple. Tapping her right foot ten times brought a calm to her spine. The wait hadn't been that bad, and surely in a few more minutes they would be ready to load her trunk. "I don't see any other passengers today, Mo. How about you ride across from me. A tufted bench all to yourself?" She scratched under the orange cat's chin, and his creamy white paws circled her fingers. "Much better than that unfortunate ride from Denver." Six passengers stuffed inside the coach while poor Moses had to ride above with the cargo.

Laney picked up the handle to her parasol and shaded her face while watching for any movement from across the way. Her fingers tapped up and down the handle. She took a deep breath before stepping off the small platform. The driver and gunmen stepped out onto the wooden sidewalk, and their gruff conversation slowed her steps. A feeling in her belly said they were not happy to have her. The older man slapped his dust-filled bandana on his dirty pants and shrugged his shoulders while the tall, younger one shook his head again. Unhappy head to toe, the taller man turned and walked toward her. Hidden under a wide felt hat, dark brown eyes slanted over her. She almost took a step backward. For such a ruggedly well-proportioned face and incredible handsomeness, he was a bit surly-looking at this moment.

"Ma'am." He tipped his hat, and everything softened a bit, making him even more strikingly attractive.

"Ahh, yes, sir." Laney prayed she didn't appear too cockeyed.

He removed his hat and raked his fingers through thick brown hair. Laney quickly looked away. Every movement he made caused her cheeks to flush, and she knew she was gawking.

"Thing is…" Even his voice meshed perfectly with his size and stance—not too soft, but not too rough either. She tried to meet his gaze, but it was almost impossible.

"Better for you to get on to Virginia City tomorrow." His finger pulled across the corner of his mouth. "There'll be another stage before noon."

She was rarely speechless but now was highly aware that her mouth was hanging open. "Sir, I have traveled from Bellevue, Nebraska. My companion, my aunt, had to take a medical leave in Cherry Springs. I assured her I could make this last stage of my trip alone." *And her body ached for a real bed.* "Are there no other passengers who are as anxious as I to get to Virginia City?"

He dropped his chin to the side and scanned the empty street. "No." He tucked his hat tight around his forehead. "Good day, ma'am." He turned to walk away.

"Sir." Laney hurried to meet his long steps. "Please. Can you explain why I'm not welcome on your stage?"

The Wells Fargo man had the nerve to keep walking until he came up to the horses. Patting the mare's sleek back neck, he checked the harness, ignoring her.

"The coach says Wells Fargo and Company." Laney started in. "Where I come from, the employees are polite and responsible. May I please speak to your elder? The man driving the coach."

The rogue looked up and ran his tongue across his straight teeth. "He's inside, we flipped a coin to tell you, and I lost." He stepped away and checked the straps on the cargo. "I heard you're the new teacher, so you must have some smarts." With a dismissive sigh, he moved away. "You'll hitch your ride tomorrow."

Chapter 2

Laney huffed as her bottom lip turned into a frown. This was exactly why she'd traveled this barren land with a harping aunt. When that finger-pointing spinster spoke, everyone listened. Aunt Lula would've had this tall drink of water on task loading her trunk this very moment. Now it pained her insides, too humiliating to mention, but she didn't have any money for a hotel. She looked again down the dusty barren town, if there was such a building. Her aunt had needed the bulk of their money for her room and meals back to Nebraska Territory. Laney had coins for a few small meals until she settled in at the B Street boarding house in Virginia City. There, her room and board would be included with her teaching contract. Glancing back, the thought of spending the night on that hard platform made her swallow hard. *"The Lord is a God of justice; blessed are all those who wait for Him."*

"Huh? Are you talking to me?" the tall, brazenly handsome man asked.

"No, I am not," Laney replied with a glare and skirted around the front of the horses, finding the driver setting his canteen on the high bench. "Sir, I am in a quandary. I have no means to spend the night here, and my position requires I arrive...." She hesitated, knowing full well what the Lord felt of liars. "I need to arrive in a timely manner. I am brand new to the position. Although I understand the town is rough and unreliable, I am truly alone here." The words poured out a little too close to her true feelings at the moment, and her eyes began to pool. "Please, sir...."

"Oh, hold up now. Don't start in with that wet face." His worn wrinkles turned red, and he scratched his stubbled jaw. "All right, all right." He handed Laney his kerchief. Taking the crusted brown rag by her fingertips, she found a small smile. "You're so kind. I do have my own." With doe eyes, she handed his handkerchief back and dabbed her face with the hankie from her pocket. "I was just telling the younger man, I've only known of Wells Fargo men to be responsible and courteous."

"Okay, okay, enough. Get in." The driver held the door open to the stagecoach and helped her in.

"My things are...."

"Yep, I know." The driver stepped near her door, hauled himself up, and landed on the bench seat.

Laney tucked her hand in her pocket and pinched her hankie ten times before tapping her toe ten times. The coach rocked side to side as it made a circle around the street and in front of her trunk. The entire coach was hers and made her feel like a child in a large empty room. Strangely, no scriptures would come to mind.

Once she had Moses inside, she could finally rest in the Lord. Laney leaned out to where the tall man had walked across the road to meet the turning stage. As the stage stopped, she opened the door. Under his hat's brim, a scowl developed just for her. He grabbed Moses' box so rough she almost flew out the door.

"Wait!" Holding her hands out, she pleaded. "Can I please have him in here?"

"Him?" The man held up the box and peered inside. "A cat. You have a cat in a box?" A paw swiped out the slat, almost catching the man's nose. He handed the box over while grumbling something unmannerly.

Pulling Moses' box close, she whispered. "Let's try not to judge." Out of the corner of her eye, she saw the tall man hoist her trunk upward while the driver pulled it into the cargo area. "But we can forgive him because he is strong and somewhat agreeable." She waggled her head back and forth. "At least in the face."

After a short time of steady rocking and nothing but dry desert to look at, Laney's eyes drooped. Having a seat to herself was pure luxury, so she curled up with her elbow under her head and slept.

Blinking awake, and unaware of how long she'd slept, Laney rose quickly. "What was that, Moses?" Had she dreamt the sound, or was it real? Trying to judge the hour by the setting sun, she leaned out the window as a loud pop cracked in her ear and a furious wind spun by her face. The flash of air was so strong she flung back into the coach, almost landing on the cat's box.

"Holy Moses, what was that!" Heart thudding, she huddled on the seat, clutching her head.

A booming voice echoed from over the horse's hooves. "Hang on, lady!" The entire stagecoach jerked forward, and she tumbled onto the floor, gripping Moses' box. "Ouch!" Laney fought to right herself as the crack of the whip and speed of the horses increased.

"*The Lord, thy God, is my sun shield and....*" Her voice splintered into a frightened whimper, holding the cat box. "*My rock and my fortress....*" Laney screamed. Another pop roared over all the pounding hooves. Her stomach clenched, and she had to swallow hard to keep it down. "*I will fear no evil, for thou art with me. I will fear no evil for thou art—*"

"Lady!"

Laney's head shot up, and her shaking hand pushed aside the leather curtain. "What?" Her response came out like a tiny kitten's.

"Door! Come out the door!"

Door? The stagecoach door? Was this a nightmare? Setting Moses' box on the coach floor, she carefully inched back to the window. "Sir! What?"

She could see the side of the driver, slapping the reins as the horses ran full speed. "What?" she yelled over the pounding hooves.

"Other side!" he yelled back. "Get to the other door and climb up!"

Laney fell back against her seat. Whimpering, she could not have heard that right and went to the other door and carefully looked out. The horses were running like a chariot on fire. Bit by bit, she stuck her head out the opening and saw the tall man's shotgun tumble off the side into a fury of dust and dirt. "What is happening?" Her screech muffled as she pulled up on the door handle, and the door flew out of her hand and slammed against the coach. Now the wild wind had her gripping the door frame with all her might.

"The Lord is…" she cried, inching outward while clutching the coach. *"The Lord is my…."* Wobbling in the wind, she reached above her head to find a strap or bar to hold. Just as she was about to retreat, her hand found a cold metal bar. "Moses, I love you!" She pulled herself out and stepped into the window opening. The dirt and air were so thick it tried to pull her skirt above her legs and her body from her perch. Sliding her hands down the bar, she quickly traded her right foot for her left on the window ledge and inched closer to the bench area. With a straightforward swing, her leg could connect with the high bench. *Oh Savior, Oh Savior, catch me….*

Slam! The stage hit a rut, and her once brave moccasin missed its mark and flung down next to the one that flopped loose from the window opening. Swinging like a church bell by a thread, Laney screamed in wild panic. Any moment her skirt or feet would tangle into the flying spokes. With shaking arms, she pulled upward with all her might, but only her knees would rise above the spinning wheels of the Wells Fargo Express. Terror thrust into every fiber when she realized her knees pressed inside her skirt, trapping her from moving. She could not pull herself upward, she was stuck, and her arms couldn't hold the pounding much longer.

"Lord, oh Lord," she cried as the stage hit another bump. Her fingers stretched to breaking. Her left hand slipped from its grip. Like a rag doll, her whole body dangled by one arm while the swirling air sucked the breath from her lungs. Four slipping fingers stood between her death, just one more bump, and it would be all over.

"Though You slay me, still, I will praise you." She choked out against the torrent of dirt and air. Laney took one last deep breath before the impending impact spattered her and broke every bone. A scream tried to escape when something flashed by her and grabbed her waistband. Like the mighty hand of God, it jerked once, and her body slammed higher against the stage. Positive it was something divine, Laney looked up through the dust and saw

the tall man's face as he secured his grip on her. Panting hard, he was pale, and his eyes filled with water.

"Pull!" He ground out against the pounding noise. Laney reached for the bench as he heaved her up by the waistband one more time. Her body flopped on top of his, in a swirl of panting and blubbering. Stunned, she quickly rolled to the left and sat on the bench between the men.

"I need you to hold him!" The driver yelled to Laney over the pounding hooves. "I can't drive the team and catch him!"

Laney, unable to fathom her survival, quickly observed the tall man next to her. Sure enough, he wavered. His watery eyes were unable to stay open. Just as he leaned toward the abyss she had just come from, she grabbed onto his shirt front and pulled him toward her. His head flopped forward and then back, and she gasped. His right sleeve was bright red, soaked in blood.

"My shotgun messenger, done been shot. Those dirty...." The driver swore in anger.

Laney could smell the blood, and she wondered who would hold them both when she passed out. Trying not to touch his wounded side was almost impossible as the stage rumbled on. She angled her shoulder behind his, wrapped her arms around his waist, locked her fingers, and braced her feet against the driver's box.

"Can you look behind us? I need some eyes to make sure they're gone." The driver shouted.

"Yes, sir!" Laney was amazed her voice worked at all. New blood filled her terrorized veins as she rehearsed the two jobs. Keep this giant man from tumbling off the seat, and keep an eye out for bandits. For some unfathomable reason, she felt capable of the task. Maybe it was just relief to have the shotgun messenger securely in front of her and the stage driver next to her. Anything was better than hanging by her fingertips from this wild stage. "Dear Lord, my Moses...." Had the cat box bumped and inched toward the open door? *"Be strong, do not fear; your God will come, He will come with vengeance."* Laney stopped. That was the verse she'd memorized after being fired from her first teaching position. She just needed Moses safe. Turning to look past the swirl of dust behind them—she spied no sign of a broken box. Or, thankfully, any bandits.

The injured man groaned and tried to move from her grip. "Be still now. I've got you," Laney cautioned. His other hand covered her locked fingers around his waist. His skin was clammy over hers, but he had little strength to separate her hands and arms from around him. She could feel him panting and saw the labored rise and fall of his chest. Wavering, his weight sagged against her and the rim of his hat touched her disheveled loose brown hair. His face rested only an inch away.

"I...I...." Clipped and cross, he tried to speak. "Tried to tell you not to come."

Chapter 3

An hour later, the sunset over the desert brought the most mesmerizing vivid orange and purples. Arms aching from holding tight to the injured man, Laney admired God's handiwork and said another quiet prayer for their safety.

The driver slowed the wagon from its pounding pace. "I got Austin Station up here in a mile. I need to drop you all off and get on to Fort Churchill. Someone will come back and take you all on to Virginia City—that is if he makes it."

Laney caught a whimper from escaping. She was well aware the front of her dress was soaked in this man's blood. "What is his name, sir? I want to be praying personally for him."

"Sawyer, Sawyer Roth." The driver tipped a frown at her. "I'd be most thankful if you would. He's one of the best shotgun messengers Wells Fargo has." He slowed the team into a trot. "We got wind there were some bandits in the area. But usually, they are after what we're bringing *out* of the mining towns, and little do they care what we are bringing *in*."

As the stagecoach was intended for Virginia City and the silver mining lode, the contradiction seemed noteworthy. The man in Laney's arms rode with his shotgun in hand for the safety of the cargo. "Will you send word to his family?" she asked. "They will want to come to aid him."

"No wife, nor youngin's. Not allowed for a shotgun messenger."

Laney saw the small soddy and corrals come into view and tried to lean up from where her back pained her. *Not allowed.* Just like teaching, unmarried was the rule. Mr. Roth must have felt her movement. He stirred, and a loud curse word escaped while he leaned forward, gripping his elbow.

"Stay with me, Sawyer." The driver stopped the team, pulled the brake, and wound the reins around it. Stepping over Laney, he pulled Mr. Roth to standing. "Help me get you down, and then we'll get you all patched up." A white-haired man and woman came out to greet the stage, and seeing the scene, rushed to help. Laney watched Mr. Roth stumble and writhe in pain as the three of them helped him inside.

Wanting to be free of this stage, Laney took a brief moment to look around. Standing alone in the driver's box, she watched as the last warm rays blended into faded shadows, and a light breeze cooled her blood-soaked bodice. *Oh Lord, what have I done? You know my thoughts and intentions. Is this from any wicked ways in me? Have I been prideful to think I could find my own way in this unforgivable land?*

A meow broke into the first moment of serenity.

"Oh, Moses," Laney gasped as sudden tears flooded down her cheeks. Using the very wagon wheel that almost sucked her to her death, she stepped down and found her cat's box just as she had left it.

"Oh, thank You, Lord, Your mercies are never-ending." Laney pulled the box to her face and fingered the neck of her beloved orange cat. "I'm so sorry I left you. You must have been so scared. I'm here now." Each word was undoubtedly spoken for her own beating heart and knocking knees. She finally straightened and looked toward the soddy. Two old hound dogs barely lifted their heads to watch her.

"The shotgun messenger is wounded." She turned back to her cat. "I will see if there is anything more I can do, and then I will be right back." Laney wiped her face with her sleeve and took in a deep breath. Glancing back at the dogs, she protectively closed the stage door. *"Those who wait on the Lord will renew their strength."*

Every shaky step reminded her how thankful she was to be off the rocking stage. *"They shall mount up with wings like eagles."* She stepped up to the porch between the lazy dogs. The front door hung ajar, and Mr. Roth sat bent over in a chair, his shirt removed. Her stomach clenched. His shoulder was a bloody mess.

"Miss, Miss."

Laney blinked and realized the stage driver spoke to her.

"Come in now. You're good at holdin' him."

Laney carefully walked in, and the woman tending the wound looked up and gasped. "Her too!"

"Oh no, ma'am." Laney shook her head quickly. "This is his blood." Regretting the quick glance at the exposed mangled wound, her eyes locked on the floor.

"Oh, fine then," the woman huffed. "Get over in front of him, and don't let him pitch forward."

Laney swallowed hard. The smell of blood and the damp soddy made her dizzy. She'd never been good at medical ministrations. She took a timid step forward. At her first teaching position, one of the children had once shown her a bloody hanging tooth, and she'd almost lost her lunch. Then there was the student with the gash over his— suddenly a cold hand reached out and caught hers. Choking back his pain, he squeezed her fingers tight.

Another surge of Christian duty weaved inside her. "I'm right here, Mr. Roth." Her heartbeat quickened, and she remembered to close her eyes and pray inside her head. *"He is the Lord that healeth thee." Oh, that slipped out.* She pressed her lips in a thin line. As the minutes ticked by and the blood continued to run down his arm, the woman finished stitching his wound and began to clean him. The older man at Austin Station had ripped up a sheet and handed the long lengths to his wife.

"Sit up tall as you can." The older woman told Mr. Roth.

He took a pained breath and forced his spine straight. "Blessed—"

Laney cleared her voice, interrupting his unsuitable words. He growled and dropped her hand.

"Thank you…" Mr. Roth strained to control the sharpness in his tone while the woman wrapped his injured arm against his bare chest, "…Mrs. Franklin." Looking out the top of his red eyes, he flashed fire at Laney, and she stepped away. *What had she done now?*

"I'd have a stiff drink for ya, Sawyer, but the Misses keeps a dry station," the older man said.

With a hung head, Mr. Roth barely nodded, and Laney appreciated that the woman had such good morals, besides her control of thread and needle.

"Let me get ya a pillow and put you on the couch," the wife said as she walked into the only other room. Laney spied the narrow sunken fainting couch with only one rounded end. He was a tall man; his feet would likely hang off. The simple room only held a fireplace, a table, two filthy round rugs, and four other wooden table chairs.

"Excuse me, sir," Laney said. "I need to get my cat from the stagecoach. He's in a box. Your dogs don't look too…too…lively. Would you mind if I brought him inside?"

Mr. Franklin scratched his white-whiskered chin with a furrowed brow. "You got a cat inside the Wells Fargo stagecoach?"

"Yes, sir." Why did that seem so far-fetched? She thought every state in the union had cats. Mrs. Franklin walked by with the pillow, shaking her head. Some folks didn't care for cats. Certainly they could come out and say it kindly.

"John's left," Mr. Roth grunted. Pained, his face squeezed tight as Mrs. Franklin helped him onto the fainting couch.

"John? Who is…." Laney searched the room. When had the driver slipped out? "Oh, no. Oh, no." She ran through the door. Shadowy, but glaringly hard not to miss, only dry landscape and sagebrush remained where the stage had been parked. Laney groaned and searched the abandoned area. Crossing her arms over her chest, she squeezed her hands into a tight fist. Now it was practically dark and what must Moses be thinking? She told him she'd be right back. Muttering to herself, she dropped her forehead onto her knuckles and knocked them together. "Now what, now what?" She jerked her hand free and stuffed it into her pocket. Ten pinches into her hankie did no good, small shudders grew until her body started to shake all over. Ten toe taps turned into five more foot stomps until a rock dug into her deerskin moccasins.

"Everything's out of order." Whimpering, she fell on her knees. "Poor Moses, he's alone. What if someone lets him go?" She pulled and twisted her loose shoulder-length hair. Why hadn't she listened to Mr. Roth? She was the one who insisted on coming. Would God rebuke her for her stubborn foolhardiness?

"Ma'am?"

Laney rose quickly to her feet and dried her face with her sleeve.

"The Missus put on some hot water for you to clean up with. Says she can get that blood out if you let her soak it overnight."

Laney looked over her shoulder and gave the kind man a short nod. Taking in a choppy breath, she reluctantly followed him. *"Thy rod and thy staff, they comfort me."* She mumbled. "Except for right now."

"Sorry, Miss, what did you say?"

"Nothing, sir. For such an inopportune emergency, it is very kind of you to help us." She followed him into the lantern-lit room. Mr. Roth leaned back on the narrow couch, each leg hanging over the side, with his eyes closed. Mrs. Franklin signaled for Laney to come into her room. Just inside, Laney stopped cold. A frail, thin woman lay asleep in the bed.

"Just my dear, old mother-in-law." Mrs. Franklin said. "Give me that blouse and chemise."

Laney slowly unbuttoned her stained blouse and untied the drawstring on her chemise, tugging it loose from under her corset. Mr. Roth's blood had soaked even into her thick corset, but she would not be removing it in this strange place.

"Here is a rag for your face and chest." Laney took it from her hand and leaned toward a small standing mirror. Cutting off a gasp, she held the cloth over her mouth. Her hair stuck out every direction as if someone had pulled it out by the roots, and her face was covered in brown streaks and smudged dirt. It wasn't a nightmare. She really did hang off the side of a stagecoach going full speed.

After cleaning her face and neck, she picked up the comb off the bureau. Laney tried small strokes to get the tangles to lay down until tremors ran up her tired arms. In all the ruckus, had she expressed her thanks to Mr. Roth for saving her life?

"Take my extra work shirt there." Cleaning the rag with the water in the basin, Mrs. Franklin nodded to the hook on the wall. Laney stole a glance at the sunken woman in the large bed. Was she alive? Certainly not aware of their talking or movement. With cold fingers she buttoned the front and tucked in the large green cotton blouse under her waistband.

"You're a thin one. That thing 'bout to swallow you." Mrs. Franklin took some soap to her stained blouse, rubbing the fabric together. "Sawyer says you're the new teacher in Virginia City?"

"Yes, ma'am." Arms crossed over the strange blouse, she rubbed her elbows, looking around, and felt the pain of the mislaid Moses. Not to mention the mislaid sense of order. She tried to focus on something else. "May I be of some help? I feel at a loss as to what to do."

"Maybe you can keep an eye on Sawyer tonight. I need the Mister to help carry mother to the outhouse. Then I help clean her and get her back in bed."

"Yes, ma'am." She chewed her bottom lip. How hard could it be to watch a man sleep?

Chapter 4

On, mother of all the living. Sawyer's gut clenched in pain as the contents of his stomach reached his throat. Now this would compete with the coals of fire burning in his shoulder. His eyes pinched tight, and his mind begged the fog to put him back to sleep. Where had the Franklins gone? Only one flickering lantern remained on the fireplace mantel revealing a womanly figure standing between the couch and the front window.

"Bucket." Sawyer croaked out and reached with his free hand to layers of fabric on his left. He'd sworn he was about to touch a swatch of dark red curtain, but somehow his hand brushed down the rounder layers below her waist. Easily, he would claim blinded agony, but the way she spun back to look at him, she'd likely not believe him. "Bucket." Sawyer panted again. A relentless wave of shivers joined in with a shoulder on fire and a churning stomach of poison.

"Oh, dear," she whispered and quickly disappeared from the window where she'd been staring into the darkness. If only the dark shadows would come back to overtake him. Why was she standing there, anyhow? Did John let the cat out? Was she searching for the animal now?

He tried to sit up a bit as a crockery bowl was shoved in front of him. At least he wouldn't lose his stomach on the Franklin's dirt floor. Clutching the bowl with his only working arm, Sawyer took a deep breath and fought for mastery over the waves punching the very life from his gut. A cooling sensation at the back of his neck rested on his flaming skin. Stealing a glance in that direction, he watched as she gently patted his cheeks, forehead, and hairline. Maybe she was an angel? Did they all smell like fresh river water and wildflowers as she did?

The cool cloth seemed to douse the fire under his skin, even calming the punching into mere pinching in his gut. His breathing evened out enough, and he rested back against the only side of the thin couch.

"Whatsoever things are true, whatsoever things are honest, whatsoever things are just, whatsoever...." Her voice trailed off, and before he could turn to find her, she returned with more cool water on the cloth. Sawyer closed his eyes. It felt so good. Not beyond the fire in his shoulder, but enough to distract him and settle his stomach.

"...if there be any virtue, and if there be any praise, think on these things."

"What…what is your name?" He panted. If it wasn't for the familiar watering station the Franklins provided the Wells Fargo team, he'd think he was in another hazy dream.

"Oh, ah, Miss Elaine Balderhoff." She answered, interrupting her scripture reciting. "Miss Balderhoff is fine, or I suppose Elaine is fine. Or after we rode the last hour with me holding you, maybe you should call me Sister Laney."

Sawyer wanted to straighten up and look hard into her face, but only his watery eyes would make contact. "What are you talking about?"

"Oh, just what you should address me by." She continued to carefully dab the cloth on his collar bone, and he realized his shirt and undershirt were gone.

"See, my father's name was Lane. I had an older brother also named Lane, but he passed when he was four or so. I wasn't born yet, so I have no memory of him. But ah, so, see how Elaine also contains Lane. Everyone's always called me Laney. If you were to remove the E from Elaine and just tack it on the back, you get Laney. Not with a short vowel, Lann-ee. That's wrong. But Lane-ee. I teach the children that long vowels all say their names. Because, like I said, my father was Lane. Similar if you were to use it in a sentence, like boulevard. The lane was covered in green grass." She scratched her nose. "So, ah, yes, that's how that works."

Sawyer wondered if she could just hold the rag tight over his ears, then nose and mouth, until it all went black again. Friendly gal, except for being a know-it-all schoolmarm, good-book quoting magpie to the stars and back. But the way her gentle touch continued to settle his raging gut, it was nothing to scoff at.

"I could make you some ginger tea. Or I saw a bowl of rolls. Would you like to try one?"

"Yes." He ground out. "Thank you, Lane-*ee*." Sawyer held her name out longer than necessary.

"Well, yes, that is right." The woman holding his cool cloth spoke from the kitchen. "I suppose you may move past my formal name for this strange time we are in."

Sawyer grunted and tried to sit up while still balancing the bowl in his lap. A roll appeared in front of him, and he took it.

"I'm sorry, I saw no ginger tea."

He noticed a cup in her other hand.

"Water is fine." He took a bite of the thick bread and chewed. Reaching for the cup, he swallowed, feeling the food push his stomach from his throat. He took a drink as she walked around the small couch and resumed searching out the front window.

"Are you worried?" He took another bite. Likely it wasn't about the cat. The woman could be fearful the bandits would attack in the night.

"Yes, thank you for noticing." She looked over her shoulder, and Sawyer caught her eyes for the first time. They were round and soft, and her brown hair lay loose around her shoulders. He shouldn't stare, but when she turned back to the window, he noticed her slight build and a glaring problem. A pretty thing, but much too young and innocent to be the newest resident of Virginia City. With her silly ways, that place would eat her alive.

"He's never been alone like this." Her words made no sense unless he was drifting off again.

"What?" He winced, his shoulder throbbing.

"My cat, Moses. He's wondering where I am. Do you think your driver will just let him loose?" Turning to face him, he could see the woman was serious. He'd almost been shot in the head, and she could've fallen to her death, but she was fearful for a cat? "Oh, lady." Sawyer moaned.

"No, it's Lane-*ee*." She accentuated.

Rubbing his hand over his face and stubble, Sawyer swallowed something gruff on the tip of his tongue. Wounded and trapped in a soddy with an addled young woman, at least the roll had settled his stomach. He held up the bowl. "Here." She took it and returned to her spot at the window.

An old itchy woolen blanket lay under his legs. The air was chilled, and he wanted to return to sleep.

"Here, Miss. Take the blanket. Go get some sleep."

"Thank you, Mr. Roth." She glanced around the small room. "It seems the Franklins allow their dogs to sleep inside. One is on the rug under the table, and one is on the rug near the fireplace." She shrugged. "I cannot sleep on the dirt floor."

"Just give them a kick." He looked back and forth, seeing the dogs spread across the rugs.

"Oh no, sir, this is their home. I can rest on a chair."

Sawyer ground his teeth and sat up. "Here, you can take the couch."

"Oh, no, never." She placed her hand on his uninjured shoulder. Her cool feminine touch on his skin made him obey instantly. "I have yet to thank you for your valiant rescue of me today. I could have died." Her soft eyes held deep sincerity. "And your selfless bravery overshadowed your own pressing injury. So, no need to be noble again."

"So one good act is all I get?" Sawyer murmured. And honestly, he'd surprised himself that he'd been able to swing the young woman upward onto the driver's seat. Shaking his head he rocked forward. "Maybe you should know this couch is a worthless piece of furniture. I've seen wagons drop tables and wardrobes across the long trail west. This thing should've been left behind."

Laney smiled, and Sawyer wondered how daft he'd gone. She was attractive, and her smile warmed her whole face. He wanted to be valiant *again*. "And because it is so narrow and without sides, I'll likely tip-off in the night."

"I'll be fine, Mr. Roth. You need your rest to heal." She stepped over to the mantel and blew out the lantern candle.

Even in the faint shadows, he could hear the brush of her skirts as she stood only inches from him, resuming her search out the window. His chest rose and fell as her comforting presence grew quiet.

"You think that cat's going to get out and come back here?" he said.

Laney turned and sighed. "I know that sounds illogical. But I have read in books that cats do have an attuned homing system."

"Like pigeons." He took a deep breath. Talking to her distracted him from the pain. And after taking a real look at the young woman, the question burned almost as hot as his shoulder. "Why would you want to be a teacher in Virginia City? It's a godless place."

"Does it have children?" Her eyes narrowed on his.

"Unfortunately, some now without fathers." He huffed. "The mine had a cave-in a while back. Killed twelve men."

"Oh, *blessed be the children, for they will inherit the kingdom of God.*" Shaking her head, she sighed.

"Matthew Farrow is one child left fatherless from the cave-in." He rubbed under his chin. "He lives with his mother and two other widows at the widow house."

"Is this house on B Street?" she asked.

"Yes, next door to the Wells Fargo station."

"That's where I'll be staying. A home for widows on B Street. What a delight to have one of my students in residence." She paused and bit the corner of her lip. "Is he an agreeable child?"

"I guess." He blinked. "Why?" She seemed troubled, but he couldn't make out her expression.

Laney turned completely to face him and tapped her chin. "Tell me, Mr. Roth, what kind of student were you? What subjects did you like?"

He grimaced with the shoulder ache and his own recollection. "Probably deemed *dis*agreeable."

She rewarded him with another smile. "And how did that happen?" she asked.

"Left too long on my own in the cornfields, probably. Or being stuck in the middle of a pack of siblings. The older ones all worked sunup to sundown planting and harvesting the corn. The little ones got some schooling here and there. Being somewhere in the middle..." He groaned, finding no place on the sunken couch that brought comfort. "Just never stayed with schoolin' too long. When I did go, I couldn't keep up, so I'd find excuses not to go." He leaned forward, resting his good elbow on his knee.

"I see." Her tone was reflective. "And your mother, a Proverbs thirty-one woman? I pray her children rose up to bless her."

"Some did." He released a huff. Many times as an adult, he'd wished an easier road for her. Now with only two daughters left to raise, her burden had to be lighter. It had been months since he'd heard a word from them. He never did miss the farm, nor pine to return. He'd shucked enough corn to last a lifetime, and the work for Wells Fargo felt right from the first stage ride. Now, what would the company do with him?

Somewhere on the road from the last station to this one, a perfectly good Colt revolving shotgun lay in the dirt along with his job and purpose. Now he couldn't even hold a gun. Frustrated, his eyes rose to meet hers. Sawyer knew firsthand this area could be ruthless. Now, seeing this naïve, tender woman, he felt concern for her future. "You have some kinda starch climbing out of that coach to reach the driver's box today."

"Oh, sir, that was highly unusual for me. I can say that the Lord is my strength and my shield, but I was also ready to make my peace and join the saints in the everlasting."

Sawyer scratched the back of his hairline. "So, you must be a Shaker or Quaker or something along those lines?"

"Umm." She shrugged. "No, Presbyterian."

"Hum." That didn't make sense. They seemed like ordinary folk where he was from. "Just remember, whatever that starch is, you're going to need it in Virginia City." He took in a deep breath and carefully rose. "Here, I want you to take the couch. You can still see out the window from here." Sawyer straightened slowly. "Me and the old coon dog can share the rug."

"No, that will never do." Laney shook her head and drew her lips in a tight line. Quickly sitting in his spot on the fainting couch, she righted the pillow under her back and tucked her left foot inside her thigh. "Come sit down, we will share."

His mouth dropped open. "What?"

"Just like on the stagecoach. Sit back down, you can lean on me, and I will hold you so you won't fall over."

Lane-ee was as flighty as a hummingbird, but he was weary. He would reason out the prudence of her suggestion later. Sawyer sat carefully, and his left eye narrowed. "I don't want to crush you."

"You won't. This seat is easier than sitting on a rocking stagecoach." Pulling the blanket over her lap, her fingers pulled back gently on his ribs, and he sucked in a stifled gasp. She should not touch him like that. Sawyer carefully inched back against her.

Even in blinding pain, he was not a pew-warmin' Presbyterian, but a pure-bred man.

Chapter 5

Peace I giveth to you, not as the world gives. No, no. *Peace I leave with you, My peace I give unto you.* I think. Laney curbed a squeak as Mr. Roth settled his head and working shoulder in her lap. Her Good Samaritan spirit might have gone awry because she rarely jumbled up her verses. Unfortunately, she hadn't thought this offer through, and his close presence caused her heartbeat to spike. His eyes were closed, and she did want him to have proper rest. But he wasn't really resting with her support. This young man was sleeping with his head on the blanket, the blanket on her tucked leg. His upper expanse covered her and the couch. She had two capable arms and nowhere to place them.

Laney rebuked her bright ideas and sighed. Number one, *thou shalt have no other gods before me.* Number two, *thou shalt not make unto thee any graven image.* She tried to twine her fingers above her chest, keeping her elbows clear of him. Number three, *"Thou shalt not take the name of the Lord thy God in vain; for the Lord will—"*

"Will what?" His eyes cracked open, looking up.

"Oh, mercy." She covered her mouth. "I didn't mean to talk aloud." The humor was notable—not taking the Lord's name in vain was the one scripture he needed to hear again and again—or in his sleep, anyway. "I often quote the commandments in order. I just need to do it inside my head." She rolled her eyes. "Please rest. I will hush."

"Quote all you like. It's distracting." Sawyer tried to stretch his back, and his hand slipped off the blanket. He tucked it back under his head and closed his eyes.

Laney felt every ounce of her being freeze. He'd slipped his hand back *under* the blanket, between that and *her skirt*—the very fabric that covered her leg. Like sparks from a campfire, little prickles landed all across her limbs. But they didn't hurt; amazingly, it was quite the opposite. Heat rushed to her face.

Remember the Sabbath day, to keep it holy. He was sleeping, and it was innocent. Number five, *honor thy father and thy mother.* She was practically a spinster. Quite normal to feel flustered in this position. She'd never even been kissed. *Kissed?* Number six, *thou shalt not commit adultery.* No, that's not right. Number six is *thou shalt not kill.* Laney smirked a frown to the side.

His intrusive hand felt strong and warm, extremely warm atop her skirt and upper leg. Had he a fever? She lightly brushed the hair from his brow and rose her hand in the air, shaking the mistake out like she'd caught leprosy. *Don't run your fingers over his hair—though it is soft and secretly touchable. No—bad, bad idea.*

A quaking started inside her. With a man, a handsome man no less, asleep on her, Laney couldn't get her hand in her pocket to squeeze her hankie ten times, so she lightly tapped her one foot that remained on the floor. Ten more would surely help—another ten.

Number eight, *Thou shalt not steal.* Number nine, and her breathing seemed to return to normal. There, she could barely feel his hand. She often slept curled, with hands tucked under her chin. And so what, she'd freely chosen the life of a single teacher, and she wasn't some wanton woman violating that now.

Laney stared long into the darkness. "God works all things for good, Mr. Roth," Laney whispered. Positive his chest rose and fell in a deep sleep, she let her fingers lightly brush through his hair. For the life of a woman with little options, the west looked hopeful and riveting, to say the least. Feeling little flecks of dried blood in his hair reminded her how easily infection could lead to death, so she said another prayer for his recovery and then one for Moses.

Resting her head on the side of the couch, her eyes drooped and then drifted closed.

***

"Well, these two figured something out," Mrs. Franklin said, walking into the room the next morning. Tying her apron around her waist, she smiled and waggled her head.

"Maybe it got cold. I should have built a fire." Mr. Franklin's eyes made a sweep over them. "He looks alive. That's a good thing." *And mighty cozy.*

"I'll get the coffee on and will see—" Mrs. Franklin stiffened as Mr. Franklin came up and wrapped his hands around her waist. "Remember when we were their age?" He nuzzled a soft kiss on her neck. "And my mother didn't sleep in our bed."

"Oh, stop all that." She swatted him away. "Heavens, you'll make me forget what I'm doing."

***

Laney thought she heard her aunt and mother talking, and her eyes blinked open to daylight. An aroma beckoned her. Someone was cooking breakfast. *And coffee.* Sucking in a startling gasp, the air stuck in her throat and she noticed Mr. Roth still slept in peace on her lap. Before panic set in, she'd have to move fast to remove the man. Pushing his head and wrapped shoulder upward, she slipped her tucked leg out and cautiously lay him down where she'd been. The quick plan went smoothly until she stepped away. Her unresponsive leg was numb and sent her tumbling onto the couch directly over Mr. Roth's lap!

"Now, what's going on in there?" Mr. Franklin said in jest, and before Laney could pull herself upward, her entire body had flushed redder than a beet. Would they report this scene, her brazen behavior? Would she be out of a job before she could even arrive in Virginia City? She huffed a short groan, trying to straighten up and shake her leg out like one of their lazy dogs would do. Praying to find feeling again, she struggled to stand and find her balance. Mr. Roth sat up and steadied her elbow.

"You are a skittish woman, Lane-*ee.*"

"Thank you for saying my name correctly, Mr. Roth." She puffed out the hair that hung in her face and tried to secure it behind her ears. God must have heard her prayers. The man had better color and possessed a smirk for her—seemingly a close cousin to a smile. Pulling from his grip and testing her balance, the tingling leg pulsed close to working again. Mr. Roth suppressed a low groan as he stood. Favoring his condition, his back curved from his usual height.

Mr. Franklin came around the corner with a shirt. "Shoulda' gave this to ya last night. But it appears as though that blood has quit running."

Sawyer looked over to his well-wrapped shoulder. The cloth remained white.

"Here ya go, Miss." Mr. Franklin handed her the shirt. "Seems you're quite the helper."

Thankfully, the man turned back to the kitchen. Laney could've sworn he was hiding a cheeky grin. Feeling her nostrils flaring, she opened the front and helped Mr. Roth thread his good arm through. The injured man appeared more muscular than she'd recalled. But, Lord knows, she hadn't been trying to study him, it was just hard *not* to notice. Standing on her tiptoes to pull it over his back, she wrapped it around his front. The way his chin stayed down, it felt like he watched her. She would not, in any fashion, be making eye contact.

Now in broad daylight, they were too close again, and the same constricting in her chest had reappeared. She tried to pull the shirt together over his wrapped arm, but her fingers felt like lead. If there were any way the man could've done this himself, she would let him. It was far too personal helping a man dress. A tiny squeak escaped. *As if holding him all night wasn't personal?*

Finishing the last button, Laney went to step back, but Mr. Roth quickly covered her hands with his, stopping her.

"Thank you, Lane-*ee*." He tipped her chin quickly as a reluctant grin teased his mouth. "You *are* helpful."

Embarrassed to the bone, Laney didn't feel the sincerity. He'd stretched her name out more than once now. "It's Miss Balderhoff, Mr. Roth," she snapped.

"Of course." His face stiffened, and his tongue touched his top lip. Her anger and discomfort had sharpened her tone. She regretted her response.

Taking in a deep breath, Sawyer lowered himself back to the fainting couch.

"Oh, dear, you're not well." Laney held the back of her fingers to his cheek. Mr. Roth seemed clammy, but cool to the touch.

"Can ya hold some coffee with that good arm?" Mr. Franklin held out a steaming mug.

"Yes, sir. I believe so."

Laney watched him sip the hot liquid and then shoved her hand in her pocket, squeezing her hankie ten times. Why did she bark at him? Where was the mercy of God that had often been shown to her? The cup began to shake, and she took it from his hand and sat next to him. "I am earnestly praying for your recovery, sir, but it will take time."

"And I will despise that." He took his coffee from her and closed his eyes, then opened them quickly. "Not you or the prayers." He backtracked. His warm, glossy gaze brought the air between them to a standstill. He looked down at his coffee. "I just meant having to recover. I have to work, and I have to do my job."

"I can understand the desperation of lost employment," she murmured. Standing, she locked her jaw, wished she could kick a hole in the soddy. *Oh, this mouth.* "That's not what I meant, just that it could happen. But it likely won't. Not to you any…how." Laney rubbed her forehead. "I've read the Wells Fargo company is very reputable. I'm sure they will allow you time for full recovery and then…then back on the job." She firmly tucked her hair behind her ears.

"Can you make it to the table, Sawyer?" Mr. Franklin asked.

Sawyer handed Laney his coffee and slowly stood. "Much obliged, Mrs. Franklin." Walking the four steps, he carefully lowered himself into a kitchen chair. Laney took the only empty chair next to him and sat. Folding her hands in her lap, she dropped her chin and waited. The silence was awkward, so she beseeched her own blessing over the food. Mrs. Franklin served Mr. Roth a plate of eggs, a chunk of ham, and a buttered biscuit.

"Tough break, that bullet gettin' ya in the right shoulder." Mr. Franklin clicked his tongue. "But it could be worse." He stabbed his meat.

With tremors, Sawyer balanced a spoonful of eggs with his left hand.

"I don't think it got to the bone." Mrs. Franklin chewed her ham. "Just laid the meat and muscle wide open."

Laney was hungry, but her fork dropped, clanging on the ironstone plate. This was to be the table conversation?

Slightly hunched over his plate, Sawyer tilted his head, spying her with deep, pained eyes. "You all right, Miss Balderhoff?"

The use of her formal name and the way she couldn't for the life of her read him, Laney went straight into ten rapid toe taps. "Yes, Mr. Roth." She stared back at him.

The challenge was on. At least in his weakened state, he didn't look away. Or maybe he didn't want to? Did Mr. Roth know he'd held his misplaced hand atop her thigh all night? Before the vapors colored her face scarlet, she had another thought. Maybe the wounded man was about to pass out? That did it, pure Christian empathy for a child of God broke the spell, and she took the knife to butter her biscuit.

"The Lord is my shield and *my* starch," Laney mumbled, taking a bite.

Chapter 6

Standing in a patch of warm morning sunshine, Laney gladly helped Mrs. Franklin dry the last of the dishes and hung the towel on the cabinet hook. The men had stepped outside after breakfast. The fresh air likely was helpful for Mr. Roth, and his distance from her was particularly helpful for her in return.

"Looks to be the wagon from Fort Churchill pulling in." Mrs. Franklin peered out the front window. "I believe your blouse is dried."

Mrs. Franklin walked to her room. Following her, Laney found the same frail women laying silent in the bed. Laney stepped into the corner and began to change.

"Thank you for the loan, Mrs. Franklin." She did her buttons up the front. "I lost all my pins on the, ah…ride here. My others are in my trunk." Laney frowned. She shouldn't be so worried over appearances when the fate of Moses pressed heavily on her heart.

"I've got a ribbon here." Mrs. Franklin pulled it out of her top drawer. "No use do I have for such a thing." She smiled at Laney. "May I?"

Laney nodded and felt Mrs. Franklin draw her brush through her hair, creating a part down the middle. Suddenly she was a child again, sitting for her mother's Sunday beautifications.

"I use to do this for my gals before they married and moved on." Mrs. Franklin's fingers laced in and out of Laney's hair. Like a master weaver, she'd created two sides of French braids and pulled them back into one. The ribbon held it all securely. Laney felt the blessed delight of each hair tight and in place.

"Thank you, Mrs. Franklin." Laney patted the sides. "This makes me feel so much better."

"Sorry, there won't be another stage till Wednesday. I suppose you'll go on to the Fort and then Virginia City?"

Laney had never thought of waiting for the next stage. "I do have an urgency to see what the fate of my cat is." Laney glanced at the poor woman in the bed and frowned. "You don't suppose Mr. Roth will leave without me?" She stepped from the bedroom, and Mrs. Franklin followed.

"Sawyer?" Mrs. Franklin gestured toward the waiting wagon and the men talking. "Not if he has a brain in his head, and I think he does." A slow smile covered her wrinkled lips. "He'll keep you in his sights—and not because he has to."

Laney blinked while a swirling overcame her stomach. The sentiment sounded endearing but farfetched. She finally found her manners. "Thank you, Mrs. Franklin, so much for your hospitality." She looked around, scratching her head. She'd already folded the blanket on the fainting couch. *Why did Mrs. Franklin's words make her muddled?* She patted her tidy hair again. Strange, she didn't even have her reticule with her. Her aunt insisted Laney keep it in her trunk to avoid thieves from snatching it. *Thieves. Goodness, if she only knew.* Empty-handed, she exited the Wells Fargo station and the Franklin's soddy.

A young man in a blue uniform tipped his hat and stepped closer. "Ma'am, I'm Lieutenant Burg."

"How do you do, sir." Laney gave him a small curtsy and wondered if he was a day over twenty. It didn't matter, he had a gun on his hip, and she was getting closer to Virginia City. She walked with him to the wagon. "Sir, did you happen to see Mr....I mean, John, the driver of the Wells Fargo stage yesterday?"

"I did not. But I saw the detail leave to find the bandits. We have some of the finest trackers in the area. I believe we are safe to go on to the Fort."

"Can we just go onto Virginia City?" Sawyer spoke behind her, landing his hat over his thick hair.

"Sorry, sir, I have to follow orders."

Laney wondered if John had dropped off Moses and her trunk at the Fort. At least she would see for herself. The Lieutenant stepped up on the wide seat of the open wagon and held his hand out to her. Holding her skirt layers, she stepped up on the wheel and took his gloved hand. Looking back, Mr. Roth thanked Mr. and Mrs. Franklin then came to where she sat.

"Scoot over, Miss Balderhoff." His tone was tart.

Laney showed forbearance as she rose and moved to the middle. He sat next to her roughly. When their legs touched, she tried to pull her skirt close. The wagon rocked forward leaving Austin Station.

"You clean up nice." His eyes lingered too long on her face and hair, and she looked away. No man had ever paid her a compliment, and she wasn't convinced that glimmer in his gaze was the result of pain or the joy of teasing her.

Dumbfounded to find any words, which was very rare for her, she swallowed hard and watched the barren, dusty road.

"Lieutenant, are you from this Nevada territory?" Laney asked.

"No, ma'am. Come from Colorado Territory." He tapped the reins and kept them at a reasonable speed. "Thought I might be sent to fight for the south if it comes to it. Hard to believe states are seceding from the Union. With President Lincoln wanting change, war is here. Wells Fargo brings the papers from back east. Read the first battle happened at Bull Run in Manassas, Virginia. North had 411 killed, South 387."

"I can hardly imagine." Laney frowned, clutching her collar. I'm from Nebraska. Bellevue. Talk of the town, this war." She felt the weight of all those men killed." I will pray that you will serve out here in the west, away from cannons and musket balls."

Lieutenant Burg flashed her a grin. "Thank you for those kind thoughts, ma'am. But I would go in a minute. We are ready to fight. That's what we signed up for."

"You are very brave, Lieutenant." Laney declared. "Are you a God-fearing man?" She thought she heard Mr. Roth groan.

"I suppose so. I've been to church as a boy."

"I just ask because of your line of work. Even like Mr. Roth's here, such danger lurks around every corner. It would make sense to want to have peace in your heart, I would think. First, you must believe that Jesus took your sins, and by putting faith in Him, you will be saved." She waggled her head. "I'm not saying to do that just because you could die. Salvation is good for all of us, all our days. Prayer is good for all of us." Laney wondered if he understood her point and mistakenly glanced at Mr. Roth. He'd rolled his eyes into a lazy droop. A burr pricked her side, and she decided if he started to fall from this wagon, she might not grab him. *But then she would feel terrible.*

"Those are kind words, ma'am. I will put some thought into it." The Lieutenant raised a half-smile.

Laney straightened up. Her training was for teaching, not preaching. Though important to see every soul saved, she wasn't naive to the fact that many men chose the life of carnal flesh over the spirit. For that, she could only pray. A bump rocked the wagon, and Mr. Roth's hip pressed against hers. "The Lord is the stronghold of my life," she whispered, clutching her elbows close.

***

Sawyer tried to pull his right arm closer to his belly. As long as his shoulder didn't move, he could feel some relief. But he knew this road like the back of his hand. The rare desert rains caused ruts, and wagon wheels made them even deeper. As expected, green foliage of the Carson River lay to the left. The brown river provided the clay for the adobe bricks, leaving Fort Churchill in a constant state of construction. After he reported the details to the commanding officer, he could be on his way to Virginia City. Would he have to take the gabby Miss Balderhoff? The way she held this soldier's attention, she would likely be the talk of the Fort.

A young, innocent teacher amid a company of women-starved men could give a call to repent and turn every soldier from their wicked ways. They'd all be saved with a twitch of her sweet smile. His breakfast flipped in his gut.

Why did he feel so agitated? The young woman was soft and smelled good. For the life of him, why did that make him mad? Was it all her holy and righteous prattle? No, he hoped her strong faith would carry her. She would need it. Was it being helpless in her arms? Of course, he didn't show weakness with anyone. But having her help hadn't riled him. Far better to be nursed by a young woman than some smelly fellow.

Sawyer leaned on his good side and scratched under the brim of his hat. Miss Balderhoff wasn't wholly harebrained. She didn't like the way he amused himself with her name. The young teacher had made that perfectly clear. Maybe that's what needled him?

She'd already moved on to make friends with the Lieutenant like he wasn't even sitting next to her. But he didn't need her to be his friend. Beyond simple gratitude, he'd no obligation to the woman. Sawyer squeezed his hands into fists against his chest, remembering how Laney had buttoned his shirt just a few hours ago. Tending to him at night and then by day felt too familiar.

The simple acts shouldn't be his undoing, but Miss Lane-*ee* was tender, selfless, and unknowingly alluring. Staring at him with her soft eyes at breakfast unexpectedly mesmerized him. The teacher was strange but purely feminine in voice, mannerisms, and touch—*definitely touch.* Beyond fetching, a womanly cuteness felt rare and interesting, like a gift wrapped in bright colored fabric wanting to be opened.

Sawyer huffed and lightly shook his head. *Stupid rambling, thinking like some lonely goat.* And lonely, he'd never been. Growing up in a crowded two-room cabin had never afforded him the luxury of loneliness. Every moment now was spent working in the stables and running the stage line with John—he was never lonely.

He watched Fort Churchill come into view. A gunshot wound and the loss of blood had weakened more than his body. His mind had gone soft, that's all.

They hit another rut, and his hand instinctively went to steady her back. He locked his jaw and slowly removed his hand, as small talk continued between her and the Lieutenant. Sawyer knew his blood had soaked her pale blue blouse with the little purple flowers. It fit snug, and her shapely form was hard to ignore.

The road into the Fort had Sawyer wishing John and the Wells Fargo stage waited for him. Instead, her entrance brought every blue-uniformed man's eyes to attention. Miss Laney Balderhoff arrived looking like a spring flower in the blistering desert. With her eager expression and the few loose dancing tendrils framing her lovely face, it was impossible not to notice her.

Chapter 7

Miss Elaine Balderhoff chewed her thumb nail while leaning in the corner of the doctor's office. Just minutes ago, before she could take the hands of the three soldiers helping her down from the wagon, the Bible-quoting, soul-saving magpie inquired about her cat. The men squinted dumbfounded at her, and she must have realized how strange she sounded. Sawyer let them wonder and shadowed the Lieutenant into a brick building on the right.

The doctor inside motioned for him to sit on a wooden table. Without greeting, the doctor pulled off the bandage Mrs. Franklin had wrapped tightly, and Sawyer winced, looking away.

"Don't see any puss. But I want to pour some whiskey over it to make sure." He moved Sawyer's arm away from his chest, and sudden stabbing pain and black spots floated around him.

"Make her leave." Sawyer ground out as the doctor went to pour the liquid.

Laney looked up as a soldier directed her outside into the courtyard.

"Sorry, son, I know it burns worse than Hades on a hot day." The doctor gave him one second to lift the bottle to his mouth first and then administered the liquid. Sawyer had every curse word he'd ever learned ready to pour out, but somehow between the sizzling skin and clenched jaw, only a low growl came forth.

"You're still sitting up," the doctor noted. "Going to pass out?" He began to wrap a clean cloth around the stitched flesh. "Proves here, the woman at Austin Station has a good hand with a thread and needle."

Sawyer caught a needed breath as the doctor tied off the strip with a knot. "The women folk are good at stitching, but I always wondered if they could handle the blood. If the country goes to war…" He wiped up the whiskey from Sawyer's chest and belly, "We may need more women to help. Likely a steadier hand than most men."

Sawyer barely nodded. The room spun when he looked up. Carefully he tried to move his elbow from where it had been strapped to his body. Mrs. Franklin was the kind of woman the army needed, he supposed. "How long will I feel like a newborn foal?" Sawyer wished his heart would quit pounding out of his chest.

"With this blood loss, maybe a week or more." The doctor put the whiskey in the cabinet. "And I know many a strong buck like yourself. No riding shotgun for a least a month."

Sawyer grunted and shook his head.

"I mean it!" The doctor said firmly, and Sawyer straightened up. "You don't let those muscles and flesh heal right, next time I see you I'll be taking that whole arm off."

"Yes, sir." The man had read his mind, and Sawyer had been put in his place. "A month."

"And no lifting anything heavy for two weeks." The doctor waited with a white sling for his arm.

Sawyer fumbled and winced painfully as he tried to get his shirt on. "Yes, sir." Without the help of a new teacher with soft round eyes, how many weeks till he could dress himself?

***

Laney sat on the bench in front of the doctor's quarters. Thankful for the shade and Lieutenant Burg's mug of water, she sighed. No one had seen her trunk nor Moses. John, the driver, must have taken them on to Virginia City. It made sense. She frowned. Wells Fargo's mission was to keep the stage on time. The cargo was important. Would he feel that way about Moses? Would someone feed the hungry cat?

"Good day, ma'am." Another bluecoat tipped his hat as he walked by.

If it wasn't for her deep melancholy, she might have found a smile for the fourth or fifth man to walk by with friendly greetings.

Lieutenant Burg came from around the two-story building on her left. "The captain is available now. When Mr. Roth is free, I'll take you on in."

Laney stood, "Thank you, I will check on Mr. Roth." Laney walked into the doctor's foyer and hesitated. The Captain? Was he going to hear of her folly and report her to the Virginia City town counsel?

Why had she agreed to help with Mr. Roth last night? Mr. Franklin could have helped, and she could have slept with the ladies in the other room? A shiver ran up her spine. How would a sensitive soul like herself fall asleep wondering if the frail, sunken woman next to her was even breathing?

A squeak escaped as she went to peek in the doctor's room. Laney squeezed her hanky ten times, murmuring, *"Be quick to hear, slow to speak."*

Mr. Roth was rolling his eyes in pain as he fumbled to insert his bad arm into his sleeve. A strange instinct inside of her wanted to aid him, but she waited. Practically barking and adamant about having her gone during the doctor's ministrations, she now decided to let him be.

"Yes, Miss?" The doctor acknowledged her while he helped Mr. Roth place his arm in a white sling. "I was just telling this shotgun messenger no work for a month, nothing."

Laney forged a smile. Mr. Roth was red-faced and disagreeable just buttoning his shirt. He would have little interest in her keeping him in check. "The captain is waiting for us," she said.

Mr. Roth pinched his lips and pushed off the table. Wobbling only a moment before he thanked the doctor, he then walked toward her. A strange odor followed him. Maybe Mr. Roth made her leave so she couldn't see how much of that whiskey went down his throat.

Standing back as he passed, she curtsied to the doctor. Everything had been out of order since she'd insisted she get on that stage. Patience is a virtue, and unfortunately, she had so little of it.

Brushing the dust from her skirts and pulling the stray hairs behind her ears, Laney followed behind Mr. Roth and Lieutenant Burg into the captain's quarters. Inside, dark, stately paneling, yet simple workmanship, greeted them. A large, older woman came from the hallway and nodded. Smelling something cooking on the stove, Laney suddenly hoped she would be escorted into a parlor for the women and the men could—

"Good day." A tall, strapping man with a crisp blue uniform came from a nearby office. "I'm Captain Adam Townes." He was younger than Laney expected. Groomed, sandy hair outlined a strong face and deep blue eyes. "Welcome to Fort Churchill."

Laney had never felt like she was in a room with such authority. She curtseyed.

"Sawyer Roth, sir. I'd shake your hand, but I just came from the doc."

"Yes, I understand. A bullet through the shoulder." The captain seemed genuinely concerned. "Word is out; a raid on a Wells Fargo Stage is concerning. I'd hoped to talk to you about the details."

Sawyer nodded and looked down at her. "This is Miss Elaine Balderhoff. She is the new school teacher for Virginia City."

"Miss Balderhoff." The captain took her hand and gently kissed the top. "As the one who oversees that Americans are safe in this area, I deeply regret this inconvenience."

Laney could still feel the tender concern on the top of her hand from his kiss. She brought it down quickly after noticing her hand stayed afloat like a dog's paw.

"Mrs. Forb has prepared a luncheon for us. Let's sit." The captain opened his hand, indicating they enter the room. A deep red and green rug was centered between two tall windows flanked by dark green brocade curtains. In the middle of the room, a long, thick table with ten chairs filled the space.

Laney pushed her hand into her pocket and squeezed her hankie ten times.

Lieutenant Burg bowed and let himself out, and Sawyer motioned for her to follow the captain into a formal dining area. Laney stepped up slowly, taking in the beautiful table setting for three. Warm aromas and the stately presentation made her insides melt, Christmas was the only time she'd eaten on such fine dishes. Sawyer pulled her chair out, and Laney noticed his dark lashes and stoic eyes observing her. Why was his presence suddenly befuddling her? Releasing a breath, she took her seat. He sat next to her.

"The new schoolmarm for Virginia City? Have you previously been to this part of the country, Miss Balderhoff?" The captain nodded thanks as the housekeeper spooned soup into their bowls. Laney heard the familiar apprehension in his tone. Each time, it made her inadvertently doubt her choice to teach in such a place. Flashing a small smile, she took her spoon and said her silent prayer of thanks. "I have not, sir, but just as when the Israelites had to flee in the Exodus, I believe the Lord will guide me."

"A cloud by day and a fire by night?" The captain grinned as he sipped his soup.

"You know your Bible, sir. How refreshing."

Sawyer grumbled, trying to get his right hand to rise above his ability to withstand the pain.

"Do you need assistance, Mr. Roth?" she asked.

A steely tension locked through his jaw, and he switched hands. "No, thank you, Miss Balderhoff." His eyes were focused on the spoon, raising it to his lips, but she could have sworn his eyes were glaring at her.

The housekeeper set a plate of fried cutlets in front of them, and Laney hid her smile. He would have to cut meat, this should be interesting.

"I'll ask forgiveness now." The captain stabbed a piece of the meat. "I'd normally not talk of bandits and shootings in front of a lady." He took a sip of cider, and Laney couldn't help notice that Mr. Roth had drunk his all in one go. "But since you were there, you might add some points to the discussion."

Laney finished chewing a bite of the salty meat and opened her mouth to recount her details when Mr. Roth cut in.

"We call it the lightning trees." He nodded to the captain.

"Yes, I'm familiar with the rock formation. Four large round pillars that rise like trees sliced off from lightning." The captain leaned forward.

"That's it." Mr. Roth gave up trying to cut his meat. Setting his fork down, he used the salt and pepper shakers and his spoon to remake a primitive map. "Thing is, I've tracked behind that very formation. The backside is steep. The stage trail is here. Austin Station is here." Rearranging the items on the table, he drew his finger across the cloth. "There's no place to hide behind it. I mean, a man on foot, yes. But a gang of three or more just can't find the coverage. I've been watching it closely for over a year now." Sawyer moved aside as the housekeeper, Mrs. Forb, reached in and sliced his meat.

"And it wasn't Indians, I believe your driver said." The captain drummed his finger next to his plate. Sawyer smiled his thanks for the help and easily forked the meat.

Sawyer and the captain pushed their dishes aside and began to reenact the details of the Wells Fargo shooting. Laney chewed on a roll.

Was anyone going to ask her about her heroics? Remarkably, she did hang by a thread from a racing stagecoach. Certainly, she didn't walk through the valley of the shadow of death— but she flung and flew through it. *And* it was *her* arms that kept the man from tumbling from his seat to sudden death. *And* she was the one who got blood on her good blouse. Laney touched her bodice. Rinsed out, it looked fine now.

Mrs. Forb cleared all the pretty dishes. Laney sighed. If she could get a word in between the men's military ramblings and exploits, she would ask if they could be on their way. Arriving in Virginia City before dark would be her preference.

The conversation finally lulled after the men's second cup of coffee. Though their discussion was detailed to what the bandits were after, Mr. Roth felt confident they were not after the new teacher. *Did he have to talk about her like she wasn't sitting at the table?*

The captain sat back, scratching his chin, and came forward for a drink of his coffee. "Forgive us, Miss Balderhoff." He blinked and chewed on his bottom lip. He was a handsome man in his own right, but curiosity stewed behind his narrowing blue eyes. Laney swallowed, wondered what misconduct needed to be addressed with her. *For thou, Lord, wilt bless the righteous; with favor...*

He cleared his throat. "May I be so bold to ask how your parents agreed to your move and employment in Virginia City?"

Chapter 8

Laney squirmed in her cushioned seat and brushed a crumb from the tablecloth. Heavens above, now both men were staring long at her. "Well, ah, you would be glad to know my father was also a military man."

The captain nodded, looking interested. Her story stalled. The table was a mess, and without thinking about it, she pulled the salt and pepper back together and placed them next to the candlestick where they had been. "He was in the navy." Mr. Roth's spoon returned to its proper place. "Unfortunately, he was lost at sea when I was sixteen." Unconsciously she brushed another crumb from where it lay, and Laney caught Mr. Roth's eyes flickering with confusion. How kind—the ungodly, shotgun messenger must be empathic to her story. She pulled her hands into her lap and squeezed them.

"We don't know many details. There was no funeral, of course." She shrugged. "My Aunt Lula came from Nebraska and stayed with us. That's about the time I earned my teaching certificate." Laney lifted a half-smile. "Then we ladies packed up everything and went with my aunt back to her home in Nebraska. Easterners were going west every day." Laney hoped that might be enough information.

"I see. So your aunt and mother are alive and well?" the captain asked.

"Yes." Goodness, she wasn't an orphan with no means. "Well, my mother suffers from a touch of sciatica. And gout. And often goiters and cankers. A bit of a hostage to her nerves. Did I mention her dry skin? That she blames on the midwest. There is a traveling doctor who sees her regularly. Once he told her the diagnosis was hysteria. She didn't like that." Laney's face crinkled, remembering how long her mother stayed upset. "And my aunt, bless her heart, made most of this trip with me. But her varicose veins were paining her, so once we got to Cherry Creek, she wanted to return."

Both men's brows narrowed, looking at her, their faces blank. The conversation seemed to fall away. *Well good, enough of that.* She owed neither of them the details, but she told the truth either way.

"Why do you wear those deerskin moccasins?" Mr. Roth had disapproval in his tone.

"It was the last gift my father gave me." She avoided Mr. Roth's scrutiny and asked the captain. "Please, sir, tell me where you are from and if you have anything you brought with you for pure sentimentality."

"Oh." The captain straightened up and blinked away for a moment. "I hail from Kentucky. All military men in my family for the last hundred years."

Laney thought she'd heard a faint drawl in his speech.

"I suppose the letters I keep." He met her eyes. "They are sentimental to me. From my mother or my sister." His voice slowed. "I see why those moccasins are special to you."

"And a Bible." Laney smiled, enjoying the kind-hearted air over the talk of wars, bullets, and disorder. "You seem to be a man who'd keep God's word close to your heart."

The captain stood, pushing his chair back. "Yes, ma'am."

Mr. Roth stood and helped pull back her chair.

The tall, neatly uniformed man walked back to the entryway, and they followed. "You may assure the Wells Fargo company that we intend to keep the routes safe. I've got extra men who will be on detail in that area." He nodded at Mr. Roth and stilled, tipping his knuckle across the end of his nose. "I have no law or command over much of what goes on in Virginia City." He stared at Laney and then looked to Mr. Roth and back to her. "As you are a fresh, new teacher, I have concern for your well-being there.

It's not safe for a single woman. I question who would approve of your position." He eyed Mr. Roth. "As a Wells Fargo man and gentleman, can I charge you, sir, with the proper watchfulness of a young teacher in Virginia City?" The captain opened the door, and Mr. Roth scratched his head before crossing.

"Of course." The injured shotgun messenger cleared his throat.

"Till we meet again, Miss Balderhoff." The captain smiled quickly. Laney curtsied and started to walk away even though she wasn't sure what had just transpired. *A fresh new teacher? What did that mean? Like an old, moldy one would be fine to live there?*

Mr. Roth hadn't taken too much of her care to heart as he walked ahead of her to find Lieutenant Burg. Within a few minutes, the captain's strange request was likely forgotten. The wagon with the young Lieutenant appeared to her left. Sawyer jumped up and before he could offer his good hand, another man in a uniform smiled and helped her onto the bench seat. Sawyer motioned for her to sit in the middle, and Laney flattened her skirt between the two men. The team jerked the wagon forward. Finally, the moment arrived to leave the bustle of Fort Churchill.

"Moses, hang on, I'm coming," Laney murmured.

***

Even with a sling, Sawyer needed to support his elbow on the rutted road to Virginia City. Mrs. Franklin's secure wrapping had served him far better than the fort doctor's. A month, two weeks, it didn't matter. If he ground his teeth down from this bouncing, dirt-filled ride today, how would he handle a day on the stagecoach? As a shotgun messenger he was like a lame horse— he'd be no use to the stage line; best put him out to pasture. Irritation was the same feeling he had the minute he'd agreed to keep an eye on Miss Lane-*ee's* wellbeing. Wells Fargo man to nursery keeper.

When her mouth remained closed, the determined young woman was fetching to the eye. He huffed, turning away to watch a tumbleweed roll by. Boom or bust was the vow of every miner in Virginia City. This was a bust.

A few green trees and brush started to follow the Carson River. Color wound through the parched land like a mismatched thread in his sister's embroidery's hoop. Sawyer grimaced, pulling his arm tighter. Maybe he should take this time off to go home. The idea held appeal for a moment until he saw himself sitting inside of the Wells Fargo stage—the preferred place for the elderly, women, and children. And then to arrive at his family's farm unable to either harvest corn or husk... his mother and sisters would offer sympathy, but his father would want him to stay and work. What if his older brothers had already left for the new war in the east? Could he sit at the family table with their places missing, wondering if he would ever see them again? Sawyer let his head drop onto the palm of his hand, his elbow resting on his knee. When could he hold a gun? The doctor didn't say he couldn't....

"Mr. Roth." Her voice was gentle but, unfortunately, brought him back to the present. "Can you abide by a few questions? Is your shoulder paining you too much?"

Of course it hurt, but he would never say. "No, what?" Sawyer kept his head down.

"This is the Carson River to our right?" she asked.

"Yes." He didn't look up.

"Is this the river that runs to Virginia City?"

"No."

"Another river then?"

He shook his head and hoped her questions would still.

"My paperwork says I will be staying at the widow house," she said. His head nodded once. "You mentioned a mother and child there." One more disengaged nod. "How is it they are there? Does the mother work?"

Face taut, narrow eyes locked onto hers. "1859, twelve men died in a cave-in, the Ophir Mine. These men left their wives as widows. Others weren't married, or their women moved on. The city had a house built for the widows with no place to go." He rubbed his fingers up and down his forehead. "You'll meet Widow Boils and Widow Canazzaro. Widow Farrow has the son. His name is Matthew."

"Widow Boils, Canazzaro, and Farrow." Laney practiced.

"The first two are older ladies."

"Widow Boils, and Widow Canazzaro are older." She repeated. "In between teaching the children, I'll pray I can be of assistance to those ladies." Quiet finally settled between them, and he looked forward.

"And are they all church-going women?"

Sawyer ran his hand down his face. "I believe so, but I don't watch the coming and going on Sundays."

"Of course." The teacher huffed. "And as to the request of the captain at Fort Churchill, I just want you to know that supervision of my well-being is not necessary. I'm sure with these other ladies in the house, we will use neighborly love and care toward one another." The round-faced, sweet-eyed woman watched for his approval. To agree presented a tempting opportunity to unload the petite, talkative responsibility. It would be so easy, but it wasn't his nature. "It doesn't work that way," he mumbled.

"Why not?" she squinted. "I was fully aware of my choices when I took the position."

The wagon wheel hit a rock, and she bumped into his good arm. Instinctively his hand rose to her back to steady them both. Like touching a hot stove, his hand made contact and he instantly pulled it back to his leg. Sawyer stretched his fingers apart and watched the dry land, wondering what that tingling was about. *What was her question?*

"Because I gave the captain my word." Sawyer could only hope that would be the end of the discussion.

"But I cannot think of how you would fulfill that. It's chivalrous, to say the least. But I will be spending the next few weeks examining the class list and visiting the children in their homes. I must create a few short lessons in reading and writing so I can begin to divide them into educational classes. Then I can prepare the books and lessons for the start of school." The eager teacher lifted a small smile. "You see, with so much to do, it's simply too much for you to monitor my whereabouts."

Sawyer knew he would not ignore the captain's orders. *Man of his word.* He wanted to scold himself. "I will accompany you to these homes. Many of them are among the miner's shacks— someplace you should not go alone."

He watched her face contort from a frown to a sneer before she finally looked away.

Miss Balderhoff turned back quickly. "On one condition." Opening her mouth to say more, her attention diverted to the faint buildings of Virginia City in the distance.

He would pay no attention to her conditions. The gullible young woman with braids rubbed the back of her neck. The magpie held no place to bargain with his generous offer.

"Mr. Roth." Her eyes narrowed. "I've heard it said that Wells Fargo men are—"

"Stop now," he said smugly. "I won't be strong-armed. Those compliments are how you got on the wrong stage."

"There's your Virginia City." Lieutenant Burg broke in. "Not much of a city, aye?"

Miss Balderhoff's eyes widened, then blinked from either dust or the start of tears. Something nicked Sawyer's conscience. For her kindness extended to him in his feebleness, he could be a bit more agreeable.

"You're right, Lieutenant." She lifted a sad smile. "It is more of a rustic mining town than a city." The wagon slowed and pulled into the long dirt center street. Miss Balderhoff looked left to right at the storefronts, saloons, as the rosy glow faded from the passing faces. One or two townsfolk looked respectable, but most filthy. Some even stopped to watch them as they pulled in front of the widow's house. The Lieutenant pulled the brake tight and wrapped the reins.

"Here, Miss." The peach-faced soldier held his hand out.

Miss Balderhoff took it and allowed him to steady her as she jumped down. Seeing the Wells Fargo building and the need to talk to John felt like a magnet to Sawyer's body. He could nod his thanks and be on his way, but his feet betrayed him as he walked to meet them on the other side. He thanked the Lieutenant for the ride today.

Taking Miss Balderhoff's elbow, Sawyer moved her away. Like separating a boy from his first love, he'd saved the Lieutenant the embarrassment of some mush-laden folly. Still holding her elbow, they watched the Lieutenant tap the horse forward. Her eyes still roamed the town, and disappointment covered her twitching frown.

"What was that condition you mentioned earlier, Miss?" He dropped her elbow and pushed his hat back.

"Oh," she scanned the block one more time and chewed on her bottom lip. Having trouble acknowledging him, she met his gaze and then looked away. "I want to ask you on your honor as a gentlemen...um...to...promise me, that you will never mention to another soul what took place at the Franklin's home."

Sawyer's eyes narrowed. "What took place?"

Laney whimpered and rubbed her hand over her eyes. "Good, praise the Lord, what you don't remember bodes well enough."

"No, no, no." He took her by the arm as she pulled away. "That won't do. Tell me what happened that you insist I, as a gentleman, take to the grave."

"Mr. Roth, really, I wish I'd never..."

Sawyer nudged her closer. He had to know why she wouldn't look at him. "Just say it so I can forget it." He lifted a sneer, that didn't sound right.

"We shared the couch. All night," she said quickly, her eyes dropping closed then wide open. "You slept on my lap?"

He dropped her arm. That was true enough, likely from her customary Christian service. Watching her out of the corner of his eye, he waited. "And?"

"You...you held your hand atop *my leg*." She whispered as if it was painful.

He jerked back as if a skunk had sprayed. "I assure you, Miss, it was not intentional. I would never have tried to touch you." *Never in my sleep or awake.* He removed his hat and scratched his hair. "Believe me, never will there be any mention of these things to anyone."

"Everything is just so out of order." Miss Balderhoff huffed.

Sawyer shook his head, wondering if Lane-*ee* could say that again. The night she remembered or felt every vivid detail was more of a blur to him, but Miss Balderhoff was flesh and blood, real and red with embarrassment. Now the very thing he'd pledged to forget stood in front of him. He'd sat idle atop the hard wagon bench too long; surely that was why his roving hand tingled again!

Chapter 9

Laney felt humiliation radiate through her. She should've never brought up that strange night, and she could tell by his expression, Mr. Roth had no memory of wrongdoing. Before Laney let her last thread of dignity unravel, she sucked in a deep breath.

"My cat. I have to find my cat. If you will—" Laney went to step away when a young man with bushy brown hair and a thick mustache ran across the dirt street toward them.

"Wait." He held his hand up, panting. "Are you in from Fort Churchill? Mr. Roth?"

"That's right," Mr. Roth answered.

"I'm Samuel Clemens, from the newspaper, the Territorial Enterprise." He nodded at Laney. "I spoke with the coach driver and heard his recount of what happened. I want to get the story set in type by dawn if I can. Can you give me five minutes to hear what happened?" He pointed at Mr. Roth. "That sling there, is that from the bandit's gunfire?"

Laney turned to leave.

"Wait, Miss, were you there? Did you come in with Mr. Roth just now?"

"Yes, sir." She searched around them. "But I must find my cat."

"Your cat?" Mr. Clemens blinked. "Is the cat lost?"

Laney rubbed her temple. "I don't know yet, we got separated after Mr. Roth and I were left at the Austin Station."

"How terrible, how did that happen, ma'am?"

"I...I..." Laney groaned. "I stayed with Mr. Roth while Mrs. Franklin repaired his injury." She tried again to leave, but the man from the paper was inquisitive.

"So you were just an innocent bystander on the stage to Virginia City? Where did you travel from? Are you here to see relatives, or...?"

"She's the new teacher." Mr. Roth rubbed the crease between his brows.

"She is?" His face lit up. "This is perfect. An innocent, young schoolmarm caught in the crossfire of good and evil on the Wells Fargo stage going west." Mr. Clemens huffed a smile. "Can you wait right here? I need to go get my paper and pencil."

"No, I cannot." Though she was flattered, sure *her* details would make a riveting story, Moses was foremost on her mind and heart.

"I'll make you a deal, Miss...Miss?"

"Balderhoff."

"Miss Balderhoff." His voice now lowered with seriousness. "If I hold off the long night of typesetting, would you agree to meet with me in the morning?" His eyes rose in hope. "I would be willing to help look for your cat."

"That is too kind, sir," Laney said, trying to calm her frayed nerves. "I have yet to meet the lovely widows I will be sharing a home with."

"Please, Miss? I will record your account with discretion and a touch of bravery on your part." A smile appeared under his thick mustache. "Wouldn't that portrayal be a helpful reassurance to the families, as you will be caring for their beloved children?"

Laney wavered. "All right." She bowed quickly, wanting to get inside the large two-story home. "Until tomorrow."

Mr. Roth's working arm slid in front of her and opened the door.

Taking a deep breath, her eyes searched left to right as she walked into the widow's home. There was a coat tree and a large mahogany banister with matching wood steps leading to the upstairs. Sadly, no orange cat ran to meet her. Restraining a whimper, she forced herself to tiptoe forward as Mr. Roth closed the door and stood far too close behind her. Shoving her hand into her pocket, her fingers searched for her hankie. The parlor to the right teamed with curious eyes as the three widows stood to greet her.

"I'm sorry. I am the rudest woman in town. But have any of you seen my cat? He would've come in a box, like this." She displayed the dimensions with her hands. "I'm sorry to be so ill-mannered, I just…just…." *Oh, Lord, have mercy.* The tears burst forth like a flood. "His name is Moses." Her voice cracked. "And he is orange." A long wet huffy sob escaped. "I'm sorry, I…I…."

"I saw 'em in your barn, Mr. Roth," a boy with brown hair said while Laney blew her nose into her hankie.

"Your barn, Mr. Roth?" She turned to face him. "Is…is…" She fought against the gulps ruining her voice. "Is it close?"

"Right out the back door." The boy took her hand, and Laney felt him tug her through the dark hall, past two doors, and into the kitchen. The widows followed like spectators of some strange mystery. Her heart pounded with worry, but she didn't want to cry. "Please, Lord, let him be okay."

The sweet boy who still held her hand took her across a dirt alley and to the large pine barn with wide-open double doors that loomed ahead.

"Did you see him today, son?" Who had left the barn doors open? She stuck her knuckle in her mouth to contain more oncoming sobs. A strong whiff of pine, hay, and horse droppings met her first, as she searched high and low.

"Moses." Her voice dipped with pained expectancy. "Moses. I'm here. Come, kitty, kitty." Her beloved companion was an indoor cat, of course, he would never…

"Meow."

"There!" The boy pointed at a high rafter before Laney could believe what she saw.

"Moses, oh, praise the Lord above." She twisted and saw the three widows, all smiling. "That's him!" Mr. Roth missed the miracle, watching her cat with little expression.

"Come here, Mo." Laney held her hands up, and the cat scampered down two beams and a ladder to be scooped up into her arms.

"The Lord is good, and I will praise Him all my days," Laney said, nuzzling into her cat's fur. "I was so worried." A flood of peace and joy settled over her, and she smiled at the ladies and boy of the widow's house. "The real Moses was put in a basket and sent downriver, safe, cared for, and raised in a palace, and here I was with such low faith." She chuckled. "I'm so sorry, ladies." Shaking her head, she pulled in a deep breath. "May we start over? I'm Miss Balderhoff." Laney approached the shorter widow with white hair pulled tight into a bun. "But please call me Laney."

"Wonderful to meet you." Caring eyes crinkled deep lines into her temples. "I am Mrs. Canazzaro." Her thick accent was unknown to Laney. "When I was a child in Italy, we had a little bird we kept in a cage. I remember being very attached to it."

"Oh, bless you." Laney released one hand from Moses and squeezed hers. "You are a close friend already, a lover of animals too."

Laney's eyes shifted to the next woman, more gray than white in her hair and lacking an assuring smile.

"I'm Mrs. Boils." She nodded, and no hand squeezing took place. "I'm the one who said to put the cat in the barn. I'm not sure I can tolerate cat hair in the house. It's been known to make me sneeze."

"Of course," Laney said wide-eyed. "My own dear mother often had the same complaint." With no intention of letting Moses out of her arms, the next woman was young and refined and strikingly beautiful. Laney moved down to greet her.

"Hello, how do you do?" The woman was a bit taller than herself, with soft gold mixed in light brown hair. She was dressed in a full bell skirt layered in solid black sateen with black buttons running up the front of her long-sleeved, form-fitting bodice. Laney gave a small curtsy. Funny how it felt appropriate in this fine woman's presence.

"So wonderful to meet you, Miss Balderhoff." She bowed slightly. "I'm Mrs. Farrow, but please call me Ava. We are so pleased to have you with us. This is my son, Matthew."

"Yes." Laney almost swooned. "A true biblical name for such a wonderful boy. I owe you a great deal of gratitude for…" A horse nickered, kicking the stall, and Moses twisted and flew from her grip. Before she could track his escape, he was back up the ladder and jumping the top rafters. "Oh, my."

"I think he likes it up there." Matthew smiled. "But I could go climb up and get him."

Mr. Roth walked to the stall with the attention-seeking horse. He rubbed the horse's velvety nose and scratched under the chin. Laney hesitated, chewing her bottom lip; she wanted Moses back in her arms, but the ladder looked too precarious for a child.

"Matthew, do you think Moses will be safe here in the barn?" she asked.

"I do, Miss Balderhoff. His chin bobbed the reassurance. "When he's up there, Moses can spy the mice running back and forth, then he plans his attack. Being all sneaky like, your cat uses those thick paws and creeps closer and closer until he swipes his claws and has them for lunch."

Laney's bottom lip curled down, struggling to see her lazy Moses in such an aggressive state.

"Now, you went and got yourself shot." Mrs. Boils piped in, and Laney realized that Mr. Roth had hung back while everyone had focused on her cat.

"That I did." He swallowed, rubbing his upper arm. Looking tired and trail-beaten, he shook his head.

"John came and told us, declaring you'd live. Now that we see who your nurse was…." Mrs. Boils' voice rose and a pouty pinch crossed her lips.

"Don't start, Widow B." His eyes narrowed. "I'm broken and busted, and mourning the loss of my Colt."

Laney noticed all three widows winced at those last words.

"A shotgun messenger without a shotgun. *Tsk, tsk.*" Mrs. Canazzaro frowned. "I have something you like—a plate of my muffuletta rolls in the warmer. Not as good as the ones I made in Sicily, but they are getting better."

"Normally, I would in a short minute, ma'am. But I had a lumpy night of sleep." Mr. Roth flashed a wink at Laney before he walked toward the barn doors. "I'm heading to bed, I'll see you ladies in the morning." Turning, he nodded once at Laney. "Don't talk to Mr. Clemens without me."

"Sounds like a date," Widow Boils said, with a coy smirk.

Mr. Roth huffed and glared at her over his shoulder. "Be nice." He dropped his chin. "This one will hit you with her Bible."

Laney straightened up. Did Mr. Roth just wink at her? She would never hit anyone. There was a tease in his eyes, but that sounded very rude and impolite. He left her befuddled and walked out. What must these widows think of her? "No, no. I would never hit anyone with my Bible."

Mrs. Boils clasped her on her shoulder. "He was teasing you, Miss Balderhoff." She scoffed. "Handsome buck only does that with women he likes."

Laney scratched behind her ear. Holding her shoulder, Mrs. Boils led her back across the alley. "How many women does he like?" Laney mumbled.

A loud snap rent the air, and Laney jumped. "What was that?" She covered her ears.

"Gunshot." Mrs. Boils stifled a laugh as Laney looked around quickly.

"The Lord is my helper; I will not be afraid. What can mere mortals do to me?" tumbled out of Laney's mouth, unaware.

"Oh, you poor innocent thing." Mrs. Boils gestured an open wave to the other buildings facing the shadowy back alley.

"Welcome to Virginia City, Miss Balderhoff!"

Chapter 10

Still lying awake in the dark, Laney counted twelve gunshots while reciting the books of the Bible in order. Some had to be from just down the dusty streets of Virginia City, and some seemed farther away. She didn't want to close the window as the lovely evening breeze cooled the prickly, warm room. Laney rose and tried to see anything happening in the barn. She should've snuck Moses back into his box and up to her room. Likely, poor Mo was just as vexed as she was with the ruckus in this strange town.

The elder widows had talked long into the evening. Laney covered so many yawns, though their life stories were fascinating. She'd finally done the polite thing and excused herself to her small bedroom. Sighing, she retraced her steps in the new room. Having three gowns all hanging in the same direction and placing her things from her trunk in proper order on the bureau had helped her tremendously to feel more settled. Laney straightened her comb and brush again to make sure the edges were even with the sides of the water stand, and then she brushed her hair one more time before replacing it exactly where it had just been.

She went back to the window. There had been a lull in the gunshots. Without Moses in her room, would she ever be able to sleep? Knowing she should have done this hours ago, she threaded her arms through her linen robe and carefully opened her door. Her conscience still pinched; she'd taken Matthew's room, and his bed had been moved in with his mother. Ava said it was of no bother. The three of them—Ava, Matthew, and Laney—now lived in the upstairs, while the other older ladies had rooms downstairs off the kitchen. The second step down brought a faint creak to the staircase, and Laney froze. She could only hope the older widows slept as soundly as her mother and aunt. Barefoot and agile, Laney made it to the back door and lifted the latch. She had been parted from Moses too long. Blessed be, she needed her cat back, but fear of flying bullets had kept her inside.

Searching long up and down the empty back alley, not even the moonlight gave her away as she stepped out. Setting her sights to the Wells Fargo barn, she winced as sharp pebbles bit into her bare feet. The barn doors had been pulled shut, but it only took a quick tug to create a small opening to slip through.

"Moses," Laney whispered. "Come, kitty, kitty." She searched along the rafters, but it was too dark to see anything. "Moses." She tried to hold her voice low. "Kitty, kitty." Squinting upward, she moved around bales of hay, saddles, and tack hanging from the wall. "Moses." She tried a bit louder, looking in every direction. What if he'd gotten out? Out of the corner of her eye, something dark and looming came close. She jumped and swung her fist with all her might.

"Augh." It fell to the hay-covered floor. "My…" he ground out through gritted teeth, "shoulder!"

"Shoulder?"

"Oh no, I'm so sorry!" She dropped next to Mr. Roth. "Oh, forgive me, I didn't know who or what it was." Wanting to help, she almost leaned over him to help him stand. Suddenly, she straightened on her knees. "Why didn't you announce yourself, sir?"

Mr. Roth tried to rise on one knee as he hunched, holding his arm in the sling. "What are you doing here in the middle of the night?" He ground out and finally pulled himself to sitting on a bale of hay, rocking, and favoring his arm.

Laney slumped, feeling ridiculous with another unorthodox encounter with Mr. Roth. "I wanted to bring Moses back to my room. The gunshots are terrifying." She spied the area again. "Have you seen him?" Like an actor taking his cue on the stage, Moses sauntered out between two bags of feed. "Oh, heavens, Moses." Reaching for him, she pulled her beloved cat to her. "What a bundle of trouble you are."

Mr. Roth croaked a humph, shaking his head. Laney stood, holding Moses. She tried to brush the hay off her gown. "I do apologize, and I pray you will forgive me for punching your shoulder. Now I will know this is where you wander at night."

"I don't wander. I live above the Wells Fargo office, but after a couple of hours of sleep, my shoulder was paining me." He pulled his hand down his face and looked up at her. "You're the wandering, senseless piece of mischief that…"

"Hey, now!" her eyes narrowed. "No need to be mean." The horse in the stall snorted, and she hitched Moses higher to her side. "Especially after my care for you," she murmured.

"Listen, lady." He pulled in a deep breath. "I'll give you that you're spirited and…and different. And you're probably much like this cat. Every time you jump with some hair-brained idea, you probably land on your feet." He stood and hung on to a barn post. "But I don't want to care about you."

Laney blinked against the darkness. Did she hear him correctly? He cares about her? But he doesn't want to?

Mr. Roth shuffled his feet. "See, my nature is if someone is good to me, then I'll repay the favor." He shook his head. "And being you're a stranger, and an agreeable woman, and you *were* good to me…." He looked around the dark barn. "So, I will help you meet the students." No kindness rose in his tone. "And then I'm back out on the stage." Mr. Roth sighed, pressing his fingers against his temple. "I'm going to say this like you were one of my sisters." His determined eyes held hers, and she leaned back. "You have no business in this town." He took ahold of her arm. "Listen to me good. This place will bind you, strip your goodness bare, and leave you without a Bible verse to quote."

Laney blinked; just like his fingers, something fearful touched deep within her soul. Would this be another humiliating failure like her last job? Would her faith be enough to prevail here like the missionaries she'd read about, giving their very lives to penetrate the darkness of Godless countries? Was she stupid and naïve to try this life alone? Though his touch spoke of something she did not understand, should she press on past his warnings?

His grip on her arm gave way until he held her elbow, then held her wrist, and slipping his warm hand down, he gripped her hand.

As soon as their connection broke, Sawyer Roth walked away, and Laney was left with only the dreadful questions and the irregular beating of her heart.

***

The next morning, a soft knock at her door made her rise on one elbow. Moses stretched asleep at her feet, and the room felt stuffy with the late summer's heat.

"Coming." She slid from the bed and peeked through the open crack of the door.

Mrs. Canazzaro smiled. "Mr. Roth and Mr. Clemens are waiting."

"I'm so sorry. I overslept." She moaned. "I will be right there." Laney hid in the corner and twisted out of her nightgown. Reaching for her light blue, cotton dress, she fumbled with the buttons. It had taken so long to fall asleep, and then she'd had a strange dream with Mr. Roth holding her hand and telling her the town would strip her bare. Laney shook her head and whirled back to see Moses. That was no dream. She had been in the barn, and she'd accidentally struck Mr. Roth in the shoulder.

She really didn't hold his hand; truthfully, he'd held hers. Laney sank onto the bed, pulling her stockings on. And what did it matter? She'd held the injured man in her arms. *Strip me bare, good heavens!* Or maybe it was her kindness, or what did he say? After securing her moccasins with their leather laces, she fingered her hair back and found her pins to secure a low bun. *Lord, forgive me for rushed requests, but please grant me grace on this first day.*

***

Sawyer licked the cinnamon and sugar off his fingers. It was a grand morning when Widow B put the grease to the pan and fried the donuts crispy on the outside, feathery on the inside. Samuel Clemens had bested him, eating ten for his eight. Matthew had eaten four. Both men stood quickly, their chairs scraping the small kitchen wood floor as Miss Balderhoff blew into the kitchen.

"I am so sorry, gentlemen." She offered a slanted smile at Samuel before her eyes jumped off him like he was a rattlesnake.

"Porridge with a side of donut." Widow Boils set a plate in front of her and poured her some coffee.

"Thank you so much, Mrs. Boils." Laney nodded. "Good morning, Matthew." The boy grinned with sprinkles of sugar on his lips.

Mrs. Boils stood close and laid a heavy hand on her shoulder. "Not here a day and already got two and a half men at the table for ya. And ya might as well call me Widow B."

Laney showed no response but to bow her head to pray over her breakfast. She'd find out Widow B had more moxie than manners, and for an older woman who should be mourning, she also had a mettlesome tongue. The stout, disagreeable widow moved back to the stove.

Sawyer noticed Miss Balderhoff's hair. Without the tight braids, her bun made her look older, more refined. But by far, her loose hair was his favorite. Her soft blue dress was nice, but would he ever forget her standing in her nightclothes just inches from him? Why did he hold her arm, her hand? Ever since they'd shared that narrow couch, a line, a barrier seem to be crossed. Being near her again, stirred his insides to want and confusion. Needing to rein in his thoughts, Sawyer reached for another donut while she finished praying.

"So, ahh." His rabbit brain fought to make words. "I told Mr. Clemens about the details."

Laney took a small bite of porridge. "The only thing I might be able to add is the hand of the Lord. Faithfully, He saw us to safety."

"The Lord did?" Mr. Clemens's pencil stilled over his notes. "Could you be more specific?"

"It's likely familiar to you. Isaiah 40:31. '*Those who wait on the Lord shall renew their strength; they shall mount up with wings like eagles, they shall run and not be weary, they shall walk and not faint.*'"

"So this *waiting on the Lord* is what happened while you were fleeing for your life on the Wells Fargo stage?" Mr. Clemens eyed her, confused. A knock at the door made them all look up.

Widow C stepped from the parlor to open the door. Coming to the kitchen, she announced, "Its Mayor Reynolds. I showed him into the parlor. He said he's here to see Miss Balderhoff."

"And now there were three!" Widow B rolled her eyes. "We've had no members of male persuasion quite like this until today. Miss Balderhoff," she said, lifting her frown to the side, "I'm glad you're here. Going to liven up the place."

Laney stood and bowed. "Excuse me, ma'am, gentlemen."

Sawyer and Mr. Clemens both stood and then sat again. "How am I going to tie in eagle's wings and walking without fainting?" Mr. Clemens frowned. "This is a front-page action story, not some Sunday women's column."

Widow B sat at the table with her coffee. "Might bide your time and do something separate on the new teacher. She's got spunk."

"A human interest piece on her and her cat?" Mr. Clemens's snickered.

"And that's too above you, I suppose? What's with this nonsense about your name being Mark Twain?" Widow B shook her head. "Who you trying to fool? If your writing's corrupt, you can blame it on Mark Twain? Is that the drivel behind it, that name in the paper?"

Mr. Clemens's squared his shoulders and flipped his note pad closed. "I'll have you know, Widow, many writers have a pen name. It's very popular. Voltaire's real name was Francois-Marie Arouet."

"I don't have a flea's brain who that is. But Samuel Clemens is a fine name. I don't even see why we need a newspaper." She puffed out a breath. "Everybody knows everybody. The mayor is here to meet the new teacher, and there was no paper to announce that."

Sawyer wished they'd stop jabbering. He'd like to eavesdrop on the mayor's conversation. Speaking of gossip, everyone in town knew the mayor's fine wife had packed up and left him and their two sons. Mayor Reynolds is now Miss Balderhoff's boss. Yet word around town was he couldn't be trusted, setting up rules and regulations for the mines that keep him in control of fines and fees for everything done.

But for himself, he loved the open road, and he'd no time for chin-wagging in this town. If the mayor cared about his children, he'd better be agreeable to the new teacher. Sawyer rose and plucked his hat from the back of his chair and stilled. *But not too agreeable.* The man had stirred the ire of many mine owners. Could the plucky Miss Balderhoff keep her Christian principals high and waving like a flag?

"All right." Mr. Clemens rose. "Thank you, Widow Boils, for the tasty breakfast. If I ever have room for the women's interest column, I'll ask your permission to print this remarkable donut recipe."

"Never," Widow B piped in. "Taking it to the grave."

Shrugging and wide-eyed, Mr. Clemens shook his head at Sawyer. "Thank you, Mr. Roth, for the detailed account. Good thing the bandits were no match for the speed of the Wells Fargo stage or your sharpshooting. Please tell Miss Balderhoff I apologize our interview was cut short, but I have enough facts to elaborate the rest." He smiled, raising his thick eyebrows. "If the teacher would like to meet with me, I would be delighted, and tell her she can bring her cat." He dropped his note pad and pencil in his jacket pocket. "The Territorial Enterprise is still in the basement of the Silver Queen, or, where I get most of my good stories, she can send for me at the Bloody Mary Saloon."

Sawyer had no words for the reporter's offer as he pulled his hat down. Mr. Clemens walked out the back door, and Sawyer tipped his hat at Widow B. "Thanks for the breakfast. I'll be in the barn."

"Yep, now I get to keep the new schoolmarm's social calendar?" She mumbled, pouring hot water into the kitchen basin. "I see how it is."

Chapter 11

Sawyer groaned, trying to balance the pitchfork and muck the stalls left-handed. He was halfway successful until he decided to flip the droppings into the wheelbarrow—some went in and some fell on his boot. Shaking it off, he wanted to bark some bad-mannered curses. Certainly, as soon as he did, Miss Balderhoff would appear scolding him with her hourly Bible verses. Sawyer lifted his face heavenward. "Thank you." As a shotgun messenger, he wouldn't marry and be saddled to anyone's harping all the day long.

Her orange cat sauntered through the barn doors and leaped up the ladder to the hayloft. Sawyer watched the cat and shook his head. Virginia City seemed to agree with the lazy cat. Miss Balderhoff possessed a foolishly deep affection for the animal, no question about that. He would say she was loyal and something else. Well, Lane-*ee* was peculiar.

Widow B had said the excitement was more than they'd ever had. So it wasn't just him. The young woman was odd in an endearing sort of way. Sawyer reached for a piece of wood about the size of his rifle. Holding it against his right shoulder rang unimaginable, so he tried to keep it against his left. Sliding his hand down where the trigger would be, Sawyer tried to grip it and lower his head to see down the imaginary barrel. It slipped from his shoulder and landed on the floor. Fighting the urge to kick it, he bent, picked it up, and set it back. Two weeks to a month to heal; he'd go stir crazy. John had left today with the Wells Fargo clerk, Albert, in his place. Albert had asked him to keep the office open, but as soon as they left the closed sign was displayed across the Wells Fargo door. Complaints of a closed office would get out soon enough, but he'd thought of a possible solution. Widow Farrow had the disposition, *and* she knew his secret. Part of his paycheck to her would be a small price to pay for—

"Mr. Roth?"

Sawyer jumped from his thoughts and checked his boot. Did he smell like horse patties? "Miss Balderhoff." She was alone, and for some reason that sat well with him. Widow B had done enough teasing for one day. He waited. Her voice usually filled every quiet second.

"What's wrong?" he asked.

She held some papers to her skirt and tapped them against her leg. His eyes bounced quickly from that scandalous leg that he'd supposedly touched.

"Oh, nothing, really." She rose a faint smile. "I have the class roster from the last teacher, and the key to the school is mine."

His chin dropped, and he watched her chew her lip from the top of his eyes. "You're too quiet. What? Is it Mayor Reynolds?"

Laney watched her cat and finally scratched her head. "Moses has shown a liking for this barn."

"My question, Miss Balderhoff?"

Her frown sat like a fixture on her face. "It's just something he said." She huffed. "He wants to make sure the school seats are filled with American children."

Sawyer stepped closer as his tongue rolled inside his cheek. "Let me guess. No colored skin, no child that doesn't speak English from their parent's knee."

"Yes." Her forlorn tone said it all.

"And you feel different?"

Her eyes met his, and her face nodded slowly. "We have a biblical mandate to go to all the nations, to invite every tribe, every nation into the knowledge of God and His word."

He had a mental picture of her standing with Bible raised, tongue wagging, and finger pointing. "But you're the new teacher, not the preacher."

"You're right." Her shoulders rose. "I need to stay in my place here. Thankfully, he said nothing of my footwear."

Sawyer wasn't sure her compliance conveyed what he was getting at. "I'll give you, you have a mighty opinion on things. But what if allowing all children to learn is right, and Mayor Reynolds is wrong."

Wilting as if she agreed, Laney sighed. "What would you do if you were me, Mr. Roth?"

He needed no time to think. "Go home."

"Besides that."

"Far be it for me to say the obvious." Sawyer went to take the wheelbarrow outside and froze. It was impossible to balance with only one working arm. Miss Balderhoff came alongside and grabbed the handle on his right. "Tell me," she asked as they pushed together, running it outside. At least the woman came in handy.

"Pray, Miss Balderhoff." He was pleased that he spoke without sarcasm. "Surely, God will tell you, of all people."

She followed him back into the barn. "Mr. Roth." Her smile spread wide, and her eyes regained their sparkle. "You are a true brother in the Lord to remind me of such profound words. Some only believe that God speaks from the Bible and nothing else. Some believe He speaks through those in authority. But you have made my heart glad." She crossed her hands over her chest. "When I read my Bible, I see time after time where the God of the universe speaks to ordinary people—even through a donkey!" Her head tipped, and she beamed playfully. "Yes, I will pray and listen for His voice. His plan is for all the children here."

Sawyer lifted a slow grin. "I'm so glad I could help." Now his tone held a tidbit of mocking, but she didn't seem to notice.

"Oh, and this also may help. I told Mr. Reynolds that you'd agreed already to be my escort as I am new and don't know the town yet, but he said he would be happy to do it."

"No." The word snapped out before Sawyer could catch it. "I said I'd do it." The mayor could probably sell her some snake oil too. *Prohibiting certain children from the town school.* Yet the miners from every nation could drop their coin in all the businesses here. His gut rumbled. "Remember, I owe you the favor and I intend to keep my word."

Laney set her papers on the bench and stepped over to the tack wall, straightening every brush, horseshoe, and tool that hung crooked. "All right." She turned, smiling at him. "After lunch, could we go to the school building? I won't be long, but a quick look over everything there would be wonderful."

Sawyer had never seen anyone straighten a barn before. "Fine." He shrugged. "I'll be in here or out in the corral."

With another quick smile and search for her cat, she finally walked out. Sawyer stood, blinking. Sweet voice, soft-touch, but was that brain all fluffy white clouds and pearly gates?

***

Sawyer finished up the work around the corrals when he saw Matthew run into the barn.

"Matthew, would you do me a favor?"

The boy stopped climbing the ladder. "Sure, Mr. Sawyer."

"Would you ask your ma to come out here? I want to ask her something without everyone else hearing."

"Sure thing." He ran back out the barn door. Sawyer paced and glared at the rows of perfectly set tools on the tack wall. It was too tidy. He walked over and messed them up. Hearing voices, Sawyer noticed Widow Farrow attempt to enter the barn. Her wide black bell skirt hung up on the barn doors. Giving the layers a frustrated tug, she came through and met him with a smile.

Matthew ran up to him before jetting out the back door. "I got a sugar cube for Blackie." Sawyer shook his head, glanced at Widow Farrow, and then looked down. "I have an unusual question for you, ma'am. Actually, it was something Miss Balderhoff had asked on her journey here." He finally met her eyes. "She asked if you worked."

Ava tilted her head to the side, confused.

"Okay, you know some nights I sit with Widow C, and she helps me with learning."

Ava nodded.

Sawyer scratched his ear and took a deep breath. "I never really did much reading and writing, and I never did care because I was either going to husk corn my whole life or ride shotgun."

Her face lightened with understanding.

"Albert is out riding for me, and I'm supposed to be helping folks in the office while he's gone. Thing is…" Sawyer rolled his eyes. "I can't. I just can't."

Concerned, Miss Farrow took a step closer, and by heaven or hell, he was going to just swallow any pride he had left. "I was wondering if you would want to work at the Wells Fargo office in my place. Just for a month, until I can go back to shotgun and Albert can return to the office."

Her chin lifted, and she looked to be thinking. "I think I would enjoy that."

Sawyer felt the burden off his shoulders. "With how fast things are growing in the town, I can't just leave it closed."

"Of course," Ava said calmly. "I would be happy to fill in. And you will show me what it is I am to do?"

"Yes, I can do that. Say after supper. I told Miss Balderhoff I'd take her to the school this afternoon."

"And if anyone else asks about my position at the office, I will say you had commitments to help the new teacher." Ava smiled and welcomed Matthew into her arms as he ran inside.

Sawyer blinked. The lame excuse would not be his choice, but what choice did he have? "Thank you, Widow Farrow."

Leaving with Matthew in tow, she looked back. "Don't give up on your learning. We never know how our lives will grow and turn." The familiar pain in her eyes glimmered. Of all the widows in the house, Widow Farrow was the only one who still wore black and carried her loss in the very tone of her voice. Just as her gown cleared the doors, he saw Miss Balderhoff waiting to enter. Had she heard?

A loud rumble shook the ground, and the two women grabbed each other, smashing Matthew between them. Sawyer wanted to run but slowed his feet to meet them.

"The ground is shaking?" Miss Balderhoff panted. "What Babylonian provocation is this?

"It's not the wrath of the Lord, Miss Balderhoff," Sawyer replied, watching Widow Farrow lessen her grip.

"It's dynamite. The blasting they do at the mines." Widow Farrow still held Miss Balderhoff around the shoulders. "You would think I would be used to it now. But each rumble terrifies me." Ava sighed and let go. Taking Matthew's shoulder, she squeezed him. "You will notice we have nothing breakable on the shelves. Some days it will rattle a picture off the wall." She huffed and held her neck. "Forgive me if I grabbed you harshly." Ava's eyes slanted with care. "I will let you get on to the school."

"You're going to the school?" Matthew asked. "Can I go with ya?"

Miss Balderhoff took a settling breath. "It's fine with me. Mr. Roth?"

"I'll put ya to work." Sawyer ruffled Matthew's hair.

"Is it okay, Ma?" Matthew asked, excited. "I can be his right arm."

"Yes, son, you can go and help." The women smiled at each other.

Annoyed, Sawyer scratched under his chin. Were there any more maladies of his that could be highlighted today? He glanced carefully at Miss Balderhoff. For some reason, he didn't want her knowing he couldn't read or write. If the teacher overheard them, she would want to come in and save him from his miserable condition. And he was fine as he was. No woman needed to point out his failures. All the widows in the house knew he had lessons with Widow C, but not Miss Balderhoff, and Sawyer didn't want anyone's pity. That he would not abide with.

Chapter 12

The next morning, Laney laid in bed, scratching under Moses' chin as he purred cozily inside her arm. At the first streams of sunlight, she'd given her prayers and requests to God. Her new school room sang in her heart like a rousing hymn on Sunday. The men from the Curry mine had built a fine building with a stove for cold winter days and large windows with cranks, perfect for stuffy afternoons. Each bench and table would hold two children. Three perfectly spaced rows that went five rows deep. Seats for thirty children, all in order. Good heavens. She rubbed her cheek. Her last position never swelled to twenty. The door behind her desk let out to an open field. Four sapling trees had been planted, surrounded with various benches for the children to eat lunch.

As much as the square school building stood ready and waiting, her usual resounding faith felt weak this morning. As long as Matthew and Mr. Roth helped her clean and count books and slates, her mind stayed occupied with the tasks needed for the next week. But as soon as the quiet settled on her, her trepidations crept in. In the past, the younger children were her delight. Even with all the wiggles and a hundred interruptions, she knew how to keep them under control. But it was the older children that had done her in last time. Laney closed her eyes and covered her face. *Pray, ask, and believe.*

Dearest Lord, I cast these cares on you. Grant me the wisdom and strength to do the mission you've set before me.

Choosing not to dwell on the past, Laney pulled away from Moses on her bed and sat up, letting her toes rest on the cool wood floor. Though he didn't have to, Mr. Roth had been a great help. Everything the shotgun messenger did, even one-armed, shone with confidence. Without asking, he found paper to clean the windows, murmuring something about the best use of Mr. Clemens's stories. Why did it feel as if they had known each other for years? Possibly his age, being close to hers, or perhaps because he had saved her life. Nuzzling her cat, Laney kissed him and smiled with a warm feeling.

She'd not think of the strange night at the Franklins. *What else should she have done with a man blurry with pain?* Chastising her rebellious thoughts that kept leading back to him, she lifted the window. Moses found the branches outside and took his leave.

Laney leaned out. Could she make sight of the Wells Fargo shotgun messenger turned livery worker and teacher escort? Watching Moses wander across the alley, he headed for the barn just as Mr. Roth stepped out, looked up, and saw her. Gasping, she pulled back quickly and smacked the back of her head on the window. "Ouch." She rubbed it. "Oh, blessed be." Covering her face, Laney pressed against her wall.

"His mercies *are* new every morning. Until I ruin them," Laney groaned, moving to the other side of her narrow room. Reaching for her undergarments laid in perfect order in her bureau, she fretted as she pulled on clean pantaloons.

Today Ava would be working at the Wells Fargo office. The need for Ava's assistance came from the fact Mr. Roth should be covering the office duties, but he couldn't run the office due to the fact he was committed to helping her. Now she felt a bother taking him from his job. Well, actually, the bandit who shot him took him from his post.

Laney finished hooking her corset and slipped her yellow and pink striped dress over her head. Why was she always thinking of Mr. Roth? The day was full enough without being distracted in thought and heart.

After finishing the buttons, she folded her nightgown in a perfect square and set it in her drawer. *In heart?* She wasn't distracted in *heart.* "Pish." Laney blew out, straightening her bed with perfect creases and a centered pillow. Admittedly, she appreciated his friendship. She'd never had a young man as a friend. Laney finished tying her moccasins. A year ago, the pastor's nephew had asked her to sit with his family one day for the church potluck. She had made some hasty excuse to get home and then moped about her decision weeks after.

Running her brush through her hair made her wince—a bump on the head to add to her addled sensibilities. God would be her strong tower. Twisting her hair around her finger, she attached the hairpins to make a bun. Laney tucked her hankie in her pocket and squeezed it ten times.

Her pink bonnet was wrapped in tissue, safely settled in the third drawer. Should she wear it out today? Would it seem she was putting on airs for some of the simpler mining families? Laney opened the drawer and held the lovely bonnet. Pressing the woven cloth flowers back and forth, she admired the ribbon of wide pink satin. Likely it was too much fluff for a spinster. Her mother and aunt had given her the bonnet for her birthday. Even if she never wore it, it was precious to her. They had little frivolous money between them.

Laney set the bonnet carefully back in the drawer. She would wait till Sunday and see how many women donned their finery. Taking up her small hand mirror, she mimicked a toothy smile. "Step out on the water, girl." She set the mirror down and drew her hands down the layers of her skirt. "You were made for such a time as this."

Twenty minutes later, Mr. Roth stood stoic, like a guard outside the Grunder's shack. During her first home visit Laney tried to hold a conversation with Mrs. Grunder. Which children would she be sending to school? Laney tried to guess their ages. There were at least five running in circles at her best count.

"You can have that one and that one." Mrs. Grunder pointed, and Laney could not see with the whirl of dirt and children's excitement.

"Their names?" Laney tried to stand taller, holding her roster and pencil.

"That one is Amina. She is seven. And that one with the yellow hair, he's Owen. You can try and teach him, but he won't sit still unless there's a plate in front of him. So if ya need to send him back, I can use him for chores."

"Very well, I will do my best." Laney lightly tapped her foot ten times and forged a smile. "We will see them on the first day. So nice to meet you, Mrs. Grunder." Before Laney could curtsy, a loud rumble shook the ground, and she felt herself sway. No one else noticed the shaking of the earth, so she smiled and walked back to where Mr. Roth waited.

"Quite the shuffle of children there." Laney tried to sound optimistic. "Only two will attend school." Without expression, he nodded as they walked down the path toward another shanty.

With a short knock, Laney smiled and introduced herself to Mrs. Slavens. The thin woman noted her Joseph needed schooling, but he worked at the mine during the day. The girls Janetta and Henrietta would be able to attend if they could. Laney introduced herself to the sisters. The two, very similar-faced siblings, seemed genuinely excited about school starting and Laney felt her hope tick upward.

The next shanty held a very pregnant woman and two small children. Laney grinned and wished her the best.

Down the path and to the left, Laney met Mrs. Santos. With her broken English, Laney hesitated—would Mayor Reynolds be hostile to the invitation she offered? The boys' names were Neville and Sampson. The young lads spoke English and Spanish. A teacher with a conscience could not pick and choose which children would be educated. The mother was kind and eager for her boys to go to school. Mayor Reynolds would have to abide by her reasoning on this one.

Mrs. McCoy met her at the door with a toddler on her hip and invited her in. The crowed, one-room shanty smelled strongly of onions and peppers on the stove. Unfortunately, the children were all out gathering wood, but the stocky, red-haired woman would see them to school. Laney blinked back the pungent smells as she thanked her and walked out.

Mr. Roth stood back from each shanty, allowing her to do the greeting and invitations. Did the women wonder who he was? Perhaps they thought him her brother? She met two more families but no one asked so, squeezing her papers tight, she walked up the path to meet him.

"I'm a bit thirsty. Shall we walk back to the widow's house?" Laney patted the perspiration from her brow.

"I know a drinking well. It's just up here." Mr. Roth led the way, and they found a rock to sit on. After he took a long drink, he rinsed the ladle and gave her a drink.

"A well is where Moses helped the priest of Midian's daughters." Laney handed back the ladle. "Word got back to their father that this man had helped protect his daughters, so the father gave Moses one of his daughters in marriage. Zipporah."

Mr. Roth tilted his hat back. "So, with my help today, I'm entitled to one of your daughters?"

"Humm." Laney smiled. "We might have to think of something else."

Mr. Roth looked down and kicked a rock. "I noticed yesterday you took the spanking paddle off the wall and set it in the bottom of a drawer."

"Yes." Laney nodded, checking her list. "I will never use it. Never."

"I'm sure you know plenty about corralling children, but some are smellin' close to criminal." He eyed her. "You use the switch?"

"No, Mr. Roth. No paddle, no switch, no ruler." Her face cringed. "Have you ever been a child on the other side of that kind of punishment?"

"I have. I didn't like it."

"And did it make you a better student?"

"Hardly." He went to the well and brought up more water. "And you likely never got paddled?"

She shook her head and wished it was only dirt and dust that stung in her eyes. "I had the ruler applied to my hands until welts were raised. My hands didn't look like hands," she murmured.

Mr. Roth stared at her. "Not a lot of things shock me, but you, Miss Balderhoff, misbehaving?"

"I didn't misbehave."

"Then what happened?" Something almost caring yet urgent in his voice beckoned her to continue. Laney's eyes drifted over the path they'd walked.

"I was seven and it was in the winter." Her chest rose and fell. "Our teacher, Mr. Watson, often had an orange with his lunch. I don't know why I was so stupid, so naive. But four of the older girls found me at lunch break and said they'd gone together to buy me an orange from the mercantile. It was so rare for winter and they wanted me to have it. As I peeled it open, none of them would take a piece. They said they wanted me to have all of it." Unmistakable pain pinched her face. "I ate it. Just like Eve and the apple, I was duped."

"That's awful." Mr. Roth glared. "And it's going to get worse, I can tell."

Laney exhaled with a frown. "When Mr. Watson wanted to know who had stolen his orange, all eyes turned to me. He called me forward, and there I stood with sticky orange still on my hands and breath." She huffed. "Ten stinging raps on each hand." Laney took her hankie to pat her temple. "I tried so hard not to cry in front of the other children. I went to my desk, and thankfully my mother insisted I carry a hankie." She held it up. "This very one. I used it to catch every tear."

"And you want to be a teacher?" Mr. Roth stood, his working hand flipped out from his hip. "How can you not hate the very profession?"

Laney shrugged. "My mother was so upset, she kept me home and didn't go speak to the teacher for a week. My first day back, he did pull me aside and apologized. That helped."

Laney blocked the sun with her hand over her eyes to see him. "You were treated as unjustly as a Wells Fargo man."

He leveled his gaze on her.

"Someone shot at you and would give no care if you lived or died. And yet you desire to go back to the profession."

"That's different."

"Have you forgiven the bandit and renewed your trust in God's care?"

"No." He twisted away. "Why do you do that? Forgive the bandit? Raps on the hand are different than attempted murder Miss Balderhoff." He clenched his teeth. "A man has a job to do. And I won't be the last one to tell you that not everything is solved in this life by a Bible story."

Crestfallen, Laney stilled and stood, then brushed off her skirt. "I believe I'm done today," she murmured before taking the path back down past the miner's shacks. Everything squeezed in her chest. Why had she told Mr. Roth her pitiful story? Was he a kindred friend? Hardly. She'd been duped again, more likely. The unwanted tears formed, and she walked faster. Another loud rumble shook the ground, and her foot twisted on a rock. Just as she reached out to steady herself, she felt a hand hold her elbow.

"Slow down, please."

Walking on, she pulled it from his grip. Before Laney could get her hankie out to swipe her face, he'd run around her and stopped in her path.

"Wait. Just wait."

Laney stopped with heart pounding, looking everywhere but at him. This is what the curious miner's children would see, the new teacher in a squabble with a man? She straightened her spine and tried to find her composure. "I apologize for all my Bible lessons, Mr. Roth. Please forgive me and allow me to pass."

"No." His voice lowered. "I was riled by what those children and that teacher did to you. Then you brought it back to me and that riled me more. And those are both pitiful excuses to be coarse with you." A low growl escaped, and he ran his hand down his face. "I think these children—I'm sayin' this honest—they're lucky to have a teacher like you. One who'd never hit 'em to make them mind, one who'd never humiliate 'em in front of others. One who cares enough about their souls to show them the truth of the Bible."

His words felt like a slow warming blanket on a bleak Nebraska winter day. It *was* her prayer to care for those God had entrusted to her.

"I'm sorry." He huffed. "I...I like you. I keep giving off that I don't, but I do." He rocked his hat back and forth before he pushed it low. Laney wondered about the streaks of red crawling up his neck.

"Thank you, Mr. Roth. I forgive you."

His grin widened. "Ahh, your forgiveness, and the way you say, Mr. Roth. All the widows in the house call me Sawyer." He scratched his ear. "As many times as you say Mr. Roth, I might start thinking too highly of myself." He turned to unblock the path.

"I…I…will need to think about it." She walked on and noticed he strode close, nearly at her elbow.

He likes me?

Chapter 13

That afternoon, Sawyer came down the stairs at the Wells Fargo office and saw Ava still at the desk. "Widow Farrow."

Glancing up, she smiled. "Mr. Sawyer, I'm just about done." She finished writing in a ledger. "The office will close promptly at five, I promise."

Sawyer picked up a card off the desk. "And you are keeping track of your work hours?" He held it up. "I see no numbers."

Her head tilted to the side, and she replaced the quill in its holder. "I know you said you wanted to pay me, but I don't feel right. I just want to help. And." Ava held up her hand. "Before you correct me, please let me say I have so enjoyed this work." She rose from the desk, and her wide black bell skirt filled the area. "I don't speak to many people about this, so forgive me."

Sawyer swallowed. A week off the stage, and he'd more females confiding in him than he'd had in a lifetime. Had he gone soft or looked pitiful with this sling around his neck? "No, say whatever you need."

"Well, let me back up. First, I've never expressed my thanks to how you let Matthew be your shadow." She smiled a rare smile, and her voice softened. "With the loss of his father, I think you have helped my dear boy tremendously."

"He's a good kid." Sawyer agreed. "I don't ever mind him underfoot."

Another relaxed grin graced her face. "And the other reason I don't want pay is that I've needed to do something different. I didn't realize how reclusive I've been. Before we moved west, it was not unusual for me to oversee servants, houseguests, parties, correspondence, and such. Then with this move, I needed to adjust to the life of a simple miner's wife. Just when I was done pining for my niceties, the accident happened." Her eyes swept to the ground.

A low rumble rattled the windows. "Those blasts have been like reliving the day it happened over and over." Her jaw clenched. "But today, when I had people coming in with their posts…." Her eyes widened. "Did I tell you I handled a transaction for funds going to Germany?"

Sawyer shook his head. He didn't really know this woman well, but he could see a difference, hear something new in her voice.

"For the first time since losing my husband, the blasts didn't make me cringe. I was working on checking ledgers for mistakes and…I did find some." She lifted one shoulder. "But when Mr. Albert returns, I don't want to offend him." She swished around the desk and over to the wall of notices. "Then I read this from the Wells Fargo quarterly." Ava stopped and turned, shaking her head. "I know I'm rambling, and I can hear common sense say I am a mother—what else could I want?"

Sawyer was lost on what the young widow was saying. Had he ever listened to common sense?

"But one day, Matthew will grow up and start his own life."

Sawyer nodded. Now she was talking about Matthew growing up?

"I want to apply for a customer service job." Ava sucked in a deep breath. "Maybe getting to know Miss Balderhoff is rubbing off on me."

Sawyer felt his jaw go slack. "Really?"

"What do you think?" She sighed. "I know it sounds ridiculous. Even when it came out of my mouth, I knew it clattered impossible. It would mean a move." She looked back to the advertisement. There are openings in Mariposa and Stockton."

Sawyer reluctantly rolled his good shoulder upward. "You should apply." He watched her eyes lock on his. "I know Mr.

Wells and Mr. Fargo want to run a good company. They have a list of—

"I read it. Twice."

He nodded. Who was he to tell her yes or no? Though he had no trouble telling Miss Balderhoff she should go home. "I think you should."

Silence hung in the air as she chewed on the corner of her lip. "You can't imagine how many hours I've rehearsed going home to Virginia, but I'm scared of the war coming. I'm scared to think of the cannons going off and men dying. I sound like a heartless coward, but I just don't think I can do that."

"No, that's understandable." Sawyer could imagine a fine businessman in California taking her as his wife. But maybe she wanted something different? There were so few impressive women like her for marriage. The situation was unusual but not impossible. He looked up to see Ava's head tilt, looking rather contemplative. "Your options are wide open, Miss Ava, but for now, I'm paying you wages. No argument.

Ava sighed, dropped her head to her shoulder, and acknowledged him with a pinched smile.

***

Past dusk, Sawyer brushed the horses down after checking their hooves. The stage from San Francisco would be in any time, and the change of horses would be ready. Something twirled at his feet, and Miss Balderhoff's cat looked up at him. "What do you want?" He walked back to the tack wall, and the cat followed. Funny how one woman needed his help to stay in Virginia City, and another asked his help to leave. Both women talked to him more today than John did in six months. He glanced at the door. It would be perfect timing for Miss Lane-*ee* to stroll in. He eyed it a minute longer, but the barn door remained closed. After his snide remark at the well, it would be a wonder if she ever wanted to speak to him. But the schoolmarm was a woman of the good book, and there was a fair amount of forgiveness required from those pages.

Sawyer walked out to the corral and leaned his good arm on the fence. He could head down to the Red Dog Saloon. They served up a cold glass of beer and a bowl of stew for a fifty-cent piece. His eyes dropped closed. It would require walking past Miss Bulette's brothel. The buxom English woman sat on a stool outside her establishment in nothing but a corset and slip. Striking up conversations with every dirty miner who happened by, they were lured inside like a trout is to a fishhook within minutes. With no desire to empty his pockets in there, he'd smiled and keep on walking every time. But it always left a sour place in his gut. Something between "lonesome" and maybe "not being man enough" came to his mind. If he never married, would he succumb to the wiles of a painted lady? Sawyer blew out a breath and watched the last pink and orange strips fade from the sky.

"Moses."

Sawyer knew the soft voice calling from inside, and he chided himself for having a hunger that had nothing to do with food. Miss Balderhoff waited till the older ladies retired and then called her cat inside. Sawyer leaned back from the fence, yet his one hand held on for dear life. He wanted to see her like a pulling he'd never known. The familiar sour feeling twisted inside, and he held the fence even tighter.

He'd gone blubberheaded over her, just in time to torture himself more. As if being a lame shotgun messenger wasn't enough, now he'd been left to the devices of women. His feet stayed planted to the ground. And this one had her devices all right—round face with sweet wide eyes, a touch that would melt butter, a heart that would outweigh a pure bag of gold. *Moccasins.* The unorthodox woman wore old Indian moccasins that her father gave her and still carried her hankie from childhood. He shook his head, then bumped his forehead on the fencing. He needed to get back on the trail. Tomorrow he would rid himself of the sling and get his arm moving.

"Mr. Roth?"

Sawyer growled, closed his eyes tight, and slowly turned. "Miss Balderhoff."

She stood in her same pink and yellow dress with her cat tucked in her arm. "Are you all right? Is it your shoulder?"

He squeezed his lips in a snug line. "I'm fine. What can I do for you?" He forced himself to meet her gaze.

"The widows said there are a few finer homes up on A and B Street." She hesitated. "I'd like to visit them tomorrow, but if you have other plans, I can ask someone else."

"I'm free. I'll be done here after breakfast." The words were short and matter of fact.

"All right then, I'll see you after breakfast." She dropped her chin just an inch, so that her smile competed with her hooded brown eyes—all focused on him.

The air seemed to tingle—or was that his skin? Sawyer went to tip his hat before he realized he wasn't wearing it. Quickly he raked his fingers through his hair. What kind of dumb, tripping ox was he?

"And the other thing you asked?" She played with the collar on her dress. "I thought, what if you used my Christian name around here." Her finger did a little dancing circle. "And then with everyone else, I would be Miss Balderhoff, and you, of course, you would be Mr. Roth."

"That would be fine...Lane..." *Don't do it, don't tease her...*"ee." It was too late. It was out.

Her head tilted with a coy smile. "Even in your great pain, you were listening. Your correct pronunciation does impress." She took a careful step back, her flawless lips relaxing.

Keep going, woman, just keep going, Sawyer pleaded inside his head. *We've spent too much time together. Take your cat and go.* "Until tomorrow." He nodded once, keeping his face stoic.

One foot crossed over the other, and she did a small dance-like twirl as she left.

Sawyer looked out across the dark corral. Guilt poked him in the gut. That modest smile, that feminine twirl— no more exaggerating her name. He glanced back as she entered the house. Teasing her for a reaction was wrong because he knew he could get it. Seeking an agreeable spinster's attention for selfish gain was not in his nature.

What kind of recklessness was this? Calling each other by their first names was a stupid idea.

Chapter 14

Sawyer rubbed his neck as he leaned against the low fence in front of the yellow house on A Street. How many chances did he have to skip out on his escort job? Why hadn't he taken it? Thirty minutes a home, just to get the kids' names and ages? The door behind him opened, and Laney bowed to the women of the house. Lifting a weary smile, she came down the stairs to meet him.

"I'm so sorry, Sawyer." Funny how his name sounded like she'd used it a hundred times.

"This is quite the opposite of yesterday." They walked side by side down the street. "Each woman wants to visit with me in her parlor over tea. Before I can get my own questions out, they present me with a list of their own. Where am I from? What do my parents do? Am I married? How many teaching positions have I had before? Honestly, this is worse than filling out the application and waiting to hear from the town council." She slowed and touched his good arm. "I'm so sorry, are you finished with this waiting? Heatstroke coming on?" His mouth went to answer, but blast it, she needed to move her hand off his arm. It was too familiar. Like they did this all the time. Which for as long as he'd known her, they really did.

"And then the children—they look delightful and curious, and I'm wondering how they will all mix." She let go and walked to the next home. It had blue paint, white trim, and flower boxes. "Why don't you come in with me? Get out of the sun."

Sawyer stepped back. "No, thank you. I'm fine out here."

Laney's mouth twisted. "I promise, after today, we are even." She fanned her face with her hand, spying the next house.

"Umm," his eyes narrowed. "Truthfully, I saved you from falling under the wagon wheels and getting dragged to your death. How are we even?" He wiped his forehead, popped his hat back, and scratched his temple.

"Oh, sir, you were a pitifully injured man unable to hold himself upright." She nodded proudly. "Without my assistance, you would have been the one trampled by four horses and left for the buzzards."

"The buzzards?" One eye narrowed. Now she teased him? Enjoying the lighthearted banter, he smiled, forgetting what he was saying. "So, I suppose we can be even." He shrugged. "But I may follow you around because I like it." Sawyer meant it as a comeuppance, but he could tell by how her face stilled, then softened when she took his words to heart.

"I'd better keep going." Laney patted her hair at the side and blinked nervously.

As soon as Sawyer saw her go inside the next house, he yanked the white sling off his neck and tucked it in his back pocket. *"I may follow you cause I like it? Ack."* He groaned. Looking for a stick to shove between his teeth, he walked in a circle.

Forget the stick; nostrils flaring, Sawyer took a deep breath and straightened his arm. Gritting against the pain, he pulled it inches from where it hung. Why did such simple moves make his body drip with sweat? He moved his elbow upward. If she was going to be another thirty minutes, he had time to make progress one inch at a time.

***

Laney thanked Mrs. Henig for the lemonade and smiled as her son and daughter clung to their mother's skirts. Their home language was German, but the children had a simple grasp of English. She would put them in group A. Looking up as she was leaving, Mr. Roth, Sawyer, was missing. Had he taken his leave? She scanned up and down the street. Was he coming back for her? Walking down the stairs, she noticed the beautiful thick green grass. Someone had taken care to plant it. It was a delightful color against—something large lay asleep in their grass!

"Mr. Roth!" Without any response, Laney knelt where he lay flat on his back, his sling missing. Had someone attacked him? "Sir, I mean, Sawyer." She leaned over him, gripped his good arm, and gave him a shake. He was white as a sheet, and just as she rose to find help, she heard him groan. "What happened?" Glancing at his shoulder, blood had soaked through his shirt.

"Sawyer, are you all right? Did someone attack you?" Laney scanned the area again. Did people jump out in broad daylight and accost people here? Another groan and he moved his head side to side. "Were you slain in the spirit? Did you see a bright light? A whirlwind knock you over?"

A long growl accompanied his eyes rolling open and then shut. "Can you please get off me?" He snarled.

Laney jumped back, realizing she'd pinned him down. "Your arm is bleeding. Did you pass out from heat exhaustion and land on your arm?"

"Stop talking." He pushed his hair back and rubbed his head. "I'm fine." Sawyer rolled up to his elbow, straining to see straight and calm his breathing. He pushed himself up to a sitting position.

"Wait here, and I'll ask Mrs. Henig for water." Laney rose and was suddenly halted. Sawyer had a firm grip on her skirt.

"No. I said I am fine."

Laney was held captive, so she squatted next to him. "What happened? Do you know you're bleeding?"

"I can...tell."

Laney wanted to ask another question, but after seeing the glare in his eyes, she shut her mouth. His frown deepened, and then he huffed out a long breath. "I raised my arm too fast."

The sling was missing. Would he be that brash? "Was there a reason? A rabid dog or...."

"No." He snapped. "I was impatient and just swung it past my chin." He swallowed hard. "And then white and black spots took over."

"Oh," she scowled. "You did this to yourself?" As soon as the words left, she saw his fist tighten around her skirt fabric. "Your good arm is working fine." She mumbled, trying to jerk her skirt from his grip. Growling, he finally let go. "Give me your sling." Laney held her hand out.

"No, I don't need it." Trying to stand, he pulled on her arm. Upright, Sawyer fought to steady himself. After a few seconds he gripped her elbow.

"You've likely busted open those stitches. Widow C does embroidering in the evenings, I'm sure she can—" Laney stopped, seeing his arm dangling down in front of him. Had the man knocked it out of joint? "Really, Sawyer, it's hot, and we have two blocks to walk."

"I'm fine." He ground out, trying to pull it back. "Start walking and just let me hold your arm." They carefully left the Henig's yard.

"My escort needs an escort, I believe," she murmured, taking careful steps with the stubborn man attached to her elbow. "I feel as if I'm under arrest." Snickering, she tightened her smile flat. "Mockery of the medical profession, so pitiful, swinging a broken shoulder is beyond...."

"Laney, I will wrap this bloody arm around your chin and hold your mouth closed." He panted, squeezing her elbow. "I will, just watch me."

"I'm sorry. You are dizzy and fainting with pain." She bit on her bottom lip. "Again." A giggle-snort escaped before she could catch it.

His grip squeezed on her upper arm.

"Ouch."

He let go and walked next to her. Laney felt a tinge of guilt; why was she being ornery? She'd prefer he hang onto her over taking another tumble. No question he was lean and muscular and far too much for her to catch. They turned into the back alley that led to the barn.

Silently, he cut away and went inside the doors.

Laney stopped at the back door. Not even a thank you? Another cantankerous thought occurred to her. Should she? It would be in the name of his wellbeing. She walked in and found the two widows drinking coffee.

"Ladies, if you have a moment. Mr. Roth took a tumble and broke his stitches open." Both women stood quickly.

"Oh, no." Widow C held her hand over her mouth.

"That shotgun cuss, he's all vim and vigor." Widow B shook her head. "Don't know what's good from bad. My Herbert was just like that at his age."

"And he refuses to use his sling." Laney couldn't help herself; it was too easy.

"We'll take care of him." Widow B nodded with a frown.

"Thank you so much. I've got to work on my school plans." Laney smiled and held up her papers. Walking to the stairs, she wanted to giggle but then something pinched her stomach. She really didn't know him that well. Except he was handsome, prideful, and stubborn. *But pride did come before the fall.* Laney snickered, taking the stairs.

On the outside he was all dark chin stubble and toughness, but what he was on the inside she wasn't exactly sure of. She turned the knob. Nothing in her heart wanted to be unkind to the man. Dropping her papers on the bed, she sat. Truth be, she knew so little of men. Often she thought he jested at her expense. Most of the time, she didn't know what it meant. Dallying or ridicule? *Lane-ee.*

Shaking her head, she stepped to the window and watched the widows. With sewing basket in hand, they let themselves into the barn. In a few minutes, he would know she sent them. Laney felt nervous regret and came back to her bed. Trying to focus on her notes, she did have a lot to do for next week. She was the new teacher at the Virginia City school. A resigned spinster. So what did it matter if he still liked her or not? It mattered little.

Her heart squeezed until she pulled her hands over her face. What happened to with '*all lowliness and meekness, with longsuffering, forbearing one another in love*'? Was his rough, worldly disposition rubbing off on her? Or just turning her head? *Oh, Lord.*

Chapter 15

The first day of school found Laney at the schoolhouse with heart thudding. Retracing her steps to find the desks and benches in the same order as she had left them, she reminded herself she'd done this many times before. Resetting the order of the room could be done again this afternoon after all the children had left. Gripping the pulley on the third window on the left, it rose. The room was stuffy, and the faint waft of fresh sagebrush began to settle her frayed nerves. *Lord bless them and keep them*, she prayed, preparing herself for the energetic little bodies that had not yet arrived.

Someone cleared their throat, and Laney looked up. Mayor Reynolds stood in the open door with two boys flanking his sides.

"Good day, Miss Balderhoff." He tipped his bowler.

"Mayor Reynolds. So good to see you. I was sorry to have missed a home visit with your boys." Laney worked up a smile. The taller boy had to be a teenager. His pants were inches above his socks, and was there fuzz or dirt on his chin? She stepped closer. "Hello, gentlemen." After she nodded to them, they kept their gaze on the clean school floor.

"This is George, and my eldest, Howard."

"Hello." She tried again, and neither offered a greeting.

"If Howard is *able.*" The mayor held out a scornful tone. "He should take the graduation test and be done. So, I have assured him you will be challenging his educational goals. It seems the other schoolmaster did not have the time to keep Howard moving forward."

"Oh." Laney straightened up. "I will do my best. "What subjects do you excel in, Howard?"

Howard rubbed his nose back and forth, picked something from the inside, and flicked it on the ground.

Laney felt herself sway. The floor was spotless. She swallowed the bile in her throat. *Was* spotless.

"And you, George?" Happy her voice worked, she continued. "What are your favorite subjects?" At least George looked at her before he shrugged. "There is the seating chart, ahh...." Laney now second guessed her student placements. She thought for some reason, they were younger.

"We had to be in San Francisco last week," Mayor Reynolds said, staring at her figure longer than needed. Laney's hand rose to her well-covered neckline. "I'd like to have another opportunity to have you to the house," he said, finally meeting her eyes. "Say Friday night? By week's end, we could talk about seeing Howard graduated."

Laney spied the Santos family eagerly coming down the street. "Friday, yes. That would work." Maybe having nose-picking Howard graduated would be worth it. "School dismisses at two. They...ahh...will, I'm sure they walk themselves home?"

"They do." Mayor Reynolds took his leave, and before Laney could greet the Santos family, the ground rumbled. "Oh Lord, all glory and peace be thine," she whispered as the Santos family came in next. Fighting her own rattle from toe to the top of her head, Laney introduced herself to new faces and spoke with the mothers as they said goodbye to their children. Ava and Matthew walked in, and it felt like seeing family at Christmas. Matthew held a small paper bag. "This is for you."

"You are too kind, young man." Laney had the worst desire to ask Ava if she wanted to stay, but she knew she had duties at the Wells Fargo office.

Laney rang the bell but saw only a few children running up the steps. After everyone looked over the seating chart and found their bench, she took a deep breath and introduced herself. "Now it is your turn to tell me your name and age."

In the first row, her primary students, with little legs swinging under their desks, recited their names and ages. Laney was proud of the bravery of the smallest ones. The next row contained a few elbow-punching boys. But at the drop of her chin and set jaw, they settled into the simple introductions. The third row had Howard sitting awkwardly in the small table-desk. She nodded to him to begin, but he rocked forward and released a loud passing of gas. The girls covered their snickers, but the rude display sent the boys reeling.

"Boys and girls!" She clapped her hands until they quieted. A rod of gumption rose through her spine. If she could survive hanging from a wild stagecoach, she could deal with fuzz-faced Howard Reynolds.

"Is that how you want to be known or would you prefer to give us a name." Laney stared Howard down.

A girl with braids sitting behind Howard leaned around him. "What's that on your feet, Teacher?"

"These are Indian moccasins." The children seemed to be interested, and she would use this for her advantage this time. "My father gave them to me."

"Was he an Indian?" a girl from the first row asked.

"No." Laney walked back to the front and took her chair and set her foot on it. The children leaned past their tables to see the worn leather, fringe, and beadwork. "But I moved here from a territory called Nebraska. Raise your hand if you have heard of Nebraska." Half the children raised their hands. "Raise your hand if you know what Indians may live there?"

Surprisingly, George Reynolds raised his hand.

"Yes, George."

He stood, and Laney wondered if the last schoolmaster had the children stand when they answered a question. "The plains Indians have been in that area for a thousand years."

"Whoa, they must be old." Another boy piped in, and the children laughed. George looked down and started to sit.

"Wait." Laney nodded to George, and he stilled. "When someone has the floor—that is the word for when someone is speaking—no one else should be speaking until he or she sits down. George has the floor now." She eyed the children in her most serious face. "Please continue, George."

"The Arapaho live in the western part of Nebraska, and I believe the Kiowa did also." He grinned and sat.

"Yes, you are correct. Very good, George."

Howard pulled his elbow behind him until the girl's slate hit the floor. "Howard, pick that up." Laney barely missed a beat. "Raise your hand if you know why Indians had to move and the name of the place they were told to live."

Four or five hands eagerly shot into the air. One boy was about out of his seat with excitement. Laney eyed Howard obeying and felt a smile rising. They were smart children and willing to learn. Little did they know that American history and geography were happening this very moment. The lesson of Indians' encounters with the new pioneers continued for over an hour, and eventually, the gift of her moccasins came back around. "Tomorrow, when you come back to school, please bring something special to you, just as my moccasins are special to me. Maybe a ribbon from your birthday or a letter from a relative." Laney remembered the handsome Captain Adam Townes. "You may share just a few words to tell us more about it."

"Can I bring my daddy's silver coin?" Neville spoke up. "He mines the silver, and they make it into coins and teapots and fancy things."

"Yes, exactly. It can be anything." Laney wondered where the morning had gone. "Boys and girls, we will take five minutes for a drink of water and the outhouse. Then we will do some math drills at the chalkboard and learn a scripture verse before lunch." A few eye rolls and moans murmured across the schoolroom. "See you back here in five minutes."

As the schoolroom emptied, Laney turned to set up the three levels of math problems on the board and felt an uncanny quiet over the room.

Turning slowly, a tall thin woman, scantily dressed in red flounces, filled the doorway. She had to be the madam that the widows gossiped about. Suddenly Laney felt a strange pity for the woman. She had large rings under her eyes, and though her face was drawn and rough, her smile seemed genuine.

"You the teacher?" Her British accent didn't fit with her appearance.

"Yes, ma'am." Laney stepped closer. "How can I help you?"

"I got a gal child. At the Bulette's bawdyhouse. Can she come to this school?"

Laney scratched her neck and glanced out the window to see if George or Howard watched. The walls shook from a mining blast, and she suppressed a groan.

"Yes, we would love to have her." She'd already broken Mayor Reynolds' rule about foreigners in school. A bit of panic tried to riddle her. What if this was reason enough to fire her this time? Reaching in her pocket, she squeezed her handkerchief ten times. "What is her name and age?"

"Leona, she turned seven." A frown pulled down Madam Bulette's tired face. "The other bloke wouldn't let her in." She shrugged. "He saying it has to do with her not having a father or mother in town."

"I see, so you are her guardian? You see to her wellbeing." Laney heard a scream outside. Howard chased the girls with something in his hand. "School starts at eight, pack her a lunch, and pick her up at two." Laney hoped she didn't sound rude as she picked up the bell, and the woman went to walk out.

"Thank you, Teacher."

"Please call me, Miss Balderhoff." Laney rang the bell. Friday night, she would speak to Mayor Reynolds. Maybe not with overt details, but a wide variety of children should be able to learn in her classroom. If he did not agree, she would have to conform against her principals to keep her job or take her moccasined feet back to Nebraska.

***

That afternoon after the last children found their way home, Laney sat wearily at her desk to prepare for tomorrow. She sighed a deep breath and looked about the room. She really couldn't concentrate until she did her favorite thing. Walking among the rows, Laney straightened each table and bench, placing each slate perfectly in the middle of the table. When the room was back in delightful order, she swept the floor, walked down the rows one more time, and said a prayer for each child. Matthew Farrow's paper bag remained on her desk. In all the activity today, she'd forgotten to look inside. Opening it, she reached in and pulled out an orange. Her eyes stung for a moment, and she blinked it away. It was just a coincidence. The boy couldn't know.

Someone was in the doorway, and like the guilt-ridden child she'd been, she dropped the orange back in the bag.

"Oh, Ava." Laney held her chest.

"The Wells Fargo stage has returned with Albert back in the office." She pinched a frown. "I don't think he likes me filling in, so I slipped out. How was the first day?" Her wide-belled black dress swished along the clean floor.

"It was…was…good." Laney smiled. "You know the adjustment of us all getting to know each other." Laney nodded back at her desk. "And Matthew's delightful gift, an orange for the teacher." The words almost knotted in her mouth. "That was so sweet of him." She tilted her head at Ava. "And you."

"Oh." Ava bit her bottom lip. "Matthew was supposed to tell you. It wasn't from us. It was from Sawyer."

"Mr. Roth?" Her tone wistful, she pulled the orange from the bag. Just holding it made her so-called starch turn to syrup. "He hasn't spoken to me for a week." She suddenly realized she'd spoken out loud.

"And yet, he sent a gift for your first day." Ava's eyebrows rose curiously.

Laney felt befuddled head to toe and dropped the orange back in the bag. She tried hard not to show it. "Well, let's see." Standing over her desk, she tapped her moccasin covered foot. "If you give me a minute, I can take some lesson work home and check on Moses." She swallowed, hoping the heat she felt wouldn't make her blush. "Would you want to walk together?"

"Please, let's do." Ava smiled and waited as Laney gathered her things and came around her desk. Laney started to walk, but Ava didn't move.

"Miss Balderhoff, don't forget your orange."

Chapter 16

The next morning, a ray of sunlight highlighted the round orange sitting like a trophy upon her bureau. Laney chewed her thumbnail and dropped the quill into the ink. *Just do it silly. Thank the man for the gift. Didn't your mother teach you anything? A card of acknowledgment is basic courtesy.* Laney paused. She'd already divided the paper in fourths. The first note sounded like the orange was thankful for the thoughtfulness. That went in the trash. And the second and third attempts also.

"Meow." Moses made a circle on her windowsill. The sun had been up over thirty minutes, and Moses wanted out. Laney lifted the window, and he scampered down the branches onto the tree outside her window. Now she only had a few minutes to get to school—maybe she should tell him in person. Forget that; Laney dipped the quill into the ink. How did she know he wasn't teasing her? Using the bureau for her solid surface, she carefully wrote his name in her best script. A flicker of hope wanted to believe his gift came from kindness. With all her focus on school and preparing lessons, there was little time for wandering around the barn to find the handsome shotgun messenger. What an unusual friendship they possessed. Ink touched down onto the paper. *Thank you for the orange. It made my day. Laney.*

Simple and to the point. She fanned the paper until the ink dried. Crossing it in half, she gathered her school things and headed downstairs.

Widow Boils stirred something at the kitchen stove. "You'd better set your bundle down and get to this oatmeal. We haven't talked much about the winters here, but if you don't get more meat on your bones, you might not make it."

Laney appreciated the woman's motherly concern, but what exactly did "not make it" mean?

"How you supposed to keep warm without any fat?" Widow B pouted a frown.

Widow Canazzaro shook her head and smiled, filling a bowl for Laney, and gently setting it before her.

"Widow C, do you plan to see Mr. Roth today? Could you give him this note?"

The older woman lifted a twitchy frown and then turned to Widow Boils. "I…I…don't think I should." She sipped her coffee.

"Oh no, I don't want to inconvenience you," Laney added. "You likely have a full day. Widow Boils, would you mind giving him this note?" When Widow Boils looked away and rubbed her chin, Laney tried to suppress the feeling that somehow they were protecting Sawyer Roth. Had he told the older ladies to keep her away after she sent them to stitch his shoulder back up? Sawyer was quite irritated that day. But then why did he offer an orange for her first day? Taking a few more bites, she stilled. The small silent kitchen felt like a closet closing in on her.

"Well, thank you for breakfast. I must be off to the full day." Blast it. Her voice wavered a bit at the end. They had always been so grandmotherly toward her. But Sawyer was here first. It was apparent they had a loyalty to him and felt the need to keep her at arm's length. She truly was often unorthodox, a fact she had accepted about herself long ago. But it still hurt when others didn't accept her. Grabbing her things, she hurried out the back door.

"Do not neglect to show hospitality to strangers," Laney mumbled, quickening her steps. All the widows had been kind and hospitable, even allowing her to read scripture to them every Wednesday night. Her skirt layers caught between her rushed steps and almost tripped her. She could not start the day with twenty-five youngsters and tears in her eyes. Slowing down, she tried to pray and caught sight of Madam Bulette standing in front of the brothel. The woman nodded to the schoolhouse, and Laney caught sight of the blonde girl standing on the front steps. Laney nodded back. It was probably better that Madam Bulette did not wait in front of the school.

"Hello." Laney greeted her warmly. "You must be Leona?" The girl shone sweet-faced, smelling like soap, and wearing a nice store-bought blue dress. Two blonde braids tied with black ribbon bows hung down her back.

"Yes, ma'am," she whispered.

"I am Miss Balderhoff, your teacher. Let me get my key from my pocket, and we'll get the doors open." Laney turned the knob and went to lay her things on her desk. Leona held firm against the open door, checking back down the street.

"Leona, would you want to meet me at my desk? I would like to ask you some questions."

Leona's eyes glanced one more time down the street before she carefully came to the desk.

"I promise these are all easy questions." Laney smiled, wondering about the home life of this sweet face in front of her. Her own confusion and hurt from the morning seemed so silly and absurd now.

"Let's start with your name." Laney offered a slate and handed her the chalk. Before she could ask if she knew the letters, Leona had already spelled her name.

"Wonderful." Laney hesitated. What if she didn't have a last name? They could cross that bridge later. "You have an A in your name, can you point to it?" Within a few minutes, Laney could see the child was bright and eager to learn. Laney glanced down at her roster she'd made from yesterday. "I would like you to sit in row one. Can you guess which one is row one?"

Leona moved to the right and pointed.

"Yes. And which table is the third table in row one?"

Leona counted, touching each table. A small smile appeared over her face. Laney couldn't help herself; she rose and came to her side and gave her a squeeze. "Very good. Amina sits here also. I think you will like her."

Leona stared at the floor.

"It's okay to be shy." Some children were gathering outside in the play area. "Leona, can I ask you one favor." Leona looked up wide-eyed. Laney held her hand on the shoulder of her new blue dress and took one glance around her spotless, perfect schoolroom. Just like life, this room in moments will be entirely out of order. That seems the way of things out west, so what could she say of comfort to this ill-fated child of God?

"Just promise me that if any student is cruel or impolite, you will come to me." Laney didn't want to name names, but Howard had so far been a great thorn in the flesh.

"Yes, Teacher." Leona stepped closer as the other children began to come inside.

"Remember Leona, you belong here, just as they do. You are loved by God." Laney patted her back and turned to greet the other children. They all bubbled with excitement over the things they'd brought to show the class. And just like children do, they excitedly welcomed the new girl to the Virginia City school.

By late afternoon, Laney walked the two blocks back to the Widows' house. The day had been so full of sharing and lessons that she'd forgotten the strange way the widows had behaved that morning. She'd prayed for them and knew better than to count it as an offense. One minute they wanted to fatten her up, the next they didn't want her sharing notes with Mr. Roth. So what, she'd held the note over the trash twice today. One time just before she let it go, the mine blasting rumbled the school. Shoving it back in her pocket, she wondered if God was trying to get her attention. Laney shifted her things and opened the front door. Widow C sat in the parlor reading.

"Good afternoon." Laney greeted, but Widow C seemed flustered half-standing then sitting. Finally, she nodded her chin once. Laney started up the stairs as Ava's full black skirt pushed her steps to the side.

"Surprise," Ava said in a sing-song voice and kept on down the stairs. Laney got to the top landing and noticed her door cracked open. Man and beast knew she was peculiar but was this widow's house even worse? She looked back to see Ava had disappeared. What is the surprise? Laney peeked in her room. Wide-eyed and panicked, she grabbed the knob and quickly pulled her door closed. Before she could find a true breath, she realized that was the wrong impulse. *Keeping the man trapped inside her bedroom?* Rocking her jaw to calm the rattling, she carefully opened the door.

"Sawyer." She squeaked. "What…what are you doing in my room?"

Blinking at the floor, he rubbed the back of his neck. "I wasn't meaning to be here. I didn't plan…ahh." He shook his head. "The desk." Sawyer stepped back and Laney noticed the small secretary desk sitting next to her bureau. "I saw it in the back room of the Wells Fargo office. Ava and I were talking." He huffed. "Not about you, but that you bring your schoolwork home and, ahh…." He gripped the wrist of his hurt arm. "I couldn't get it up the stairs myself, so Ava helped me."

"Oh." Laney set her things on her bed and held her cheeks. "It's a charming desk." She finally relaxed and took a step closer.

"The top comes down." Sawyer showed her. "And there is a spot for the ink well and paper and what…ever else."

"I don't know what to say." Laney blinked, still in shock. The man she'd held while sleeping in her arms was cornered in her room, and the gift was so…. Before the butterflies took flight within her, she pivoted and quickly swiped the orange off its pedestal. It was too late. He must have seen it and the embarrassment flowed into her fingers.

"You didn't eat it?" His question carried a faint smile with it.

"I…I was going to." She shoved her hand in her pocket. "My mother taught…we should never use a gift until the thank you note is delivered. So here." She offered the crinkled note, and he took it.

Sawyer shifted foot to foot, holding the note in front of him. "Even for fruit?" He squinted.

Laney rolled her head. "Here." She snatched it from his hand. Her words, *'It made my day'* now felt like sour milk in her veins. *Foolhardy woman thinking a shotgun messenger would share her sensibilities.* "Did I say thank you for the desk? I can't remember."

"Just don't put it in a note." Sawyer tried to move toward her door. The room was so small Laney pressed back against the bed trading places with him.

"Forgive me." She swallowed, already missing the end of their strange time in her room. "I wonder, how your arm is doing?"

So unlike the women of the house, his rugged stature filled the door, and he turned. "Better." He scanned around the landing and looked back. "I was wondering about Saturday?"

Laney blinked, wanting to fill the silence with questions. *Saturday?* But the way his face struggled to speak was worth the wait.

Sawyer rocked his jaw. "If you want, I was going to see if you wanted to go for a picnic?"

"Picnic?" Laney pushed her hand in her pocket and pinched her hankie ten times.

"Yeah, there is a place I go fishing. Water, a tree, a blanket, food." He fingered his hair to the side of his forehead. "Picnic, right?"

"Yes. That would be nice." Her voice dipped. "Who else would be going?"

Sawyer shrugged his good shoulder. "I guess we could ask Widow Farrow and Matthew?"

"That sounds wonderful." Laney straightened, intertwining her fingers at her chest. "I think we would all enjoy an outing. Maybe Matthew can join you in fishing?"

"Sure thing." Did his tone hold a twinge of disappointment?

Laney's mind whirled. Friday night, she was expected at Mayor Reynold's home and Saturday a picnic with friends, Sunday church. This was the most social time she'd had in a...a...*ever.* "The Lord is good." She sighed and met his gaze.

Sawyer shook his head, as a smile crept up his face. "If you say so."

Chapter 17

Waiting nervously, Laney paced between the parlor and front door Friday evening. She'd donned real lady shoes tonight and could feel a pinch in her toes. Mayor Reynolds would be here any minute to escort her to his home for dinner. It was just a simple parent-teacher meeting.

Then why did her stomach hurt?

First, Howard, his eldest, was difficult. Trying to ignore her tight heeled shoes, she rolled the tension from her shoulders. On more than one occasion she'd had to pull the young man aside this past week trying to win his cooperation, to no avail. One thing Laney knew about children, they all had their currency. The little ones had earned the reward of a special guest on Monday.

Moses loved coming to school. The rough and tumble middle age boys would sit still and complete anything she asked to be able to play with the new ball and bat that the Ophir mine donated. Baseball had found an eager group at the Virginia City school. But Howard Reynolds could care less. His goal in school was to make things difficult. No wonder the last schoolmaster had no time for him.

And then there was the mixture of ethnic children attending and the fact that Mayor Reynold was her boss. "Ahh." These jittery nerves called for something in order, something calming. "But the *fruit of the Spirit is love, joy, peace, gentleness*. No." Her finger tapped her lips. *"Love, joy, peace, longsuffering...."*

A knock at the door made her jump. *"Longsuffering, gentleness, goodness."* She opened the door. "Mayor Reynolds, good evening." Laney glanced over him. It wasn't even dark yet.

"Miss Balderhoff." He tipped his bowler. "Would you like me to come in, or are you ready?"

"I'm ready." She grabbed her wrap off the hall tree. Laney had never had anyone come to the door for her. Was it impolite not to invite the middle-aged Mayor inside? Before she could cross the threshold and close the door, he had offered his elbow. Hesitant, Laney hooked her hand under and over it lightly touching the fabric of his brown suit jacket. Heading down the wooden walkway, she felt her every step protest. Devil may care, she wasn't that naïve. It appeared as if they were stepping out together. But if she removed her hand, would he find her rude? The street of saloons leered ahead; certainly, they would turn off C Street and take another road to his home.

"Howie!"

Laney looked to see the furry-faced Mr. Clemens run across the street. "And Miss Balderhoff." Samuel Clemens bowed. "See you are out for a stroll tonight, Miss. No more hanging from the Wells Fargo stagecoach?"

Laney rolled her eyes. Some of the children knew of his newspaper story and begged her to tell her side of the story. "No, I like walking now." She let her hand slip from the mayor's elbow. Finally, she could reach in her pocket and squeeze her hankie.

"So, I just wanted to check." Mr. Clemens pulled his fingers across his bushy mustache. "No cards tonight at the Bucket?"

"I am otherwise engaged." Mayor Reynolds nodded toward Laney." You'll have to keep the drunk southerners from shooting the northern men without me."

"Won't that be a feat beyond a poor newspaper reporter?" Samuel chuckled. His eyes met Laney with a lift of his thick eyebrows. "But I will not detain you two any longer. Have a wonderful night." An amused expression glimmered across his face, and Laney couldn't help speaking up.

"We are having a parent-teacher meeting tonight." She didn't mean to sound terse and lowered her tone. "I'd missed a home visit with the Reynolds' when they were out of town."

"Well, yes." Mr. Clemens stepped backward to leave. "Then, enjoy your meeting." He waved, striding across the dirt street. "If I had a child, I'd want a meeting too." His jovial smile soured over Laney as he walked back down to the Territorial Enterprise.

"We can turn here." The Mayor held his elbow out again.

Holding a frustrated breath, Laney reluctantly took his elbow and walked with him up two blocks to his house. "This is just the first floor." He broke into her uneasy thoughts. "I plan on building on."

Laney flattened a half-grin as they walked up the wooden steps, thinking it was grander than most she'd seen. He opened the door for her, and thankfully a tiny older woman in a brown and white piped dress met them and took her wrap and his hat.

"This is my mother," the Mayor said loudly. "And this is the boy's teacher, Miss Balderhoff."

Laney curtsied. The older woman must be hard of hearing. "So nice to meet you, ma'am." She leaned close and spoke clear and loud into her ear. "Your home is lovely." Laney finally felt a bit more relaxed.

"I believe I've seen you at church." Mrs. Reynolds blinked and rubbed her ear.

Laney could reach out and hug the woman. "Yes. Of course. I saw you Sunday. What a wonderful sermon it was, the loaves and fishes. I thought the reverend did a…a fine discourse." Laney smiled at George and Howard standing at the large table to the right. "Hello, young men." The smell of food and bread made her countenance rise. "What a beautiful table, Mrs. Reynolds. Thank you for having me." Laney thought she pronounced her words vibrantly, but they all stared uneasily at her. Walking to the table, the Mayor pulled out her chair. She brushed her red skirt layers back and took a seat. Chiding herself for feeling scandalous earlier, she took the napkin and placed it in her lap.

The food was delightful, and the conversation mostly flowed around the pleasure she'd had teaching this first week. Howard pulled at his bow tie, and his grandmother glared at him before she left the table. George piped in about the baseball game, and Mayor Reynolds seemed talkative, less intimidating in his own home. A maid cleared the dishes, and the boys stood to excuse themselves. Laney teased them about the home reading she required, which was probably what they were eager to get to.

Mayor Reynolds poured himself an amber liquid in a small glass. "I'd offer you some, but according to your contract—" He paused with a crooked smile. "I believe it states, 'No teacher can cross the threshold which is not clothed, from the crown of her head to the sole of her foot, in garments of virtue.'"

Laney felt her shoulders raise. No one could count her neglectful on that account.

"You spoke of reading, writing, arithmetic, a little geography, and history?" Mayor Reynolds finished his first drink and poured one more before he sat at the table's head.

"Yes, sir."

"And none of the children are using anything but English?"

Thankful she sat in the middle of the table, Laney straightened the salt and pepper before she pulled her hands to her lap. "Yes, sir."

"I want their mouths washed out with soap if they try to speak anything but English."

Laney wanted to help a sagging candle stand straight on the table. How did the informal conversation at the table turn to the Mayor's wishes? If she did not speak up, she would be out of a job by morning.

"Sir."

"I want you to call me Howie when we are alone."

Alone? Laney brushed her fingers across her cheek and held them over her mouth. "I hoped to talk about Howard and any ideas for me to reach him. I've done as much tutoring as I can fit in." She tried to find her words gently. "He seems to have a loathing for school."

"It's his mother's fault. She spoiled the boys rotten." He sniffed hard and swallowed the last drop of his drink. "You're not to coddle them, Miss Balderhoff." His eyes narrowed. "May I call you Elaine in private?"

Private? "I think he is smart. Your son just lacks motivation." When was it going to be overtly obvious she had ignored two of his questions? "What does he do around here? In his spare time?"

"Close to nothing." His lids drooped halfway. "If the south declares war—we are late in our news, it may have already begun—he can go into the military. It will help make a man of him."

Laney bit her tongue. He was so young and awkward. "Yes, sir, ahh...," her lips twitched, "Howie."

"Elaine, there are a few other things to address."

At least when he said it in such a commanding way, it appeared far from personal.

"I've tried to build a school board, but the town is growing so fast that the school's burden has fallen on me. I would have preferred to get to know you like the young lady you are. Rather than being your boss."

Laney lowered her chin. Something was coming.

"I do feel it's important that we meet often. And as you can see, my mother, though hard of hearing, runs a tight household." He hesitated. "Wouldn't you agree?"

Often? Alone? Names in private? Laney refused to agree.

"Friday nights, you have the week behind you, and we can discuss any needs you may have. Oh," he rose from his chair, "I almost forgot." The mayor lifted a wooden box from the corner. "I ordered the Webster's blue-backed spellers." He set them on the table, and Laney rose. One minute she was certain she was going to dread their boss-teacher relationship like the influenza; the next, his generosity was dumbfounding.

"The students will so enjoy these." She held one up. "Thank you."

The way he smiled made the gray in his long muttonchops stand on end. Laney was ready to go.

"Maybe I could ask Howard and George to come along and carry the box home for me?"

"No." He frowned. "I will have them delivered on Monday." He moved to open the lace curtain. "It seems like a lovely evening. I look forward to walking you home." He stepped to the hall for her wrap.

"Will you tell your mother the meal was wonderful?"

"Yes, Elaine. She'll await your return next Friday." The Mayor straightened her wrap along her back, his hand lingering on her shoulder blade longer than needed.

She stepped from his touch, and he reached for the door just as she did. Unfortunately, their hands collided, and there were only inches between them.

"You have very round, kind eyes, Elaine."

"Thank you." She pulled away. "Just as you do too. Nice eyes, I mean. Maybe more oval, but nice." Laney was falling into her own mud puddle. "As do Howard and George—eyes, nice eyes." Opening the door, they stepped out. Thankful the night air had cooled with a breeze, and even with pinched toes, she had the worst urge to run home. His elbow reappeared and she knew what he was up to. He was prancing around town with the young schoolmarm hooked to his side. For the first time in all the whirlwind of moving to this desert land, she didn't care for Virginia City. With every step in step with his, the loud banging of pianos and brawling made her miss the quiet of Nebraska. There, five or six people lived in a one-room soddy, farming from sunup to dusk. Never would they take their meager wages and waste them on drink, poker, or a romp at Madam Bulette's. Laney pulled her shawl tight. Poor Leona, what was she doing right now? How could the child sleep with this late-night revelry?

"I am disappointed, Elaine."

Laney's eyes shot to the right and found Mayor Reynolds grinning.

"I was hoping to see the famous moccasins."

Laney's upper body froze. How her legs continued walking was beyond her comprehension.

"George loved the discussion on the tribes of Indians." His voice sounded calm. "The boy is fascinated with them. I haven't the heart to tell him they are unmanageable savages."

Laney heard night crickets somewhere above the noisy streets as they walked closer to the widows' house. His summation of all Indians was incorrect, but at least he wasn't going to shame her over the strange footwear. "For a teacher meeting with the Mayor, I felt these shoes were more appropriate." She nodded once. "At school the children keep me running."

"I would commend you for finding the comfort you need for your profession." They stopped at the dark stoop, and he pulled the edge of her shawl higher on her shoulder. Like the school bell being rung in her ear, the man was far too attentive.

"There is one more thing, Elaine. There is no best way to say it." His brows crossed, and Laney could smell the alcohol on his breath. Wanting to move away, she was trapped with only a few inches with her back to the front door.

He sighed and tilted his head. "Your teaching contract had to be adjusted. I'm sorry that the posting did not reflect the current pay. Mr. Feldon was more experienced than you, and the fact that you are a woman...you understand." Now he touched her elbow. "The pay is a third of what the posting noted. I do apologize. I should have corrected the amount before it was posted. But then we didn't know who would respond."

Laney stilled. How he dare look so contrite over such a significant oversight? How was she going to be able to send her mother and aunt money every month?

"God will provide," she said stoically.

"I knew you would handle it sensibly." The mayor touched her back and ran his hand down just past her waist. "And if ever money is an issue, I want you to come to me." He winked and turned to leave. "Until next Friday, Elaine."

Laney gritted her teeth until they hurt, and before she could step through the door, a shiver ran up her spine. Flinging her wrap at the hall tree, it landed on the floor. Stomping up the stairs, she continued to her room, ignoring where it lay.

Chapter 18

Sawyer looked up and thanked Widow Boils as she poured him a second cup of coffee.

"The teacher was out with the mayor last night, ya know?" She set the pot on the stove and came and sat at the breakfast table.

"Uh-huh." Sawyer took a sip wishing she was frying some of those donuts he loved. "Can you make me a basket? I'm taking Miss Balderhoff, Ava, and Matthew to my fishing lake for a picnic."

Widow Boils tapped her finger on his arm. "It might interest you to know that last night I could hear them across the floor. Our little miss teacher was wearing shoes." She pinched her wrinkled lips together for Sawyer to respond. "Shoes. Real lady ones."

Sawyer gave up. The widow wanted to talk about Laney and the mayor. "I suppose she was trying to impress him—being her boss and all."

Widow Boils huffed and sat back in her chair. "Miss Balderhoff is as innocent as the sky is blue." She frowned, shaking her head. "I'll get that basket ready."

"I'm going to hitch up Blackie." Sawyer rose and headed out the back door. Miss Balderhoff was innocent and genuine, some of the very appealing things he needed to get out from under his skin. Widow C said the new teacher could not be married, and he could not be married, so that was that. He'd laid awake last night rehearsing what it would be like to spend time with her today. As long as they were apart last week, he could stay busy and quit thinking about her. But being in her room with her and seeing the soft, pink flush on her face brought everything back up. The way her eyes filled with gratitude over an orange and a desk. Her small surroundings were plain yet homey. Every dress on the peg hung in perfect order. Now that bedroom swirled in his mind making him desire the things he could not have. Sawyer pulled the bit taut in Blackie's mouth.

"Mr. Sawyer." Ava and her full black dress stepped from the back door. "I'm hoping you'll forgive me." She tilted her head. "With the work at Wells Fargo and Matthew starting school, I've fallen behind. I need to stay and clean today, and then I promised Matthew I would play catch with him."

"No, that's fine. I understand." Sawyer bumped his hat above his forehead, thinking this might work to his advantage. "Hopefully, Miss Balderhoff will still want to go."

"I know she is getting ready. I will send her out back right away." Ava smiled and went inside.

Sawyer spied the Wells Fargo building. A better idea flashed in his head, and he removed his fishing gear. Walking it back into the barn, he came out and went into the back of the Wells Fargo office. The guns were kept in a locked box. He found the key and removed the leather-covered 12 gauge coach gun. "Perfect." Sawyer stepped out to the wagon and laid it under the bench.

The dust swirled at the end of the alley just before Laney appeared with a basket hanging from her arm. She wore her blue dress, one of his favorites. Her hair hung over her shoulders except for the front strands she'd pulled back with a bow. Seeing her and thinking of them alone, he corralled a grin as Ava stepped out behind her.

"Take my parasol." She handed it to Laney.

"We can share it." Laney set the basket in the back of the wagon.

"I've decided not to go." Ava frowned. "Please forgive me. I have too much to do."

Laney's head swung to him, the wagon, and back to Ava. "Oh," she whispered.

"I know you'll have a wonderful day." Ava squeezed Laney's arm before stepping inside.

Laney gave Sawyer a crooked frown, and he had to contain a snicker. Why did he enjoy seeing her uncomfortable? He held his hand out and helped her on the bench next to him. She straightened her skirts and popped the black parasol open. "How far is our travel today?"

Favoring his healing shoulder, Sawyer tapped the reins, and the horse jerked them forward. Settling in with the reins in one hand, he rocked a little closer to the middle, and Laney leaned to the edge drumming her fingers over the parasol handle.

"Maybe about an hour there." He waited. A Bible quote of some kind should be next from her mouth, but instead, a deep breath exhaled. She faced forward with her usual straight back resolve.

"How was the first week of school?" he asked, leading the wagon from the town.

"It went well." Her head tilted side to side a bit. "The children are bright and, for the most part, cooperative."

She didn't seem her talkative self, and now the silence started to bother him. "And your dinner with Mayor Reynolds, how did that go?"

Laney curled her shoulder upward while her face shot him a gape of annoyance. "How do you know of that?"

"Widow B."

Laney rolled her eyes.

"What?" His eyes narrowed on hers. "You live in a house with three other women. They talk."

"Then tell me, what do they talk about? Maybe you would know." Her tone turned a bit surly. "I asked them to give you my thank you note and no one was willing."

Sawyer inched away from her and tapped the horse into a canter. "Hard to say."

"Even *you* said not to write you notes. Are thank-you notes scandalous here in Nevada territory, and no one told me?" She leered at him. "And buggy rides alone aren't." A defensive tone escaped.

"I don't think so." He needed another point to bring up quick. She was smart, nosey... and—

"I'm sure a Wells Fargo man is able to read?" She questioned confidently.

"So, how do you like the desk?" Blast it, that was a good question, then why did her eyes narrow on him. A circle of wind with dry, dusty heat swirled toward them. Sawyer grabbed her parasol and blocked the dirt from spinning onto them. "The wind sure can kick up out here," he insisted. Within the shadow of the parasol, her eyes bored into his, and he released his grip.

"Sawyer, what does N-e-v-a-d-a spell?"

"Now, I have to be one of your students?" He huffed a quick laugh. "Can't you take a day off?"

Her pious Bible-quoting head slowly wobbled no.

"I'm better with numbers." He pulled the corners of his mouth together. "Always have been so. I told you I was stuck in the corn fields."

"You can't read. That is it. You cannot read. You can't read my notes, and the widows didn't want to tell me." She sat back and stared ahead as if she knew it to be true. Her body jerked forward. "I can teach you."

"No, thank you." He groaned from deep inside. Now that he'd admitted his secret to Miss Balderhoff, a teacher, she would never let this go.

"Why not? It's nothing to be ashamed of."

"I'm not ashamed." He barked, holding back a swear word. "I just don't want to talk to you about it."

"I suppose a shotgun messenger doesn't need to read," she murmured. He'd hoped she could heed a warning and she would be silent.

"Ava!" Laney dropped the parasol from blocking the sun. Wide-eyed, she looked like she'd struck gold. "That's why Ava had to fill in at the office for you." She nodded proudly of her deduction. "All the bank drafts and sorting letters to which routes. It would be difficult if your reading was poor."

"Hey, just one short minute." Sawyer fought the urge to pull the wagon to a stop. "I'm a shotgun messenger. Not some office clerk. That's not my job and never will be." He locked his jaw and reset his hat on his head.

"It is limiting, though." Laney sighed.

"Did you hear me say something about not wanting to talk about it?"

"Yes, I do apologize. It's information that you wanted to keep to yourself. Though it sounds as if all the widows know." Another gust of wind came from the side, and she leaned into him before the parasol could block the dirt and wind.

Normally he would enjoy her being close, but now Sawyer second-guessed this picnic. His elbow gave her a nudge back to her side of the bench.

The needed quiet finally settled into the wagon ride, and he took a deep breath watching the dry, flat landscape.

Silence, a good thing. *For three minutes.*

"I'll tell you a secret that I didn't want anyone to know." Her tone sounded contrite.

Must be something horrific, like losing her Bible in the snow. He tried to swallow his judgment. "Go on," he coaxed.

"Everyone has seen my moccasins." She pulled her skirt up. They were on her feet, as he would have suspected. "I used them for a lesson with the children. I thought before they offend anyone, I could use them as an educational tool. As an excuse, really, to fend off the naysayers."

"Your moccasins offend people?"

"They're not appropriate for women to wear. As Mayor Reynolds reminded me, the teacher must be covered from head to toe in virtue. For quite a few moments, I'd wondered if my sentimental keepsakes would mean my dismissal."

"Virtue, he insists?" Sawyer scowled. "Interestingly, he doesn't require that for mayors."

"As the goodness of the Lord would have it, his son, George, has quite an interest in American Indian culture. To my favor, the Mayor seemed accepting of my oddity."

Sawyer felt something fiery rising in him. *There is more than moccasins that louse would like to accept from her.* Sawyer must have inhaled too much dust. He spit off his side of the wagon. "So, what's the secret?"

Laney huffed and rubbed between her brows. Brushing some wild hair strands behind her ear, she spoke. "I was fired from my last teaching position and on the list of infractions was a woman who wore Indian attire."

Sawyer frowned as he studied her. "They had a list against you?"

Her eyes widened as she took a deep breath. Exhaling, she finally gave him one curt nod. "Things are different in Nebraska."

"What else was on the list? Too many Bible quotes?"

Chewing on the corner of her lip, Laney watched a fast-moving tumbleweed roll in front of the wagon. Had he offended her? He didn't mean that against her.

"I think Virginia City is lucky to have you." Sawyer pulled the reins to the right, catching a smaller road to the lake. "I suppose most of life's tribulations are to make us stronger."

She finally looked at him and offered a small smile. "*Behold, I will do a new thing; now it shall spring forth; shall ye not know it?*" Dramatically, Laney waved her palm in front of them. "*I will even make a way in the wilderness and rivers in the desert.*" She shrugged. "One of my favorite verses."

Sawyer gave her shoulder a small bump. "That's the girl I know."

Chapter 19

Laney held Ava's parasol to the side and blinked back the dust and dirt rolling off the road. The expansive flat blue-brown lake spread before her. "This is it?"

"Water in the desert." Sawyer pulled the reins back and set the brake. "There's our shade." He tipped his hat and nodded to the shoreline.

Laney stood and scanned the area. "One tree? The entire lake has one tree?"

Sawyer jumped down and held his hand out.

Laney finally brought her attention to him. "Is this not your injured arm, Mr. Roth?" She took his hand and held it. It felt warm and strong. A strange flutter tickled her insides. Certainly, she was happy to see it healing.

"You can hold my hand as long as you want, Miss Balderhoff." His lips formed a narrow smile, teasing. "Just don't try to raise it too far."

"Of course." She held her skirts and stepped down. Sawyer grabbed the blanket they were sitting on and tucked it under his arm. As Laney went to get the basket from the wagon bed, she noticed him pull a shot gun from under the seat.

"Are you suspecting bandits in the area?" She tapped her bottom lip, scanning the desert landscape.

"No," he said casually. Stepping away from the wagon, Sawyer kicked a rock from under the tree. After spreading the blanket, he reached for the basket. "I thought maybe you could help me practice shooting." He set the basket down. Leaning his weight on his back leg, he hooked one thumb in his front pocket.

Laney tapped her fingers over her knuckles, thinking of how sweetly personal his invitation sounded when he asked. Now it seemed his picnic had a higher purpose. "So, what happened to the fishing?" Her eyes narrowed on him, trying to temper her question.

Sawyer shrugged. "Wrong time of year. I was going to fish if Matthew wanted." He stood holding the gun at his side, waiting.

Laney wasn't sure if this was how she pictured her time with him. "I doubt I can help you shoot that gun." The west may be wild, but not for her. *Well, minus hanging from the stage.* Remembering her body bouncing off the stage, she sat on the blanket, straightened her skirts around her, and brushed off the road dust. *Blessed Trinity*, nothing wrong with holding to propriety as long as possible.

Distracted, Sawyer didn't hear her. "Let me set something up," he said before he jogged out to a set of large rocks. Laney watched as Sawyer set a series of smaller rocks on top. He jogged back and offered his hand to help her stand. "Could you just hold it up while I try something?"

Laney reluctantly took the shot gun in her hands. It was heavier than she imagined.

"Now, hold it up near my good shoulder."

"You're going to try to shoot left-handed? She sighed, reasoning that after he'd helped her, it was her turn to help his profession. Carefully she held the butt of the gun to his left shoulder while he forced his right hand to come up under it.

"Okay, I think I've got it." Sawyer stepped away and aimed at the rocks. Closing one eye, the brim of his hat notched lower, and his tongue touched his top lip before he shot.

Laney jumped at the loud crack.

Sawyer's frustration seemed held back behind tight lips as he aimed again. After the third shot and no movement from the rocks, Laney squeezed her hankie ten times, saying a silent prayer for him. Noting the sweat on his temple, she felt the discouragement he must be feeling.

"Laney, can you help me again?" His voice sounded calmer than he looked.

As she approached, his eyes watched hers. "Can you hold it against your shoulder? I'll help." Laney faced the rocks. They blurred with sizzling waves in the bright sun. Sawyer came behind her and set the gun against her shoulder. He stood a hair's breadth behind her and brought his left hand around to hold the barrel. "I need to change out our hands. Can you hold it another minute?"

Laney swallowed and barely nodded her head. Sawyer Roth smelled like fresh pressed cotton and hovered so close that she could feel his breath on her neck. If she had goose feathers, every one of them would be ruffled. Was he dallying with her? *Oh, blessed be,* helping him out was much easier when he was weak and wounded.

"Hold still. I'm going to pull the trigger, and it will kick your shoulder a bit."

"I...I...don't think...."

Crack! Laney popped back against him. When she opened her eyes and thought to rub her shoulder, he'd cocked the hammer and another shot rang out. The smaller rock jumped from its spot, and the second also. A high-pitched ringing rattled her ear, and she shook her head.

"It's getting better. I knew it." He stepped back, the rifle at his side.

Laney staggered without his support. "I assure you, I was *not* aiming. I had my eyes closed." She turned to him, then scanned the area, thankful the landscape was empty.

"Are you all right?" Sawyer smiled, "Do you want to shoot for yourself?"

"Heavens, no." Laney rubbed her shoulder. "That's enough for today." She walked back to the shade and sat. Sawyer continued to try to shoot with the rifle hanging at his right side. One of the rocks spun into the air. Heart still erratic, she watched him. He was too familiar, devil-may-care handsome, and should not hold her so close.

Her nearness hadn't seemed to affect him, however. She was just a stand to practice his shooting. Unfortunately, his unawareness made him all the more attractive. Laney pulled the loose strands behind her ears and watched him another minute. Maybe in her heart, she wished for someone who'd care for her in that special way. More than a perch to shoot from. The way Jacob had fought for and loved Rachel—a biblical love.

Laney rolled her eyes with the silly Saturday picnic ponderings. Sawyer knelt behind a rock and used it to hold the rifle in place. She couldn't nag him about learning to read and the better jobs it would make available to him. That gun in his hand was like the way her soft moccasins felt on her feet. It truly was like second nature to him. Just as her first job was removed from her, the discouragement of being without your passion can make a heart sick. Her expression softened, watching as he set more rocks up to practice with his right arm. The picnic was for shooting practice, so what? Sawyer Roth was still her neighbor, and neighbors loved one another. *Well, biblically speaking.*

***

An hour later, between talk of the Wells Fargo routes and the children at the school, they sat and finished the cheese and rolls Widow Boils had packed. Sawyer took an apple from the basket and shined it on his shirt. "Would you like a bite?" With teasing eyes, he held it close to her mouth, and she had the worst impulse to snatch it from his hand. Opening her mouth slowly, Laney fought the red heat coming up her collar. He watched her, his mouth ajar, a partial smile arising. Keeping her eyes steady on him, she took a small bite. Chewing was fine, but the embarrassment made it hard to swallow, and she averted her eyes.

"We're okay, Lane-*ee*. We're not Adam and Eve." Sawyer took a large bite and chewed.

"You know of the Bible." She gave him a curious squint. "It's the word of God, freely given to us; wouldn't you so love to read it for yourself?"

He rolled his eyes and handed her the apple. "You can have it."

Laney spied the shared fruit in her hand, then out to the flat water. "I'm sorry. You said you don't like to talk about it. Please forgive me."

Sawyer rolled his tongue inside his cheek. "Forgiven."

Laney reached for a cloth to wrap the apple core, chiding herself for ruining the quiet lunch they shared.

"Just toss it for the animals." Sawyer nodded to the dry land.

"No, I can't. I don't like leaving things out like this."

Suddenly Sawyer leaned close, his eyes seized on hers.

She inched back. "What?" Her tone was wary.

"Toss it." He challenged.

"That makes me uncomfortable. If I can control…" a small tremor shook her hand and the apple in the cloth, "…where things go, if it's in my power… I…I…." She went to reach for her pocket, and he captured her hand first.

"Just toss it."

The stare-down was on. It was just a half-eaten apple. Laney squinted, feeling her lips purse into a line. How dare he pick at her queer behavior? She was fine with who she was, but when other people pointed out her strange patterns, it bruised her feelings. A get-even notion occurred to her. "Read Genesis One to me, and I will toss this." She loved her idea and glared back at the assertive man with smoldering brown eyes.

Sawyer released her and sat back. "Deal." He answered with the intensity of a man who'd traded off his best horse.

Laney fisted her hands before opening the cloth and took the half-eaten apple. Rolling her shoulders, she tried to picture how the school children loved the new game of baseball.

"Just toss it!" Sawyer exclaimed, wide-eyed.

Laney jumped and pitched it behind her as hard as she could. Expecting Sawyer to be a disgruntled loser, his expression stiffened. Studying something behind her, his lip twitched, eyebrows rose and then narrowed.

"Elaine Balderhoff." He huffed, still staring past her, mouth forming a tight frown. Sawyer jerked his head back. "Oh, girl."

Ignoring his remark, she reiterated. "It's only Genesis One. One chapter and I'll help you." She countered, finally turning to see what captivated him. Her hands rose to her mouth. "Are those bees?"

"Only you would hit the *only* nest in the *only* tree in miles." He took her wrist and pulled them to standing. "Watch…oh no…they're not happy." Sawyer pulled her closer to the water's edge and yanked off his boots.

Laney could not believe her eyes as the swirl of buzzing darkness came closer. How could so many bees come from that hive? "This is your fault!" She grabbed his shirt as they tried to weave opposite the swirl and swarm coming closer.

"In the water, now!" Sawyer drug her in, the cold water soaking her moccasins and skirt layers.

"No, Sawyer!" Laney panted, clinging to him. "I can't swim!"

He pulled her further, the water covering her waist. "You don't need to swim." He leaned to the side, and the bees buzzed inches from them. "Get under!"

Sawyer jumped upon her until they both went under. Rushing prickles of cold water covered her and went up her nose. She would drown at this man's hand or die from a bee attack. Fighting against his hold, Laney finally pulled her head above just in time to feel a sting on her cheek. Taking a quick breath, she went back under and found Sawyer with round eyes and rounded cheeks. They pulled and grabbed each other to stay under while her skirts floated like dark clouds around them. When the panic in airless lungs was too much, they rose and took another quick breath before going back down. Sawyer's leg wrapped around her knee while her other leg fought to find the lake bottom. His hands grabbed her waist and kept a hold on her to keep them under. Her lungs were not as strong as his; she needed air and pushed with all her might. Finally, they both rose with only the top of their heads showing. Clinging to each other, their chests rose and fell while their eyes skimmed around. Sawyer rose a hand from the water and swatted around them. "I think the swarm has moved on."

Laney's cheek stung, and she wasn't ready to surrender to his observation. Staying low as possible, she dodged left to right, seeing the remaining bees circle them. Gripping his neck, she realized her legs had somehow come around his hips, securing them together. Humiliated, she flicked her feet in the water, trying to find the lake floor.

"I've got you." His arms tightened around her while making sure the buzzing pests were gone. "I think we are okay." His eyes finally dropped on her, and he shook his head.

Mute and wide-eyed, Laney's body floated back against his. Sawyer fingered her hair out of her face. "You never have to throw an apple again." He winced, trying to pull the stinger from her cheek. "Does it hurt?"

"It does." Laney huffed. "I'm not sure if I want to laugh or cry."

Sawyer stood, the water at his chest and Laney still floated in his arms. A bee buzzed by. As one, they leaned low to let it pass. "Let's wait just another minute." His eyes warmed with something she couldn't look away from. "I think you," he whispered, "even hapless and soaked to the bone, are beautiful."

Laney felt his sweet words snuggle next to her heart. No one had ever told her that. Water ran down her stung cheek, but she didn't want to move from his eyes. Something still simmered there. As she went to take a nervous breath, his lips unexpectedly pressed against hers. Before she could pull back, he held her tighter and kissed her again and then again.

Only seconds passed before Laney realized she was unknowingly kissing him in return. Her insides spun, and she felt as if she was floating. Strong hands massaged down her back and around her waist. Without thought or permission, her fingers ran up into his wet hair. Every kiss shot overwhelming, glorious joy through her. Breathless, he finally pulled back and rested his forehead on hers.

She wondered if this new feeling could be right. "I don't think...that...ah...." Her chest rose and fell, the words slow in coming. *Schoolteachers cannot be married.* "You shouldn't... have kissed me."

Sawyer traced his finger along her hairline. "And I don't think you should have held me on your lap all night, Miss."

Laney opened her mouth to refute, and something occurred to her. She really was floating; her feet were somewhere behind her. "You were in need," she whispered.

"And I still am." His rogue smile and perfect lips were a thread away, but it was the way his eyes tenderly watched hers. His wet hair made him look younger, more earnest, and more desirable. If love was an overwhelming feeling young people truly had, without meaning to, she had just floated right into it.

Chapter 20

Sawyer held Laney's hand as he pulled her to shallower water. Rolling his eyes to the sky, Sawyer bit on his bottom lip. Surely, there weren't many smarts in him because he just went and kissed an innocent, soaked, young teacher. How did she get in his arms? Weren't they just dunking themselves to avoid bees?

She jerked her hand free as she twirled to the side. "I still see bees." Laney grimaced and swatted her hand in the air.

"Just don't make them mad." Sawyer spied the swarm circling the tree. "I think they've calmed down." He fought a humorous expression at Miss Lane-*ee* standing on the bank. Arms hung low, she was practically hunched over from the weight of water on her dress.

"You can take your dress off."

Laney's head snapped up, and she clutched her collar. "What did you say?"

Sawyer eyed her, keeping his voice even. "Take your dress off." Now that he thought about it, her wide-eyes and open mouth matched how that sounded.

"You must have water inside those ears that has loosened your brain." She sneered.

"Take the blanket or my shirt." He unbuttoned his shirt. "I'll squeeze the water from your dress. After wringing his shirt out, he tried handing it to her.

Ignoring his outstretched hand, Laney pulled on her dress layers and tried to twist the fabric. With each pull, it exposed her legs. She bent lower at the waist, struggling to rid the water from her dress. "Crossing the Red Sea was likely not this much trouble." She mumbled.

"My way is quick-like. Just roll the whole dress and give it one big squeeze." He enjoyed watching her brown hair drip on to her shoulders. Belly still warm from her touch and her kisses, Sawyer knew in his heart he was being brash. His man-logic had some other carnal motives for sure. In only her underclothes, he imagined her skin feathery soft, and cool to the touch.

Mind racing like a wild bull, he turned in a circle. A simple kiss was one thing, even harmless, really. Sawyer pulled his socks off and twisted the water from them. But her innocent lips touching his were enough to spark a wet forest.

At first, her mouth had stilled with shock, but he was glad he hadn't given up. The way he'd held her tight hadn't given her much choice. Did he just take something the teacher didn't want to give?

Before a growl could leave his throat, Sawyer remembered slender, curious fingers coming up his neck and entering his hair. That was not forced. Miss Balderhoff had kissed him back, and though timid, she did it quite well. He shook out his shirt and pulled it back on. The heat from his insides would have him dry in minutes.

Rubbing the water from his hair, he watched her. Moving away from their picnic, she sat on a rock in the sun and wrung her hem. Carefully she untied her moccasins and pulled them off.

He'd give a week's wages to know what she was thinking. Did she want to be more than a friend? Did she regret what had just happened? Should *he* regret it? As a man, not one bit; as her friend…he scratched his forehead. He probably had some explaining to do. A Christian woman like her, with all her high and mighty principles, would want them to marry. But shotgun messengers were not allowed to be married. Interesting how he felt fine with that rule an hour ago. All he wanted was to get back on the Wells Fargo stage bench and do his job.

Sawyer knocked the water from his ear and went to get his boots and hat. The horse rattled the reins back and forth, anxious to go. It was just a kiss, not a proposal or anything of the like. He *was* the one who teased her about throwing the apple. He *was* the one who grabbed her underwater, and he *was* the one who kissed her. As of this minute, all he owed her was an apology—and the reading of some chapter in the Bible.

Searching for angry buzzing creatures, Sawyer snatched the blanket and basket from under the tree. The horse reared from a few irritating bees.

"Whoa, now! You're fine." He flipped the wool blanket on the bench. "Settle down, settle down." Sawyer stepped up and released the brake, and before he could let go of the basket, the horse reared one more time. Sawyer dove for the reins, but the horse had been agitated long enough. It bolted so hard that he was knocked backward and tumbled off the wagon.

Jumping up from the sand, he took off running after the wagon, but it was of no use. His good-natured Blackie, a retired Wells Fargo horse, had galloped off at full speed, leaving them in the dust. Sawyer stood in the road in the middle of the desert, with nothing but heat waves as far as the eye could see. Sighing, he rolled his tongue inside his cheek. "I shouldn't have kissed the teacher." He glanced skyward. "Is that what You're trying to say?"

Laney jogged toward him and stopped cold. The shocked expression on her face said everything. Embarrassed for not restraining Blackie, he had trouble looking at her. They were stranded in the hot desert, and it was his fault.

"Will he stop and come back for us?" Laney swallowed hard.

"I doubt it." Sawyer pulled his hat off and set it on her head. "I think it best we start to walk." He squinted down the road. "We might catch up to him." An awkward silence lingered between them.

"I need my gun." He walked toward the tree of good and evil.

"Thank you for your hat, but maybe we should stay near the water," she droned, following him. "Would the widows know where to find us?"

"Ava knows of this lake, but none of them ride that I've ever seen. I suppose they could get the sheriff or someone to come after us."

Laney choked on her breath and felt her puffy cheek. "But then we will be exposed, and I will lose my job." She closed her eyes and dropped her chin to her chest.

"They can't fire you because my horse bolted. Bees are not your fault." Tipping his hat upward to see her, his eyes slanted on her troubled face. "Well, a little your fault."

Laney whimpered.

Blast it, she was adorable with his hat resting above those sad round eyes and swollen cheek. Should he ask permission to hold her again? He would be happy to comfort her.

"I'll be fired for being found out here with you," she cried. "A schoolmarm is to be above reproach. Clothed in dignity, not murky lake water!"

Sawyer bit his bottom lip. He would not smile, and he could not laugh. "Let's start walking." He pointed ahead. "We might get into town past dark, and all this can be kept under the roof of the widow house." Starting down the road, he looked back to where she stood. "Come on, Laney. We don't have much choice."

She frowned, closing her eyes.

His fingers signaled her forward. "Come on. You can quote me all the verses you know."

Still forlorn, her bottom lip pouted crooked, and she started to follow him. Sawyer had the worst urge to take her hand but shifted the gun over to cover the void. Should he act like their stirring, sweet encounter had never happened? The thoughtful thing would be to put it to rest, just like the trip out here. She was too worrisome.

"I want to say I'm sorry." The sun beat down on his head, but wet clothes would aid with the heat. "For everything." He cleared his throat. "You're prim and proper, and ahh…." *Come on words.* "And I know that I tease you, and I'm not sure why." Sawyer scratched his neck. "Well, from the first time I met you, you had such a stubborn jaw."

"My jaw?" She leveled him with her gaze.

"Okay, chin, I should say. When you went past me and got John to agree to take you on the stage."

"I just wanted to get to Virginia City. My aunt had turned back at the border. I was sure I would be fine to travel the last leg myself."

"That's not what I mean." His brow furrowed. *What was his point?* "Just that you have a lot of spunk and energy. Traveling with a cat in a box? I think you are even braver than what you think."

"And so you tease me?"

Sawyer admitted defeat. "I tease you because I like you, Laney. I like you a lot." There. The truth was out. And there was one more thing he would never say aloud. If she were to be judged or fired by anyone, he would marry her and set it all upright.

"Genesis one." She said in her best teacher's voice. "In the beginning, God created the heavens and the earth."

"Hey, one short minute." He touched her shoulder and shot her a halfhearted frown as they walked. "I haven't heard the words from you. Where is your forgiveness for me, Miss Balderhoff? Do you know what it takes for a man to say he's sorry? You are a one-sided preacher." They walked on in another minute of silence. Was he fishing for forgiveness or hoping she would say how she felt about him?

"I believe everything works best for me in order." She clutched her hands in front of her. "For any wrong you are admitting to, though confusing, I do…do forgive you." She lifted a quick smile. "How many more *short minutes* do you say we'll have before…" Laney followed his gaze. "What is that?"

"Horse and riders." Sawyer squinted past the desert heat.

Chapter 21

"Paiute Indians."

Laney watched Sawyer's chest rise and fall quickly. He straightened his shoulders, groaning. "Just keep walking and praying, like we do this every day."

"Indians?" Laney let out a squeak, unable to see for herself. "Are they going to kill us?"

"Don't panic," Sawyer said firmly. "They likely heard the gunshots and might just want a closer look and be on their way. You need to know, we are at their mercy. I used up most of my ammunition on target practice."

Laney gripped above his elbow. Suddenly her damp dress turned into a sweltering, heavy coat. "I don't want to faint," she whimpered.

"Then don't. Remember, brave and all that," Sawyer said, searching the flat desert. Laney could feel his muscles taut and alert. It was a small comfort, but if she were to die, they would go together. "Sawyer, you believe in God and the everlasting?" Her voice cracked. The Indians would be upon them in minutes.

"I do. I was baptized when I was ten."

"Praise the Lord above," she panted. "I will not fear for your soul. And I suppose Fort Churchill is nowhere near?" Laney's heart beat wildly, pressing herself to him as if ready to take an arrow any minute.

His arm wrapped tight around her. "Nowhere near."

They stopped walking, and Laney buried her face into his shoulder. The horse's hooves came to an eerie quiet. She peeked up from his shirt. One skinny brave reminded her of a scarecrow, possibly a youth, and she dared a glance at the other. Possibly brothers? Sawyer held the gun at his side; it seemed a peaceable stance, but he couldn't raise it to shoot without her help anyway. She tried to pull a prayer or scripture from somewhere, but her mind rattled as hard as her teeth. The Indians spoke their language back and forth, and Sawyer shook his head. One brave jumped from his horse and circled them. The sun reflected off the large knife in his hand, blinding in her eyes. Laney pressed herself into Sawyer, blinking back tears.

"No." Sawyer piped up, shaking his head. "She stays with me."

Laney missed the hand signal exchange, but knowing Sawyer would not trade her off, she would adore this man into eternity. Unable to take her eyes from the large Indian knife, she saw the skinny youth point it to her moccasins. Carefully Laney rose her foot to show him. The young man's eyes narrowed into disgust, and he snapped angry words to his brother.

Before she could take another breath, his fierce eyes blazed on hers. His knife came up so fast, she jumped behind Sawyer. In that split second of commotion, she reached forward to the trigger on the gun and fired it. Sawyer jerked to the side, and the brave on the horse fell to the ground. The one with the knife yelled and ran to pull his brother from the dirt as his own horse bolted down the road. The young braves rounded up the remaining horse and jumped on together. Kicking and whooping, the horse sprang forward, kicking gravel in their faces.

Laney's heart pounded so hard, and she couldn't find words. "I...I...what just happened?"

Sawyer pulled her down the road, searching side to side. "I hope you didn't just bring the entire tribe down on us."

"I...I...didn't mean to shoot him," she cried. "Do...you did...he—"

"Breathe, Laney, and keep walking. You didn't kill anyone." Sawyer stopped abruptly, and she bumped into him. "Be still, girl. No crying," he said in a hushed voice. Laney closed her eyes and rolled her shoulders inward. Certainly, they were going to be attacked at any moment.

Sawyer clicked his tongue. Laney opened her eyes as he pulled on a clump of sagebrush. "Please, Lord Jesus," she whispered, watching the Indian horse come closer to investigate.

"Come here," Sawyer pleaded gently. "We need your help." Cautiously, Sawyer reached up and took the mane. "Come to me easy." He waved Laney closer. Bending one knee low, he looked wide-eyed at her. "Take this step and carefully swing on."

Laney wasn't sure her legs would cooperate, but she stepped onto Sawyers' knee and swung her leg over. He handed her the gun, and he gripped the back of her dress. In a fluid jump, he landed on the back of the horse and pulled close behind her.

"Grab the woven rawhide." Sawyer reached around and took it from her. "Hang on, Miss Balderhoff. We need to get out of here." He kicked the horse into a gallop.

***

In what felt like an hour, with bones jarred and legs that could barely hold her upright, Sawyer finally brought the Indian horse to a trot. "Look over there."

"Please say it's Virginia City." She panted from the heat.

"A rogue black horse and wagon. Just out playing with the lizards. That scoundrel." Sawyer jumped off the horse. "Hold tight until I can secure him."

Laney immediately felt the loss. As long as his arms were around her, she had a safe place to lean on. She tried to raise her legs to regain feeling. Sawyer walked Blackie around to the road, and Laney tapped the Indian horse to the side.

"Can you step over to the bench? The brake is set," he asked.

"I need to walk a moment." Laney went to slip off the horse, and Sawyer caught her inside his good arm. They were both hot and dusty and needed a second to feel the ground. "I might've taken another swim about now." She lifted a weary smile, thankful he held her close again.

"You want to walk?" Sawyer tipped his hat back that rested on her head. His eyes were doing that longing look again. Laney wondered if she just inched ever so slightly closer.... His head lowered, and he pressed a hungry kiss to her lips. The glorious tingles returned, thankful it wasn't just from cold water. Yet without cold water, it seemed more real, more heated, and urgent. Sawyer pressed her closer, taking every kiss with more passion and need. Breaking the moment, he pulled back, breathing hard. "I think we're happy to be alive."

"Yes, of course." She squeaked, embarrassed at how he could ignite her body with his touch. Moving from his hold, she covered her mouth. What kind of proper woman brazenly offered the invitation to a man?

"And what of this horse?" She needed to break the tension.

"Git!" Sawyer slapped the rump of the Indian horse. It took off, leaving a whirl of dust.

Sawyer offered his hand as she took it, sitting up on the bench. "Look." Laney gave a hollow laugh. Ava's parasol was still on the floorboard. "You may have your hat back." She reached up and placed it on his head. He tipped his hat and winked at her.

"This turned out to be a bit different kind of day than I ever thought," Sawyer said, tapping Blackie down the road. Laney popped open the parasol. Certainly, she would awaken from this dream any time.

As dusk fell, Sawyer led the wagon down a side road and into the back alley of the Wells Fargo corrals. Laney shoved her hand in her pocket, realizing she hadn't squeezed her hankie all day. Ten toe taps followed. With all the chaos, you'd think she would have worn her hankie out.

Sawyer stopped the wagon and helped her step down. "I know what you are going to say." He scratched his chin and then tucked her undone hair behind her ear. The sweet gesture melted her. Laney waited curiously.

"I promise never to say what happened today." He dropped his head to the side. "Well, the personal stuff I will take to my grave." His eyebrows rose quickly, and his finger traced a cross over his mouth.

His lovely mouth was—

"There you are!" Widow Boils hurried down the back steps. "We were all pacing, wondering if you'd run off with the circus."

Ava and Matthew followed her out. Matthew looked up at the widow. "You said maybe they'd run off and got married."

Laney whimpered and handed Ava the parasol. "I'm so sorry. It's a bit worse for the wear.

"What...what..." Ava searched her up and down. "What happened? Your cheek is red and swollen."

"I gotta' care for Blackie." Sawyer turned.

"Oh no, you don't." Widow B piped in. Sawyer stopped mid-step and twisted around. "Go ahead." He gestured for Laney to tell the story.

"The picnic included a beehive." Laney sighed. Widow C had joined them out back, and all the women shook their heads. "And then a swim to avoid the bees."

The widow's faces pursed with empathy.

"Then, Blackie got spooked by the bees and took off."

Now the widows were wide-eyed. Even Matthew's mouth hung open. "What did you do next, Teacher?"

"I shot an Indian, and we took his horse."

The wide-eyed shock paled the ladies' faces.

"But I didn't mean to. I really wasn't even aiming." Laney didn't want it to sound that simple and heartless.

"She didn't even graze him." Sawyer huffed. "Just knocked him off his horse, is all.

"What the devil is the teacher doing shooting at Indians?" Widow B protested. "Last I heard, *you* did that for a living."

"The gal just fired my gun while I was trying to keep it all peaceable." Sawyer pleaded, then shrugged. "They were young, likely brothers."

"The one didn't like my moccasins." Laney urged. "I thought he was going to stab me." Oh, how she wished the story made more sense. "Ladies, I pray none of you will ever face such fright."

"Didn't like your moccasins?" Widow B scowled. "The beading not to his pleasure?"

"I think," Sawyer circled his head, "he assumed she'd taken them off...a...another..." he censored his words, "...ahh, unfortunate tribe mate."

The widows oohed and ahhed like the closing act of a theater show.

"Can I tell George about the Indians you shot at, Teacher? He loves to play Indians."

"No!" Laney stepped forward, placing a hand on his shoulder. "I can't have another story in the paper, Matthew. I'm too afraid others will share, and then we could have a...a...war. You wouldn't want to start a war, would you?"

"Oh, no, Miss Balderhoff. That would be bad."

Sawyer gave them a tired, tight-lipped nod. "Now, you know all about our day." He tipped his hat, and Laney felt her stomach flip. He began to unhitch the horse, and she wondered if the affection they shared was over. It had to be. She blinked, took a deep breath, and smiled at the widows. "Now for a hot bath and to check on Moses."

"I've been thinkin' all along, those moccasins you wear are trouble." Widow Boils blew out a breath.

"Yes, ma'am." Laney's heart clenched tight as they went in the back door. If she only knew the deep trouble her affections were in; her footwear was the last of her problems.

Chapter 22

The Wells Fargo stage rode in just as Sawyer had Blackie brushed and fed. Sawyer unhitched the team while John and Albert loaded the mail and parcels into the back of the office. Forking the team hay and hanging up the tack, he looked up as the men walked into the barn.

"We gotta' talk, Sawyer." Covered in dust, John slapped his hat against his leg. I can't listen to Albert bellyache anymore."

"And I can't leave the care of the mail and freight to a woman." Albert fired back.

"With the Army regiment watching the route, I don't see any reason you can't get back on the road with me." John nodded once. "I know you need more time to heal, but—"

"I'm ready," flew from Sawyer's mouth. "I'll ride with you tomorrow."

"Sunday is Sabbath." John scratched his beard. "Plan on hitting the route on Monday."

"I'll be ready." Sawyer stilled as they left. All he'd wanted was to be back on the road. Finally, the wait was over. Charged with the good news, he pounded his fist into his hand. The pain shot up to his shoulder. Today's target practice hadn't been great, but at least he wasn't as weak as before. Sawyer turned to muck the stalls. Crazy, he'd never really feared getting shot again. Just like today, he could've used the butt of the gun for protection if Laney hadn't fired the gun first.

"Lane-*ee*," Sawyer whispered. Setting the pitchfork aside, he sank onto a bale of hay. Scratching the back of his head, he rested his elbow on his knee. The woman was like none he'd met before. And even if he was in another profession, could he be happy with a perky cat-loving Bible-thumper? They were as different as fish and birds.

Leaning back against the stall and covering his eyes, he sighed, recounting how she stilled in his arms. Her round eyes held his like it was the first time she'd seen the stars. Heaven above, he liked those eyes, and the curve of her waist and how her hands felt in his hair. When she rose up for a kiss, how could he not oblige those soft lips? He wanted to oblige her and then oblige her some more.

Sawyer stared long to the darkness outside the barn doors. Her ornery cat had left minutes after he'd walked in tonight. Deep inside, he wished she might come looking for the cat. That might turn into more obliging. *Obliging,* Sawyer snickered and shook his head. Holding her would be all he'd think about.

Sawyer blew out the lantern. Before leaving the barn, he stopped and glanced up. Her window was dark. What must that spirited girl be thinking? Does the young woman think he's now her beau? Should he be? Sawyer let the title sink in. It stirred warm and honest in his gut. To know someone cared for him, wanted him, the way he wanted her. It's likely how God intended. *God?* "Ohh," he wheezed and walked through the Wells Fargo back door. He needed to get back to work and quit mollywollin' in this stupid barn.

***

"Time for church, lazy Mo." Laney pulled the cat from where he slept on her legs. Truth be known, she was tired too and moving slowly. Muscles in her back ached with each step. Laney carefully opened the window, and Moses took his usual leave. A morning breeze crept through the opening, and she leaned a little farther out. There was no man with brown hair and warm eyes moving below. Laney sighed. The Wells Fargo stage had rolled in last night as she prepared for bed. That and gunfire from town had added to her restless sleep. Dreaming of falling from the stage, being carried off by Indians, then held underwater by Sawyer, only to realize it was Mayor Reynolds holding her when she came up for air. Her insides cringed as a shiver rang through the side of her body. Rest had been challenging, to say the least.

Matthew jumped off the back steps and ran to the outhouse. The widows were up, and as bad as she wanted to watch for Sawyer Roth all day, she needed to help with the breakfast preparations.

A few hours later, Laney waited as the widows took their time to visit with the other ladies outside of church. A few of the school children's families nodded and waved to her as they passed. Fingering strands of hair over her cheek helped to hide her swollen bee sting. At least the pastor gave a good sermon, she thought, as people thinned out to go home. They were to lay up treasures in heaven, where moth and rust could not destroy. She'd loved those verses herself and....

"Mr. Reynolds, Howard, George." Laney curtsied as they stepped in front of her. They were all dressed in suits and bow ties.

"We saw you standing here, looking deep in thought." Mayor Reynolds smiled.

"Oh no, just ruminating on the sermon," Laney said casually, searching to see if the widows were ready.

"I've also done some thinking myself." The Mayor narrowed one eye. "I've a surprise for you this Friday night."

"Oh no, sir—I...."

"Call me, Howie," he cut in, squinting at her.

"No need for surprises." Laney fingered her hair around her cheek wondering if that sounded right.

"All right, then." The mayor lightly brushed his hand down her arm, and she almost jumped from her skin. "I have a gift for you. I felt it necessary after our talk last week."

Laney felt her head wobble, and she could not imagine receiving a gift from him. "Something for the school?" The books were a wonderful gift.

"Or something for the school teacher?" His smirk grew upward to a sly smile.

Laney suddenly wished to leave without the widows. "I've done well as I am, a humble servant of the Lord, rarely in need." She stepped back. "I'd better get along home to set up for school tomorrow."

"Wait." He went to touch her hand, just as she pulled from his reach and shoved it in her pocket. "I'll be by Wednesday after school," he said, forcing her to stop and listen. "Your gift is to be worn Friday night. I've invited Mr. Hearst and his wife to dine with us. They are the wealthiest couple in town." His eyebrows rose, and his forehead wrinkled into his thinning hairline.

Laney swallowed. At least she would not be alone with him like last time. "Really," Laney forced the word past her teeth, "Howie." Her face sobered. "I'm sure your distinguished guests would rather have your full attention. They would have nothing in common with the town schoolmarm. I'd best bow out and let you all discuss town business."

"And how would poor Mrs. Hearst be entertained?" He smirked. "With my mother's lack of hearing and the spunk and charm you possess, certainly, you can give an evening to balance the conversation?"

Laney's eyes followed the widows starting down the sidewalk.

"I'll be by on Wednesday." He tipped his bowler. "You'll like the gift. I'm sure of it."

Before Laney could find another rebuttal, the three of them turned and walked away. Frowning, she noticed Howard's stockings sagging down from his pants leg. Why is the man buying her anything? His son has obviously grown near four inches without any new church pants to wear.

Laney hurried to walk behind the widows and Matthew. Maybe she could gain more favor with Howard. Last week she'd had to pull him aside daily to reprimand his behavior. He teased the girls by cracking open any bug he could find and pressing the insides close to them. As hard as she tried to make his lessons interesting, Howard found himself avoiding any of the schoolwork that would see him graduated. There must be something a prudent teacher could do. Laney brushed her swollen cheek, seeing the school down on the right. *Pray*, of course. She needed to pray for him.

The widows chatted about news in town. Alarmingly, another shooting Saturday night had left a miner dead. The war between the states was heating up the men in Virginia City. Widow B mentioned that in their drunken state, southerners should not carouse with northern sympathizers. Their shenanigans would run wild until something tragic happened. All the widows shook their heads. Laney knew nothing of the deceased, but these women understood the loss of husbands and income.

Entering the two-story home, the ladies went to their own rooms to change. Laney closed her door, set her Sunday things aside, and peered into her hand mirror. Even after parting her brown hair to fall over the sting, her face looked uneven and atrocious. Mayor Reynolds was so pleased with his invitation that he hadn't even asked her what happened. Pulling her hair back behind her ear, Laney stepped carefully to her window. Lifting it open, she thought that if Moses didn't come in soon, she might have to take a stroll to the barn. Would Sawyer make himself scarce today, avoiding her and the mischief of yesterday?

Mischief? That was an interesting word for their behavior. One minute she was in prayer for Howard. The next, she was the one who had caused mischief between the Wells Fargo shotgun messenger and the single school teacher. Laney pulled back from watching the barn and sunk against her little desk. Chewing her thumbnail, she hated this uncertainty. Without a doubt, her inexperienced heart was captivated by the man. Laney leaned to the side to glance out the window again. But her life also riveted on being a school teacher in Virginia City. Life versus heart.

"Oh Lord," she sighed. "You have given me life and blessed me with this home and position." She twisted to see nothing moving from the back of the Wells Fargo building. "Please, Lord, help me not ruin it." A movement brought her gaze back to the window. Moses sprinted up the skinny tree and onto her sill.

"Hello, Mo." Laney picked him up and held him close as he raised his head for a good chin scratch. "Did you see anyone we know in the barn?" The cat rubbed his ears into Laney's chest. "Tall, a bit lean, but muscular." Moses scanned her room. "Ruffled brown hair, warm piercing eyes. The kind that looks into you and makes you feel like you're the only person in the world."

Moses pulled away and jumped on her bed. "I know, enough gibberish, you're the only male in my life."

Moses stretched leisurely and rolled on his back. Laney felt the weight missing from her arms and something else missing from her heart. In the silence of her small room, yesterday felt like a strange dream. They'd both just got caught up in it all. *Just adult mischief.* She frowned.

Looking down at her empty hands, the melancholy felt as real as the loss of her first teaching position. How could she know the power of a man's touch? She'd never been held before. How could she be prepared for how his kisses melted her down to her knees? She'd never been kissed before. Why in this minute did her chest hurt, and tears form in her eyes?

Laney sat on her bed and pulled her fingers down Moses's soft fur. Wiping the tears off her cheek, she winced, having forgotten the bee sting. She wanted to pray, and God had always been her refuge and strength. Certainly, He understood the pain in her heart. She sniffed and pulled out her hankie. Kicking her real shoes aside, Laney laid on the bed and pulled Moses close. Prayer wouldn't come—she was too confused to form words. Her hankie lay limp between her fingers. What kind of grown woman finds comfort from pinching a hankie and tapping her moccasins? Laney rolled her eyes and squeezed them shut. Fatigue meshed her body into her bed.

Mischief. She yawned. Her breathing deepened. It was all just spur of the moment...mischief.

Chapter 23

Laney startled, thinking she heard something, and rose on one elbow.

Ava was peeking around her door. "I'm sorry, I didn't want to wake you." Her soft voice and kind eyes brought Laney up to sitting. Moses rose and jumped to the window sill, letting himself out.

"No, no, I didn't mean to fall asleep." Laney stretched and blinked back the fog. "I'm sorry I didn't even help with supper."

"We knew you were likely worn out from yesterday. We saved you a bowl on the stove." Ava came in and held the door. Her full black dress filled the small space. "I'd forgotten in all the commotion of yesterday a letter came, from Nebraska, Bellevue—your mother?" Ava handed it to Laney, and Laney thought she saw a hint of hesitation in her eyes.

Was she here to reprimand her for her outing with Sawyer? Widow Ava Farrow was a school parent, and the schoolmarm should be above reproach. Laney scanned the envelope, likely her mother's response from Laney's last letter. *Wait*—Laney looked up from the top of her letter. Ava did back out yesterday and insist Laney go ahead.

"Is everything all right, Ava?" Laney held the letter with her two hands. Might as well have the truth spoken. Maybe she could confess her confusion with Sawyer—Ava would be sympathetic. Laney cleared her throat. The words wouldn't form, and it didn't seem wise.

"Oh, I..." Ava shrugged. "Well, you might understand being a working woman. The widows don't recognize what I'm feeling. They think I should be happy."

Laney blinked and tilted her head. "Please take the chair at my desk." Maybe it had nothing to do with her?

Ava's thick layers ruffled together to take a seat. Laney had often thought the pastor's wife in Bellevue was the primmest, godliest woman she'd known. Ava sitting before her straight-backed and without a hair out of place, was by far the most beautiful, refined woman she had ever met. "Please, I hope you'll confide in me."

"Maybe it's silly." Ava began. "But I've so enjoyed the work at the Wells Fargo office." She sighed. "And I knew Albert would want his position back soon enough." The crease in Ava's brow returned, her face pinched. "I've applied for another clerk position with the company."

"You have?" Laney could feel the loss but tried to hide it. "It would take you from here?"

"Yes, I answered the advertisement for Mariposa, California."

"And have they responded?" Laney tried to keep her voice enthusiastic.

"No." Ava shook her head. "I feel it's a longshot in the breeze. Why would they give it to a widow when everyone expects a man in that position?"

Laney sat up straighter. "Because you have experience here in Virginia City, a bustling office, I might add." Ava's head hung down, and Laney leaned forward, touching her knee. "And you like the work, yes?"

"I do." Ava glanced up, allowing a faint smile. "While Matthew is in school, it gave me something to look forward to. I hadn't realized how melancholy I'd gotten until I had to pick up my heels and get to the office. And once I was there, I delighted in helping the people with mail and booking passage, really everything." Ava huffed. "I know I'm rambling, but the confidence it built in me is like nothing I've ever known." Ava gazed out the widow gathering her thoughts. "You see, I come from a very staunch southern family. There was a prevailing, unseen wall there that I could never have gotten over." She held her finger over her mouth. "And I chastened myself every day for why I couldn't be more thankful. I had wonderful parents who only wanted what was best for me. My southern breeding and schooling were priming me to become the perfect hostess and wife. I was taught how to oversee the slaves, put them in their place." Her nose flared, and her face tremored. "But I just couldn't do it. None of it agreed with me." As her face paled, Laney could see the strain.

"I had two older sisters who loved the attention, and I got away with being in the shadows. Then they became engaged. The parties, the dresses…the first one married, then the second, and I was expected to follow suit. The only blessing was that at one of their engagement parties I met Zackary. He was so friendly and kind. He never saw me in light of my family's influence."

Laney listened close. This is the conversation she had hoped for. How *did* Ava fall in love with Zachary?

"We would go for walks and talk for hours. Zachary's desire was to come west." She grinned. "My mother said he was full of nothing but fanciful daydreams, and I should wait for a man with more security, one my father would pick for me."

Laney hung on her words, wondering if it would be rude to stop her and ask questions.

"And funny that at my mother's insistence that he wasn't a man of means, is when I agreed to marry him and come west." Ava chuckled. "My parents were so upset that I promised we would not leave for a year." She exhaled. "After we were married, I was expecting Matthew, and it turned into two years. But we did come west." Her tone seemed to drop suddenly. "Sorry, I don't know why I'm going on like this. Zachary Farrow was a good man, and he believed a woman could do more than flit a fan." Her chin shook with emotion she could not hide. "Maybe my work at Wells Fargo makes me feel his approval—that I could be more and he would be proud of me." Her eyes filled.

"I couldn't agree more, Ava." Laney reached out and squeezed her shoulder. "My work as a teacher means everything to me. I know my calling, and I feel the pleasure of the Lord each time I see a child's eyes light up." She sat back. "No wonder your work agrees with you." Laney handed Ava her hankie. "You have your own path, and even though it may be uphill, I believe the Lord will use you, even if it means employment. You have the gift of education. You're cordial and helpful—what establishment would not benefit from someone like you?"

"You are being kind, Laney." Ava set her hankie on the bed. "I've taken enough of your time. I know you have things to ready for school tomorrow."

Laney started to open her mouth, but with Ava's tearful ending, asking questions about how a man should love a woman seemed out of place.

Ava rose. "I hope my strange confessions haven't made you uncomfortable. The older widows think I should be open to a genteel wealthy man for my future." She walked to the door, opened it, and looked over her shoulder. "Maybe there will be a rich one in Mariposa." Ava flashed a half-smile before she left.

Maybe Mayor Reynolds could ask Ava to a meal? A cringe coursed through Laney's skin. She liked Ava too much, even to imagine that working out.

***

Laney closed the book, finishing the lessons she needed for the week, and tucked her mother's letter in the small drawer in the desk. Mother and Aunt Lula were doing fine if you didn't count bunions and itchy scalps. Prattling on about the gossip at their church in Nebraska caused Laney to realize how completely different her life had become. The wilds of the west were nothing anyone could prepare for. Drumming her fingers over the new book from the mayor, she mused over Ava's confession today. As working women, they were more kindred than she'd first imagined—minus the fact her hair was brown, she was shorter with a rounder face, and not a mother or a widow—not to mention Ava was perfect. Laney stood scratching her head. Actually, they had very little in common.

Sounds came from below. Laney carefully leaned to the window to see John and Sawyer walking into the barn. Gasping a small breath, she exhaled. She should be relieved. There would be no talking to Sawyer alone.

What was her speech to Ava just hours ago? Her calling, her teaching a gift from God. Laney hung back, watching. The woman in Proverbs 31 worked making and selling linen, and her husband praised her. Why couldn't female teachers be married? Ava had never neglected Matthew and her obligations here at home. Certainly, most women worked sunup to sundown caring for their own homes and still had time to help others. Laney felt the afternoon sun stream a narrow line across her face.

Why was she musing on marriage anyway? No one was asking. Laney jumped, seeing John and Sawyer walking out. John said something and then headed into the back of the Wells Fargo office. Before she could move away from the window, Sawyer looked up and waved her down. Laney flattened against the wall. Too late, he'd seen her watching and had the nerve to beckon her down. With her heart thudding in her chest, she could not look again. He would think her a ninny.

Picking up her mirror, she frowned at her reflection. The bee sting looked like a swollen pimple. She tried to brush her hair and only ended up unfastening more pieces from her messy bun. Squeaking out a growl, she pulled the pins from her hair and gave it a real brush. It had been presentable for church, but Sawyer wouldn't know because he did not attend church. Laney found a ribbon and pulled her hair securely back. Unable to quench a groan, she walked to the door and pulled it open. She didn't want to continue all week in this misery so this was high time to have another truthful conversation. The one with Ava had gone well enough, she comforted herself.

Thankfully, the widows were all preoccupied as Laney let herself down the back stairs and walked toward the striking young man waiting with a twinkle of coy happiness in his eyes. Shoving her hand in her pocket, she stopped cold. She'd left her hankie on the bed. Slowly she turned to fetch it.

"Wait. Where are you going?" Sawyer asked.

Laney stilled, feeling like her fingertips were on fire. She'd come this far—for the glory of God, just look at him!

"Nowhere." She blinked, clenching her jaw. "How are you?"

"Really good." He bit his bottom lip, his smile growing. "I have great news."

"Oh, please tell." Laney appreciated how positive she sounded.

"I'm back on the stage at dawn tomorrow." His eyes rounded. "Well, maybe I should say after John's second cup of coffee."

"As the shotgun messenger?"

"Yes, ma'am." He nodded. "Albert and John don't make such good bench mates."

Laney opened her mouth. Of course, Ava was out of a job, and Sawyer was getting back to his. One saddened and one delighted. "I'm...I'm so happy for you, Sawyer."

His eyes narrowed. "You don't sound happy."

He stepped closer, and Laney inched backward. "It's just, I...I...spoke to Ava this afternoon. She is going to miss her time at the office. She enjoyed it." Before she could take another step back, he reached for her hand and secured it inside his.

"Come here, Laney." He pulled her toward the barn.

Laney stumbled behind him, looking side to side in a panic. What if someone was watching? "Sawyer, please, I shouldn't."

He led her inside and tucked them around the corner and pulled her close. "I know it's Sunday, and you're going to say this is sinful," he brushed a kiss along her temple, another one down her jaw and several along her neck, "but I don't care."

Laney's knees were melting again, and she felt powerless to move. "We shouldn't," she whispered as his lips found hers. Oh Lord, that request went silent. It only took a second until she found his soft yet wanting desire burning into hers.

Chapter 24

Sawyer suddenly broke the kiss and hugged her tight. "I'm past ready to be back on that stage, and I couldn't wait to tell you." He leaned back, gazing inches from her face. "Your poor cheek. Does it hurt as bad as it looks?"

Laney didn't realize she'd been on her toes until her feet flattened. "It looks that bad?" She released him and brushed her fingers over her jaw. Did all men kiss women when they were happy? "Oh, Sawyer," Laney whispered, confused.

"I know, you're going to miss me something bad." He winked, and she had to smile at his teasing. "But I'll be back Wednesday." Fingers played with the ribbon around her hair.

"I wish that was it." She sighed.

"You think I'm trying to get out of our bet? I promised you could help me read that chapter in the Bible."

He winked, and Laney sensed he was still teasing.

"I should be back before supper. I can…take you to the café." It sounded too much like a question, and Laney slowly shook her head no.

"Bucket of Blood saloon better?" His eyebrows rose.

Laney forced a smile. He was in a good mood, and she couldn't fault him for that. Sawyer Roth was returning to the job he loved. Grace and mercy, she would hold her burdens back. Why not be happy for him.

Matthew walked into the barn, and she quickly stepped away from Sawyer's hold.

"Hey, Teacher, suppose your cat's in here?"

"Wonderful question Matthew, I was just telling Sawyer I needed to find him, and he was going to help me search." Laney quickly brushed her hands down her waist like she could erase his touch.

"You didn't look too hard. He's right there." Matthew started up the loft ladder. Moses lay stretched out at the entrance.

"Well, that silly old Mo, I don't think he was there a minute ago." Laney's jaw dropped, and she rolled her eyes at Sawyer. Now she'd lied. "Lord, help me," she whined as Matthew stood at the top, petting Moses. Sawyer reached out and grasped her hand, and she scolded him with her eyes. The harder Laney tried to pull free, the harder the rogue pulled her towards him. Matthew turned, and Sawyer suddenly let go. Laney almost fell to the side, and she swore Sawyer poorly restrained a snicker.

"You okay, Miss Balderhoff?" Sawyer feigned a pressing tone. "A mouse scare ya?"

Laney's tongue touched her top lip. Had she just agreed to let him have his happiness?

"Matthew, bring Moses down. I'm ready to take him in."

Sawyer's delight vanished, and his eyes locked on hers. "Come back, after dark."

"Oh, no." Laney watched Matthew balance the cat and step down the ladder. "That is not prudent."

Sawyer straightened and helped Matthew take the last steps. "Miss Balderhoff, I just asked so we could read together."

Now it was Laney's turn to chuckle with wide eyes. "Maybe that will be saved for Wednesday." She shrugged and took Moses from Matthew. "I hope you have a…a…" the right words would not come, "a pleasant return to your shotgun job." Laney huffed, walking out with Matthew. *Shotgun job?* What kind of heedless woman would kiss a man who's so clearly her opposite?

The back stoop of the widow house was only five more steps away. Matthew scurried to open the door as Laney held Moses with one arm and gripped her skirt with the other. *Don't look, don't look,* she ground with each step. Then just as she went to cross the threshold, her eyes betrayed her, and she glanced back. Cavalier expression missing, he leaned against the barn door and studied her intently. Why did her body waiver like she was never to see him again?

Move, just one step. Laney closed her eyes, walked in, and closed the door.

***

Sawyer waited, watching the empty back stoop. He'd made a mistake in there somewhere. He likely shouldn't have teased her with Matthew so close. Had he ruined the goodwill she had for him? And why did she have to be so soft and agreeable? Like a man lost in the desert, kissing her satisfied a thirst more than water ever could.

He slowly turned and entered the barn. Reaching for the newest Wells Fargo shotgun off the rack, Sawyer needed to clean it after Albert had used it. He held it in his hand and considered the fact that the gun he'd taken Saturday had had more use than this one. He'd clean them both.

In an hour, Sawyer finished with the guns, and his stomach was growling. Sunday, the café was closed, and he sneered at the old bread he'd had from last week in the Wells Fargo kitchen. About now, he might have snuck in the back door of the widow house to see if Widow B left anything for him. If she hadn't, she would at least make him hot flapjacks and eggs. Tonight, it didn't seem like a good idea. Neither did his bright idea of taking the teacher out for a meal. Miss Balderhoff wasn't allowed male social time, at least where the whole town could see.

Blowing out a long breath, he lit a lantern to clean up. What a fine kettle. He wasn't going to kiss her as he did earlier and not make a plan to court her properly. He wasn't out to dally with the woman. The weeks he'd known her, she'd appeared sweetly *undallyable.* Was that a word? But her heart, it was tender, soft, and it deserved the utmost care.

Sawyer tapped his fingers on the workbench. Blast it all, if he claimed to be so well-intentioned, then why had he held her and kissed her like she belonged to him? *Just tell her the good news—*

a simple enough plan. But she'd kept backing up, like a skittish foal about to bolt. Once he pulled her by the hand, his wild nature took over. Well, that and those last unredeemed intentions.

Sawyer dropped his head and raked his fingers over his face. The open road would be his reprieve. He might even be able to get her out of his mind. The life he lived had run fine before a certain woman demanded her way onto his stagecoach.

Sawyer tossed the supplies he and John would need for the next day into a pile. He was ready to get back to what he knew best. Being a shotgun messenger on the Wells Fargo stage pumped life into his blood. He enjoyed the dry wind in his face, a sore backside, watching like an eagle from every angle, and seeing the caretakers and folks from different areas. Freedom and hard work pulsed in him—not to mention, the time had come to get his brain back where it should be. Sawyer blew out the light. As he went to leave he had to step aside. Moses sauntered past the barn opening like the cat owned the place. Sawyer shook his head and rubbed his brow.

"My shift here is up, Moses. It's all yours."

***

The next morning, the kitchen window was half open and the cooler fall air felt a welcome relief. Laney sat with the other ladies finishing her biscuit and jam. Sounds came from the alley to taunt her. The men's voices and the crack of the whip couldn't be missed. The Wells Fargo stage was heading out and taking Sawyer with it. Laney picked at the few crumbs on her plate. Even Ava seemed somber. Getting up, she poured the last of her coffee into the waste bucket.

"Matthew, I have time to walk you to school." She sighed.

"Okay, Teacher." He licked his fingers. "Can I have biscuits and jam instead of a biscuit and ham in my lunch?" He wiggled his eyebrows at his mother.

Laney smiled. He was such a good boy. She caught Ava's expression sparkle with love. "How about both?"

Widow Boil's eyes narrowed. "Are you going to have a word with that scoundrel who took your job?"

"Widow B." Ava's voice was stern, but kind. "It was his job all along."

"And what about the ledger with missing sums?" the widow said, wide-eyed. "You better believe me, he's ready to see you gone. Then, nobody knows what money is coming and going with all these mine owners."

"Mark Twain, I mean Samuel Clemens, reports on the Comstock Lode in every issue," Ava said, pouring hot water into the basin. "If the mine owners want to send the silver back east for the Union formation, it's not against the law." She took a rag and scrubbed the dishes.

"I just never did like Mr. Carrillo, the snooty clerk." Widow Boils pursed her lips. "How many folks at church told us how much they enjoyed having someone friendly behind the desk at the office?" She nodded to Widow C.

"It's true, dear." Widow C sipped her coffee. "I just worry that attack on Sawyer and the stage might become common now. All that money and silver moving back and forth." She frowned, dabbing her lips with her napkin.

Laney stood and walked her dish to the basin. "The soldiers at Fort Churchill are to guard the routes."

"We'll have to see what condition Sawyer returns in." Widow B dropped her chin. "If the attacks continue," her eyes narrowed "then we'll know whose hand is feeding whose mouth. I believe there's a large rat next door."

"Mother, where's the large rat?"

Ava flipped the towel over her shoulder. "It's all just women being women." She ruffled his hair. "Wash up, and we can walk with Miss Balderhoff."

"Yes, ma'am." Matthew ran down the hall to the washroom.

Laney looked around at the women in the small kitchen. "Do you ladies think Sawyer is in danger?" The forlorn dread in her voice gave her worry away.

Ava shook her head and went back to drying the dishes. The older widows looked long at each other, and Widow B tilted her head. "If you tried to warn him, do you think he would listen and do anything differently?"

Laney knew the answer and felt her shoulders slump.

"But God will watch over him." Widow C smiled. "Look how God sent you to his aid."

A strange eerie quiet settled over the kitchen as the widows all slowly turned away from each other. As Christian women, hadn't they all believed that God would watch over their hardworking men? Laney wanted to sit down and hold them and cry, and yet nothing had even yet happened to Sawyer. She took in a deep breath and announced, "*The Lord is my light and my salvation—whom shall I fear? The Lord is the stronghold of my life—of whom shall I be afraid?*"

"Amen," Widow C whispered.

Chapter 25

By Tuesday afternoon Laney contemplated how to expel Howard from school. Beyond mad, she felt tired and frustrated. The fall wind whipped her skirt layers back and forth as she rang the school bell. The children formed a line to come inside.

"Children, you will have 10 minutes to quiz each other on the spelling test, and then it will begin." She stood over Howard, where she insisted he wash his hands with lye soap.

"Give me the knife." Laney held her hand out, the warning in her tone. He pulled the pocket knife out of his pants and set it in her hand. It still had slimy goo from where he had cut the dead mouse open. Laney swallowed the lunch that rose in her throat. She let the small pocket knife slide onto the washing bench and reached for the soap herself.

"Howard, how would you feel to be sent home for the rest of the week?"

He shrugged and wiped his hands on his pants leg.

"What do you think your father would say?"

Another shrug. "I'd rather stay at school."

"And I would rather have you here too!" The pleading wasn't missed in her voice. "But, every day you disobey my rules."

"What rule?" He blinked, chin down.

"The one where I have asked you not to cut open bugs and dead animals and show them to the girls. Have you missed their screams and my scolding's?"

His lip twitched, and he blinked rapidly. "I don't know why they scream." The ground rumbled from a mine blast, and Laney took a deep breath and let it out slowly.

"Because they don't like dead things anywhere near their faces," she answered.

Howard rubbed a finger under his nose. "Why not, it's hard to see all the insides unless you look close."

"Howard." Laney lowered her chin. "They are afraid of dead things."

"But why? They're already dead."

Laney wanted to grab his arm and give him a good shake, but she sighed and took a glance over him. His shirt, as usual, was half untucked, and his pants were too short. With chapped lips and greasy tousled hair, he had pox marks over both cheeks, as many adolescents do, but it was his eyes that caused her to pause. Their vacant amber pools drained the anger from her and replaced it with pity. So he was odd and backward. Hadn't she felt those things a hundred times?

"Howard, if I make you a deal, do you think you could keep it?"

"Why, what is it?" His chin notched sideways.

"I will keep your knife, and for every recess that you don't show any girls bugs or dead animals, you can have it after school." Laney pushed the words from her mouth. "And I will go with you, and you can show me what you find so interesting."

"I could do that." He stood taller. "Can we go after school today?"

"I...I..." Laney searched for an excuse. "Yes, we can go today." She lifted a tight smile. "Let's just hope you pass your spelling test, or that will have to come before...hunting for...dead things." Dropping her hand on the back of his neck, she led him into the schoolroom, wondering what she had just agreed to.

***

After the last student left for home, Howard walked back inside the schoolroom. "I don't see any hawks."

Laney looked up from grading papers. "We are hunting for hawks?" She stood and set her work aside.

"No, Miss Balderhoff, the hawks circle and that's where I find the dead animals."

"Oh, yes, of course. Well, there's always tomorrow." She locked her jaw as the walls rumbled from a blast.

"I passed my spelling test?" He came up to the desk.

"You did. Thirty out of thirty. That is one hundred percent." Laney eyed him closer. "That's the best you've ever done."

"You said if I passed we could go look. Sometimes I can find a lizard or rat before the hawks get it."

Laney pulled her key from her pocket. Howard's penmanship was atrocious, but every word was correct. Maybe she had found a way to reach him. "I've got thirty minutes before the widows will worry about me." Laney headed for the door. "Let's see what we can find."

***

Twenty minutes later, without shade or water, the usual Nevada Territory afternoon wind blew her hair from her pins. Was she half-brained to come to this dry land? And certainly the only teacher who would traipse through the hot sand with a student searching for dead things to cut open. Holding her hand to her forehead to block the sun, she wondered where Sawyer was at this minute. Picking up people and packages at Austin Station? Howard stopped and pulled a snake from between two rocks. Laney stepped back, scowling. The tiny reptile's tongue flipped in and out as it coiled around Howard's hand.

"It's not poisonous, Miss Balderhoff."

"I know. One time, my cat had a snake like this in his teeth."

"Did your cat eat it?" Howard didn't seem to mind how the snake wound around his hand and fingers.

"No, I made him release it." She watched the ground for any relatives looking for their lost loved one. "Just like now. I think you should let it go free."

"Ya." Howard set it back in the rocks. "This one would have a lot of blood, and then it's hard to see the organs."

Laney glanced away, ready to be done. "So, if they are dead, they are easier to examine?"

Howard nodded. "My father has a medical book with drawings of people all cut open. You can see the muscles and bones, even the vessels."

"Are you sure this is a medical book?" Laney mumbled, starting back down the dirt trail they had taken. Mayor Reynolds had bushy muttonchops. She always thought men with those had greater potential for being devious. "This has been an interesting outing, Howard."

"Can you bring your cat to school again?" He interrupted her.

Laney gripped her scalloped collar as they walked. "Why would I do that?"

"The doctor has one of those long wooden tubes. A stethoscope he called it. Maybe he would bring it, and we could listen to your cat: the heart, the lungs."

"Moses can be touchy." Laney hesitated. "I'm not sure he would allow it."

"What if we make a deal." Howard stopped, and Laney turned to eye him. The awkward teen was using her own tactics. "You keep my knife." He scratched his nose. "And if I pass my school exams this week, you bring your cat to school."

"Humm, schoolwork done correctly." She pointed a single finger at him. "No teasing the girls." She pointed two fingers. "And then I will bring my cat." *And she would have his knife in her possession.* Before Laney could say she would think about it, Howard piped up.

"Deal." He stuck out a hand with dirty, jagged fingernails.

Laney felt her hand prickle as she took him and gave it a shake. One cat visit for a week of cooperation. She looked down, holding back a desire to run her contaminated hand down her dress. Who knew where that hand had been.

***

The next day at lunch, Laney sat at her desk, finishing her cheese and crackers. She brushed the crumbs onto her hand and tossed them in her waste can. So far, the Howard 'deal' had worked to her benefit. She looked down to find the chapter from Moby Dick she would be reading as the children came back in. A few minutes into scanning the first paragraph of chapter seven, a shrill scream rent the air, and Laney rolled her eyes and set the book down. Why had she been so optimistic? This time it was poor, sweet-faced Leona being escorted in by two older girls. Laney handed her her handkerchief. "A fall? A braid pulling—or someone putting a bug in your face?" Laney rested her fist on her hip noticing that the child didn't seem worse for the wear.

"Caleb Rodriguez went to catch the ball and knocked her over." The friend on the right, empathic Corine, said.

"My, my, my...." Leona sucked in a sob.

"Her sandwich went flying in the dirt," Vella said from the left. "I tried to brush it off, but it had sand all in it."

"Ahh, I see." Laney sighed. "Are you hurt, Leona?"

The pretty round eyes blinked, and she shook her head no.

"Then, the loss of your lunch is all that's paining you?" Laney thought to offer the two crackers she had left.

"Howard gave her half of his lunch," Corine said. "It looked like pot roast. His grandmother packs a good lunch."

Laney stood bewildered. "So, will you be fine to eat that?"

Leona perked up with a small smile. Her comforting side guards tucked her back inside their folds and walked her outside. Laney almost couldn't believe what she'd heard until she went to the long window and watched Leona take a seat on the bench next to Howard. Like they were kindred friends that shared every day, he handed her the food in a paper wrapper.

Who was this young man, and where had he put the other Howard?

***

Bolstering her scientist's sensibilities, Laney took a long drink of water before heading out the door with Howard. Just as they stepped out, the Mayor and George stood on the porch.

"Miss Balderhoff. Did you remember I was coming by today?" The Mayor tipped his bowler.

"I do apologize, sir. I had forgotten. And I promised Howard we would hunt for--." The word *dead things* would not leave her mouth.

"Very well, this will only take a moment." He motioned for her to take a seat on the outside school bench. Like a king presenting a queen with jewels, the mayor gently set a brown wrapped package on her lap. He was so pleased with himself, Laney could swear his chest enlarged.

"Really, I'm in no need." Laney forced a crooked smile at George and Howard as they observed her pull the string from around the paper. Gently falling open, a shiny green taffeta dress with white ruffles and puffed sleeves lay before her.

"I knew it would make your eyes widen in delight!" The mayor tugged on the lapel of his suit jacket. I had it ordered from San Francisco."

Laney was barely able to lift the fabric; the skirt must've been six feet wide. "Sir, this is far too extravagant." And need she mention, her eyes were wide because of shock. *Blessed be.* The pompous nerve of the man to pick a garment out for her! Gritting her teeth, she pulled the paper back over the dress.

"It's for Friday night. The dinner with the Hearst's. Trust me, Mrs. Hearst will be dressed well, and I didn't want you to feel out of place."

Laney went to open her mouth in protest. But she stopped when he raised his hand close. "I realized after you left last week that it was slightly unfair to pay you a third of what the last teacher made. So there is no need to go on with thanks. I think you should see the dress as part of the salary you are missing."

Pinching her lips tight, Laney slowly ran a hand over her healing cheek. What kind of misguided logic was he up to? A dress instead of wages? Whatever it is, she would not participate. Something came around the side of the school building and jumped up on the landing. All four of them turned to see Sawyer come to an abrupt halt.

Laney rose so fast the paper and dress slipped off her lap. "Sawyer!"

Howie looked cross at him and back to her as she pulled the dress up from the ground.

"Mr. Roth." The mayor's tone dropped as he licked the corner of his mouth.

"That's what I meant to say. Mr. Roth." Laney panted, squeezing the overflowing layers of fabric together at her chest.

"I...ahh...um." Sawyer's dark eyes narrowed under his hat. "The widows asked me to check on you." Sawyer's clothes were peppered with dust and dirt from the trail.

"Of course. Thank you, Mr. Roth." Laney fought for a full breath. "Didn't I just tell Howard yesterday, they worry when I am late?" She nodded at Howard, eyes begging him to agree. Instead, he scratched his belly and turned to leave.

"And, ah, so, yes, I'd better go." She dipped a curtsy at Howie. "Don't want those sweet ladies to worry."

Before Laney could get two full steps away, Howie called after her. "I look forward to Friday's dinner together—and to see you in that dress."

Mortified, her stomach fell to her feet. If a hawk came now and took her away or left her in a snake den, it would be fine with her.

Chapter 26

Sawyer stalked away in full man aggravation. Even despite her inexperience with men, Laney could see his ire clearly from staring at his backside. His long legs marched in front of her, and she could barely hold the heavy dress from tumbling to the ground, let alone keep up. He jumped up onto the sidewalk in front of the widow house and stormed past to reach for the Wells Fargo door.

"Wait!" Laney gave up and dumped the dress in front of the widow house. He froze with his hand on the door but would not look at her. Straining to catch her breath, she waited, but no prayers or scripture would come to mind. "Can we just talk about this?"

"I don't think that's wise." The veins on his neck strained against his skin.

"Sawyer, please, the Friday night dinner is about the school, the community." She panted and jerked back when he swung to face her.

"You expect me to believe that hogwash?" He sneered, and his face reddened. "You can't be that stupid."

Laney's mouth fell open. Did he really call her stupid? That was rude. "Sawyer, I'm the towns only school teacher, and Mayor Reynolds is my boss. He oversees the school."

He shook his head, still glaring at her. "And that makes it all the more wrong." His hand flew up from his side. "You don't see John out buying me dresses—I mean pants or—oh, you know what I'm sayin'." He jerked his hat from his head and slammed it back on. "I told you we shouldn't talk now."

The thumping in her heart needed to settle, so with a deep breath, she took four cautious steps toward him. "Sawyer." Her tone softened. "Believe me, that looked like something more than it was."

He rolled his eyes and placed his hand back on the doorknob. "Just stay back, Laney. I can't even feel my words coming out right."

Eyeing him guardedly, she slowly rested her hand on his arm. He stilled. "I told you to go on now."

"You know," she edged in a tiny bit closer, "I won't hurt you."

He released a sad huff and glared down at her. "Humm. Then take that dress and the Friday night invitation back to the Mayor's doorstep. Decline all of it, and then I'll believe you."

Laney's soft and gentle approach had just stung her on the other cheek, and she dropped her arm and stepped back, "I can't. He's invited another couple and…and…I can't. *And* you should trust me." That last part had to be help from the Lord. *He should trust her.*

"And maybe I should." His mild tone and deep stare were causing her nerves to jumble. Was jealousy a good thing because Sawyer had deep affections for her, or bad, like when he called her stupid? He finally spoke. "But I don't trust him."

Laney went to rebut those last words when Albert flipped the sign on the door to "closed" and leaned out. "Could you two take your lovers spat somewhere else? I need to sweep."

Sawyer took such a deep breath, she wondered if he would reach in and take Albert by the throat. Instead, he pulled the door open and let himself through. Without so much as a nod, he left her standing outside the Wells Fargo building. Her body slumped as she turned back to the widow's door. She thought being a teacher in Nevada territory was challenging; being a young woman was worse.

***

Laney sat with the widows around the table that evening and finally blurted out what rolled around in her mind. "Could we skip the scripture reading tonight, ladies?" She forged a smile. "I…I have other things with work and school and…

"No, bother." Widow Boils waved her off. "We only do it for you."

Laney wondered if her face looked as crestfallen as she felt.

"It's been good for all of us." Ava patted her hand. "You have a love and enthusiasm for God's word like…like…ah, not many I know."

Laney rubbed her ear. Dear Ava meant something in between those gracious words.

"Did I see a new dress come in on your arm earlier?" Widow C said, agreeably.

Now Laney knew her face dropped.

"What, dear?" Widow C asked. "Did you have it made here or ordered? Not to your liking?"

"Probably doesn't go well with Indian moccasins." Widow B rolled her eyes.

"Oh, a hem." Widow C piped up. "Might take a while, but I'd be happy to hem it for you."

"If you had it made down at the shop on C Street," Widow B went at it again "they should hem it for you." All three women waited for Laney to answer.

"I understand it's from San Francisco," she murmured.

Widow B shook her head. "Whew, spent those first earnings, I suppose. How much did the silly frock set you back?"

A low groan crawled up Laney's throat. "I didn't buy it."

Now all three faces locked on her. "Did Sawyer bring it back for you?" Ava asked, hopefully. Widow B frowned. "Our Sawyer? The shotgun messenger for Wells Fargo?"

"She did save his life," Widow C countered.

"And the man forgets to eat and shave most days." Widow B scowled at all of them. "Buying a dress, ridiculous." Widow B paused long enough for Laney to shrink when the widow's eyes bore down on hers. "Wait up a minute. Is there a young rooster out loose and setting his sights on the teacher with the cat?"

Laney couldn't believe they were all talking about her like she wasn't sitting across from them. "It's from Mayor Reynolds!" The words popped out louder than she meant.

Leaning her elbows on the table, she held her hands over her eyes. That news would bring the roof in on all of them.

"Mayor Reynolds?" Widow B said, appalled.

Laney looked up. "He has two boys in the school, and you know I was at his home last Friday for dinner." Laney wondered if it was too late to divert to the parlor and read the scriptures anyway.

"You said that was because he missed the home visits you did to meet the other students." Widow B rolled her eyes. "And now he's buying you dresses?"

"He said it was part of my salary." Laney knew that sounded beyond pathetic—no wonder Sawyer was done with her.

"What's wrong with the paper money he owes you? Is the town out of money?" Widow B's face lined in deep annoyance. "Are we to be pushed from our home next?" She growled. "It's all that Madame Bulette's fault if you ask me. A brothel owner is putting up the money for the town's new fire cart." She shook her head so hard her sagging chin skin could not keep up. "I heard rumor they were going to make her the queen of the Fourth of July parade next year! I'll likely fall over dead before a woman of ill repute is the queen of anything in my town."

"Slow down, slow down." Widow C patted her hand. "Laney was saying something about her salary, not the town going under."

Like a nightmare Laney could not wake from, they all looked curiously at her again. She began, "I do understand the last teacher was a gentleman."

"Humph." Widow B piped in.

"And so, he made three times more money than I did. Mr. Reynolds said he felt bad about my pay being so much less and that I should accept the dress as a…subsidy?" Laney gave up and dropped her face in her hands.

"Was I born with a nose on my face or not?" Widow B pushed her chair out, and grasped her ears before slapping her hands on the table. "He is a manipulating, greedy pig. You deserve the same wage for the same job." She rose and paced the small kitchen. "Oh, that fries me like grease in a hot skillet."

"As women who are left to support ourselves, equal pay sounds logical to our ears." Ava sighed. "It is just not the way of things."

"And it gets worse," Laney mumbled from her hands. Spreading her fingers to peek out, she whispered. "I'm to wear it Friday night. He's invited the Hearst's to dine and insists I attend." The silence in the room began to scare her. What conclusion were they all coming to? Before she could calculate an escape plan, Widow C caught her gaze.

"Do you want to go, dear?" she asked gently.

"No." Laney sighed. "I tried to tell him. I have nothing in common with wealthy people. But he's my boss, and I don't want to be seen as obstinate."

The small kitchen table stilled. Finally, Ava rose and took a deep breath. "I'll say goodnight. Matthew is waiting for us to say prayers."

Laney reached up, and they squeezed hands. Ava knew how difficult it was to work in a man's world.

"He better not try any silly business." Widow B's tone was still surly. "You wear those real lady shoes Friday night. If he gets too *greedy...*" She looked hard at Laney through the top of her eyes. "You just put your heel to the top of his shin and rake it down as hard as you can." She nodded. "That will teach him a thing or two."

Laney tried to visualize the action. Somehow, she'd made it from Nebraska to Nevada Territory without raking anyone's shins.

Widow C stood with her and took her hand and kissed it. "I'll be praying. I know God lives big inside you, young lady." Laney leaned in for a hug, and they patted each other's backs.

Widow B huffed. "Nothing wrong with prayer, but believe you me, you'll need the right shoes."

Laney took the stairs to her room like her feet were encased in mud. Opening the door, she sneered. The dress took up half her bed, and she happily tossed it off the end. How did her life get away from her so fast? Just teaching in this wild mining town should have been enough.

But then there was Sawyer. He was strong and masculine, and there wasn't an hour that she wasn't thinking about him and how she'd felt in his arms. Laney lifted her window and waited for Moses. The widows had talked much longer than she'd wanted. If only Sawyer could settle down and talk to her.

Laney flopped back on her bed. For this week, she just needed to keep her job. That was the reason she'd come this far. Oh, and the children at the Virginia City school, they were gems. Even Howard had found her helpful. This appointment was far better than the last one, with the boys teasing her and moving her things to annoy her. The older students had threatened to tell their parents what a crazy odd woman she was and report that all she did was teach them the Bible.

It wasn't true—she taught all the subjects with the same vigor. Just because the Bible was her favorite didn't mean they should create falsehoods about her and plan to undermine her character. Laney turned and squeezed her pillow.

Sawyer was already back to what he loved. He'd never have to stand in front of the mayor and sheriff while the parents repeated lies about him. Being fired was the most humiliating thing she'd ever been through. And even though she'd prayed long for forgiveness, the pain and crushing to her spirit was too fresh. Laney tried to shake off the dark shadow.

Now God had redeemed her circumstances for good. So, if the new teacher had to dine at a fine table Friday night, smile, wear a puffy dress, and make polite conversation to keep her job intact, she would.

Chapter 27

Sawyer flipped over on his back in bed and rubbed his eyebrows. He'd expected a warm, wide-eyed greeting when he saw Laney at the school. He'd planned the reunion in his mind from the moment he left Virginia City. It couldn't have gone more wrong than if he tripped and shot his other shoulder.

Sawyer crossed his good arm over his eyes. First, he'd been so shocked to see the Mayor showering her with gifts, he'd lost his head with Laney. Albert must have saved up his wrath for days until Sawyer came back from the stage route. He felt his chest pound with what he wanted to do to the man who had yelled and ranted.

Rising on one elbow, Sawyer listened in the darkness as a door click closed. Albert had a room off the back, making it easy for him to come and go. When he drank on Friday nights, the man's tongue ran amok, spouting about his regular visits to Madam Bulette's business. If that's where he'd been, maybe now the disgruntled office man would calm down.

Sawyer rolled his eyes. It was no secret. Being on the road was Sawyer's life, and Albert had hated every minute on the stagecoach. Albert couldn't fathom how Sawyer would allow a woman to touch Wells Fargo property. Was it necessary to explode and imply the office had been left to meddlesome females? Nobody ruined all his hard work. In fact, Ava's keeping the ledgers in order was helpful, Sawyer had tried to counter. The educated widow had done an excellent job. Sawyer flipped over to his good side. Somehow that point became an accusation against Albert's abilities and made him all the madder. After he called Sawyer a few bad-mannered names, it was a good thing the warthog had stormed out when he did.

Sawyer would never find sleep; his heart hadn't calmed down one bit. He'd retaliated that he was *not* hired to do office work. And since it was left to him, choosing Widow Farrow to help was his decision. Of course, Albert had shouted, he was never hired to ride shotgun.

Sawyer thought of a good payback to tonight's scolding—Ava knew just how well the ledgers had been kept *or unkempt.* It might be high time to meet with her and have a little discussion in that direction. Maybe there was more behind Albert's anger than a female who dared touch Albert's fine work.

Sawyer raked his fingers through his hair and punched the pillow under his head. Maybe he should do something different. Here in Virginia City, he could have a job in the silver mines in five minutes. You don't have to read to pick rock. He groaned.

Why not go home and harvest corn for the rest of his life? At least he'd be above the earth. Rock, or corn? But as a miner, he could marry. His eyes dropped closed, and he rubbed the bridge of his nose. Why would a school teacher who could hobnob with the well-to-do want a filthy miner coming home every night? Sawyer flung back his blanket—the fall evenings were only a bit cooler than the summer. He closed his eyes.

He needed to think of something else, something to aid sleep. Soft lips came to mind. Elaine Balderhoff was easy to pull close. She smelled like soap and flowers, and he was lost—no, he was captivated with her touch. When did he turn so sappy? His eyes flew open. Lord of mercy, he didn't like the idea of the mayor entertaining her—or being anywhere near her. *School business, my backside.*

Sawyer sat up and rubbed his chest. He'd made no declaration of his intentions, but he'd held her tight and wanted her like a man whose heart belonged with his one and only. The spunky, doe-eyed gal had asked him to trust her. That spoke of some kind of attachment, he was sure—or not?

Sawyer wondered if his mind would ever settle. He walked to the window and looked out. He'd promised himself he'd not dally with the lovely, pure, cat lovin' Miss Balderhoff. A faint frown smirked over his face. But was he positive the beautiful Bible-thumper wasn't dallying with him?

***

The next day, Laney sat at her desk while the children worked math problems on the board. She wanted to ask Sawyer about finding dead animals, but they hadn't spoken since he'd walked away from her in front of the Wells Fargo office. Slumping her chin into her palm, her elbow rested on her desk, and she rehearsed again what she could have done better. No doubt, she was imprudent and naïve, and after the way the widows had drilled her, it was obvious she would sell her soul to keep her job.

Sell her soul? Where did that come from? She would never, ever do such a thing. *Lord, forgive me.*

Laney wearily lined the paper and books in crisp, orderly lines on her desk, rolling her eyes up to make sure no one watched. Heavens, she would take the first stage back to Nebraska before she would backslide that far. The school windows rumbled from the mine blasting, and she didn't even flinch.

"Miss Balderhoff? Ahh, Teacher?"

Laney jumped. How long had the child tried to get her attention?

"I'm done. I finished my sums on the chalkboard, now can you check it?"

"Yes, yes, I will, Henrietta." Laney rose, rubbing her eyes.

"I'm Janetta. My sister is Henrietta."

"Of course, forgive me. I didn't sleep well last night, and all my thoughts are jumbled, and..." Laney went to the chalkboard. "Does that ever happen to you?" She lifted a smile.

"No, ma'am." Janetta blinked. "It happens to my grandma all the time. She couldn't remember where she put the fire poker, and we found it out in the chicken coop."

Laney tried to focus on the crooked number problems. She'd never even had a chance to be a mother, yet now she sounded like an absentminded grandmother. What if this got back to the school parents?

Oh, Lord, come quickly.

***

Later that afternoon, Howard and Laney waited while a team of horses drove down the road they were waiting to cross.

"Howard." Laney straightened. A thought arose, inspired by their searches. "Have you ever thought about being a farrier?"

"And shoe horses?" He frowned.

"Well, yes, but where I'm from in Nebraska, those men are the ones people call when their animals are sick."

"But I don't know anything about caring for sick animals."

Laney tapped her chin as they approached the school. "But you do have an interest in dead animals and their insides."

"Yes." He answered with a weary tone.

"Then let's think together. What would be some reasons animals would die?" They stepped up to the school, and she reached for the water bucket and drew up the ladle. He stood with his mouth open until she bobbed her eyebrows and gestured toward the water. Taking a sip, she waited.

"Like not having water?" Howard got her hints.

"Yes! Very good, what else?"

"Maybe they die without enough food," Howard said after he took a sip.

"Yes, keep thinking."

"Maybe they have a disease?"

"Yes, true. We know animals can get sick like us, and…"

"Injury." Howard was engaged now. "Other animals attack or some animals attack their own kind."

"True." Her brows rose—*just like humans.*

"Sometimes they travel together, and they leave the weak behind."

Impressed, Laney hadn't even thought of that. "You know a lot, Howard!" That praise made his face light up. "I've read stories where entire herds of cattle were found dead, and no one knew what to do," she noted.

"Did they cut them open?" Howard's eyes grew wide.

"Maybe they did. Maybe they thought they could study the parts and find what was killing them. What if the town had eaten the meat and everyone died?"

Howard shook his head slowly, taking it all in.

"So maybe not a farrier," Laney said. "But maybe God intended you to help animals? Help them before they die or have the constitution to look closer and find out why they died."

"I would like that." A twinkle replaced the usual dullness of his eyes. "If I finished my schooling here. Do you think I could go to a school where they would teach me how to doctor animals?

"I do. I think you are plenty smart. I think you are brave in the face of...ah...death." Lizards and bugs, particularly. "Things that make other people nervous and squeamish don't affect you at all."

Howard looked away. Laney could tell something else stirred behind his excitement. "Miss Balderhoff, do you think you could find one of these schools? And after we talk about it, could you help me talk to my father?"

Laney felt a bit taken back at the prospect of mediating with the mayor. She had been hoping to have *fewer* Friday nights and *fewer* things to talk with him about. She could still hear Sawyer's accusations in her ear.

Howard's entire future could be blessed by finding something that he loved. The Lord had done that for her with teaching children. Smiling quickly, she nodded to him and straightened her shoulders; it was her God-given call to see every student succeed. Howard being so unique, it was well worth the try.

Chapter 28

Early Friday evening, Laney stood at the foot of her bed and gaped at the pile of green toile and flounces that lay on the floor. It was so unlike her to leave anything unkempt or messy that she had to blink back the shock. Bending over, she grabbed the dress off the floor and laid it on her bed. Annoyed at being awoken, Moses stretched out further and swiped at the fabric. Mayor Reynolds would be here shortly. The time had arrived to face the Red Sea and either cross over or die in Egypt.

Laney released a deep sigh, dropped her head to her chest, and started to undress from the plaid dress she'd worn to school.

After finishing the last button, Laney tried one more time to get the giant green puffs on the sleeves to lay flat.

"Meow." Moses chimed in on Laney's frustration.

"I know it's ridiculous." Laney rubbed her forehead. "The hem is too long, and these sleeves look like watermelons waiting to bang into each side of the door." She sighed and tried to push them into manageable puffs. A knock sounded at the door.

"Laney? Mayor Reynolds is downstairs waiting."

Laney opened the door to Ava's sweet face. "Oh, my," Ava said, eyes opening wider. "The dress is lovely?"

"For someone else," Laney whimpered. "But not for me."

Ava scanned the debacle. "Step back, Miss Balderhoff."

Laney had to pick up ten yards of fabric just to make a small step backward.

"The sash needs to be pulled wider." Ava flattened, tucked, and then tapped her bottom lip. "Where are your lady shoes?"

Laney pulled the fabric up until her foot appeared. They were already on. Ava leaned back and scanned the outfit.

"I think it's your hair. Come to my room. I know just the thing."

Laney followed. Maybe Mayor Reynolds would be offended at her lack of promptness and leave without her.

Ava opened her wardrobe and pulled a hatbox from the bottom. Laney gaped and leaned closer; the woman had two gorgeous dresses with tissue wrapped around them.

"I know. It's a wonder they made it west. We should've burned them to stay warm." Ava pulled the midnight blue one from the wrappings. "This is what I was wearing at my sister's engagement party when I first met Zachary."

"It's stunning." Laney sighed. "No wonder he was smitten with you."

"And this lovely ornament was from that era of my life." Ava pulled a large blue and green gemstone comb out and began to pull and tuck it around Laney's hair.

"This brings the balance to the size of the dress." Ava handed her a mirror. If anything took the eye from the peacock costume she wore, then she would not argue.

"Thank you, Ava." Laney lifted a sad smile. "I wish I didn't have to be someone I'm not."

"Did you ever play dress up as a girl?" Ava redid her bow at the waist before they left her room.

"Never." Laney frowned. "Was I supposed to?"

"No, no. You'll be fine." Ava followed her down the stairs as Laney had to lift the ocean of layers to find each step.

Laney looked over her shoulder and squeezed her hand before she greeted the wide-eyed Mayor Reynolds. "Thank you, Ava."

No amount of the Mayor's drippy compliments would ease Laney's discomfort. She'd almost grabbed a shawl off the hall tree, but couldn't figure out how to hold the hem and the shawl at the same time. Why hadn't she tried the gown on and had it altered before she grappled with the expanse of it? Thankful again not to be paraded down C Street with everyone to see, they took B Street as they'd done before.

"Are the Hearst's waiting at your home?" Laney asked.

"I told them seven-thirty. I wanted a chance to enjoy this lovely dress before everyone else was smitten with you." A fly buzzed by her nose, and Laney took the opportunity to swerve from where he held her elbow. "Will the boys be part of our dinner?"

"I had the maid feed them early. They would be bored with the adult conversation." He returned her hand to the inside of his elbow.

Laney was determined to make teaching the reason for this absurd charade. "You know I've had a few after-school outings with Howard?"

"Yes." He cleared his throat. "Though I would encourage you to do more tutoring with George. Howard will be leaving soon. His mother is from Maryland, and even though it's considered a border state, he will have to be like other young men and take up arms for our country."

"So, after graduation, you will be sending him back to his mother?" Laney wondered if a letter to this woman might be the ticket for Howard's future. Or did Howard resist his school lessons to delay the military? "Are they close?"

"Who are you talking about?"

"Howard and his mother." Laney noticed the Reynolds home brightly lit a block away.

"What does that matter?" The Mayor scolded. "If the woman wanted to be close to her children, she should've never left." His brows narrowed in a tight line.

Laney looked away. Somehow she stepped on a hot coal of the Mayor's—good thing she'd wore the right shoes.

***

An hour later, Laney was making small talk with the Mayor's mother and Mrs. Hearst, who preferred to be called Phoebe. Laney had liked her new acquaintance immediately. The lovely woman was younger than she expected, a Presbyterian, and had wanted to be a teacher before she married. Phoebe had just started to share an idea when they were all called to the table.

The evening hadn't been as insufferable as Laney thought it would be. The food tasted delicious and Mayor Reynolds appeared happy having George Hearst to converse with. At one point, Mayor Reynolds reached over and squeezed her hand. It was profoundly disturbing because she didn't know why he would do such a thing. Had he referred to her and she'd been too entranced by the well-ordered table and the serving of dessert to pay attention? From now on, she would keep her hands in her lap. As the men rose to take drinks and cigars in the other room, Phoebe moved into the chair next to her.

"I can imagine you are busy with the children and the school, so I want to tell you my idea, and I just want you to think about it." Phoebe's eyes lit up. "In Franklin County, we used to do the quaintest fundraiser. I was thinking we could reimagine it for Virginia City and have all the proceeds go to the school."

She had Laney's full attention. "It's a bit like the old church pie auctions, but we could do lunch or whatever you think would work. So many people are coming to this area, and we need to offer something more appealing than the Bucket of Blood Saloon and mining talk. Something after church that would get people visiting, and who knows?" She waggled her eyebrows. "Good people finding good people."

Laney smiled. It was true; there was far more abuzz in Virginia City for the sinners than the saints. "Wonderful idea. I could ask the widows I live with to help."

"Perfect." Phoebe beamed. "Shall we have our first ladies' social visit after church on Sunday?"

"Yes." A cool wind swept inside her, and she chewed on her bottom lip. "You seem to have such a generous heart," Laney murmured.

"Oh, thank you, dear Miss Balderhoff." Phoebe gripped her hand. "But your face saddened just now."

"Oh my." Laney ran her hand down her cheek, and her full sleeve nicked her berry pie plate. The stain made the words more necessary. "I feel a bit of an imposter tonight." She took her napkin, raised her elbow, and tried to rub it out. "The thing is, this isn't my dress. I wear serviceable dresses for teaching and I have one favorite for Sunday. They're all from Nebraska."

"Of course." Phoebe nodded. "I completely understand."

Laney wanted to swallow the dear woman's empathy. But Mrs. Hearst herself was fluffed with the most beautiful silk and lace. "I only wore this for the Mayor."

Phoebe's chin notched down. "Are the two of you a couple by any chance?"

"Oh, no. No." Laney stretched to see the men still in the parlor. "The mayor is only my boss, and he should not be buying me expensive gowns. But I think it a kindness since he wanted me to look better," she frowned crookedly, "than I usually do." Laney hesitated. "For tonight anyway. But this is not how you will see me again."

"All right." Phoebe blinked, mildly confused. "I won't expect to see you in this dress again." Both their eyes turned to see George opening the door from the kitchen.

"George! One of my students." Laney rose and pushed her chair back. Perfect break in an awkward moment. "George and his older brother Howard," Laney went to step away, struggling to get the layers of her dress free from the chair leg, "are both smart students." Proud, she held her hand out for George to join them as she still fought to free her hem. "In fact—." Giving the fabric a solid tug, her dress caught on her shoe and as if someone had pushed her, it snagged her step, and she tumbled forward, landing on the floor.

"Oh, no." Laney huffed, trying to rise. Just as she thought she was free, another layer caught under her foot and she fell forward onto the carpet again. Quickly covering the bodice, Laney's hand slapped only bare skin. The tugged hem had pulled the bodice lower than it already was, and Laney looked down mortified.

"Good grief, Miss Balderhoff." The Mayor stepped in and reached for her arm, trying to lift her from a pile of fabric. "What are you doing on the floor?"

Laney yanked the bodice higher to her chest and fumbled to stand. "I…I thought I'd dropped something." She glanced up seeing George and Howard wide-eyed. This was their Bible-quoting teacher with the heart of a missionary? Were they staring at her chest? Just by the heat she felt, her face must be as red as the wallpaper. "I'd better get home. Howard, would you like to walk me home?"

Laney didn't move except to keep her hand locked over her chest. "Mr. and Mrs. Hearst, it was so pleasant to meet you." She nodded and gathered the layers in front.

"You don't have to be in a rush, Elaine." The Mayor said close to her ear. "I want to walk you."

"No, no." Still cringing head to toe, she forged a smile at all of them. "I'd hoped to have a word with Howard about a school project anyway."

Howard, bless his strange soul, opened the front door for them to exit.

"I will see you Sunday. Until then, Mrs. Hearst." Her voice quaked. "Mayor, please thank your mother for me. Her hospitality is always delightful."

Before she could read their shocked faces, she hurried out with Howard." The cool night air was like a splash of cold water on a sunburned face.

"Thank you, Howard." Laney flung all the front toile, skirting, and green fabric over her arm. "I don't know how women do it." She gripped his arm, walking toward home. "This is far too much work."

"What project did you want to talk about Miss Balderhoff?"

His question calmed her rattled blood a bit, and she took a deep breath, thankful to be away from the humiliating scene. "Do you write to your mother, Howard?"

"Sometimes." He shrugged.

"I was thinking about finding a college that trains people for animal science."

"Yes." Above the crunch of their steps, Laney could hear the rise in his tone.

"Might you write to your mother and ask her if she knew of any colleges or academies back east—ones that train for animal doctors? Do you think she would do that for you?"

"I could ask." Howard squished his nose between his fingers. "Did you talk to my father?"

The young man was far wiser than he appeared. "I did try. Just a brief moment."

They walked on until the widow house came into view. "Why aren't your parents married anymore?"

Howard shrugged. "She didn't like it here, and she didn't like my father. And he didn't like her."

Laney stepped up to the porch of the widow house. That seemed a prudent enough account. "Thank you, Howard, for the escort. I will see you at church."

He looked down, and even in the shadows, Laney could see the discouragement. "Pray to God, Howard." She patted his shoulder. "Many times when I could not see a way, I believe God made a way for me. I believe He will do it for you."

Chapter 29

Sawyer stood outside the Wells Fargo office door on Saturday, watching in every direction. The owners of the Ophir Mine preferred to come inside when the office was empty to secure the silver that headed east. Sawyer stood sturdy with his shotgun in hand. Little did they know he still was slow as a gun-slingin' slug when it came to his still-healing shoulder. But in the past year, not even a hot, dusty wind interrupted the miner's transactions.

He chewed on the corner of his bottom lip as his eyes searched up and down. Was Laney still sleeping? Most likely, she was tired after an evening out at the Mayor's home. Sawyer huffed. Would he find the time to see her today? After their words on this very sidewalk, did she want to see him again? His stomach growled. Maybe he'd just ask Widow B to set a place for him at supper.

"Ah, keeping the civil peace there."

Sawyer noticed Samuel Clemens striding toward him. When thinking of his last encounter with Laney, he almost balked at Samuel's words. "I try." Sawyer nodded as he approached.

"Just got this hot off the press." Samuel handed Sawyer the paper. "You hear about those claim jumpers who shot up a bunch of greenhorns?"

"I had not." Sawyer lifted the paper and dropped it against his leg. The news—just another bunch of letters taunting him. Why did those simple words often seem to change directions when he tried to put them together to read?

"And the news back east isn't much better." Samuel shook his head. "It happened in August, but it's just now getting to us. Battle of Bull Run lasted three days. The Union Army of Virginia suffered 14,000 losses. The army of Northern Virginia lost over 9,000."

Sawyer covered his face and rubbed his forehead. His own brothers had talked about signing up. Had they done it?

"Renders you speechless." Samuel blew out a long breath. The men stood quietly, the severity of the numbers silencing both in sorrowful thought.

"I got more deliveries." Samuel turned. "Good work keeping that stoop safe." He mocked Sawyer as he smiled and walked away.

Straightening his pained shoulder, a wave of guilt rolled through him. Here he stood out west pining over a hungry belly and his own ridiculous woes, while in the east they were filling grave pits with slain men atop men. Sawyer glanced up at the brilliant white fluffy clouds placed in a flawless blue sky.

What if he was flat on his back on the battlefield of Virginia, full of lead and making his peace before his eyes closed for good? Wasn't that what Laney had asked him as the Indians came near? And his answer still rung true. No, he didn't attend church or read well. But he'd promised the Maker years ago that he would live upright to the best of his ability. Sawyer felt it in his bones to be a just man and do right to others. Truth be told, as a kid, he didn't feel a whole lot different when he came up from baptism at Tawny Creek. Sawyer caught himself looking skyward two more times and then around him to make sure no one watched.

Lord, if I've taken You for granted, please forgive me, and show me differently. Some, I know, make talking about you a way of life. A very pretty round face entered his prayer. *I heard somewhere you came to help sinners.* Sawyer shook his head and rubbed his jaw. Now he confused himself. *Anyway, I pray for the fighting in the east. May it end quickly. Amen.*

***

Later that afternoon, Sawyer and John finished off some stew before they started checking the silver load and padlocks.

"This will do nothin' but weigh us down," John growled as Sawyer took one end, and he took the other. Sawyer strained with only one good arm, as the men struggled to stack the silver shipment. "But I heard talk there might be a short line rail train coming," John said, making Sawyer stop in his tracks.

"Here?"

"Yep, with all the gold and silver coming out of the mine, they want to move it faster." John grabbed another container, and Sawyer followed suit. "The Virginia and Truckee Railroad. A group of surveyors were having drinks at the Delta Saloon talkin' it up. Then the Union Pacific will hook into that." John shook his head in irritation.

"And then what?" Sawyer didn't like where this was headed.

"Then we're out of a job." John huffed. "I'd suppose we'd keep the smaller routes over to Truckee Meadows and any mountain passes. But the bulk of the contracts we have will be gone."

"How long to lay track and get the engines out here?" Sawyer asked.

"Heard it will be completed in five years."

"Five years." Sawyer scratched his stubbled chin. What he planned to do for a lifetime now had a limit.

"Gonna' hurt Wells Fargo stages all across this land." John's expression soured. "I suppose they will keep the banking company. But why would you send your folk or your letter on a stage when it could go by train?"

"Trains would be safer." Sawyer rubbed his arm. "I appreciate the Wells Fargo company, but I'll never be a banker in some stiff suit. Don't have the constitution to sit in an office."

"Me neither." John smirked, "I guess we can stamp tickets on the train or shovel coal." John reached for another container of silver.

"I'd feel like a Wells Fargo traitor." Sawyer snorted a short laugh. Funny how he'd never thought much about his existence until recently. "John, you ever think about settling down?" They stacked the last box on top of the others.

"Like with a gal and a house and barn, ya mean?"

"Well, yeah." Sawyer wondered if that was none of his business.

"I have a gal. Just need to build a barn, I suppose." John scanned the shipment list, dragging his finger over the clipboard with the list of goods.

"You have a gal? I never knew that." Now Sawyer was shocked.

"Well, you never asked before." John snickered, looking up. "This askin' have anything to do with a teacher next door and a cat that lives in our barn?"

"Maybe." Sawyer scratched under his chin.

"She's pretty enough." John nodded. "And that teacher got more grit than what appears from the outside." He snickered. "I don't think I'll ever forget her hangin' from the stagecoach. Either you were going over them wheels, or she was going under. Hoo wee." John chuckled. "I'm gonna miss the fun we had."

Fun? Sawyer wanted to correct his interpretation of fun. "Hey, it's not over yet. We have a few good years left in us."

"That we do, son." John slapped his back as he turned to leave but suddenly stopped.

Sawyer waited. John's face held the deep creases of wind and sun. The man was as hard-working as they come, but he often struggled to say what was really on his mind.

"Thing is," John cleared his throat, "you're like a son to me." John rubbed under his nose. "And if you find a gal who is good to ya, loves ya, and has a tone of kindness toward ya, you do whatever you have to do. I mean it. Move the stars or build a barn, I don't care. Just don't let pride or hankering for fortune lead you astray. Every dirty fellow down at the Bucket of Blood Saloon had an opportunity to do it right. But they messed up. I've heard it with my own ears. They wouldn't bend their opinions or say they're sorry and look what it got them—a cold glass and cold shanty." John frowned. "And that's no life. You're young and can do better. And believe me, you're going to make mistakes."

Sawyer felt that truth like the breath in his lungs.

"We all promised things we can't provide," Rubbing his chin, he continued. "But we say sorry and try harder next time." John tipped his head. "That's all I wanted to say. I'm sure it don't make no difference."

"It does," Sawyer said, tersely. He'd made a mess with the kind Miss Elaine Balderhoff, and she was worth more than a fleet of Wells Fargo stagecoaches. "It makes perfect sense."

***

From her second-story window, Laney's eyes went wide as she watched the wind swirl and a large tumbleweed roll down the alley. Sawyer had just walked into the barn. She'd hoped to catch him all afternoon. She'd prayed and read her favorite verses, but this contention with him would not leave her be. If he wanted to see her, wouldn't he have stopped and looked up to her window? Or just walked into the back of the widow house *and*—Laney jerked back.

Sawyer walked toward their back door. Every stride was just like him, lean and confident. She pulled back as far as she could but saw his hand reach up to knock on the back door. Did he usually knock? Laney swore she didn't know when the knocking stopped because her heart was thudding so loudly in her chest. Like one of Howard's lizards, sneaking out from a rock, carefully she reached for her doorknob and opened it a crack. Straining, Laney pulled the door open another notch to try and hear what he wanted.

Blast it, she couldn't make out the words. She slipped out and leaned down the stairwell. Clutching the wooden rail, she tried to lean closer just as Widow B shot her head up toward the stairs. Laney gasped, and her stockinged foot slipped off the top step. By the grace of God, her hands remained on the rail, and only her legs slipped out from under her. Her arms strained to hold her weight while her body became a stiff board. What was wrong with her limbs of late?

Widow B cocked her head to the side, smirking. "If you can find a way to *walk* down the stairs, there is a young man at the back door to see you."

Laney pulled a loose strand behind her ear and stiffened on the top stair. "Thank you." The words spoken were far more refined than how she felt. Reaching her hand into her pocket, she gave her hankie ten quick pinches. "I walk by faith and not by sight," she whispered, carefully taking the steps down. "Oh, and by sight." Thank the Father above, she'd put the tripping over the green costume far from her mind. *Well, until this minute.*

Laney reached the bottom and lifted a small smile to Ava and Widow C as they read in the parlor. Taking extremely slow steps, Laney ambled down the hallway toward the back door. Should she invite him in? Crossing the threshold to the kitchen, she saw Sawyer already standing inside by the stove. His dark, soft eyes and handsomeness struck her hard as she felt her chest constrict in his presence.

"Sawyer." She nodded once, unable to read one thing from his expression.

"Laney."

Not Lane-*ee*? But he didn't say Miss Balderhoff either. "Would you like to sit?" She held her palm out to the table. "Some coffee?"

"That would be kind of you." Sawyer sat, and Laney wondered about his choice of words. Certainly, he thought her *not* kind by going to the Mayor's house. She set a cup of coffee before him reminding herself just to breathe and not fall over. Sweeping her hand across her backside, she sat gracefully. His hand gripped the mug while her fingers swiveled over the wood table. No one spoke, and Laney shocked herself with allowing such a long silence.

"So, I was wondering." Sawyer took a small sip and set the coffee down. "If tomorrow, maybe after church, you'd want to go for a wagon ride or a picnic?" One of his hands rose quickly. "Not where we went before." He rocked back in his chair, looking away.

A warm blanket covered Laney's insides to see him so uncomfortable. Should they behave as if the dinner at the Mayor's never happened? Hadn't she rehearsed her defense? She really had been there to converse with Mrs. Hearst.

"Oh, no." Laney pinched her frown tight. "I made plans after church."

"That's fine." Sawyer rose and walked his mug to the basin. His Adam's apple rose and fell as he swallowed. "Maybe another time."

"It's a ladies' meeting!" Laney blurted out.

"Okay." Wide-eyes and a faint smile teased his lips. "Good to know."

Laney felt a panic rise over her being. He was going to leave, and they'd not found goodwill restored. Maybe a walk after the meeting? *For all the town to see?* Her shoulders slumped as he headed for the door.

"Sawyer—" Laney paused as Matthew walked in.

"Hey, Sawyer." Matthew searched around the kitchen.

"Hey to you, Matthew." Sawyer messed up the boy's hair.

Laney tried again, "I wanted to—"

"Teacher, do you mind if I have this last apple turnover?" Matthew already had it in his hand. "I'll eat it outside, so all the crumbs fall in the dirt." Sawyer held the back door open, and Matthew went out before she answered.

Sawyer walked out, and the wind kicked up around them as Laney followed. *What was she going to say?* Laney took one step down. Wasn't it an apology? Or an explanation? Why did her words feel lost in the wind? Another repeat of awkward seconds ticked by before Sawyer nodded at her and walked away. Matthew skipped along after him. Grabbing her hankie from her pocket, she grimaced in defeat and tossed it in the air.

Chapter 30

"Sister Balderhoff, would you be so kind as to close our time in prayer?" The pastor's wife asked.

Laney sat unmoving.

"Laney, she meant you." Suddenly Ava's whisper and bump to the elbow woke her from her stupor.

"Yes, of course." Laney sat taller on the church pew and cleared her throat, trying to sound attentive. "Heavenly Father, we thank you for our time today. Thank you for the insight that Mrs. Hearst has brought to these last two hours." Laney hoped her weariness over the overly drawn-out meeting didn't show in her tone. "We pray for Your hand to guide us as we make preparations for the Fall Frolic this next Sunday. Grant us Your blessing as we ask that our plans may please You and for Your favor, dear Lord, in all that we do. Amen." Laney rose her head from prayer. Sliding out of the pew with Ava, they offered their farewells as the other ladies continued to talk and share their ideas.

"That was a short prayer." Ava smiled as they walked toward the church door. "I mean for you." She tucked her elbow inside Laney's, hugging her arm.

"It was such a long meeting." Laney sighed as they stepped up onto the sidewalk.

"Did you expect anything less with fifteen women all planning?" Ava asked.

"No, I just have to set up lessons for tomorrow and…" Laney exhaled and looked away.

"Tell me." Ava nudged her elbow, giving Laney a little pull.

"No, really, I just have a lot to do." Laney hadn't told anyone about her feelings for Sawyer. Or about their strange tiff. And as the parent of a student, Ava was the last one she should confide in.

"How was the dinner at the Mayor's?" Ava's voice was kind, and Laney felt thankful for the friendship.

"Two things," Laney said as they approached C Street. "First, thank you for the help with the dress and loaning me that fine pin for my hair." Laney had returned the pin first thing and left the dress shoved under her bed.

"Anytime." Ava patted her hand.

"Second, meeting Mrs. Hearst was a delight. As you can see by today, she is a natural philanthropist." Laney's face softened. "I really do appreciate how Mrs. Hearst can plan socials and find a way to raise money for the school. And as you saw, I volunteered to get the word to the parents, but the food and decorations were left to everyone else. I was worried that maybe she had wonderful ideas but that I would be left with all the work."

"You're right about Mrs. Hearst." Ava agreed. "We've had little here in Virginia City to bring our town together." Ava squeezed Laney's elbow. "And don't mention Madam Bulette's purchase of the fire wagon." Ava rolled her eyes. "That sets Widow Boils a-boil every time."

Laney sighed, wishing she could enjoy Ava's jesting. This town was riddled with rough and ready misfits. It was no wonder Laney felt she fit in so well. Ava stepped aside and opened the front door. Laney watched her full black skirt cross the threshold. Ava, on the other hand, was a perfect lady, and so was Mrs. Hearst, and then there were her students—they were all darlings.

Two men on horseback with guns resting off their legs rode by and tipped their hats to her. Rattled by their greeting, Laney turned quickly and shut the front door behind her. Finding the parlor a safe haven, Laney sat and stretched her head back on the back of a soft chair.

After a few minutes, Ava peeked in the parlor. "I can't seem to find Matthew," she said frowning. "Widow Boils said that he'd been with Sawyer earlier."

"I'd be happy to check the barn," Laney offered quickly.

"I called for him a minute ago, but he's not here. Maybe they went for a ride." Ava headed back down the hall, and Laney followed. She knew Matthew was an obedient boy and wouldn't wander off alone.

"Mrs. Boils, thank you for watching Matthew while I attended the ladies' meeting. Did Sawyer say they were going anywhere?" Ava frowned, brushing a strand of hair behind her ear.

"No." The widow shrugged. "They came in for sandwiches, and then I heard Matthew ask for a ride on Blackie. I figured they were in the corral."

"He likely couldn't hear me when I called." Ava's tone softened. Smiling, she walked out the back door and out to the barn.

Laney wanted to see Sawyer, even if it meant she hid sheepishly behind her friend's black skirt. Laney moved away and pushed back the barn door. "Matthew!" She called. Not even her lazy cat made an appearance. "Moses, where are you?" Laney climbed the loft ladder. "Moses. Kitty, kitty." She scanned each direction, finding the barn empty of child or animal life. Had Moses tired of her lack of attention since school had started and found a new barn to lounge in?

Ava came inside. "They're not in the corral, but Blackie is."

"Did you see Sawyer?" Laney asked.

"No, and the stage is here. I checked inside just in case Matthew was playing in it." Ava drooped. "Will you stand with me to knock on the back door? Mr. Albert makes me uncomfortable."

"Yes, of course." The women walked to the back stoop of the Wells Fargo building and knocked.

Albert, the disgruntled office clerk, opened the door. "What? It's Sunday, and we are closed."

Laney felt her body wanting to shield Ava and smack that rudeness off his face.

Ava lifted a small smile. "I understand that my son might be riding with Sawyer. Have you seen either of them?"

Albert rolled his eyes and stepped back. "Sawyer!" he yelled up the stairs.

Laney heard the wooden floors creak from above, then a set of loud footsteps headed their way. Shrinking back behind Ava, Laney suddenly felt embarrassed and guarded. Too nervous to greet Sawyer, she decided to do another sweep of the alley to look for Matthew. She turned and walked in the other direction. As Sawyer approached Ava, she overheard Sawyer telling her they'd gone riding about an hour ago and he later left Matthew playing in the barn with Moses.

"Moses is gone too," Laney said with sudden alarm.

"I'm sure he's close." Sawyer nodded. The way his eyes flashed at her, she understood. Clearly, he meant Matthew. "Ava, check the house one more time, Laney check the barn, and I'll jog around the block."

They all took their assignments and did as told. Laney retraced her steps and gave the loft a thorough search, along with every corner, while calling for Moses. Maybe she'd better check her room. Had she left her window open? Laney came out and met Ava in the back alley.

"Where could he be?" Worry lines covered Ava's face. Widow B and Widow C came from the back door. "We'll help. Maybe the child found a friend to play with." Widow C patted Ava's back. "One of my boys did that once, forgetting to tell me."

"Of course, he has many friends at school." Laney hoped to ease some of the tension in Ava's face and body.

"Wouldn't Sawyer have returned by now?" Ava searched up and down the alley. Like a woman with tuned instincts, she tilted her head and listened. Pulling her thick black skirt layers close, she marched toward the barn, but twisted right and walked the road between the corral and barn. The other women followed close on her heels. Dirt, brush, and scrub trees filled the hill in front of them, and Ava hiked like a mule, straight up. From afar, Laney saw Sawyer about the same time as Ava did.

"Look there! Sawyer!" Ava called and began to run.

Laney ran behind her and slowed, wondering why Sawyer unbuttoned his leather suspenders. Such a strange feeling accompanied his undressing that Laney had to stop. For heaven's sake, at least Ava was married before and knew more about men and their strange behavior than her.

Sawyer ran, jumped, and flung his legs around a bottom branch, pulling himself up.

"Matthew! Hang on!" Ava shouted.

Finally, Laney could see poor Matthew gripping a thin branch extended high atop the old tree.

"Mother! I think the branch is breaking!" Matthew cried.

"Hold still, Matthew! Sawyer is coming." Ava covered her hands over her cheeks.

With heart pounding, Laney placed herself under the tree with Matthew above. If he fell, she would catch him. She looked again between the high branches. Certainly, she would *cushion* his fall when it all collapsed on her. *Angels of mercy, please, please...*

"Hang on, boy!" The widows called to Matthew. "Sawyer is coming."

Watching Sawyer cling to the tree with one arm, he extended himself outward, swinging his suspenders toward Matthew. "Wrap the straps around your arm." He called to Matthew.

Sweat and dirt smudged Matthew's face as he reached for the leather and missed. Laney held her breath until, with the second swing, Matthew reached out and grabbed the straps. Sawyer had thought ahead to have the boy secured to him in case the limb gave way. Laney inched back and stopped to watch. Sawyer held the tree with his good arm. Thank goodness Matthew was able to shimmy backward.

Crack!

The women screamed as the branch suddenly snapped and crashed to the ground. Laney jumped back and blinked away the leaves and dirt. *Oh, praise the Lord above.* Matthew still gripped the safety strap that Sawyer had given him. Sawyer had already pulled the dangling boy to a lower limb, and Matthew wrapped his arms around the tree. A painful strain pulled Sawyer's face taut. The boy's weight hung from Sawyer's wounded shoulder.

Sawyer reached for Matthew and pulled him onto his back. As Matthew clutched his neck and back, Sawyer did the rest of the work as he lowered them limb from limb to the ground. Ava took two steps with her arms extended to her child. Falling on her knees, she gripped Matthew to her chest. Laney swallowed her emotion at seeing mother and child safe. The widows stood wide-eyed with their hands over their mouths. Sawyer bent over to catch his breath, resting only one arm on his knee. With his lips pinched tight, he raked his fingers through his hair and finally looked up to see Laney watching him.

All she could see was deep red covering his face. "Are you all right?" She wanted to reach for him but hesitated.

He cleared his throat. "Fine now." He winced pulling his shoulder back, then tried to straighten taller.

"I saw Matthew hanging from your bad arm." Laney drew her hand over her mouth and wanted him to know she understood his pain. "I meant to say, that was very brave." The man hated to be pitied. Hadn't she learned that from the first moments after he'd been shot?

Sawyer nodded to Ava as she stepped over to hug him. "Thank you, Sawyer. This boy is my world." Her words stilled, and her eyes filled with pure gratitude. Moving from Sawyer's arms, she grabbed her boy's tousled head and kissed his cheek.

"Good thing you can climb a tree," Widow B said, patting Sawyer's back. "No ladder was going to get my old legs up that high."

"I was going after Moses, Teacher." Matthew frowned. "He jumped from this tree and left me out on that limb, then I couldn't get back."

Where had Moses gone? She wanted to turn from the group and do her own search, but the moment was too special. Matthew could have fallen and broken his neck. Every person in the circle felt the weight.

Laney forged a smile. "I'm so glad you are safe."

"Sorry I worried you all," Matthew said. Ava wrapped her arm around his shoulders and helped him down the hill. Everyone followed, and Laney hung back. *Where is Moses? Is he all right?* Her stomach pinched with worry; Moses was like her child, except with...orange fur. Stepping to the side to search more of the area, over grown dried sage bush caught her skirt, and she tried to pull it free.

"Your cat will be fine."

Laney glanced up. Sawyer had pulled away from the group and stood before her. Heavens above, he was easy on the eyes in his dark green shirt and brown canvas working pants. Something warmed her top to bottom, and she looked away.

"I've neglected him." Laney stepped back to the tree and found Sawyer's suspenders. Coming back to where he waited, she handed them to him.

Taking them from her hand, he buttoned the front and back, leaving them hanging down. Finally, he regarded her with a curious expression.

"Only the cat?"

Chapter 31

Laney pouted with each step down the hill. Seeing the back of the Wells Fargo barn, she slowed and eyed Sawyer. "Well, no, I've neglected my Bible reading. I've neglected Bible memorization. I've wanted to have more fellowship with the widows. And yes, Moses is used to having more of my time." She felt like snarling at his question. Was he trying to tell her he felt neglected? Why had he walked away offended after she said she had a meeting at the church? Laney stopped and slapped the dust and leaves off the bottom of her blue skirt. "Sawyer, I like my job." Pulling her hem higher, she picked a thistle from her moccasins. "It's actually going better than I thought."

"Really? "He tilted his head, his eyes confused.

"Do you remember what you said? Virginia City was no place for someone like me. Well, I tell you, I've flourished despite dealing with an insensitive mayor with certain prejudices. Howard and the bugs, and then sweet Leona walked in." Her nose crinkled.

Mute, Sawyer scratched the side of his head.

"Oh, forget it." He didn't know it was a pure joy not to have students making up lies about her. "Believe me, it's just going better than I anticipated, and I want to keep it that way."

Sawyer leaned his backside onto the corral fence and rubbed his healing shoulder. "In order to keep your job, you're saying we should just be friends?" He blinked, scratching the ground with the toe of his boot. "Is that what you're trying to say?"

Laney could not open her mouth nor find it within herself to remind him that, as a teacher, she was *not* to marry. If she made that point, it would sound like she assumed he wanted to marry her. Because she knew nothing of the male brain—including Sawyer Roth's brain—it seemed far-fetched to mention anything about marriage.

His question broke into her fretting. "Do I mean anything special to you?" Soft brown eyes found hers quickly before he glanced out to the corral.

"Yes, you do mean something special." Speaking complete truth, Laney was rewarded with a slight grin when he looked back her way.

Sawyer bit on his bottom lip, restraining a broader smile. "You mean something to me too. That's why I got so riled over your evening with the mayor. I don't like the idea of you meaning something to anyone else. You know what I mean?"

Laney wondered if she'd caught the meaning of *meaning*. "I think I know what you mean if it's what you mean." She shook her head. Was this word communicating anything? "You were feeling jealous?" She came out with it.

"No." Sawyer kicked his boot against the fence post, stirring up a stream of dust. "I think you told me I should have no reason. Didn't you?"

"Yes, exactly. The evening went just as I'd assumed, but better, really. I met Mrs. Hearst. We, shockingly, did have quite a bit in common." Amazement laced her wide eyes. "She'd planned to be a teacher before she'd married her husband. She's Presbyterian and has quite the heart to help others. The meeting today was to plan a Fall Frolic at the church." Her perky tone revealed her excitement. "We're having a boxed food auction, and all the money will go to the school. You'll have to come. Maybe I can figure out how to bake something." Her eyes narrowed. Chewing on her bottom lip, she sighed. "But don't bid on it."

With the discouragement in her voice, she frowned. After a few minutes of silence, something like tingles of flashing pleasure feathered up her spine. Sawyer's fingers had come around her ribs, and her body froze. The warmth of his hands made her thoughts blur.

"Why can't I bid on the box you donate?" He gripped her waist tighter.

Laney pressed her hand against his chest to avoid falling into him. "I said," she whispered, trying not to focus on the tan skin around his neck or how firm his jaw was, "I like my job." She pushed harder, needing the space from how good his chest felt next to her hand. Finally, his hands fell away. "And I do like you a lot." Fighting for the right words to keep her from sounding like a dingbat, Laney pressed a finger over her lips. "I don't know what to do. Just promise me you won't bid on it."

Sawyer blinked and released a deep sigh. It seemed he was struggling, or maybe she shouldn't have pushed him away. "I don't think you want to hide in barns or alleyways any more than I do," she said.

"I don't," he huffed. "And I leave in the morning." His eyes were tense as they met hers. "But I think about you every day. More like every hour."

Laney couldn't hide how the sweet words melted her. Her smile gave away her pleasure, and before she realized it, she tilted toward him. This time his hands rose gently on her cheeks and brought her lips to his.

His kisses were soft, and she nestled closer. Without temperance, her blood quickened throughout her body, and he wrapped her in his embrace. Deepening her kiss, she wondered whether it would always feel like nothing else in the world mattered when their lips met?

"I'd like to stay like this forever," he whispered, lingering soft kisses around her neck. His sweet breath tickled her ear. This man, these feelings were so powerful, she was utterly defenseless against them. They rested foreheads, and a sheepish grin covered his face. "I'll be back Wednesday," he said. Laney closed her eyes and gave him a tiny nod.

They separated and looked around like two people caught stealing from the store. Laney walked swiftly from the side of the barn to the back door of the widow house. She wanted to watch Sawyer but forced her eyes on the door. Conflicting desires still swirled around her as she stepped inside. *How would she hide the flush on her face? Didn't they agree neither wanted to sneak around?*

Laney entered and caught Widow B at the basin. "I…I was taking a few extra minutes to find Moses." The last of her words trailed off as she headed down the hallway. Words? More like half-truths. Still winded, she jogged up the stairs and went into her room.

As soon as she lifted her window, Moses jumped up on the sill. Laney frowned at him and pulled some dead leaves and stickers from his fur. "Moses." She pulled him into her chest. "Matthew could have been hurt." Laney stroked under his chin and thought about how Sawyer seemed to always know what to do—whether it was bees or boys who climbed trees. Even though her life felt out of order when she was with him, she also believed in her bones that she could trust him.

Suddenly, Moses twisted from her arms and jumped to the bed. "Moses, I didn't mean to scold you." Laney sat on her bed and scratched around his ears. Again he moved away from her and spread out at the end of her bed. "Are you mad at me?" It was unusual for Moses not to want her attention. "I know I've been distracted." Laney glanced at the pile of books on her desk. She had hours of work ahead of her creating her lessons for tomorrow. Watching Moses lick his paws, Laney could tell he'd changed. "You've found your own life here, I suppose. You must like Virginia City."

Even though she was used to doing all the talking, a mumbled sadness tinged her voice. Moses was her best friend, her confidante, and companion. But her busyness and lack of attention had caused Moses to rove around wandering off with Matthew in his wake.

Laney unlaced her moccasins and kicked them aside. Curling her legs up, she leaned her back against the pillow with her head against the wall. Even her room was out of order. A green mob of taffeta remained stuffed under her bed. She had a pile of laundry that needed to be done, and her own cat had found a life away from her. Laney reached forward to pet the orange fur. "It's always been you and me."

Moses pulled away and jumped back to the window sill. Laney felt a strange loneliness settle within her. Moses ambled from the windowsill to her desk, stepping atop her books.

"The children have asked me to bring you to school again." Moses' long tail flicked across her desk, snapping her quill from the inkpot, and dripping ink over her school things.

"Moses!" Laney chided, grabbed him quickly. She stared at the mess. In her rush out the door for church, she should have put the cap back on. "What am I to do with you? I'm sorry. I suppose I've changed too." She set the cat on her bed and went to blot up the mess. Schoolwork loomed, needing to be done before it got too dark to read. Laney began to organize her lessons and create a plan for Monday.

I like my job. Isn't that what she'd declared to Sawyer? Most days, she enjoyed the demands of teaching the different ages of children from diverse backgrounds. Laney dropped a stack of books on the floor to make room for the worksheets she needed to create. Shaking her head and blotting up another drop of ink, she stared at the stain it made in the wood. It really wasn't her cat or her job. It was Sawyer Roth.

She rubbed her finger over the blemished wood. If she loved him, then why did she feel so sad? Wasn't love supposed to feel grand and charming? Laney shook her head and started her lesson plan. Should she introduce Moses early to the students tomorrow and then ask Ava to retrieve him? Maybe she could tie in a Bible lesson about Noah and the animals on the ark.

Laney rested her hand on her Bible. Was she in love with Sawyer?

Her mind drifted back to the moment she'd held him as he slept and then when she found him passed out on the Henig's lawn. The man was so funny when he was angry with himself. She glanced up at her bureau.

The orange he'd given her the first day of school sat as a sentimental memorial stone. Would she become like Miss Havisham in Great Expectations and leave her orange shriveled up like the untouched food in the grand dining room? Would cobwebs fix onto her orange, like her foolish untouched youth strewn across her room telling the tragic tale?

Laney jumped up, grabbed the orange, and set it in her top drawer. "I need to focus," she whispered. Feeling riled inside, she sat and took a deep breath. Laney knew the antidote was prayer. "Dear Father, You know my love for the children of this town. I believe they are a gift from You. My teaching position is a gift from You. Grant me the grace to prepare and teach well. In Your name and for Your glory, I pray. Amen."

Laney took the quill and started in again. After five pages were completed, she looked back at Moses sleeping. "He said I *mean* something to him." Laney tilted her head. "What does that mean? Mean something?" She sighed. "Ava and Matthew mean something to me." Laney turned back to her work, coming up with questions for her Bible lesson on Noah.

The way Sawyer took her face in his hands made Laney feel the tingles down to her toes. She hadn't planned on kissing him. In fact, she'd successfully pushed him away. Because they *"mean something"* to each other, they could kiss like there wasn't a care in the world? And for sure, there must be something broken in her, because she didn't feel guilty. In fact, his kisses just made her dreamier and wanting. Undoubtedly, she was a full willing participant. And yet Sawyer said he didn't want to sneak around.

Hiding and lying are what made it feel wrong. But it wasn't right either. They'd made no declaration. Laney's shoulders slumped. Then she shouldn't be kissing him! She was in Virginia City, Nevada Territory, to do a job! Her God-given assignment teetered precariously. This sneaking around with Sawyer wasn't a difficult choice to stop.

Laney groaned and stood up. She did love her job. She could not spoil all that God had given her. "And so what?" she frowned at Moses. "So what if I think I love him? There, I just said it. I think I love him. Now it's out. Yep, in the open, for everyone to see." Her arm swung wide in the air. Owning her predisposition for the dramatic, Laney reached for her moccasins and set them neatly next to her bureau. "Wouldn't every spinster at least want to know once in her lifetime what love was?" She glared at the disinterested cat. "God gives strength to the weary." She paused in the silence. "He does. Even to weary, lovesick teachers." Laney let out a long huff and sat back at her desk.

Sawyer had asked her earlier if she wanted to be friends. She hadn't been strong enough to answer then. But friendship seemed like the most reasonable solution. And it would quell the problem of sneaking around.

Laney grabbed a book from the floor. Friendship was good. Like Jonathan and David, or Paul and Timothy, or Elizabeth and Mary, though they were cousins. Still, friendship appeared like the obvious answer. Laney took one more glance back at sleeping Moses. Gloomy stuffiness overtook the small bedroom and her virtuous intentions.

Chapter 32

Even with the excitement of Moses coming to school and Howard reluctantly agreeing to lead the four science lessons on animals, Laney felt the school week drag on like cold molasses. Sawyer was back on the road. After he'd held her face and kissed her, he'd said something about Wednesday. Today was Wednesday; would Sawyer Roth come through these school doors? She shouldn't be seen in public with him, yet she couldn't control which parents or whether the town mayor came to talk to her. Before she went down this winding road again, Laney stood in front of the class.

"Boys and girls, remember, next week we will turn in our news articles and have a tour of the newspaper. Mr. Clemens said he would print *one* of the stories we submit." The room was abuzz with excitement. "Please make sure your stories are true and accurate."

Leona's hand flew up, and Laney acknowledged her. "Should we ask permission to tell something about someone else?" Leona confirmed.

"Yes." Laney swallowed. What news this child was privy to at Madam Bulette's house made Laney's teeth clench. But at least Leona knew to ask to retell it. "That's all for today, children. Practice your spelling words tonight."

The room moved with children talking and gathering their things. George came to speak with her. "Miss. Balderhoff, can I go hunting with you and Howard today?"

Laney did one thorough glance out the windows of the schoolhouse. No tall, strapping shotgun messenger lingered near. "Yes, George. You are always welcome."

"I was hoping to search for Indian arrowheads."

"Sounds like an interesting pursuit." She nodded. "I need fifteen minutes to straighten the schoolroom."

"I know." George smiled. "I can help get the rows and benches just how you like them." He went to the front of row one and bent to survey the row. Carefully he nudged each desk and seat straight. Laney blushed, thankful for the consideration. Of all the children who sought her out, she wished they didn't come attached to the Mayor, but his boys were nothing like him.

After Laney had her desk in order, she grabbed her bonnet and they headed out. They took a trail from the side of A Street that led past the new building site of a Catholic Church. This Sunday was the frolic and fundraiser.

Laney chewed the side of her bottom lip. Would people come and participate? Would she be able to spend the funds on the books and items the children needed? Howard watched the sky for hawks or buzzards while George took a stick and dug around rocks. Laney walked ahead between the boys, wondering if she would see Sawyer tonight. Did she have the courage just to be friends? Isn't that what he'd given her the choice to do?

George yelped, and Laney spun quickly. Before she could reach him, the terrifying sound hit her. A rattle. Laney froze as her eyes darted side to side. "George, where?" she cried, inching forward.

"By my foot!" George practically jumped and landed in her outstretched arms. They both held each other as they backed away from the sound. Laney turned in every direction while she gripped George. "Did...did it get you?"

"I felt something hit my boot." Laney still had him in a death grip as she pulled his pant leg up. She sucked in a terrified breath to see the venom running down the leather of his ankle boot.

"But your skin? Did it bite your skin?" Now shaking, she saw Howard meet them on the trail.

"I don't think so," George grimaced. "I think it just struck my boot."

Howard started back from where they'd come.

"Howard, don't!" Laney screamed. "Get back here now."

Howard looked up wide-eyed. "I wasn't going to touch it. Just get a stick and bring it out to see." Howard stepped back to where she still held George.

"This…this is my fault." Fear and regret lined her words. "There are too many snakes in this area." *A bite could have killed George*. The thought of bringing a rattlesnake-bit child back to their parents made her dizzy. "I'm sorry, Howard, but we can study inside." She scanned back and forth; there was a wide road to the left. "Boys, head over there and keep your eyes on the ground. We stepped right by and never saw it."

"I think it bit me before it rattled." George skipped ahead, seemingly unaffected.

Laney tried to focus on her steps. Of course, they would tell their father. If she asked them not to, it would be asking them to lie. *Thou shall not lie.*

They carefully stepped back onto A Street. "George, I might ask you to be in charge of the play yard. Would you be willing to leave class a few minutes early each day and make sure the play area is free of snakes? Then I will feel better having the other children outside."

George nodded wide-eyed. "I will, Miss Balderhoff."

"Flicking his stick and hunting for arrowheads is what stirred it up," Howard said as they went past the school and toward their home.

Laney wanted to beat herself with a stick. She was often mindless throughout the day, daydreaming like some flitting bird. Branch to branch, Sawyer to Sawyer. She repressed a groan as they approached the steps up to the Mayor's house. Laney squared her shoulders. Now to admit her poor supervision of the mayor's children.

Howard walked in. "Grandma? The teacher's at the door. George got bit by a rattlesnake." Nonchalant, he continued into the kitchen.

Laney dropped her head, clutching her temples as George stepped inside. A housemaid ran around the corner with a dust rag in her hand. "What? A rattlesnake!"

"It bit my boot, not my skin, Mrs. Garcia." George lifted his pant leg, and the woman pressed her hands into her chest in thankful relief. "Your boot! Gloria Dios!" she exclaimed while making the sign of the cross. "Your father is at his office, and your grandmother is still at the seamstress."

Laney stood frozen. George looked to her, to Mrs. Garcia, then back again.

"Miss Balderhoff, do you need a drink of water?"

Laney drifted off in a daze again. She should be the one to talk to the mayor or his mother. Her cheeks puffed wide with air before she blew it out. "Please tell your father to come to the school in the morning. I will be happy to explain what happened."

"We can explain what happened." Howard crossed between them and into the parlor with a mouth full of bread and jam. Laney stilled. She was responsible, and she should have never let them out of her sight. This, right here, could cost her job. Wilting inside, she exhaled. "George, I'm glad you are fine. I do pray for each of you by name."

"I know." George patted her arm.

Now, who was reassuring whom? Laney glanced at Mrs. Garcia. "So, I guess I'm free to leave now?"

"Yes, ma'am. I will tell the mayor you walked them home to see them safe."

"Perfect," Laney whispered. "I mean, thank you." She turned and heard the door click behind her. Struggling to find her legs sturdy and cooperative, Laney strode back to the widow house, drifting past the saloons and people. The sounds, the elements, the west was obviously too wild for the likes of her. But George was okay; she shook her head, offering her thanks to the Lord.

***

Before Laney could untie her bonnet, Widow B called down the hall. "Sawyer Roth was just here. He invited himself to dinner." The white-haired woman stopped halfway, drying her hands on her apron. "I'd like to amuse myself thinking it's my fine cooking he's after." She smirked a half-grin. "But I gather it has something to do with you."

"Or maybe he wants to join in our Bible reading tonight." Laney shocked herself with the prickling words. *Oh, the draining afternoon.*

"Sawyer Roth, the tall drink of water from next door? Are we talking about the same man?" The widow dropped her fists on her square hips.

Laney had found her end. She needed to head up the stairs. "Yes, that one." She stopped halfway, keeping her voice in check. "It was a rough afternoon at the school, but I'll be down in a bit to help."

"No need," Widow B called back.

***

An hour later, Laney had redone her hair, donned a clean dress, and sat in the parlor with Ava. She recounted the details of the rattlesnake story and stopped when Matthew ran into the parlor. "Sawyer's here."

"We'll be there in one second." Ava waved him on. "And George is okay?" Ava asked with motherly concern. "His leather boot possibly saved his life."

Laney nodded, wondering why she'd spilled the story. Unfortunately, it was like reliving it over for the second time. She stood and took a deep swallow. Now for dinner with Sawyer and the widows.

After running her hands down her dress, her eyes reached up to see Sawyer in the parlor opening. He'd shaved, and his hair was shorter and wet from his bath. Something in her belly flipped over. He looked so fine in his pressed white shirt. What had widow B called him? *A tall drink of water.* From the way he made her feel this very moment, it was more like a tall drink of something intoxicating. Though she'd never tasted alcohol, she assumed it made one dizzy. Their eyes must have locked on each other because Ava murmured something and skirted out around him.

"You look nice." He smiled and coyly eyed her up and down.

Heat rushed to Laney's face, and she held her hand to her cheek. "Thank you. You look very nice—I mean handsome—

too." She scrunched her face. Would she stumble all night long? "How was the stage route?"

"Fine." He glanced around the parlor. "How is the school doing?"

"Fine." Laney rubbed her temple. They'd agreed not to sneak around, but standing in her home felt just as odd. Or worse!

"Would you like a seat?" She held her hand out to the settee. "I could get you something to drink."

"I'm fine." He took a seat. Leaning his elbows on his knees, he intertwined his fingers.

Two "fines." Laney felt the pressure to bridge the gap with an acceptable conversation. Maybe dinner was ready.

A knock at the door made her jump. "Excuse me." She turned as Matthew flew by.

"Miss Balderhoff." Matthew met her in the hallway. "Howard and George's father is here for you."

Laney felt her stomach ram into her throat and quickly stepped in front of Matthew. "Mayor Reynolds." She stepped out to the walk and pulled the door closed behind her. Had the mayor seen Sawyer through the front window, sitting in the parlor?

His brows rose and his chin dropped. "Call me, Howie, please, Elaine." He drew his hand down her arm, and Laney flinched, wondering if Sawyer was watching them.

"I know why you are here." She panted. "I will never step off the road with the boys again. I...I feel terrible and responsible for what happened."

"I knew you would." His tone held a slice of endearment. "That's why I came straight over."

Laney inched back. Why wasn't he upset and ready to fire her?

"You've been attentive to my boys. I've noticed the special interest you've taken in them. A rattlesnake bite is not your fault. My boys go outdoors every day. It could happen tomorrow."

Laney squinted toward the sidewalk, confused by what he said. Good Lord, his forbearance was shocking. If it were her child put in harm's way, she would have come after him with an ax.

"I know how smart you are, Elaine. You have singled out my boys for a reason. I just wanted to come by and tell you it's working."

Laney felt her face drop into a deep frown. "Mayor." She ground out the word. "Howie, I have not singled out your boys. I hope you believe what I say. I try to find the gifts that God has given each of the children under my care. Howard had very little interest in following directions or school or graduating until *I* showed interest in his desire to cut open things." The words sounded wrong as soon as they left her mouth. "I believe he is a scientist at heart."

"Scientist?" the mayor huffed. "Little good that will do him on the battlefield."

Laney had a rebuttal burning on her tongue but closed her lips quickly. "I must go. The widows are holding dinner for me."

"Wait, Elaine." His touch to her elbow made her freeze. "I feel I've said things to upset you, and I don't know how that happened." He frowned and blinked. "But I wanted you to save me a dance at the Fall Frolic. It is a wonderful thing you and Mrs. Hearst are putting together. Virginia City is lucky to have this kind of event."

"I wasn't aware there would be dancing," Laney mumbled. "Just believe me, I thank God for watching over George today." She nodded before turning the knob. "Have a good evening."

Laney carefully closed the door and looked once up the stairs before she glanced in the hallway. Like a feeling she was already dreading, she knew Sawyer was missing. Walking down the hall to the kitchen, the small round table held three widows and a brown-haired little boy. All of them were staring at their plates.

Their silence spoke volumes.

Chapter 33

Laney wondered if her voice would work. With a croaking whisper, she said, "I think I'm not as hungry as I thought. I'll just finish up my lesson plans." Not looking anyone in the eye, she held her hand over her face and slumped back down the hall.

"Funny, Mr. Sawyer said he wasn't hungry either." Matthew's voice carried from the kitchen table.

Laney grabbed her skirts and ran up the house stairs. Fighting the urge to slam her door shut, she carefully closed it behind her. Her eyes slowly shifted to the right where her decomposing orange had retaken its rightful place of honor. Pulling the pins from the new bun she'd worked on for over twenty minutes, she set them on the bureau.

Why did she manage to fall into such poor happenstance? This was the hour the mayor had to show up? Did Sawyer hear the conversation or see the man touch her arm? The weight of her poor luck and the thought of hurting Sawyer made her drop to her knees by her bed. Her hair fell forward as she buried her face in her blanket hanging over the edge.

"Lord, I know you love me. And You know I love You. But I can't seem to do anything right. I don't want to hurt Sawyer," she whined. "I think I love him. Ahhh." Her buried face slid downward with her crumpled shoulders as she heard the words said aloud. But so what. God knew everything anyway. There is no place on earth to hide from Him.

Laney pounded her forehead against her bedding. "Ouch," she said as her forehead came into contact with the wood frame. Maybe the only way for them to stay safely distant was to hold an offense. Her knees hurt from kneeling, and she was already distracted from her prayer. Flipping around to sit on the floor, she leaned her head on her mattress, staring at the ceiling. Stay offended. That didn't sound right. Being mad was the only way they'd keep their hands off each other? *Or lips?*

Laney dropped her face into her knees and groaned. Moses was so much easier to love. Longing to hold her cat, Laney rose and lifted the window. The shadows fell low, and she couldn't help wonder if Sawyer lingered in the barn this very minute. Standing back, she searched the back alley. Was he waiting for her? Would he listen to her explanation and understand that the mayor's innocent visit was only a father's concern for his child's welfare? *Save me a dance.* But *was* the mayor's visit innocent? Moses ran from the barn and up the tree next to her window.

"Hello, friend." She held him close and kissed behind his ear. "Does Wells Fargo have anyone in the barn tonight?" Moses lifted his chin until Laney gave him a good scratch. Watching the barn out of the corner of her eye, there didn't appear to be any movement. Laney looked at her bed as Moses jumped over to his favorite spot. Would she be able to sleep tonight? What if they could just clear the air? The rattlesnake story *was real* and very frightening.

Widow C stepped from the back door and tossed out the dirty water.

Maybe she could clear up the silly mistake with Sawyer and grab a sandwich on her way back in. She spurred herself to move. Laney took a deep breath and pushed her hair behind her ears. "Do not let the sun go down on your wrath. Trust in the Lord," Laney reassured herself as she stepped from her room.

The fall evenings were getting colder and darker, and Laney had wondered if she should have grabbed a wrap. Pulling the barn door wider, she released a sigh. It seemed empty of the man she searched for. A few interesting memories of being with Sawyer came upon her. When did they go from tolerating each other to kissing? The bee attack was quite unusual. The man had wanted her help him to shoot his gun again. But then she'd been submerged in the lake, held close, and soaked to the bone. That handsome expression of concern mixed with humor had been impossible to turn away from.

Should she have pushed him away? Indeed, surviving the Indians and the desert heat had made them light-hearted. Did that make any sense for the second kiss? Laney stopped halfway in and straightened a pitchfork from its crooked stance. Wasn't he supposed to express his feelings before he kissed her?

Shaking her head, she realized her mind rattled with confusion again. No wonder she'd had little peace. Taking one last look around the barn, Laney walked out and stood staring at the back door of the Wells Fargo building.

"Waiting for your man to come down?"

The voice in the dark made her jump and hold her high collared dress. "Good evening, Mr. Carrillo."

"You can call me Albert." He seemed to stagger toward the back door. "Here, I can let you in. You can sneak right up the stairs and into his room."

Laney had just about taken a step toward the Wells Fargo back door when her moccasined feet froze. "Excuse me?"

"Or better yet." He licked his bottom lip. "You can come to my room. It's just through there."

"Sir," her voice trembled. "I will not be in any man's room. I find your proposition revolting."

"They were only suggestions." He shrugged. "I doubt a prude like you would ever imagine the joy of such liberties." Wobbling, Carrillo took a step up. "Trust me, Sawyer has." He reached for the door and fumbled. "Maybe Sawyer could teach you a thing or two." He snickered.

Laney backed away. He'd been drinking the devil's concoctions, and surely his lips spewed lasciviousness from the fiery pit. Appalled and ashamed, she couldn't get away fast enough. Reaching her room, she paced and found herself giving him a tongue lashing—he was blunt, vulgar, rude, and had ugly muttonchops far more unpleasant than the mayor's. Running out of meanness, Laney sat on her bed. His words were like deep shards of glass to her heart—the young schoolmarm out pining for Sawyer after dark. Sawyer wasn't out looking for her, so maybe she deserved his accusations.

Lord knew she'd prayed long and hard for another chance to follow her call as a teacher, and Virginia City and the men here had been hard opponents. There was a certain godly standard, a diligence she had not kept high enough. That was why everything had gone wrong. The mayor thought she purposely favored his boys! Like she'd devised a way to the man's heart. Ridiculous!

Mr. Carrillo assumed she was just an object of fornication with the shotgun messenger. Laney stood again. That one made her see red. Pacing, she gritted her teeth. "It's a good thing I don't swear." She boxed her knuckles in the air. "Without strict standards everything goes wrong," she shook a finger at Moses.

"I'm thankful for what he said," she said, her tone clipped. "No, I really am." She untied her moccasins. "I've got to keep my shield of faith higher. When I can feel the fiery darts wound, then I need to do better." Kicking her moccasins to the corner, she undid the buttons on her dress. "Tonight was just a splash of cold water." The memory of Sawyer holding her in the cold lake flashed by. "Or better, a swift kick in the rear." That didn't work. She pulled her dress off. It was impossible to kick one's self in the rear. "Or an awakening from a deep sleep." Laney nodded victoriously at Moses, and her stomach growled.

"Oh, blessed be, Moses, I forgot to make a sandwich."

***

An hour later, with an empty stomach knocking her ribs, Laney laid in bed wide awake. There *was* a fight to her faith. She was so concerned with not having a repeat of her last position that she had become a puppet in her desire to do well. Yes, God ordered each of her steps, but He'd also given her a heart and sound mind to protect herself. Her mind circled this over and over, and she wondered if she would ever fall asleep.

First, the mayor had decided there was no one else to serve on the school board—that seemed a bit too convenient for him. After one night of meeting the Hearsts, Phoebe was already planning a school fundraiser. The Hearsts would be excellent school board representatives. Ava would be also. She was educated, smart, and the mother of a student.

Laney snuggled into her pillow. What about the reverend or his wife? "Yes!" She swung her finger in the air. What would they all say about her pay being a third of what the last teacher made? Well, that may have to be for later. The first order of business was to ask them if they would be willing to serve on the board this Sunday at the frolic.

Mayor Reynolds had no checks and balances. He should not be escorting her to his home or buying her dresses or showing up unannounced at her door. A new fire lit in the back of her throat and she growled. What if the new school board members overturned the rule of the teacher being unmarried? Laney gripped her blanket to her mouth and bit it. That felt like too much of a dream.

She let out a deep breath and tried to get her heart to settle. The next thing would be immigrants. Mayor Reynolds could not pick and choose which children were deemed teachable. All of God's children have capabilities. Their sweet faces swam before her, and she began to pray for each student row by row. This would help sleep to come—until she pictured Sawyer. He'd looked so ruggedly dashing tonight. His usual confidence and swagger seemed tame inside the widow's parlor doors. This Wells Fargo man was calling on her simply because they meant something to each other. It must have taken a great deal of courage for him to invite himself over. He'd adamantly agreed that he didn't want to sneak around either.

Laney nestled deep under the covers. Sawyer's sweet eyes on her tonight brought tingles in her belly that were not aiding sleep. One minute she was going to let the distance between them stay, the next she couldn't sleep for thinking about his smile, his voice, his arms around her. Was he done with her?

She sighed and flipped over to her other side. With her heart set in God's great field of labor, she had too many traditional standards. Sawyer had probably already convinced himself of their many differences. Their whole relationship was like a wide river that no one should cross. It was better that they both stayed safe each on their own side. Laney stretched her neck side to side. What was the old hymn they often sang in her childhood church?

Guide me, O my great Redeemer,
Pilgrim through this barren land;
I am weak, but You are mighty;
Hold me with Your powerful hand.
Bread of heaven, bread of heaven,
Feed me now and evermore, she yawned.
Feed me now…and forever more.

Chapter 34

A hot, dry wind swirled up the dust and dried leaves throughout the churchyard, but the parishioners set up tables and chairs outside anyway. Laney was impressed by how everyone stayed after church to see the Fall Frolic come to life. On the grass to the left of the church, men were laying down a wood floor for dancing. Curious as to who had ordered the musicians, Laney walked toward the building. Pulling her shoulders back, she decided a dance floor wasn't going to bother her as the Hearsts had agreed a few minutes ago to become school board members. Coming inside, she sought a piece of paper. She would have all the possible school board members names ready for the mayor and then spend the rest of the day enjoying the children and their families. Ava came from the vestibule, carrying a cake tin.

"Ava." Laney eyed a piece of paper. "I'd hoped to have all the names for school board members ready. The reverend and his wife have agreed and also the Hearsts. I think it's important to have a parent's input."

Ava peeked side to side and set the cake tin down on the communion table. "I would love to serve." She hesitated. "But you know I've also applied for a Wells Fargo position." She silenced, smiling at a gentleman carrying a stack of chairs out the door. "I can confide only in you." Ava held her elbow and turned away from the people coming and going. "There was another position they sought me for."

"That's wonderful!" Laney forgot to keep her voice down. "Where?"

Ava chewed on the bottom of her lip. "Austin Station," she said warily.

"Oh, I've been there, "Laney exclaimed. "You will be helping the Franklins."

"No, the Franklins want to move back east. I understand Mr. Franklin's mother has passed away."

"Of course." Laney's brows creased, remembering the bedridden woman.

"So you don't think it's ridiculous?" Ava's brows narrowed, and Laney caught Ava's concerned expression,

"I suppose it would be difficult." Was Ava talking of running Austin Station by herself? "It would be just you and Matthew?"

Ava released a shaky sigh and waved her fingers at Laney. "It's too strange. I completely understand why it would be impossible. Say no more."

Laney stilled, surprised at her abrupt reaction. "Ava, this means something to you. Tell me. I don't think it's ridiculous." Laney waited while Ava looked around the church building and shook her head.

"The whole idea of my employment with Wells Fargo in a barren desert area is scandalous. Especially if you knew the family I come from." Ava's lips formed a line that squished into a frown. "But, I applied anyway." She blew out a fast breath. "I'm certain I won't get it. I tried to convince myself that knowing that Sawyer and John ride through each week would make it some grand adventure from the pages of fiction—except with a strong heroine."

"Yes! I love those books." Laney's tone delighted. "And God hath seen the Deborahs and…and Esthers and Abigails and Marthas." She held Ava's arm. "You can be just like them."

"Didn't they all have husbands or brothers?" Ava lowered her chin.

"And you will have a Glorious Father!" Bright-eyed, Laney nodded with inspiration. "He will watch over you."

"Oh, you sweet girl." Grinning, Ava hugged Laney. "Put my name on that paper. I will be here and happy to serve the school."

"And I will pray for the right Wells Fargo position for you."

Both women turned to hear the pastor make an announcement. "They are about to start the food auction and bidding. I'd better get my cake out there." Ava picked her cake up and headed for the door.

Laney stayed back and smiled as another couple went by. Widow Boils insisted on bringing her famous donuts and entering them in the auction. That was fine, except she entered them with Laney's name. Scooting towards the door, she peeked out. Sawyer stood under a tree talking to Samuel Clemens. Would he bid on her counterfeit donuts? Sawyer knew they weren't from her hand. But he did love them. Laney huffed. *And* she'd told him not to.

Two girls from school waved at her, and she came out to greet them, reminding herself that this day was for the school. Regardless of her bruised heart, things were going to go better for her job and the school. She just knew it.

Two apple pies and one cobbler had been actioned off. Ava's cake was next. Even in her fine black dress, the woman projected a vision of charm and beauty. Many a single man might be able to look past her state of mourning to see the delightful woman she—

"One dollar!" The pastor shouted. "The highest bid goes to Sawyer Roth. Congratulations."

Who? What? Laney watched Ava pick up her cake tin, smiling towards Sawyer. Everybody knew the highest bidder would get to share the yummy fare with the top purchaser. Laney pulled her mouth closed as Sawyer and Ava walked to a blanket under the tree.

No, she didn't want him bidding on her goodies. But a dollar? And Ava? Would they talk and plan for her new adventure working for Wells Fargo?

Laney watched nervously as the other items were auctioned off. Two brothers from her class proudly purchased their mother's sugar cookies, and everyone clapped.

Her sham donuts were next. Her eyes wanted to bore fire into Widow B. Why did she agree to this? Forging a smile, they called out her name, and her eyes roved over her sweet students. Maybe there was a family who would have mercy on her.

"Two bits." Samuel Clemens held up his finger.

Of course, Mr. Clemens was being kind. The children had so enjoyed the trip to his newspaper office. He'd taught them the various duties of the newspaper shop and let the students crank the handle of the printing press. Reading all their stories, he'd picked Henriette's on the boiling water that flowed under the mine shafts. It really was a very insightful piece after the tragedy that took the miner's lives last year. He said he would include it in the next print setting.

"Sold."

Laney glanced over and nodded toward Mr. Clemens. But he wasn't moving or looking at her. Howard stepped forward and handed the money to the pastor then walked toward Laney.

"My father has a blanket over there." Howard pointed, holding the plate of Widow B's donuts. Laney strained to swallow and shoved her hand into her pocket. Her handkerchief was missing. Everything careened out of order again. Except she held the names of the new school board in her other hand. "All right." She squared her shoulders. "I needed to speak with him anyway."

By the grace of a merciful God, Laney didn't have to walk to the mayor's blanket with a hundred eyes on her. After one more item was sold, the auction ended, and everyone began to move and visit. Thankfully, Ava and Sawyer sat on the other end of the churchyard. A gust of dirt and wind tossed her skirts around. Now, if Howard could just trip and drop these pastries.

Phoebe Hearst came to walk next to her in a striking pink and gray fitted skirt and vest. The voluptuous feathers on her hat swayed back and forth in the wind. "A grand success, I would say. I counted almost twenty dollars." She bit her lip with a coy smile. "I mean, George did bid ten of those dollars." Phoebe intertwined their elbows and led them away from the men talking. "I've been dying to confide in another woman my age."

Laney looked back. Phoebe's husband, George, *was* much older. Was that something popular out west?

"I believe I'm expecting," Phoebe whispered.

"Oh." Laney sucked in a breath and remembered to be glad. These miracles often happened with married people. "That is so wonderful. You must be so happy."

"I am." One-shoulder tipped upward. "George wants a boy, of course." Phoebe rolled her eyes. "Men, all they really care about is mining and making money. I think I should have a girl to keep me company."

Laney listened, but her eyes drifted to the other side of the churchyard. Sawyer and Ava seemed deep in conversation. What confidences were they sharing with each other? The widows stood not far away, talking to other women.

"Did you approve of dancing and music?" Laney asked.

"It was the mayor's idea." Phoebe released her arm. "I understand that he sent for the musicians from Sacramento."

"Sacramento?" Laney frowned. "They will want to be paid."

"My husband said he would cover it."

Laney bristled inside but tried to keep her chin up. Right now, the children were laughing and playing, and the fundraiser had gone well. The Hearsts would be a blessed family to have their own child. Children are an arrow to the future. Blessed is the man whose quiver is full of them. She grinned at Phoebe and pointed to the students who ran like the wind, freely in and out of the churchyard.

Virginia City was more than saloons and brothels. It held families and children from all parts of this country. Today counted as a success just to see her students' families socializing and taking a much-deserved break from the hard work of mining.

"Elaine." The mayor lightly touched her back, and Phoebe moved to her husband. "Come join us. My mother has packed a wonderful luncheon."

Laney hesitated as she watched the Hearst's take a seat next to Howard and George.

"Could I speak to you first?"

"Say anything you'd like." He nodded.

Something about his benevolent tone irritated her. "I know you are very busy with the town dealings, so I took it upon myself to gather some names of people who would be willing to serve on the school board."

"Really?" Now his edged tone matched his suspicious muttonchops.

"I think a meeting once a month would suffice. We could meet at the school." For one brave second, Laney met his eyes.

His bottom lip twitched into a faint frown. "I'll think about it."

"It would help with your load, I'm sure. Here are the names of the willing volunteers." She tried to find a breath. "The pastor and his wife have agreed."

"I can read it, Elaine." He folded it quickly and shoved the paper in his pocket.

She swallowed, finding her voice. "Just as Mrs. Hearst has so graciously taken on the care to raise funds for the school, we will now have a board to discuss and oversee the best use of that money."

"The Hearst's are waiting." He took her elbow. "Come sit down."

"Oh, I apologize." She found a small smile. "Widow Boils made the donuts. Would you like to enjoy them with her?"

"No, I would not. Your name was read for the bidding. The boys were wanting to have lunch and treats with their teacher. Is that going to be a problem?"

Laney felt a chill on the warm day and sighed. Howard and George were finishing off the plate of donuts. Dare she mention they would hardly miss her? Without looking, she could feel the mayor's eyes drilling her for the right answer.

"Your mother is a wonderful cook," Laney murmured, walking around to a free spot on the blanket. Remembering to speak loudly, she yelled toward Mrs. Reynolds, "Your lunches are renowned at the school!"

Mrs. Reynolds rolled her eyes and turned away.

Chapter 35

The festive Sunday afternoon turned to calm at dusk. As the first stars appeared, a few families had said their goodbyes while most of the crowd stayed to enjoy the music. The Spanish men played their guitars and violins while someone lit the dance area with pole-like torches. Laney separated from the Reynolds group and stood with the widows.

"Does it seem strange to have music and dancing on the Lords' Day?" Laney watched some of her students chase each other on the dance floor.

"Everything in Virginia City seems strange to me." Widow B shook her head. "I prefer knee slappin' American music."

Laney didn't know Spanish, but the serene song seemed to have a sad origin. Two couples joined the children and swayed back and forth in each other's arms.

Ava joined their huddle. "Aren't we the woeful?" She sighed. "Three lonesome widows and a schoolmarm."

Laney flashed a quick smile before she returned to watching the couples dance. She did feel pitiful. The music wasn't helping. "I'm just staying to help clean up."

"Very good," Widow C said. "My feet are aching, and I'm ready to go.

"Me too." Widow B huffed. "I'll walk you home, Beatrice, and you can make me a cup of tea."

"Don't be too late, ladies." Widow B smirked with flashing eyebrows.

Laney stilled, feeling a hole about to burn through her tongue. She wanted to ask Ava about her talk with Sawyer. It was unusual to see him stretched out on a blanket, resting on his elbow, and talking with Ava. So relaxed and yet attentive—what could it have been about?

She didn't need to know. It was a terrible curse being born this curious. Her neck hurt from talking to the children and families while straining to watch them all afternoon. Sawyer had to be done with her. Not once did he glance her way. Not once did he—

"Laney."

She jumped and tried calmly to turn to the voice that made her heart melt. Sawyer Roth simmered so close and so handsome that her mouth went dry. Looking down, he scratched his temple and then glanced up. "Do you want to dance?"

"I...I...." What was her new plan to keep her shield of faith up? She finally met his eyes. "I would." Sawyer held his hand out, and she took it. Tingles of warmth radiated up her arm, making her forget her name. Quenching a small squeak forming in the back of her throat, he walked her past people talking, and she kept her eyes unmoving from her steps. *So what. It was just a dance.* Laney released a deep breath as they stepped up on the wooden floor.

"I've never danced." She bit on her bottom lip. "Our church back home would never allow dancing." Couples moved around them as they stood regarding each other.

"I just figured this was better than asking you to go for a walk with me." Sawyer held his hand up, and Laney carefully took it. His other hand rested on her back. Before she was ready, he nudged her close and danced them back and forth. Laney tried to imitate what the other couples did, but her feet often moved the opposite of his. "I'm sorry." She almost stepped on his toe.

"You're fine," Sawyer said.

Laney wanted to gaze long into his eyes. He carried that unreadable expression again. Taking a glance around, she moved back and forth, feeling sheltered inside the circle of other dancers. "I'm sorry about the other night. George Reynolds had been bitten by a rattlesnake."

"I know, Ava explained." He nodded once.

Ava. She was her friend, but she guessed the two of them were better friends. Laney watched the man strum the guitar, trying to ignore the way Sawyer smelled like linen soap. Focusing on moving with the dancers proved enough. And why hadn't he come to her for the explanation? Maybe he'd come to have supper with Ava? Her foot collided with his.

"I'm just not good at this." They stopped. "I really only waited around to help clean up."

Sawyer dropped his hand from hers. "I only waited around to talk to you."

"I've been here all afternoon." The words came out snippy.

"And you spent most of it with the Mayor and his friends."

Laney shoved her hand in her pocket. Thankfully, the other dancers moved around them without notice. Blast it! Where had she left her hankie? A warm, thick grip took her free hand and led her off the wooden floor. "Let's have some punch." Sawyer suggested.

Laney knew she could not be seen holding his hand and quickly let go. The punch table was empty of people. Sawyer took the ladle and spooned her a cup. Winded and edgy, she took a large drink and scowled. "It's warm and spoiled, I think."

Sawyer filled his cup and took a drink. His eyes widened, and he flattened a smile. "It's spiked."

"What!" Disbelieving, Laney took another drink, and Sawyer grabbed her wrist.

"You'd better be careful, Miss Balderhoff."

"Who would do that? At a school fundraiser? On the church grounds?"

"Someone's hoping for a better time."

Laney set her cup down and spied the remaining crowd. "Oh, this town." She grumbled.

"I tried to warn you." He shrugged, smiling. "You are, by far, the most respectable pillar we have."

"How can you say that?" Her lips began to feel strangely puffy. "The reverend and his wife are over there."

"Okay, you are the most respectable pillar *I* know."

Laney felt her stomach sink with his words. "Hardly," she whispered, knowing what being in his arms did to her crumbling pillar-*ness*.

Sawyer tilted his head. "Two innocent swallows of alcohol won't turn you from your honest ways."

"You're right." Her eyes simmered on his. "But that's not what I'm talking about."

***

Sawyer stilled and watched two boys chasing a little girl. Had he been foolish in playing tag with the pious teacher's affections? Lifting the bowl, he gave the punch a toss into the bushes. Had their kisses spiked something in him that could only be satisfied with her? *Blast it.* There just wasn't anyone like her. She was different. And she'd snuck unaware into his heart. He scratched the back of his head. And truth be told, he liked it—a lot. His eyes went back to her and found her setting empty cups into a bucket. Far more than a sweet, round face and a heart of gold, she was a prize, and everything in him wanted to fight, to earn her love. He'd pushed past his pride and invited himself to dinner with the ladies. After watching her visit with everyone else today, he came to her and asked her to dance. Laney went to lift the bucket, and Sawyer took it from her hands.

"There's a sink in the church kitchen." She led the way, and he followed. What they had, what they meant to each other, seemed to change course without warning.

Entering the simple kitchen, Laney tapped her fingers on the kettle, checking the temperature. "There's some hot water left. I'm going to wash and dry these cups." She pulled an apron off the hook and used it to grab the handle. "I'm sure you have better things to do." Setting the kettle on the washboard, she tied the apron around her waist.

"I'll help," Sawyer paused, "if you'll let me."

When her eyes met his, he couldn't ignore the pound in his chest. He was asking about more than dishes.

Laney glanced away and then softly met his gaze. "I'd like that."

When she turned around to fill the tub, Sawyer touched the bow on her apron. It wasn't enough. He wanted forgiveness for his jealousy and mostly her soft, pliable body in his arms. An older woman carrying the punch bowl came in, and he dropped his hand.

"How can I help?" she asked

Sawyer took the bowl and gave it to Laney.

"I suppose you can bring me anything that needs washing." Laney nodded a smile. She went back to washing the cups, and Sawyer wanted to kick himself. He'd seen his sisters do this a hundred times. Finding a towel folded on a shelf, he took it and began to dry the cups. When he'd caught up with drying, Laney placed the rinsed cups in his hand. Without meaning to, his fingers wrapped around hers and they both froze. The pounding in his chest was back.

"Come here," his voice beckoned low and husky, "Lane-*ee*." Sawyer gave her hand a tug toward him. Unmoving, something akin to concern and desire flashed in her eyes. He released the cup in her grip. Stretching his fingers along her wrist and under her cuff, her skin, the softest he'd ever felt. Gingerly reaching up further, her arm was his for the taking.

"Ahh!" Laney jumped back, and the cup went flying in the air. By the shocked look on her face, he realized they weren't alone. Her hand flew over her mouth, and she bent to pick up the cup.

"Praise the Lord!" She panted, swinging up with her hand held high. "I'm so clumsy. Luckily, it didn't even break."

Sawyer moved to the side as a woman set down two trays and another bowl.

"Teacher." The woman looked between the two of them. "I've seen you work all day. I think you should go on and let me finish these few things. The reverend's wife is my sister. I promise to put everything back as they like it."

Laney searched around the small space and rubbed her chin. "That is very kind." She pulled the apron off and hung it where she'd found it. "I do have school tomorrow." Holding her flushed face, she smiled quickly and walked out.

Stepping out behind her, Laney slowed and then they paused. Sawyer noticed the shadows had melted into darkness, and the evening air had cooled. The Spanish music still floated from the right, and without thinking, Sawyer reached for her hand, and she sucked in a loud breath. Laney gripped his hand hard, then let it go and cleared her throat. "I need to say goodbye to Mrs. Hearst. This frolic was all her idea."

"I'll wait right here to walk you home," he said matter-of-factly.

Laney hesitated, her mouth open, ready to argue, but suddenly she closed it. "All right," she whispered.

Townsfolk were folding up their blankets and calling for their kids. The day's event was like something they'd never seen before, and it was all due to Miss Balderhoff and her godly influence— something else Virginia City wasn't accustomed to. He'd no wish to change what everyone thought of her. A walk home was the gentlemanly thing to do.

Albert and the mayor stood back in the shadows smoking their thin sweet-scented cigarettes. If he could see better, he would have sworn they were both watching him. Anger grated in Sawyer's chest. Albert's poor bookkeeping revealed more than bad mathematics. The only problem was, it was Ava who knew the bulk of the truth.

They had talked today about the possibility that Albert was skimming off funds from the Wells Fargo Company of Virginia City. But he was at a loss as to what to do. He didn't read or write well enough to contact the branch manager. After some convincing, Ava agreed to report the discrepancies she'd found while filling in for him. He didn't want to put her in the middle, but hopefully, someone would come to investigate. If it was true, Albert would be gone. Laney stepped past the men and lifted a wave to say goodnight. Was the mayor part of the ring of theft? Since Fort Churchill regularly protected the stage route, the bandits trying to get the Wells Fargo stage had disappeared. How would anyone know if it was a random attack on the stage that almost took his life? Or if now the silent thievery took place unannounced in the back alleys of Virginia City?

Sawyer sighed, wishing spiked punch was the worst crime in town.

Chapter 36

With the smell of sagebrush wafting in the evening air, Sawyer took slow, purposeful steps from the church and down along to the Wells Fargo corral. Laney stayed close by his side but quiet, which was not like her. He wanted to have strong faith that she had the same feelings he had for her, but Sawyer didn't want to be one of those men who only prayed when he was desperate for something he wanted. Should he try again to take her hand?

The moonlight and their footsteps made Blackie think they were here to see him. The horse moved along the fence where they walked. "Now, the turncoat wants to be with us." Sawyer stopped and rubbed the tall black forehead. Laney reached up to scratch under Blackie's chin.

"Thank you for your help with the dishes." She drew her hand down the horse's nose. "I'm sorry I'm such a poor dancer." Withdrawing her hand, she looked away. The cool evening surrounded them with the faint sounds of Spanish guitars in the air.

"I could care less about dancing." He drew his hand down her back and rested it below her waist.

Turning fast from his touch, her wide-eyes were hard to miss. "No kissing, Sawyer. I mean it. I'm powerless when you kiss me."

He suppressed a laugh inside his pressed lips. "Okay. I won't kiss you. And just for the record, I'm powerless when you kiss me."

"And that's the problem." Stepping back, she tempered her anxious tone and lowered it. "I don't *plan* on kissing you. I should know better at my age."

Her age, Sawyer swallowed another snicker. Like she was one of the old widows.

"But you say something sweet or do something chivalrous and it just happens."

"I'm what? Chivalrous?"

"Like when you saved Matthew from falling," she explained.

Sawyer stood narrow-eyed and confused. "And that makes you want to kiss me?"

"Well, yes. Like when I was about to fall to my death from the stage, and you reached over and yanked me on top of you."

"You wanted to kiss me then?" Sawyer stilled, and Blackie bumped his arm for more attention.

"Well—no. Not right then. I thought you were dying."

"But later?" He rubbed the horse behind the ear. These were things he would have never guessed. She seemed far too virtuous to have such thoughts.

"Oh, forget it. I'm double-minded," she huffed. "It's not just kissing. It's really *all* the things I like about you." She closed her eyes and rubbed between her eyebrows. "I like how your eyes remind me of warm chocolate drops on a cold day. And your voice is tender when you talk to me. Well, not at first, you said Laney in a strange way. But now when you say it makes me melt instead of cringe. And regardless of being wounded and still healing, you are as strong as nails, and I feel safe when I'm with you."

Shocked, Sawyer quickly closed his mouth; she was rambling, and he enjoyed every minute.

"And the orange, I won't ever eat it because it reminds me that you heard my childhood story and not just that, you did something kind to show me you heard me." She gripped the wooden corral fencing and rolled her eyes. "And the feeling of being heard and understood is like what my Bible is to me. Because I know I'm different. I know I have strange habits. Tap squeeze, tap squeeze. Oh, the desk reminds me of you, too." Groaning, Laney dropped her forehead on the railing. "And I understand why the mayor's presence upsets you." She glanced up quickly. "Even though, believe me, I really don't care for him. I understand because I felt jealous of..." she murmured something into her hand.

"What? What did you say? Jealous of what?" These were amazing insights, and Sawyer didn't want her to stop now.

Laney shook her head. "It's humiliating."

"Just say it." He cupped her cheek to have her look at him.

"Ava," she whispered. "I was jealous all afternoon." Her face squinted uptight as she pulled his hand back. "It really is the worst feeling. And I forgot my handkerchief."

Sawyer blinked and then blinked again. Jealousy and forgetfulness? "I wanted to support the school. You told me not to bid on your items."

"I know." Her hand flew up and banged her palm on her forehead.

Sawyer leaned back, fighting a laugh, then twisted her close to him and wrapped her in a hug. "Ava and I were just talking about Wells Fargo and the Virginia City office." He said near her ear while his heart raced in his chest. "I could never have romantic feelings for anyone else but you." His fingers massaged the back of her lovely neck. "I'm in love with the schoolteacher." The words were so soft and honest. Did he say them aloud? And now what? Perfect warm lips and gleaming wide eyes were coming closer and closer...

"Shouldn't you two at least go in the barn?"

They jerked apart, and Sawyer saw Albert making his way to the back door.

"Apologize now! Or you will be sorry." Sawyer marched across the dirt alley.

"Go ahead, weakling." Albert sneered. "John told me that poor shoulder has left you a cripple."

Seeing red, Sawyer grabbed the man by the collar and tossed him to the ground. "Get up! Let's see if this arm works or not."

Albert got up on one knee, but before he stood, he rammed his shoulder into Sawyer's gut and knocked them both to the ground.

Teeth clenched, Sawyer pushed him off and got in a good right hook that sent Albert flying back on his backside.

"I said, get up!" Sawyer wanted to put a boot in his face but preferred a real fist fight.

Seething, Albert spit blood and held his chin. "I will see you fired." He staggered to his feet. "Then you can go live with your teacher friend and be one of the ladies." Albert held his fists up and swung at him. Sawyer ducked and jerked his arm back for another quick punch to the—Sawyer's elbow came in contact with something, and he heard a yelp before a flurry of fabric and ruffles were at his feet.

"Laney!" His arms came around her to pick her up. "I...I...Lord Almighty." Setting her on her feet, she wavered dazed, and tears rushed to her eyes. "I'm so sorry! I didn't see you there." Sawyer held her tight as Albert snickered and staggered to the Wells Fargo back door.

"Look at me." Sawyer searched her face, brushing the dirt off her backside. "I'm so sorry." He could see the bright red coloring forming on her face. Sawyer prayed to heaven he'd not broken her nose. "What hurts?"

"I would place the bet on you for the win." She croaked and gingerly rubbed her face. "You are not crippled."

Sawyer's eyes swept the back alley. "Let's get you inside." He held her snug as they reached the back door. "Laney, don't you know? Never, *never* approach men who are fighting." He tried to keep his voice even though every inch of him was on alert.

"Ahh, I know now." She grimaced.

Sawyer helped her sit at the kitchen table and went to light the lantern. A small trickle of blood came from her nose. Grabbing a rag, he dipped it in water, and his hand trembled as he held it to her cheek. "Your nose doesn't look broken." He came down on one knee to examine her.

"I think my teeth are rattled."

"Oh Lord," Sawyer grumbled. "I'm sorry. Can I wake someone up? Do you want me to get the doctor?

Little by little, she made tiny movements with her chin, cheeks, and nose, and blinked each eye. "I think I'll be okay."

"Let me get Ava to see to you."

"No." Laney held his arm. "I'll be fine."

"I'd take you to your room, but I probably shouldn't." In the lantern light, it was hard to tell if she was blushing or swelling. "Now, I think you can have that word back. What was it? Chivalrous? It doesn't describe a man who pops a woman in the face."

"You didn't mean to." She touched his cheek. "It was dark, and I panicked, thinking I could stop the two of you."

"Oh, girl." Sawyer stood up and pulled her into his arms.

"He's a mean, awful man," Laney sank into his chest, rubbing her hand up his back.

Sawyer pulled back, and his jaw rocked to the side. "Because of just now?"

Rubbing her cheek, her mouth hung open. Sawyer gripped her upper arms as his eyes pierced hers.

"He is in general," she mumbled.

"Has he done anything to you?"

"No." She looked away, but he held her arms firm. "He's done nothing, just said some unsuitable things."

"Like what?"

"It's late, Sawyer, and you shouldn't be in here." She tried to pull away without luck.

"Tell me, Laney. What did he say?"

Her shoulders slumped. "It was the night you came for dinner and left angry. I'd tried to go to my room and pray, but…"

"What did he say?" Sawyer growled.

"I can tell you are angry, and if I tell you, will you promise me you won't go start another fight?"

"Start?" Sawyer released her. "I didn't start *that* fight. His rude remarks about us started it. He was asking for it, really."

"Shush." She frowned. "Keep your voice down. The older ladies are just down this hall."

Sawyer shifted his feet, wondering if he could keep a promise like that. "Okay, I promise not to pound him to a pulp."

Laney dabbed her red, tender nose. "I don't remember. Oh, I was outside the back door, hoping I could talk to you. For some reason, he alluded that I should go up to your room." She closed her eyes.

Something was missing; she wouldn't look at him. "That's all?"

"Or that I could come into his room," she whispered.

Sawyer jabbed his fingers into his hair. "The no account, worthless snake. I'm going to hang him from his toenails."

"Sawyer." Laney pulled on his arm. "He'd been drinking. Mr. Carrillo likely doesn't even remember what he said."

Blood boiling, Sawyer rehearsed what he'd do over again. After what he'd just heard, the man wouldn't have gotten away without another fist to the jaw and a broken...

"You tried to warn me." Her shoulders sagged. "This place is ungodly."

"His days are numbered." Sawyer wasn't listening. Albert had hurt someone he cared about. Her pinch to his arm brought him back. A faint purple ring under her left eye appeared, and he winced. "I'm sorry, Laney."

Biting on the corner of his lip, he wondered how to make this better. "But I *was* listening earlier. Before the fight, you said some very kind things about me." His mouth went dry. Now to recall what he'd said in return. "I told you...you...how I feel. You don't ever have to wonder about anyone else. My heart is set on you. And I know I don't deserve anyone as good and smart," he gently ran his finger under her chin, "and as respectful as you, because if you knew how badly I wanted to kiss you this instant." He took a step back and held up a finger. "And I won't." He backed up to the door handle. "So, I'm going to leave now." He smiled, turning the knob. "Just going to say goodnight." He backed out and almost closed the door until it flew open again.

"I'll be back on Wednesday. Don't go even to get Moses by yourself. Anywhere."

She nodded, but must have been in pain. With sad, glazed eyes, she turned to the hall leaving him without confidence she would follow his sincere instructions.

Chapter 37

"Oh, Ava." Laney wanted to cry, holding the mirror to see her face the next morning.

"Hold still, just a little more powder, and we'll have those two black eyes covered."

Laney didn't have to ask. The grimace on Ava's face as she applied the powder said it all. How would she conduct school with two black eyes? The children would be shocked. And every child would ask who hit her in the face. "Maybe I should shut down school today." Laney held the mirror out, hoping from a distance it was better.

"Just use it as a lesson on not walking into things in the dark. Maybe you don't have to mention you walked into two men fighting. Or that Sawyer's elbow was the cause of this suffering."

"Lessons on walking in the dark?" Laney appreciated the plan. "It might work."

"I know you need to get to school." Ava tilted her face and raised one eyebrow, "But I want details when you get home."

"Yes, ma'am." Laney sighed, picking up her school bag.

"Matthew!" Ava called for her son. "Miss Balderhoff is ready for her escort."

***

The children jabbered all morning at school. Laney kept her back to the students as she wrote their assignments on the chalkboard.

"Everyone take your seats, please." She turned, ruffling some papers on her desk. "Who would like to open our morning in prayer?"

"Hoo wee," Guthrie said from the front row. "You got two shiners, Teacher."

Laney looked out to a sea of student's faces, most of them wide-eyed. "Before we pray, let's play the three-word game." Laney saw Leona's raised hand begin to tip her out of her seat. "Yes, Leona."

"Boys against girls, Teacher?"

"Yes, boys against girls." She spied the eager faces. "Let's start with Matthew. Matthew, in three words, what did you like about the fall frolic yesterday?"

Matthew twisted a smile. "It was fun."

The girls turned to one another, abuzz to come up with more.

"Sarah, you're next."

She wiggled in her seat. "I played with—" Her face fell. "Oops."

"That's not a three-word sentence," George interjected.

"Yes, next try goes to Neville." Laney pointed at him.

"I like dancing!" He stood and bowed as the other boys clapped. Laney grinned, remembering him spinning around the wood floor without a partner.

"Henrietta."

"Neville can't dance," she said proudly, and the girls clapped as the boys booed. "That's not about the frolic," Joseph yelled from the back.

"It's a point for the girls, but keep the three words on the topic." Laney continued with the game until each child had shared. The younger ones missed a word or two, but in the end, the girls won and were rewarded with an extra five minutes for lunch recess.

"Now, for my three words." She stared at the eager faces and held the moment longer to engage them.

"Darkness hurts faces." She made a circle with her fingers around her face.

Some children frowned sympathetically, and others nodded. "I did that once, Miss Balderhoff," Santos said. "It was dark, and I walked right into a hitching post."

"What did you walk into, Teacher?" Sweet Leona asked with sincere concern.

Laney was so close to victory, but every eye gaped at her.

"Three words." Her eyes scanned over the attentive faces. "An unseen elbow."

"Ouch." Sarah held her hand over her mouth.

"Children, slates out. George, will you pray and thank the Lord for our wonderful day yesterday? And then we need to get to work."

***

The morning went well as far as the education of young minds, except for the few times Laney rubbed her finger under her nose and felt the pain up behind her eyeballs. Giving the girls a few extra minutes at lunch gave her time to draw a baseball diamond on the board. The game supplied a great way to do addition with the boys.

Ava had been right. Children didn't need the entire story. She finished the last bite of cheese she'd packed. Her students were so bright and eager. How could she properly thank God for the blessing of having such a wonderful class? From different countries and abilities to different interests and gifts, each one had an open heart to learn all they could. Somehow as hard as Virginia City had been, this teaching assignment had rekindled her confidence in God's call. A clump of dirt from someone's shoe spread under the second desk in the third row. It didn't even move her to action. She could leave it there until after school, and she would be fine.

The joy was unspeakable. Even with two black eyes, her mission sparked a flame within her. This Friday she would be paid, and she'd be able to send most of her money off to her mother and aunt in Nebraska. Laney stood to call the boys inside.

And what about that man, she sighed. He'd said he loved her. Slowing her steps, she allowed the warmth to rush over her again. She knew she loved him—her own feelings weren't just silly. Oh, but Wednesday felt like forever. Taking in a deep breath to settle her heartbeat, Laney rang the bell in her hand. *Goodness and mercy shall follow me all my days.*

***

That afternoon, after the schoolroom had been returned to clean and tidy, Laney waved goodbye to Howard. Little did he know all their afternoon tutoring and help had paid off! The unique young Howard Reynolds passed the graduation exam she'd just finished grading.

A blast from the mine rattled the schoolroom, and she froze. With a school full of busy children, she hardly noticed anymore. She looked up and found Madam Bulette standing at the schoolroom door.

"Miss Balderhoff." Her refined English accent competed with the jagged dark lines on her face.

"Yes, please come in." Laney leaned to the right. Leona wasn't with her.

"Is everything all right with Leona?"

"She's fine. But the child mentioned you got yourself a couple of black eyes. Madam Bulette drew closer and frowned. "Dodgy teacher. I've been on the side of those myself." Shaking her head, she pulled loose strands of brown hair to the side. Laney felt her heart sink from the weight of the life she must live night after night.

"You don't have to tell me how. Blimey, my working girls tell me *too* much." Madam Bulette rolled her eyes. "I just wanted you to know if anyone ever is too...*too* aggressive...." Holding Laney's gaze, she clenched her hands together. "You take your strongest knee," she patted her knee "and bring it up real fast like—right into the man's crotch." Her skirt and foot flew up. Laney's eyes widened, getting the visual message.

How to disable a man was certainly nothing they ever discussed in her ladies' Sunday school class. "I...hum...thank you," Laney stammered.

"It will give you time to run. Best behind a bloody locked door." The businesswoman nodded. "Some men can't get up at all."

Laney blinked, trying to blur the image. Undoubtedly this was one of those special Virginia City moments she'd likely never forget. The town's brothel owner giving her a lesson or two. "Leona is a good student." It seemed to be a sound redirection.

"The child loves school. Talks about you all the time."

"I've never asked her." Laney wondered, "but her mother, does she come back or visit her?"

"She's long gone." Madam Bulette shrugged. "Her new bloke promised her a wagon load of bull—*patties.*" She stopped. "Those kind don't want a kid in the way."

"And so…" Laney couldn't find the words to ask the next question.

"So, is the fair-haired child destined to be a repeat of her mother?" Her fine accent held a certain new decorum Laney was thankful for.

"I suppose, yes, that is what I'm asking." Laney's heart would crack in two if prostitution was to be Leona's future.

"I got a letter. Her mother has a sister coming from back east." Madam Bulette shrugged. "Family," she huffed. "My ladies have a better life working for me than they ever did with their bloody families."

Laney could hardly fathom the thought. But at least Leona may have a different path. "I understand you are donating the first fire wagon and uniforms for Virginia City."

"That I am."

"How very generous of you."

"The men in this town paid for it," she snickered. "But as a proprietor of a renowned business, I can do what I want with my money."

"True, you can." Laney wondered how she held this conversation like they were two women discussing the price of thread. "And I appreciate your help. I was not attacked myself, but I did get too close to two men." She swallowed, remembering. "They were engaging in fisticuffs."

"Over you?" Madam Bulette asked.

"No, more over things that should not be said in a lady's presence." As soon as the words left, Laney wanted them back.

"I heard talk. The good people of Virginia City liked the frolic after church." Madam Bulette flinched as the ground rumbled. Of course, the painted women of the town would not be welcome at such an event. "If you ever need anything for the school...." She looked up and moved to leave. "You can write a note and have Leona deliver it." Something in her forlorn tone pinched inside Laney. "I would be happy to donate." She walked to the door. "And no one would have to know."

Laney felt something burning on her lips as the woman moved to leave. What would the Lord want her to say? "Madam Bulette, wait." Laney moved closer and touched her sleeve. "I don't understand much of how things are in this world, but your kindness to help me protect myself means a lot to me. I know we are different." Laney felt her chin quiver—the woman's hard life penetrated from under her sleeve into her hand. "I count you as a friend, and I admire the care you've taken of Leona. She is always on time and ready to learn. It is another thing you don't have to do, but you do."

"Do you think all the immoral are void of common sense?" Madam Bulette's tone dropped cold.

"No." Laney fired back. "Will you let me compliment you?"

Madam Bulette released a small huff and closed her eyes. "If you must." She opened them with a cheeky grin

Laney smiled back and squeezed her arm before she released her. Stepping back, she twisted her lips with determination and popped her knee up fast. "Like that?"

"Practice, practice, Teacher. With your size, it needs a bit more spite and force." Madam turned and waved her fingers over her shoulder. "And those bruises will fade by tomorrow."

Laney watched her walk across the street. Two different men called out to her, and Madam Bulette waved back.

Oh, Virginia City. Laney sauntered back toward her desk and popped her knee up hard. Narrowing her eyes like she was angry, she tried it again.

Chapter 38

The next day while eating lunch, Laney jumped from the rattle of three giggling students looking for the jump rope. Her focus had been off all day—not that focus had ever been her strong suit. Taking a deep breath, she nodded a smile as the girls ran outside.

Without fanfare, Sawyer had come back to eat last night. She had to give him credit, except he seemed talkative with the other widows and less attentive with her. *But he came back.*

The whole evening left too many things unsaid. How many more weeks could they keep their secret? Rolling her eyes, Laney poked a hole in the roll on her desk in front of her. Maybe to avoid the hopeless path with Sawyer, she'd gotten too involved with Howard's education. *His future.*

The mayor had made request after request for *his own* benefit. Laney sighed. Had she been catering to him, convincing herself that a school board would fix everything? Maybe the painful reality was too hard to face. If she was fired, it would take her from the widows, the children, and the wish of her heart, Sawyer Roth.

Laney dropped her face into her hand. Her rituals and need for order had been fading. In one moment, she felt proud of herself, like a child who could hold her own cup. But wasn't there an obvious correlation? When she didn't have her rituals, life spun like a top on a crooked table. Laney forced her head upward. It was time to call in the children.

Remembering the disappointment the night before, Laney stood. As the widows had been about to retire to the parlor for her to read the Bible after dinner, Sawyer had thanked them all for the evening and let himself out. What was she to do, standing there with her Bible and all the eyes on her? Run after him? Laney reached for the bell and groaned. Now she was dissatisfied with being proper?

***

By the time Laney walked home, she had a headache and was ready to spill everything to the widows. Certainly, God had assigned these housemates together and she loved these three precious women dearly. If Laney confided in Widow Boils, the no-nonsense widow would scold her for allowing the mayor to control her decisions. If she told Widow C, she would comfort her in the dilemma and probably advise her to keep the peace, and in the end, Laney would get what she wanted. Both were valid points.

Then there was Ava. Laney sighed and stepped up the wooden sidewalk to the two-story home. Ava, her dear friend, always brought peace and calm to her soul. The young widow, herself, was trying to defy the odds against her by applying for a position with Wells Fargo. Laney let herself in and hung her bonnet and shawl on the hall tree. Taking the stairs slowly, she decided that speaking with Ava was her safest bet.

Exhaling from her overactive brain, Laney entered her own room, sat on the bed, and closed her eyes. *Lord, I know you live in me. I know you lead me.*

Another dreaded test and trial loomed from the Sunday frolic when Phoebe Hearst asked if she would go shopping with her in San Francisco and help her prepare for the nursery. Like a numbskull, she'd answered too quickly with her unprepared yes. Maybe she should've asked who would be going? Regret in putting things off sunk within her. Not even a polite excuse could be found at this late notice. *Please grant me the grace to get through this weekend.*

***

Friday at the school lunch break, Laney went over her notes and set her desk in order. Sarah's mother had arrived, kindly agreeing to take the class for the afternoon. With a weak smile and gratitude, Laney had to say goodbye and grab her carpet bag from under her desk. The most elegant black carriage in Virginia City waited outside for her. It looked like a square box with large black wheels and doors with glass windows. Suddenly she didn't want Sarah's mother to see her enter such a grand display.

Embarrassed, Laney held herself back and thanked Sarah's mother again for taking the class for the afternoon. As soon as Howard came from the play yard, she slipped behind him and gave her bag to the driver. Through the glass, she spied the Hearsts sitting together and the mayor sitting across. "Howard, you get in." She pushed him in front of her. "This way, I can talk to Mrs. Hearst."

Entering the carriage, Laney nodded to Phoebe and straightened her skirts. Having Howard in the middle worked perfectly. She tried to relax her shoulders as the carriage rolled forward.

Phoebe apologized, fanning her face. She hadn't felt well this morning and almost canceled, but she knew how much this trip would mean to Laney.

Laney held her tongue. It was only for Phoebe's benefit she'd even agreed to this—*and* to pick a date for the school to board start. San Francisco held no appeal, and she would've been happy to stay home.

"I do want you to see our new home." Phoebe tried to brighten her tone. "Three stories, six bedrooms, two kitchens, and servants' quarters. It overlooks over the ocean. It's breathtaking."

"The mayor said it was *being* built." Laney felt her brow stiffen.

"Oh, it's done. We will stay there tomorrow night. I don't have all the furnishings in yet. Some are coming from Europe."

Laney blinked, trying to remember what the mayor had implied.

"Are you happy for me?" Phoebe reached forward and touched her knee. "This sweet girl—" she waggled her head and patted her belly "—or boy, will have the most beautiful nursery."

"Oh, please. Yes, I'm happy for all of you." Laney swallowed hard. "I guess I thought when you agreed to be on the school board, you would be in Virginia City for a while still."

"Not too much longer," Phoebe sighed, "since the house is ready."

Laney felt as if someone dropped a brick inside her gut. Slowly she glanced over to Howard. He looked down, picking his nose. Turning to watch out the window, the brick flopped hard. It didn't help that she rode backward while the road snaked down steep curves.

"George wants to run for office—the State Assembly." Phoebe fanned her face again.

Laney stole a glance at Mr. Hearst puffing his cigar and speaking with the mayor. His long gray and white beard gave him a certain astute profile that seemed to command authority. "Won't that be a stimulating life for your family?" Her tone didn't sound believable.

"The Ophir Mine has done well." Phoebe brushed a hair back near her temple.

Laney had to clench her jaw. Did the woman realize the widows she lived with had lost their husbands to that same mine? Where were *their* homes? Now two bricks lodged in her chest, remembering the day she'd walked to Zachary's grave with Ava. A sweaty dizziness was rolling over her. She tried to swallow down the contents from her stomach.

"Stop! Let me out." Laney rocked forward and grabbed the handle on the door.

"Wait, wait!" Phoebe grabbed her arm.

"I need to be excused!" Laney cried as the door flew open. She'd hung from a rocking stagecoach before. Out of the corner of her eye, she saw the mayor lean over Howard and grab the layers of her skirt.

"Woman! What are you doing?" He yanked her back.

Gripping the sides of the door, Laney resisted him and pulled herself closer to the door. The wind and dust rose in her face. Anything was better than being sick and suffocating in a place she didn't belong.

"Stop, driver! Stop!" Mr. Hearst pounded the roof of the carriage.

The carriage slowed, and Laney saw the deep, jagged cliffs on each side. As soon as the mayor let go she put a foot to the gravel road, gripping the door. Her heart pounded, making it hard to breathe. The mayor flew around the back of the carriage and gripped her arm.

"What are you doing? My God, you could have fallen to your death!"

"I'm sorry." Laney panted. "I can't do this." Her eyes rolled in the back of her head. "I can't go on this trip. I don't belong here." Searching, she sought for footing away from the carriage. "These are your friends and I...I...just can't." The way the mayor's eyes bore into her with alarm, she felt the need to explain. "I wouldn't have fallen from the carriage. I'm very strong." Laney pushed off the sizeable black rig and stepped to the back.

"Are you sick?" He followed her.

"Yes, a little." The curvy road and smell of the cigars had made her woozy. She scanned the area. "I don't want to disrupt your trip with the Hearst's. I will walk back to Virginia City."

"Walk? Woman, we are going to be in California in another hour. You can't just walk back!" The mayor groaned and pulled his fingers down his muttonchops. "Elaine. Something must have upset you. Just tell me, and I will reassure you."

Laney took in a deep breath. She would give him a passing mark for trying to lower his voice.

"No, nothing that anyone would make sense of." Laney looked to where her carpetbag was tied to the back. "I'll just take my bag now, and you all can be on your way."

The mayor shook his head and huffed. "Elaine, please. The Hearst's have a wonderful weekend planned for us. I brought Howard, as you asked."

Her eyes widened, and she pinned a weak smile. "Perfect. You can spend time with him in San Francisco. He is close to graduating, and if you are to send him back east, this will be—"

"Stop." The mayor pointed a finger at her. "I don't want to holiday with Howard. I want to be with you."

A fast, dry wind swirled up, and Laney covered her face with both hands. *She knew it.*

Warm hands rested on each of her arms. "Elaine, I'm not good at these types of things, but I find myself enamored with you."

"I am only here to teach school and that is it." She mumbled behind her fingers.

The mayor tugged on her wrists until she had to unveil her face. "I know you are young and are inexperienced in life," he said. "But I will be patient with you. If you want, I will allow you to continue teaching."

Laney felt herself sway. *Now he'd change the rule for his benefit?*

"At least until you are with child."

Whether by wind or the hand of God, Laney swooned and fell backward so fast her feet could not catch her. The gravel edge gave way and she tumbled from his grip. Her rump, back, then head knocked on a rock or two before her body skidded to a halt in a swirl of dust. Grimacing, she sat in a pile and rubbed the back of her head. A bump or two felt better than being close to the mayor. Seeing Howard hanging from the carriage, Laney jumped up and dusted herself off.

"I'm fine." She waved at him.

The mayor met her halfway down the steep edge and offered his hand. "Miss Balderhoff, I have never seen such strange behavior in a woman!" Pulling her to level ground, he flipped his handkerchief from his suit pocket and dabbed a scratch of blood above her temple.

With his touch, Laney jumped back like he was a snake ready to strike. "Sir, you either turn this carriage around, or I'm walking."

With mouth ajar, his face reddened, and he stared at her speechless. "Fine." He glared and stalked away to speak to the driver. Walking back to her, she could see veins popping out from his neck. Gripping the handle of the door, his jaw rocked to the side. "Now get in. There is a spot past the next ridge where the driver can turn the carriage."

Laney didn't dare look to see the shocked expressions from the Hearst's, but she could feel the steam pulsing from the mayor. "Go ahead." She stepped away. "I'll wait here."

Chapter 39

The ride back to Virginia City was thick with numbing silence. The only sound made was when Howard fell asleep, and his head flipped back against the window. Oh, and Mr. Hearst exaggeratingly cleared his throat three times. Phoebe, the gracious friend, kept her head down, picking at a loose thread on her dress. The mayor sat fuming. Coming to a stop and without anything reasonable to say, Laney stepped out and stood alone on the sidewalk in front of the widow house. The driver handed her her carpetbag and wished her a good evening.

Stepping inside the widow house, Matthew bounded past her down the stairs as she was laboriously climbing upward. "Teacher, hey there. I thought you were gone on a trip?"

Laney held back a growl and shook her head.

"Sarah's mom was a nice teacher. Look there, Miss Balderhoff, you've got a tear on your dress." He grimaced. "And dirt."

Laney patted his head and took the last steps like her feet were encased in mud. As soon as she dropped her bag inside her room, she fell on her knees beside her bed. *"Lord, do you remember me asking for your help? Help to get me through this? Not that it was your fault…but…but I…can't do anything right."* Her whiney voice fell into a broken sob.

The silence in the carriage ride had spoken her fate. The mayor would fire her come Monday for sure. Laney felt sick to her stomach and began to unbutton her blue and brown checkered vest while tears streamed from her nose and face. A small knock was at the door.

"Laney?" Ava whispered. "Are you all right?"

She rose to her knees and stood. Opening the door a crack, she dabbed her face dry. "I'm okay, I just had a strange attack and didn't want to continue to San Francisco."

"Oh no, friend. What kind of attack?" Ava said gently, her frown pulling to the side.

Laney opened the door wider. "The kind where my heart starts pounding, and my stomach hurts, and I can't breathe."

"I'm so sorry. Can I get you some tea or something to eat?"

Laney sighed. "No, not now, maybe after I find Moses and have a long cry."

"Don't be hard on yourself." Ava patted her elbow. "I'm sure they understood."

Laney gave her a sad, frozen expression.

"So, they didn't understand?" Ava asked timidly.

Laney slowly shook her head no. "I'm fairly sure I've gotten myself fired."

"No." Ava gasped. "Why would you say that?"

Laney left the door open and sat on her bed. "The mayor said something about being enamored with me. But even before that, I felt like a trapped mouse in a cage. I had to get out."

"Laney." Ava stepped closer. "Do you do this in every carriage or wagon?"

"I guess I do." Her face crumbled before she dropped her chin to her chest.

"And I'm guessing you don't have feelings for the mayor?"

"No." Laney's head shot up. "Never."

Ava huffed and locked her hands on her hips. "There are so few upstanding eligible young women in Virginia City. I mean, I could see it happening."

"But the mayor is the one who said the school teacher would have to be unmarried and above reproach. Then he tells me I could teach until…acck." Laney choked and rolled to her side, burying her face in her pillow.

"Until what?"

"I was…" Laney felt her cheeks flush red. "With child." She groaned and covered her face while she whined.

"Ew!" Ava shivered and sat next to her. "That is an appalling thing to say."

"I love my job," Laney whined. "It's me. I keep messing up everywhere I go."

"How can that be true?" Ava rubbed her back. "The children and parents love you. You were the talk of the Fall Frolic."

"I love teaching. It's the one thing I don't mess up. But the rest of my life is such a mess." Laney groaned.

"Well, now." Ava tapped her chin. "I have this friend who always leads people to believe what God believes about them."

Laney rubbed her temples. "Ouch." She hit a scratch or bump from her fall. "I'm not sure I remember her." Laney released a long breath and stood to open her window. "Listen, Ava, please forgive me for whining. My troubles are nothing compared to yours." Laney found her hankie and gave her nose a blow. *Oops.* "I didn't mean that you're going to have trouble."

With her forgiving expression, Ava stood. "If it matters or not, I've seen a big change in you. Here you were, the new teacher in town, moving in with your Bible recitation and ready to lead everyone to the eternal glory."

Laney grabbed Moses as he came off the sill. "I'm sorry you all had to put up with me."

"You are who you are, Miss Balderhoff. There is nothing to be sorry for. But I wondered how the rigors of Virginia City would affect you."

"They wore me down. I think that's what happened today." Laney dropped her face in Moses' fur. "I was in the carriage, but it wasn't me. I was tolerating lies and inconsistencies I never saw myself tolerating. I tried to convince myself my motives were higher than the things that were wrong."

Laney set Moses on her bed. "But today— in my gut, it just hurt. I don't know how to say it."

"I think I understand." Ava bent to pet Moses. I know I've done some hard things myself. And you should be proud right now. When you felt that pain, you didn't ignore it. You found yourself again and that is wonderful. The Lord did give you strength."

Laney looked long out the window. "I suppose the Lord cares more about my heart than my job."

"He cares about both." Ava waited at the door. "What if I thought there was a certain employee of the Wells Fargo Company who is happy you didn't go to San Francisco?"

Laney scratched the outside of her nose before her eyes met Ava's. "I'd be happy if he was happy," Laney said shyly.

"Okay." Ava smiled. "I'd had my suspicions." she bit down on her coy grin. "Come down and eat when you are ready." She turned to leave. "And don't fret about your job. You are a good teacher, and for that reason, he cannot fire you."

***

An hour later, Laney couldn't ignore the pain of an empty stomach as it competed with her crumbling future. Slumping down the stairs, she stopped at a knock at the door. Would it be Sawyer? Had he heard? Maybe Matthew told him she was back? Pulling her loose hair behind her ear, she took a deep breath and opened the door. A thin man with a white handlebar mustache pulled his bowler from his head and held it in his hand.

"Mrs. Farrow?"

"No, sir, but I can fetch her." Laney went to turn.

"I'm Charles Spade. I'm a Wells Fargo Superintendent." He nodded. "I need to get back next door. But if you would be so kind as to give this to her." He handed Laney a large brown envelope with a tied string.

"Of course, thank you, sir." Laney closed the door and looked at the thick envelope. It had a large Wells Fargo stamp across the center.

Searching into the parlor, she noticed Widow B stepping closer. "Who was at the door?"

"A Wells Fargo gentlemen, delivering a package for Ava." Laney continued inside the parlor where Ava and Widow C sipped tea. Wide-eyed, Laney handed the envelope to Ava. Ava set her cup and saucer down, and searched each woman's face. Pressing her lips flat, she turned the envelope over and untied the string. Pulling out a thick package, she held the top page in front of her face.

"Oh my, oh my…" Ava held her hand over her mouth and stared at them like she'd struck gold.

Laney leaned over her. "What? What does it say?"

"I've been awarded the position at Austin Station." Ava's mouth hung open, and her face paled. "Oh, blessed assurance, what have I done?"

Widow B shook her head and clucked her tongue. "You went and did it now. You got yourself a job all right." She dropped her fist on her hip, and Laney wasn't sure how to react either. This meant Ava and Matthew would be moving.

Matthew came in with a cookie in his hand. "What job?"

Ava took a large breath, blinking with the shock. "Interesting, this letter is for both of us, Matthew. It says; '*To the Widow Farrow and her son. The position of Wells Fargo station keeper has been granted for your immediate occupation.*'" Ava held up a smaller piece of paper. "Oh, my." She swung her head in disbelief. "This is a check for twenty dollars. My first month of wages and extra for the stocking of the post." She thumbed through the pile of letters. "There is a list of pantry items to be kept on hand, feed for the horses, cow, and chickens." She lifted a cautious smile to Matthew. "You'll have to help me with the horses."

Matthew jumped up. "I can help John and Sawyer?"

"The schedule." Ava scanned the papers. "The Wells Fargo philosophy." She read aloud.

"*There is one very powerful business rule. It is concentrated in the word courtesy.*" Ava blinked. "*Proper respect must be shown to all—let them be men, women or children, rich or poor, white or black.*" The words felt sacred, and hush filled the parlor as they looked at each other.

"I can see why you'd want to work for their company." Widow C patted her shoulder. "Forgive us for not showing our excitement." She creased a frown. "We all will be sorry to see you go."

"I saw that man going in there earlier today." Widow B piped up. "I think something is going on next door, and it isn't good." Her eyes widened. "I caught Sawyer going in when I gathered wood. Invited him in for supper. He said they had some big meeting going on."

Laney and Ava's eyes met.

"When that boy can't find time to eat, it's either important or bad." Widow B huffed.

Ava stood frozen, holding her assignment. "I think I'm in shock. I...I work for the Wells Fargo Company."

Laney felt proud of her sweet friend. "You're going to make history, Ava. You may even be the first woman to run an office."

"Whoa, now." Widow B huffed. "Before you get her petticoats floating in the clouds. This ain't no office with banking and such. Nothing like what you did next door. It's going to be pure dust and back-breaking labor. Cooking for the drivers and all those people coming from back east. Hauling water and taking care of stock." Widow B snipped. "Her only neighbors are going to be coyotes and Indians."

Laney watched Ava swallow, tears filling her eyes.

"I've been to Austin Station." Laney tried to sound positive. "Yes, it is primitive. But all those things are just what you read." Swaying her head, she tapped her chin. "Yes, it will be hard, too." *What was she saying?* "But all that about courtesy and showing respect to all people—that you are overqualified to do. You've been a hostess and...and...." Laney could no longer sell Ava. It was going to be a strange place for a beautiful southern belle and her son. Ava had steadied herself by wrapping her hand around Matthew's shoulder.

"Thank you." Ava pulled her hankie from her sleeve. "You all have given me important things to think about. I suppose Matthew and I have some talking to do." She fingered her son's hair, and he gave her a bright grin.

Pasting a smile, Ava dabbed her cheeks and bid everyone goodnight.

Widow B scrunched her face as Ava left. She shrugged at Widow C. "I'm not changing the sheets. I'll give her one month, and she'll be back."

Chapter 40

It was Saturday morning, and Laney stretched in her bed and finally closed her Bible and tucked it under her pillow. Somehow the light of Ava's employment and the dawn of another day helped her spirits perk back up.

She took the next hour to bathe and wash her clothes. Hauling her wet things outside, she began to toss them over the drying line. Sawyer stepped from the back door, and Laney jumped. His eyes smiled, soft and personal as he stepped closer.

"I'm surprised to see you." He took the blue dress from her hand and helped her to pin it on the drying line.

"I didn't make it to San Francisco." Laney scrunched a frown.

"I have to walk to the café and order food for the Wells Fargo men. Walk with me."

Laney took a gander at the length of the back alley. It frustrated her, knowing she could only walk part way. She didn't want to be seen strolling Virginia City with Sawyer, putting the final nail in her coffin.

Nodding in agreement, she walked with him toward town.

"So, what happened?" His words held sincere concern.

Laney felt his hand softly touch her back. Sawyer Roth seemed to sincerely care about her. Why had she behaved so thoughtlessly?

Hoping to leave some parts unsaid, she explained the attack of panic. "They turned around and brought me back."

"I'm sorry." He looked apologetic. "Were you disappointed? Not to shop with Mrs. Hearst?" Sawyer rested his hand on the round of her shoulder. It felt too warm and sweet to mention she'd tumbled and hit a rock in that same spot.

"No." Her feet stilled, and she rubbed between her brows. "I'm glad I didn't go." Her fear of being fired would not come from her mouth. "Say, what do you think of Ava getting the post at Austin Station? Are the men still discussing it?"

Sawyer dropped his arm, and she immediately missed his touch. "No, that meeting is to figure out what to do with Albert. I told you Ava suspected some poor accounting of the banking drafts and the mine owners' funds. She didn't see just a few things wrong—he's been doing a lot of things wrong." Sawyer glanced back from where they'd started walking. "There is one man here from San Francisco, just writing down everything that's being said."

"Oh, my." Laney had a hard time working up sympathy for the clerk. "Do you suppose that if they are to let him go, Ava could have the Virginia City job?"

"I couldn't say. This may take a while. It involves the mine owners and what was agreed upon and…." Sawyer smiled and drew his finger down her cheek. "I have to sit through it and hurry back with food. But I want to see you before I leave Monday morning."

"Just knock on the door. I worried about Ava knowing." Laney squeezed his hand.

"Knowing what?" He squinted his eyes on hers and pushed her fingers entwined with his.

"That I'm sweet on you." She confessed with a coy smile.

His expression melted with delight, and Sawyer pulled her hand up to his lips. "I'm going to tell you, I'm very sweet on you." His kiss on the back of her hand gave her the tingles down to her toes.

"But, I have to run." He released her and jogged on. "Sunday, I'll come by."

***

The Sunday sermon was wonderful—full of hope and grace for all who call upon the name of the Lord. Laney chewed her thumbnail as the congregation stood for the last hymn. The Hearst's were missing. They likely had headed back to San Francisco for shopping. But the mayor and the boys sat up two rows to her right. Apparently, they had gone home after she did.

Laney tried with all her might not to stare at the back of their heads. The mayor's declaration was too disconcerting. *Enamored* wouldn't have been a problem. *Lord knows she was enamored with her cat.* But it was the other remark about being his wife, and he'd allow her to teach.

From the moment she'd set foot in Virginia City, he'd placed demands and dictates on her. He said which children she could teach. He said why her salary was not what had been promised. He told her what to wear and when to come to his house. The only thing she'd done on her own was to show interest in his children's education.

In all her flighty behavior, she'd believed he'd gotten the hint. Laney looked around nervously as her row moved into the aisle. The last thing she could tolerate was...

"May I walk you home?"

How did the man get by her side so quickly? The line of people inched slowly toward the door where the Reverend shook each hand.

"I think I'll walk with the other widows." Laney smoothed her hair flat as she set her bonnet on her head and tied the bow under her chin.

"You likely think I'm angry at you." His elbow brushed hers. Laney searched side to side, people visited, and there was no escape from the center aisle.

"I do apologize for ruining the trip." She kept her eyes forward.

"I accept your apology and forgive you. I've already spoken to my mother. If you could come for Sunday supper, I think we should talk more."

Laney sucked in an irritated breath. "Howie, I must ask you to forget about me. I don't feel our social interactions should go further than the care of the school." She made sure to keep her voice lowered. "I will only call you Mayor Reynolds. I should have never agreed...." She stuck her hand out and gave the Reverend a quick shake. A nod to his wife and the open air was hers. Finally.

A glance over her shoulder found him a few feet back. "I am sorry." Laney pulled her skirt away from her moccasins and caught up with the ladies. Her heart pounded like a drum in her chest. It should feel good to set him straight once and for all. Then why did she want to run to her room and cry?

The afternoon crawled by like a snail on an icy pond. Sawyer was nowhere to be seen. Her only distraction came in helping Ava. The woman poured over the needs of Austin Station with confidence and flair. But then the next minute, she would stare into space with pale doubt and dread.

"I don't think I can do it." Ava leaned against the wall, her trunk open before her. "You should have seen the letter I wrote to my mother. It was filled with gaps and vague notions of this Wells Fargo job. If the woman knew the truth, half the Confederate Army would be sent out for me." Ava's soft blue eyes filled. "And what about Matthew? He's just a boy and thinks it all a grand adventure, but there will be no school for him." She shook her head and pulled things from her bottom drawer. "Is that what a godly mother would do to a child?" Her eyes pleaded with Laney. "You will tell me straight. I know you will." Ava dropped her things on the bed. "All I wear is this black crepe and the black sateen." Distracted, Ava huffed.

Laney reached out to still her arm. "Matthew will be fine. I will have his lessons sent with Sawyer each week. The boy will never fall behind. And when he misses his friends, have Sawyer bring him here. I'll watch him and...and do what mothers do." Laney supposed if she could run a class of twenty-six children, she could keep track of Matthew.

"My parents barely tolerated my husband wanting to come west." Ava held up the black, wide-belled crepe dress. "So far, my sisters have only birthed girls. Matthew is the heir to my father's estate." Ava folded the dress. "My year of mourning is far past. Should I purchase more serviceable dresses for Austin Station?"

Ava set the bundle in her trunk. "According to Widow B, I'll need them for mucking stalls."

"Oh, pish on her." Laney helped push the fabric inside the walls of the trunk. "Buy some pretty dresses that look like you and a good, thick work apron."

Ava stopped. "Thank you, Laney. That is a wonderful thought."

"Austin Station is about to be born again." Laney nodded with a smile. "Wells Fargo and their cargo." Laney waggled her eyebrows at the pun. "They won't want to leave when they've had a taste of your southern charm and flair." Before Laney could flinch, Ava wrapped her in a warm tight hug. "You are the dearest friend." Ava hugged her tighter. "You make me believe my dream isn't ridiculous."

It's a tiny bit ridiculous. Laney held back, remembering nothing but desert as far as you could see. But so was her desire to come this far from home to teach in a wild mining town. She admired Ava, a protective mother with a child still to raise.

"I won't be ready by Monday to leave with the company stage I work for," Ava said matter-of-fact, folding a shawl. "I hope to have the supplies ready by Tuesday. There is another wagon Matthew and I can catch."

Laney felt herself wilt. It would be too soon. "I will miss you desperately."

"I was thinking." Ava turned and grasped her hands. "Come for Thanksgiving." Her eyes held such hope. Widow B would have expected her back home by then.

"I would love to." Laney began. "I suppose we could have wild rattlesnake."

"Oh, no!" Ava grabbed her cheeks and laughed. "Please tell me there are better things with which to celebrate the harvest within this Nevada Territory?"

Lizards? Laney bit down on her bottom lip.

"I saw you talking to the mayor after church." Ava changed the subject. "I'm sorry I won't be able to be on your school board."

Laney sighed and shrugged. "I learned that the Hearsts can't either. They're waiting to move to San Francisco anytime. I find, once again, my best-laid plans falling short."

"Mother?" Matthew stood at the doorway. "Widow Boils says if you want to learn her secret to donuts, you'd better come now."

"What?" Laney's eyes grew wide. "She is showing you her magic recipe?" The snarly old widow was such a contradiction. Scorning the young mother one minute and giving her a hand up the next. "You may have to open a dining hall if word of these donuts and your gracious service gets out."

Ava walked by and smiled at Laney. "Maybe, I will." One-shoulder lifted. "Right after my mercantile gets going."

Chapter 41

Laney fought her disappointment Monday as she strode across the street to the schoolhouse. Sawyer hadn't knocked on her door Sunday. At least she knew the reason why. The Wells Fargo office was still under investigation. Maybe the timing for Ava and Matthew to move on fared better for them. With Albert under investigation, he could want to blame her or retaliate.

Pulling her book bag higher on her shoulder, Laney glanced back. She knew the Wells Fargo stage was already gone, but somehow just the sight of Sawyer would have made her day.

By afternoon, the children enjoyed another visit from the newspaperman, Samuel Clemens. He loved the student's ideas for a new article in the Territorial Enterprise. He brought the latest edition and wowed them with the stories of the battles of North and South—carefully editing some of the harsh details. At the last hour of the school day, it was with a heavy heart she handed out paper and asked the children to write a farewell card to the beloved Matthew Farrow.

He proudly stood in front of the class and shared the new adventure of moving to Austin Station with his mother. There, Matthew assured the children, he would be in charge of the Wells Fargo horses. On the way out, the boys made a line and shook his hand while the girls curtsied goodbye. Finally, with everyone gone, Laney plopped into her chair to grade the papers from the morning's spelling test.

A sound at the door made her look up. Mayor Reynolds pulled on his muttonchops and glared at her. Taking a few steps in, he tightened his lips in a pinched white circle and released a deep sigh.

"Miss Balderhoff."

Laney stood. She didn't like the scowl on his face, but at least he'd gotten her name request correct.

"It all makes sense now." Nodding his head, his disapproving frown deepened. Taking another step toward her desk, he scratched the top of his forehead. The walls rumbled from a mine blast, and he crossed his arms over his chest, puffing a cynical laugh.

"I saw the two of you, myself." His jaw twitched to the side. "Dancing poorly." He mocked. "I guess I thought you understood what your contract means when it says 'our school teacher must be above reproach.'"

Laney's eyes flashed out the window, and a shiver ran up her spine. "What are you talking about, Mayor?"

"The Wells Fargo shotgun messenger." He scoffed. "I'm sure the two of you are on a first-name basis."

"We are." Laney shoved her hand in her pocket. Heavens, she'd left her hankie in her room. "And, there is no reproach in that."

"Yet, going from each other's rooms *is*." His nostrils flared. "Now, I finally understand why you were so odd around me. Your affections were being pulled in two directions. Keeping me dangling while you were entertaining him."

Laney felt her skin flash hot. "You are very wrong, Mayor!" Her hands began to shake at the implication that he was ever a prospect for her regard.

Stepping around the desk, he lowered his chin. "Has he been in your room? Don't lie, Miss Balderhoff. I have witnesses."

"To deliver a desk." Her tone rose firmly. "I find you are out of line with these questions, and I must ask you to leave."

"I don't have to leave." His brows drew together. "This is public property, and you have broken your teaching contract."

"I have not." Laney clenched her jaw. "You have been thwarted by me, and these are falsehoods to put me in my place."

"The Wells Fargo clerk has seen you in intimacies with the shotgun messenger."

Albert.

"I am still above reproach." Laney straightened taller. "I love him." She leaned forward, ready to fight. "And that has nothing to do with my ability to teach children."

The mayor's eyes narrowed. "I have a right to protect this town and the children from a hussy who would…would…." He stopped inches from her. Laney could smell stale cigar. "Who would lift her skirts and Jezebel—." His spittle hit her face as he reached toward her neck.

"Oof!" His eyes bulged round.

Laney didn't realize her knee had flown upward and made contact until the man collapsed in half. Mayor Reynolds made such guttural, pained sounds that Laney wondered if she should steady him before he fell forward on his head. His hand reached out and gripped her desk, then he fell forward flat on his chest, choking out groans while thrashing on her papers and books.

"You are fired!" He ground out and pushed off with an elbow, knocking half her things to the floor. "Never will you teach again. Never!" Her boss moaned and writhed as Laney took a step back. Madam Bulette was right. Now should she run?

"And I will tell you one more thing." He growled like a bear and tried to stand. "You will leave this town and never look back. If you so much as show an inch of yourself, I will throw those widows out on their ear. That widow house belongs to the town." He panted. "And a scathing letter of debauchery will be written for the dismissal of Mr. Roth." His chest rose and fell as he jerked down on his suit jacket. "Get your things, and never let me see your face again." Holding on to the children's desks, he wavered, released a curse word, and let himself out.

Laney stared motionless at the disordered papers on her desk and floor. Her heart pounded so hard, little air reached her lungs. Like a strange person she used to know, her shaking hands began to straighten the desk. Everything needed to be in order. She bent and gathered the children's work off the floor.

How *could* she let things get so out of order? *"Even though I walk through the darkest valley, I will fear no evil, for you are with me."* A whimper escaped, and Laney clasped a hand over her mouth. What had just happened? Why did she knee the man in the groin? The impulse wasn't intentional, was it? He'd only called her a Jezebel. That could be forgiven. Her eyes shot up to the door. What if she could apologize? He'd seen her do rash things before.

Laney pulled the desks into a perfect row. Biting hard on her lip, the tears wouldn't stay back. A bottomless sob broke free as she turned to gather her things. Should she leave a note for a mother to take her class? The quill and ink were still upright and within reach, but her hand tremored out of control. Laney knew in the deepest, loneliest place of her heart she would never be back. Without her hankie, her tears streamed down her face. The reminiscent sound of the children's giggles and eager bright faces were silenced by thick sobs. As if she was there, in her mind's eye the widows chatted around their table, and Sawyer sat high atop the stage bench, proud, with his hat pulled forward and his shotgun over his knee. The mayor had drawn a heavy line with dark, burning coal. Laney could see her shriveled orange packed away in her old carpet bag. Her last token of a strange time in her life. There was no fear in her decision. She hiccupped a sob. These faces, these loved ones, their well-being outweighed her desire to teach. *"Thy rod and thy staff, they comfort me."* Another deeply pained gulp escaped as she dropped her key on the desk and walked out.

***

Wednesday, Sawyer had counted the minutes to return to Virginia City. He'd hated missing out on seeing Laney before he left. The meetings had been tense but also amazing. Albert, the Wells Fargo clerk of only sixteen months, was told to go, and if he caused problems, they would file charges against him. Another trained clerk from Sonora was transferred to the position and began to set things straight.

Before the superintendent left, Sawyer asked a question burning on his heart. Could Sawyer have permission to keep his job and have a wife? Funny how his nerves never got the best of him. If the answer was no, he was happy to hand over his resignation on the spot. But the superintendent had slapped him on the shoulder and snickered. Something about, "Of course you can marry." He chided him. "If you can survive a shotgun wound, you should be able to handle a wife."

Sawyer heard those words anew. *Were they a warning?* It didn't matter. Miss Lane-*ee* Balderhoff was worth all the trouble. She was as gentle to the touch as anything he'd ever known—or wanted to know—for the rest of this life. He rubbed the scruff on his jaw. He'd been smiling so much, thinking of her reaction that his jaw hurt. Together they would approach her new school board to have the same permission given from them. Sawyer unhitched the team and led them into the corral. He looked up. Her curtain was drawn.

"Hey, Moses." Sawyer entered the barn and forked some hay over the fence. "Moses?" Sawyer listened. It was too quiet. He took one last look for Moses in his usual sleeping spots but found them empty. Sawyer stopped in the middle of the alley. He wanted to get cleaned up and do this all proper like. Stepping toward the Wells Fargo back door, he stilled. He didn't want to wait.

It had been three, no four, days since he'd seen her. Far too long. And the good news of their future life together couldn't wait another minute. Sawyer turned on his heel and walked to the back of the widow house. Knocking, he took in a deep breath and dusted the trail off his pants. He was dropping his hat down to his knee when Widow C answered the door.

"Ma'am." Sawyer nodded, fingering his hair down flat. "Could I trouble you to call for Laney?"

The widow blinked and glanced to the ground. Something about her reaction made his stomach drop.

"I'm sorry Sawyer, she's not here." The soft-spoken, older lady still wouldn't look at him.

"When will she be back?"

The widow rolled her lips tight and glimpsed over her shoulder. Widow B appeared at her side. "That foul mayor let her go. Made her leave town." Widow B snarled. "The teacher was so upset we couldn't get a straight word from her."

"What? When? When did this happen?"

The forlorn ladies stared at each other. "Monday." Their tone faint.

"She must have told you where?" he questioned. "Is she staying in town?"

"No, the teacher packed everything. Put that cat back in a box and kissed us goodbye."

"What about Nebraska? She's from Nebraska." Sawyer felt like he'd been sucker-punched. "Did she say she was going home?"

They both lowered their heads and sighed. "That silly gal sure did love teaching. You'd never seen or heard such a bawl. You'd think that cat had died or something." Widow B huffed. "Maybe she'll get another try at teaching somewhere."

Sawyer stood frozen and stunned. "And Ava, has she already left?"

"Bright and early, Tuesday morning."

Sawyer stepped off their back step. Had he heard these two correctly? They would never tease him—would they? "She might not have left me a note. Did she leave anything and ask you to read it to me?"

Slowly they both shook their heads no. "Pitiful thing. Pitiful town," Widow C murmured.

"Nothing but pain and sorrow." Widow B added. "I'm sorry, Sawyer, I think we will all miss her. She was a magpie like no one else."

Sawyer felt his gut rip anew. He'd never told the widows he was in love with Laney. How could he expect them to know how badly he needed them to give him something he could hang on to? "Do you think she confided in Ava?"

"Possibly." Widow B shrugged. "I know we all did our best to get her along to Austin Station."

He took another step back up. "Will you come and get me, if you think of anything?"

"Yes."

"We will." They quietly closed the door.

Reeling in waves of shock, Sawyer walked back to the Wells Fargo door. Did she care about him at all? Was it only him who'd thought they would have a forever?

How did his life and hope just fall off a cliff in only five minutes?

There was one possibility left.

Chapter 42

Into Nevada Territory, Sawyer rode hard and looked ahead to see the glow of Fort Churchill. The oncoming darkness didn't bother him. He could run this road with his eyes closed. He knew every landmark and layout of this desert landscape by heart. He hated to push Blackie like this, but there was a small chance that Ava knew Laney's whereabouts. He needed to know and couldn't wait for more valuable time to pass. Swiping his brow of sweat and dust, he pressed Blackie on.

Pulling the horse back into a trot, he spied the lit widows of Austin Station. The pitch-black night blanketed the desert with a cool breeze. A woman, a young mother, hired on as the postmaster. It hit him anew that this didn't seem like the right place for Ava and Matthew. Sawyer jumped down and tied Blackie to the hitching post. How would he knock without scaring the life out of them? Shaking his head, he knocked gently. The curtain flipped back from the window, and Ava peered at him before she opened the door.

"Sawyer? Is that you?" Ava didn't seem to know how to welcome him. Matthew jumped off the floor. "Sawyer!" Before Sawyer could lift a smile at the boy, his eyes landed on something orange.

"Is that Moses?" He stepped inside and closed the door. Not meaning to hold his breath, he searched the shadowy room.

"Sure is." Matthew went to pick the cat up and brought it to Sawyer.

Sawyer scratched under Moses' chin while his eyes narrowed on Ava. "Is Laney here?"

"She's out back." Ava nodded. "She wanted to leave you a note, but…"

Sawyer moved before Ava could finish. He remembered that through the bedroom, a back door was cut into the sod. Opening the door carefully, he saw her back, where she sat on a round of wood. Her hair hung loose to her shoulders, but her body quaked with unrestrained weeping. Something in his chest squeezed, a crushing pain like he'd never felt before.

"Laney," he whispered.

Her mouth hung open as she turned. Wiping her face with the back of her sleeve, she blinked and stood. "Sawyer, what are you doing here?"

"I had to see you." A surge of protectiveness rose within him, and he wanted to grab her and pull her close, but something in her drawn face froze his feet. "The widows said you got fired. But why did you leave so fast? I would have…have…."

"There was nothing you could do." She frowned and shook her head.

Sawyer took a hesitant step forward and tried to calm the pounding in his chest. "You could have talked to me. Anything."

"Please believe me." Her voice and face crumbled. "I never wanted to hurt you."

"Laney." He took her hands. They felt like they'd come from an ice-cold river. He squeezed them with his. "Please don't leave me."

Thick tears rolled down her cheeks, and his discomfort worsened when she would not look at him. "I do love you." Her words choked within a sob. "But it's time for me to go home." She pulled her hands loose and wiped her wet face. "I've made such a mess." She wept, holding her hands over her face. "I never learn. Why can't I hide the things I shouldn't say, and say the things I should?"

"Oh, girl." Sawyer held a grin back as he pulled her into his arms. "Life is messy." He pulled his fingers through her hair and kissed her hairline. "I know how much you like things in order. If you want to go home, I'll take you."

She waggled her head *no* against his chest. "You have a job—and a life in Virginia City."

"I don't have a life without you." He pulled back and brushed a thumb over her wet tears. "I got permission from the Wells Fargo superintendent. I can be a shotgun messenger and be married."

Laney squeaked the saddest chuckle. "I can't live in Virginia City. Never again."

"Then I'll find another job. And you'll find another teaching job." Sawyer felt her body crumble inside his arms.

"No," she murmured. "I don't have the strength."

Sawyer felt his muscles pull taut. There had to be a way. "Laney." He pulled away to search her eyes. "I know I don't deserve you. You are kind and good, and…and should have been a disciple." He smiled as her head fell to the side. "But I want to marry you if you will have me…." His approach couldn't be right—she still looked miserable. "Laney, will you wait here with Ava? Wait and pray." Those last words brought her eyes to his. "Will you give God a chance to work something out?"

"Of course, I will." Agony laced her voice. "But I don't want you to quit a job you love."

"Can you give God a chance?" he asked again.

"Yes, but…I know what that feels like and—."

"Can you?"

"Will you promise not to quit your job?" Her chin tipped up.

The woman he loved never missed anything. She was quick to put him to the test. "Yes." Sawyer agreed, wondering why he felt less confident. Did he just propose? And all he had to show from that heartfelt offer was a faint promise to let God work something out? Now his threadbare faith questioned his logic. Sawyer stood, resting his head above hers. He rubbed her back as she held onto him.

"Did I see an old couch by the front window when I walked in?" A warm remembrance infused his skin.

"The one and the same." She released him and stepped back. "I'm surprised you remember."

"I told you I would never tell." He took her hand. "But I rode hard, and my shoulder is paining me something awful." Rewarded with a slight smile, his teasing succeeded.

"That is terrible. And what did you have in mind?" A small light glimmered in her eyes.

He pulled her closer to the back door, and they walked in together. Ava and Matthew sat at the Franklin's old table. "I'm sorry to show up unannounced," he told them.

"No, no, please have a seat. " Ava stood and poured him some coffee. "Matthew and I were just saying how worn out we are with setting things up today." She pulled her apron off. "Would it be rude of me to bid you two goodnight? I have a feeling there is more you want to talk about." She motioned for Matthew to join her.

"Thank you, Ava." Sawyer sat and sipped the coffee.

Ava reached out to hug Laney before she took Matthew's hand. "Sit and listen to Sawyer," She whispered in Laney's ear.

Laney turned into the small open kitchen. "Are you hungry?" She pulled a bowl off the shelf.

"Anything would be fine." Sawyer couldn't help but watch her every move. He still needed more answers, but her face couldn't be sadder. She sat a bowl of chunked ham and greens in front of him. "Laney, I need to know." He took her wrist and pulled for her to sit. "Do you want to be away from me? Is the thought of marrying me not what you want?"

"You should eat." She shook her head, looking away.

"I know I don't know the Bible like you or always believe the best as you do."

"No, Sawyer. You are all that God has made you. I don't need us to match like twins." She dropped her elbow on the table and rested her chin on her palm.

He waited and chewed a bite. "Talk to me. Start by telling me how you got fired."

Now she rested both elbows and covered her face. "The mayor accused me—us—of being immoral."

"Immoral?" He swallowed another bite.

"*The schoolmarm is to be above reproach.*" She stared at the table, frowning. "I told him it's not immoral to love someone." She huffed. "Then, he got angrier and came closer." She whined. "I don't know why...." Moaning, she dropped her head to the table. "I kicked him in the groin."

Sawyer felt his body jerk back, and he choked on the food. "You what?"

"I kicked him. Well, no, I kneed him." Her tears burst forth, and she slapped her hand over her eyes. "That *will* get someone fired." She rasped, rubbing her eyebrows back and forth.

Sawyer drank the last two gulps of coffee and stood. "So you are saying, the man accused you of sleeping with me? And then, when you denied it, he became angry? Did Mayor Reynolds make a pass at you?" Now he felt his skin crawl.

"No, I was standing next to my desk telling him to leave. But he was saying such disgusting lies...I...I don't know, he came closer, and I just reacted."

Sawyer paced the small kitchen and went over to the fireplace to stoke the low embers. He needed to settle himself before he rode back to Virginia City and took the man by the neck. Approaching the front window, Sawyer pulled the curtain back and felt his chest pumping with anger. Hadn't he just asked her to pray and believe for what God would do? Hearing the faint hiccup of her sob, he glanced over to the table. With slumped shoulders, Laney rested her face on her hands on the table. His anger would do her no good. Taking a deep breath, he called to her from the lumpy fainting couch.

"Come here, Lane-*ee*."

She wiped her face with her sleeve and came and sat next to him. "He demanded I leave town," she whispered. "Said he'd kick the widows out of their home if I did not leave immediately."

Sawyer locked his jaw. Maybe Mayor Reynolds could fire her, but he couldn't force her to leave town. That was criminal. "I'm sorry." Sawyer wrapped his arm around her back, but it wasn't enough. He released her and pulled his leg to the other side, so he could bring her against his chest. Leaning back on the one-sided couch, he pulled her close and held the warmth that was such a part of her.

"Now you understand why I can't live in Virginia City." Tucking her legs up under her skirts, she rested and exhaled a broken sigh.

Sawyer looked out over the darkened room and gently kissed her cheek. "There are other towns that need good teachers. I'm just sorry for your students. They've never had a better teacher nor likely ever will."

"I will miss them." Laney whimpered.

Sawyer remembered sitting with her like this in the dark. "I suppose the pain inside a person surpasses the pain from something sustained on the outside." An ember popped in the fire, breaking the extended silence.

Laney peeked up and ran her hand gently down his cheek. "Last time we were here on this very couch, you were in a bad place."

Sawyer had to smile. "Last time we were like this, I thought you were the oddest young woman—looking for your cat and quoting all those Bible verses."

Laney poked his arm. "*Judge not, lest ye be judged.*"

"My judgment didn't go deep. I liked the way you tended to me." His fingers trailed lightly over her hand. "I didn't want you to know, but you had my attention in a bad way."

"*Oddest* and *a bad way*? Just one short minute, Mr. Roth. You forgot peculiar."

Sawyer didn't need to see her smile to know she was teasing. "From my heart, I've told you I love you, and I would walk across this desert to marry you." He sat forward, and she sat up. "But when I kiss you" his fingers rose into her hair, and he brushed his lips gently to hers, "everything in my being wants to convince you that I mean it." His lips were careful not to take, but when she pressed forward, meeting each of his kisses with soft sighs of breath and desire, he could easily lose his patience. Sawyer laid back and pulled her close. Resting on him, she ran her fingers around his jaw and into his hair. Lifting her eyes to his brought a clear vision of the future he wanted.

"I came to teach," she whispered. "And God gave me the love of a great man."

The air stilled as Laney's eyes filled, and two tears ran loose and dripped onto his collar. Gently touching her damp cheek, he brushed them aside. A fierce primal protectiveness pumped through his veins—something words could not express. Inching to the left, he tucked her inside his arm and kissed her forehead.

"Rest now. God will make a way."

Chapter 43

The following Saturday, Sawyer stepped from the Wells Fargo office's front door and saw Samuel Clemens walking toward him. "I've heard a few rumors around town that the new teacher left on account of you."

Sawyer never had a reason to want to hurt the newspaper reporter, but his irritation grew by the minute.

"It can't be that scandalous since you're on the road most of the week," Samuel joked, "but you might find this week's editorial interesting." Samuel slapped the paper into Sawyer's chest.

Sawyer looked down, holding it against his chest. If it had anything to do with Laney, he wanted to read it. *Blast it.* His reading was poor and his patience worse. He turned on his heel and knocked on the widow's door. Widow C opened it and greeted him.

"Do you have a minute to read me something in the paper? I think it might have to do with Laney."

"Yes, of course. Come into the parlor."

Sawyer removed his hat, greeted Widow B, and took a seat. Widow C took the paper and scanned over it. "Here it is, in the letter to the editor." She read to herself while her eyes showed interest and delight. "The children have all written letters asking to have their teacher back. It is very well done and persuasive. The Henig and Grunder families are asking for a meeting after church. They're asking the mayor for an explanation."

Widow B seemed excited and militant. "I'll tell the parents the truth if the mayor does not."

Sawyer thought of what Laney had said about the mayor kicking them from their home. "Promise me, you'll let the meeting run its course."

"But she can't speak for herself." Widow B narrowed her eyes on him.

Sawyer stood. "No worry, I'm going to be there, and I know the truth."

***

Just like the spiked punch at the Fall Frolic, Virginia City loved anything that had a kick. The church had standing room only Sunday, and Sawyer squeezed by some dirty miners that seemed too old to have children in school. He found the widows and stood with them. "Who are all these people?"

"I think, like me, they are hoping the mayor will face the chopping block." Widow B nodded hard.

Mayor Reynolds stood at the front and raised his hand. "Everyone, please quiet down. I understand that the children are missing Miss Balderhoff. Everyone quiet." He spoke louder. "I would be happy to answer any—"

"What'd she do wrong?" some old miner yelled from the back.

"Read her Bible too much," someone else heckled.

"Please." The mayor pulled on his collar. "I have her contract in my hand. It states the new schoolmarm is to be unmarried and above reproach at all times."

For some reason, the crowd seemed to settle down. One of the mothers, with her two girls on each side, stood and rose her hand. "I am Mrs. Slavens. My two girls have learned more with Miss Balderhoff, and they now can help me learn," she said with a thick accent. "I am confused. Did she marry?"

"No. Not that I'm aware," the mayor said with a sour tone. "But I felt the company she kept was not as moral as she presented it to be."

The Reverend raised his hand. "The company of three widows?" Snickers and laughs popped across the room.

"Reverend, I'm sure you can appreciate that I do not intend to stand in a public place and slander the teacher. But I assure you, the widow house is not as reputable as it looks. I have witnesses that stated there were men in Miss Balderhoff's own quarters."

Sawyer felt himself lunge forward, and a hand quickly pulled him back.

"And I am a witness," Widow B shouted, "that the only man near her room was delivering a desk. And I also know you, yourself, had her in your home many a Friday evening. Even provided a dress you wished her to wear."

The mayor went to open his mouth, but the whistles and wolf calls echoed across the room.

"Order! I demand order!" he shouted. "The only people allowed at this meeting are the parents of the children. They are the only ones I need answer to. The rest of you get out!"

The sheriff stepped down the middle aisle and shooed the rowdy folk out the back door. He waved the widows and Sawyer out. Sawyer walked the widows home before he beelined it back to an open window. Staying back, he could hear the Reverend say he'd been asked to be part of the school board and should be allowed to stay.

"I can't imagine Miss Balderhoff doing anything sinful," Mrs. Santos spoke softly. "I know she is a good teacher."

Mr. Grunder stood. "It seems to me, Mayor, if the woman was allowed to marry, it would quell any rumors. You would have to agree, a husband and family is a protective place for all women."

Mayor Reynolds pulled out his pocket watch and clicked it open, then shut. "We will have a new teacher in place soon, and your children will be back in school."

"Will the new school board be part of that decision?" the Reverend asked, "or will that be up to you only?"

"Unlike you, Reverend, I am a parent of two students. So beyond being the city's mayor, I have a very personal interest in finding quality people for our growing town."

"Just hire her back, Dad," Howard bellowed from the back row. Rising from where he crouched, he huffed. "You won't find any teacher better than her."

The mayor's face reddened. "I think I've been fair in answering questions. Thank you all for your concern."

"Maybe she did get into mischief. I don't care if it's with a mayor, miner, or mailman, there wasn't one day she didn't show up to educate and love children. How many in this room think she should be given another chance?" A woman spoke from behind some people standing. The parents looked at each other and began to raise their hands. The children jumped up and raised both hands. "And if she wills, she should be allowed to marry." The parents nodded to each other, an obvious answer to the misconduct charge.

Sawyer tried to peek through the corner of the window. The parent standing in the far back appeared to be Madam Bulette. Funny how her words took command of the room.

"And, Mayor, the new school board would like to have more say," the Reverend piped up. "That way the burden of proof will not fall on you alone. With Widow Farrow moving, I'll need four more volunteers." Four parents raised their hands, and the Reverend acknowledged them.

"Excuse me!" The mayor's nostrils flared. "A few inept voices do not get to decide on school decisions. That is my job!"

"Who are you calling inept?" Mr. Henig rose with shoulders as broad as a bale of hay. "We are the people who give you a job. Shall we wait until we vote you out?"

The mayor paced the front with tight fists at his side. "Fine, have your board, have your promiscuous teacher back." He flung his hand outward. "I'll wash my hands of it!" The room went silent at his tirade.

"Howard! Get home now." The mayor pointed his son to the door.

Sawyer turned from the window and leaned against the church. What had just happened? Did he hear what he thought he heard? Stunned, he raked his fingers through his hair and looked up to the heavens. He hadn't even spoken a word. People and children milled out the door, talking excitedly amongst themselves.

Madam Bulette sauntered out closer to the side of the church, holding the hand of a young girl with long yellow braids. She glanced over her shoulder. "You'd better go find her and get her back, Mailman."

Sawyer jerked to attention. "Yes, ma'am, I will."

***

Three days later

Laney stood in the kitchen of the widow house as Ava heated the iron for curling her brown hair. "This is so fun." Ava fingered another strand. "I haven't styled hair since I was back home with my sisters."

Laney chewed on her bottom lip. "I don't know what I'd do without you. When Sawyer said he wanted to marry this Sunday after church, it made sense to get that settled so I could start teaching again. But three days... Oh Lord." She huffed. "I didn't leave myself much time to think it through."

"I told ya, with her and the boy gone," Widow B walked in and checked the cooling cake, "you and him could have the upstairs." She brought out a tray and flipped the cake over. "You know us old gals don't hear good." She snickered, and then Ava snorted a laugh.

"What?" Laney frowned. "What is funny about that?"

Widow B shook her head at Ava. "You want to tell her or should I?"

"Mrs. Boils." Ava gave her a censored frown. "It's prudent for a young wife to learn with her new husband."

"Learn? Learn what? Just tell me." Laney started to turn, but Ava pressed her still.

"I'm not quite finished."

"Then talk while you do my hair." Laney felt her nerves prickle.

"Let's see." Ava set the iron back on the stove and combed another strand. "The reason I fell in love with Matthew's father was because he was the only man who asked about me."

"Oh Lord, this is going to take a while." Widow B sighed and whipped the butter before adding some sugar.

Ava continued. "I say that because most men who tried to court me, all they did was talk about themselves. Zachary would talk, but then he would always stop and ask me how I felt or what I was thinking." She narrowed an eye on Widow B. "These are the things that make the marriage bed successful."

"Yes." Laney stood taller. "Get to that."

"Even after supper, I know how hard it is only to see dirty dishes and crumbs on the floor. But stop and talk to your husband. Even if he doesn't ask, begin to tell him about your day. Start at the beginning of your marriage to really listen to each other."

Laney rubbed her temples. "Supper, dishes, ignore. Talk and listen. Okay, what else."

"Yes, Miss Southern Belle, what else?" Widow B began to frost the cake.

"In the evening, sit close to him as he relaxes. Rub his shoulders if they're weary."

"Hmmm, now you're getting there." The widow murmured.

Laney felt the heat of the iron and Ava making another curl.

"So when you retire at night, you feel close to him; you want to be his lover."

"That's the bread and butter," Widow B piped in. "My old grannie said, angel by day, wildcat by night."

"Wildcat!" Both Ava and Laney exclaimed at the same time.

"What are you talking about, Widow?" Laney stood and faced her. "With claws and pouncing?"

"I do believe men like their women to pounce." Widow B nodded confidently.

"Oh my Lord, I can't...I can't..." Laney searched for an open door to bolt through. Ava held her shoulder again and sat her back down.

"Forget that wildcat image." Ava huffed. "I'll say it fast. Don't be shy, a husband cannot read your mind and you cannot read his. So talk. In all ways a young couple should be caring and courteous with each other. That is the foundation of a good marriage."

Widow B stepped closer, handing Laney the spoon with a bit of frosting. "But cut the prattling when you're under the sheets."

Wide-eyed, Laney swallowed a groan and pushed the spoon back. "I have to go! I'm going to be late!"

***

Feeling like a pincushion of adornment, Laney walked with the widows to the church. With her brown hair pulled and prim, her Sunday dress was pressed and tucked with a bit of lace and ribbon from Ava's things. Her hands were covered in white gloves, and, as she explained to the ladies, the moccasins would stay on her feet. The feeling of having her father walk her down the aisle was important today. Laney took in a cool breeze before seeing that the churchyard was full of students and their families.

"Miss Balderhoff!" Janetta and Henrietta waved.

Laney couldn't help herself. She hugged each child that came forward. Even Matthew got in line with Moses in his grip. A lovely woman in a gray and gold suit stood smiling with Howard and George by her side.

"I don't want to interrupt your important day. I saw your handsome groom enter the church a few minutes ago. I'm Howard and George's mother, Mrs. Reynolds." She extended her hand. Laney took it, standing amazed. "Howard wrote to me about you, and I completely agree with you. I feel his gifts should be given a chance at university." Laney watched tears fill her tender eyes. "Their father wouldn't allow me to take them when I left, but something has changed his mind. I don't know what it was exactly, but I just want to thank you."

Laney knew her mouth hung open in shock. "I've so enjoyed being their teacher. They are remarkable boys." Laney reached out and squeezed Howard's arm. "Please forgive me, *young men*."

Howard took her hand from his arm and kissed it. Never looking up, he shuffled his feet, and Laney felt his thanks straight into her heart.

"Congratulations!" Someone yelled from the crowd.

"Three cheers for the teacher returning!"

"Hip, hip, hooray! Hip, hip, hooray! Hip, hip, hooray!"

Laney noticed Leona jumping up and down with delight. Madam Bulette stood to the back, nodding with a coy wink and a smile. Even Samuel Clemens tipped his hat from where he stood near a tree.

Still bewildered and speechless, Laney struggled to believe they had all come out to welcome her back and congratulate her on her wedding day.

"What will we call you on Monday, Teacher?" Little Owen asked.

Laney tried to rein her smile in to speak. "Mrs. Roth. Starting Monday, I am Mrs. Roth." She announced, then laughed. "Or just *very blessed* teacher."

Author's Notes

great place for writing

Oh, **Virginia City**, what a start you had. From the earliest writings of Mark Twain to the Wells Fargo routes, to the beginning of the Hearst fortune. Most of those mentioned in my fiction are familiar names to us today. What some readers of inspirational fiction may not know is that Madam Bulette was an English-born young woman who, at one time, was the only female in Virginia City. As you can imagine, she was greatly sought after and quickly established prostitution. As the proprietor of her own business, she went on to gain respect in her town by supporting the miners when sickness or Indian attack was imminent.

She also raised funds for the Union cause during the Civil War. On July 4th, 1861, the firemen in Virginia City elected her the Queen of the Independence Day parade. We will pick up with Madam Bulette and Leona's Aunt Naomi

coming back to collect Leona in Book 3 of this Wells Fargo series.

Book 2, *The Station Keeper's Surrender,* is going to continue with lovely Ava and her boy, Matthew. What happens to a young widow and son out in the isolated desert of Nevada? Nothing, if Captain Adam Towns the Commander Fort Churchill has anything to say. He is also a southern gentleman who cannot allow the lovely belle to live alone in the wild desert.

Even amidst strange travelers and surrounding Indians, she is a woman who will fight to hold her position with the Wells Fargo post. Will the commander surrender the Fort? Or will the station keeper surrender her post? Will either surrender their hearts to love?

Please sign up for my newsletter at. www.juliadwrites.com

From there will be entered in all my drawings, learn of release dates and receive very infrequent emails.

Here's a fun answer to put on the email contact form. For some reason I felt like Laney's song would go like this: The B I B L E, yes that's the book for me. I _____ (five letters) alone on the word of God. The BIBLE.

Know the answer? Put it in the contact form. I'm going to do a drawing for a $50.00 Amazon card for one lucky winner with the correct answer.

I really do write for you to escape to an *Era Where True Love Prevails*. My last series, Love's Pure Gold, had darker themes and I was determined that this round of escape held a little more humor and lightheartedness. Please remember to always give your heart a balance. Life can be hard and messy. Only you know how important it is to go to coffee with a friend, get outdoors on a walk, and listen to peaceful music. Laugh at yourself. Jesus wants to carry our burdens, but often we think we'll do a better job. *Ugg*

Just this week in my journal I noted when my trust was wavering, my joy wavered downward. TRUST that He is savior, healer, redeemer, restorer and FOR you.

Good place to rest-

Thank you, dear one-

Julia

Made in the USA
Las Vegas, NV
06 April 2021